More praise for Mary Lee Settle's *I, Roger Williams*

"Mary Lee Settle's *I, Roger Willi...* [....] l novel at its best. . . . Her experienc[e] [....] ay that she spins her dense multi-layered narrative of old-world tyranny at war with the religious and political ideals of the new world."
—*Seattle Times*

"This novelist's great power—manifest in all her work, from the celebrated *Beulah Quintet* to the National Book Award–winning *Blood Ties*—has always been the ability to evoke place and mood with uncanny realism, and to transport the reader into the world she recreates. Here . . . that power is undiminished." —*Book World*

"A compelling piece of imaginative autobiography." —*Booklist*

"Roger Williams is truly one of the unsung American heroes, who lost everything in his life three times for the sake of a simple ideal that we now all take for granted. Settle's Williams speaks to us with a real sense of that loss, a pathos underlying the matter-of-fact tone of his recollections. . . . *I, Roger Williams* is a rich read."
—*Providence Sunday Journal*

"Branded a traitor, a heretic, an Indian lover, even 'divinely mad,' the founder of Rhode Island smelted his ideas about the primacy of conscience in the flames of England's religious controversy. In re-creating him, Settle demonstrates remarkable fidelity to his passionate voice."
—*Christian Science Monitor*

I, Roger Williams

A FRAGMENT OF AUTOBIOGRAPHY

I, Roger Williams

A FRAGMENT

OF AUTOBIOGRAPHY

MARY LEE SETTLE

W. W. NORTON & COMPANY / NEW YORK / LONDON

For information about permission to reproduce selections from this book, write to
Permissions, W. W. Norton & Company, Inc., 500 Fifth Avenue, New York, NY 10110

The text of this book is composed in Garamond No. 3
with the display set in Aquiline
Composition by Sue Carlson
Manufacturing by Quebecor Fairfield
Book design by JAM Design

Library of Congress Cataloging-in-Publication Data

Settle, Mary Lee.
I, Roger Williams : a fragment of autobiography / by Mary Lee Settle.
p. cm.
ISBN 0-393-04905-1
1. Williams, Roger, 1604?–1683—Fiction. 2. Colonists—Fiction.
3. Puritans—Fiction. 4. Rhode Island—History—Colonial period,
ca. 1600–1775—Fiction. I. Title.

PS3569.E84 I3 2001
813.'54-dc21   00-050046
ISBN 0-393-32383-8 pbk.

W. W. Norton & Company, Inc.
500 Fifth Avenue, New York, N.Y. 10110
www.wwnorton.com

W. W. Norton & Company Ltd.
Castle House, 75/76 Wells Street, London W1T 3QT

1 2 3 4 5 6 7 8 9 0

The sweetest soul I ever knew.

—EDWARD WINSLOW,
governor, Plymouth Colony

Under this cloud of darkness
did this child of light walk.

—WILLIAM HUBBARD,
historian, Massachusetts Bay Colony

I, Roger Williams

A FRAGMENT OF AUTOBIOGRAPHY

I

---

*I was unmercifully driven from my chamber to a winter's
flight. A monstrous paradox that God's children should
persecute God's children, and that they . . . should not suffer each other to live in this common air together.*

— ROGER WILLIAMS

I, ROGER WILLIAMS, ONCE CALLED PASSIONATE, PRE-
cipitate, and divinely mad, New England's gadfly, firebrand in the
night, do slump upon the ground this day in late June of the most dis-
astrous year of my life, 1676, like a stove hulk. Now in my age I am a
little old spindled weak bruised man, with rupture and colic and lame-
ness in both my feet. I own nothing, no fine house, no fame, no power
men care so for they act the brute in their God's name. Well, at long
and blessed last, I care not nor need any of these temporaries and triv-
ials. I would keep my mind on the business of eternity, if my memory
did not play me impish tricks.

For it was only three months ago that this work of smoke, flame, and
blood of those I loved was done. Oh Father of Lights, we went to war.
I too went to war, and that lower self of me, dress, sword, and gun,
called myself as they did captain, Captain Roger Williams. For the last
time that still brings heated anger and tears, I tried to treat with the
Narragansetts who for fifty years I had loved and protected against the
fear and greed of my own people.

Even while we parleyed as I had done with their fathers, their grandfathers, the young warriors ran with torches and touched thatch,

hayloft, home, hearth, cut the throats of what beasts we had not hid, killed and killed. Oh how delicately did this begin with a little lick, a kiss of fire, and then a wild destruction, providence aflame, and I old fool still did not give up, parleyed on with the heat upon my back.

Tribe. Tribe of the English, the Yengees as they called us. I had known the Indian fathers and even the grandfathers, but the sons and grandsons knew not me. They had, for cheating, stealing, and betrayal on both sides, grown as dangerous as wolves, more dangerous than wolves for as men they suffered hurt.

As I did. I betrayed them out of fear and fury. The flames flew up as we say prayers do and burned all love from my soul. I killed. I even, God help me, went along with selling the captives, who I had loved for all the years. In weak explanation, I did insist that they be sold only as indentured servants for eight to fourteen years, as white prisoners were, not into perpetual slavery as the other colonies did.

When I think of it I want to crawl to the light of the Father of Lights and bay like the wolf I accused them of being when they went mad with grief and slaughtered us. Our turn. Their turn. Our turn. Their turn.

So once again, as it was so long ago, my home for this fine morning is a sycamore as old as Adam, so huge that four men span it with their outstretched arms. Its hollow trunk is always cool in summer and warm in winter. Many a family have lived in it while they built their cabins. Truth to tell, many a man has come here to sleep when he has quarreled with his wife. Though it is on the land parceled to me it is free for all, a cave to pray and live in.

As we try to rebuild after the burning, it is our town meetinghouse, as it was forty years ago before a house was built. My neighbors sit along the ground and argue as fiercely as if they spoke in the great halls of Westminster, it, too, by the water, there the Thames and here the Moshassuck. I know both rivers like the palms and calluses of my hands. This one has written a history of paddling mile on mile on mile through summer and winter on my lawful occasions of teaching and trading. The very bark against my back makes me remember, as I do often when I stay here, when once I burrowed here in the deep snow of winter, before Mary came to be with me.

My work with my native friends lies failed, all failed, since I made

friends with what my tribe, the Yengees, call the savage native men. I
have spent years with them, a profligate of time. I slept by the filthy
smoke holes of their wild houses, warmed by their barbarous fires, and
often wrote my passionate arguments by their firelight while they slept
around me, and I argued with the night. My life was saved by them
when the other savages, my own countrymen, condemned me to a
white death.

I was driven from my house in Salem, from Mary and the children,
at twilight of a winter day forty years ago into a storm of snow, in January of a New England winter when I was already sick abed from the
persecution of my own kind. I had suffered since I was a child until I
heard God's reasons for my suffering. My body was so impatient for
guidance that three times in my life I have sunk into a futility and a
heartbreak that took my strength and froze the sinews of my back and
feet.

But I have had, every time, light and voices to save me, oh, not fan-
tastic visions and holy ghosts, for I am, and have always been, a practical man. No, my voices were those of my conscience, ever lodged
within me, two above all to guide and save me, one called heretic,
another called arrogant and proud-tongued.

That time I remembered to my strength that Sir Edward Coke, the
greatest lawyer in England and my own mentor in my youth, was sent
himself to the Tower and accused of treason that near cost him his
blessed head in the same unjust way. His real crime, so long ago, was
that he was too much honored by the people. He saved himself by wit
and knowledge, and those fine-honed weapons of anger and memory.
Ever to his death he taught that to accuse and then seek out a cause is
the greatest perversion of the law. He thundered it; he wrote it; he suffered for it. And by his life and work struck the first blow to bring
down an absolute monarchy.

The Saints of Boston, to rid themselves of me, their gadfly, imitated the very intolerance that sent their own selves forth from lost
estates, lost lands, lost preferments in England to such a wilderness as
this. "Tolerance" is a word they, too, despise. They accused me of heresy
and thrust me out. At least I think they said heresy, that or another
thing or many things; there were many words to cover their act. It is
hard to remember what it was truly about so long ago. I was sent forth

over a mass of separate argument. But the true reason that boiled beneath it was that I pointed out that in law the Indians owned the lands the Saints of Boston said God had given them, God or the king, sometimes I forget, and that they should pay the Indians for their land. That was my real heresy in their Christian eyes, heresy in their worship of God Land.

I am sick at heart when these memories come unbidden, even though I felt the warmth of someone's love when Governor Winthrop sent me a secret warning that a ship rode anchor at Nantasket and had sent men by pinnace to arrest me and take me back to England. Every child here in Providence knows how I last saw my house as a ghost blown by the wind, then fading into night. I trudged and fell and trudged and fell again in snowdrifts to my waist in a hell that was frozen and white, not burning. The burning came in my life both earlier and later.

I walked long after dark into the night. I knew my way and God guided me. When the moon rose and reflected on the snow it was like some day in night without warmth or kindness. The wind blew ghosts in my path, but it was so familiar to me that I could not be lost for I had thought of it as my private road to those who loved me for I had spent six years becoming their only friendly tie with the avalanche of English, hungry or God-driven, thief and saint, that were pouring onto their shore. They were as honest and full of guile as animals, as far from us who are as strange to them as the infidel Turk or the Chinee of Cathay. My long friendship and curiosity about them saved me, as John Winthrop and I and Governor Winslow of Plymouth Colony knew they would. That is, if they found me in that snow-covered sleeping time of winter, for the tribes and their villages went into the swamps in winter to quarters where they were as warm and safe as bears in their caves, or the legions of animals underground. I remember sensing, with a kind of other hearing and smelling, the vast life hidden under and around me as I walked my road, as formal as a carriageway for a king, among the virgin trees so vast that no undergrowth could chain me.

My road, which had long been my own private shortcut to Boston, away behind the settlements where few English ventured, took me by a small, poor village of Pennacooks. We knew each other well. It was empty, the wigwams long gone, leaving only a clearing in the woods.

I found a place beneath a tree, lit a small fire from fallen branches, and rolled in my bearskin coat, lay and watched the stars that came and went with the wind above the forest ceiling. No sleep. I lay in a kind of shock at what had happened. Gradually my mind cleared and I saw my way ahead toward Narragansett Bay, where Mary and I could make a home.

I walked on through days and nights, I never knew how many, for after a while I was simply there and then not there and no time passed any more, only the rising of the sun and its lowering or the day storms or the night storms of snow, or the moonrise or those blessed nights under a black sky filled deep with stars. Some friendly Indians of Massasoit, sachem of the Wampanoags, an old friend, found me asleep at midday, as one given up and waiting to freeze to a quiet death. They carried me to Massasoit's village. It saved my life.

How can I forget my exile? My feet froze. I walk upon my exile every day of my life. And must needs walk lest I become a chairborn crippled man, even forty years later. I had traveled several hundred miles, who knows how much, like a ship's captain by the place of the sun, the growth and waning of the moon, and by a small compass which I still have. It is ever in my pocket, for once it led me when I was lost I could not ever part with it. More than anything else the feel of that small metal disk in my pocket has reminded me that the Father of Lights watched over me.

It was the Indians who guided me to the Narragansetts and my dearly loved old man, Canonicus, their sachem, and Miantonomo, his nephew. That was near Seekonk, which they call now Rehoboth in the patent of Plymouth. I found not until years later that Massasoit had made a contact for me with Governor Winslow there, and Indians took my bearings to him and to my dear John Winthrop, so that I was less abandoned than I knew while I was walking toward where I sit now.

John Winthrop's part was secret for he was the head of the colony, its governor for most of his life in America. But he never lost touch with me until land hunger forced him to an opposite camp. The other Visible Saints in Boston were not so kind. Mr. John Cotton wrote me, "Had you perished your blood would have been on your own head; it was your sin to procure it, and your sorrow to suffer it."

I would not think of this on this fine morning late in life but that the word of the burning of Providence has reached Boston. It seems that after forty years, those who were taught with their mothers' milk that I was a dangerous firebrand in the night, whose fathers had once conspired to throw me back into the teeth of the English law, which was in those days Bishop Laud, God rest his sorry soul, have offered me a home in Boston! That is, of course, as they point out, so long as I keep my dirty contentious old mouth shut. But alas for their kind offer, I am still as young, still as disputatious, and I fear as much a master of passionate prolixity as when I burned my bridges so long ago in England lest Archbishop Laud tan my heretical hide. His Orthodox Church of England Christian solution to what he termed heresy was a room in prison or a whipping at the cart's tail, H branded on both my cheeks, or to have my ears cropped like a pit bull.

For fourteen weeks I wandered south from Salem, mile after mile, from tribe to tribe, shelter to shelter. In the six years I had been in New England, I already spoke their language, and could serve them as peacemaker between the tribes, for the Father of Lights gave me the art to pick up languages with ease, or better, taught me to listen, which is the same. In their filthy hospitable sinkholes I had long since found a lifelong friend, yet another of the fathers God has sent me for my guides. Canonicus, sachem of the Narragansetts, was a shy, wise man who distrusted the new foreigners who came to his shores. Thanks be to God he never saw this day.

So I did then come to this place by the water, and here I will stay until death releases me and gives me glory. That is, of course, if I have earned it. Who knows? Who ever knows?

I plowed and rowed and built and taught and wrote and begged peace between the English and my friends the native savages. I did save many lives between them over the years until it was too late and came at last to this day, when I and my dear wife, Mary, live with my son, Daniel, who plows the far fields while I keep watch lest those I loved and love with all my heart fall on us again like wild beasts. On this long day while I lie here against my home tree, I am the watchman as I have always been while he and the others work the fields around me as far as I can see. There has been many an ambush. Some have been murdered as they worked and left along the ground, poor souls, without their hair, some in their kitchens, some with their mouths full of chestnuts, some asleep.

But the English who have hated the natives as savage beasts came from a place where they took as a fact of life that men made holidays of watching living men be cut into quarters like meat at Tyburn, and baited bulls with dogs, and had a king who, being king, baited the lions in the lion tower as dog after dog died in service to his majesty's ease and pleasure. Men were whipped from Westminster to Paul's Cross while a crowd jeered as if it were their duty, or beheaded at Westminster like Raleigh or so many others whose heads were cured by weather at the gates of London as a warning to obey King James's and then King Charles's law

King James took pride in his thinking on grave matters. He really saw himself as the defender of the faith when in truth he was the defender of his own opinions, for like God, as he said so many times, he was sent to judge but not to be judged as ordinary men. In other men such leanings would have sent them to Bedlam as mad as beasts in cages, but when the king spoke I saw men I was taught to honor bow before his words.

I, to my shame, when a boy, twisted and shoved my way through crowds watching men drawn and quartered alive, when I was delayed on my own errands. Annoyed at the delay, I said a learned prayer, as thoughtless as a hiccup, for one who had not ceased screaming. We take the world around us without thought. It is our shame to be blind and our sin to care not.

Now I look out on these ash-strewn, ruined house shapes, with only the mud and stone chimneys, spires of loss against the sky, left of Providence. All through the spring we strove to build our houses back, not brave, not despairing, having no choice. I have seen God's insects do this, build back when their homes are destroyed by a careless foot. Daniel, who, like the rest, must depend on hope of a late winter, is trying to plant in early June, praying that enough grows in the rich burned ground to feed us this winter. He and his mule Hiram plow a straight furrow, their minds only on that.

I tried to stop it happening but no one listened. After the years of English stealing and lying and breaking of promises to the Narragansetts, the men of Massachusetts Bay Colony came upon them in the late winter and massacred them in the swamp where they thought their wives and children safe. Those they captured they sold for slaves to the new plantations in the Bermudas. No Indian nor anyone can be sold as a slave in Providence Colony, being equal before the law.

After over forty years of resentment built up by English greed, the Narragansetts were maddened with grief, and they ranged up and down the new colonies and set our little hard-earned world afire with their fury, not knowing that their true enemies were not these weak and distressed souls who have flown thither over perilous seas, as I know well. They are the ones who have plowed and planted and hoped and prayed, not those who worship God Land and God Money and want more and more and more.

Many an impotent man says, "I have tried." I have tried. I can hear the empty sound of those words.

Now I must know within my soul that I have as gain only what the Father of Spirits who loves me leaves me. A stick to chastise me. A little stick that Joseph carved for me in winter with a wolf head for a handle. The children call me the old man with a stick. Fine title for a man who cast away preferment, ease, and all ambition to follow a voice often too faint to hear. Or to be honest, since I am alone and it is late in life, preferment cast me away.

If only I could have saved the books. My only jewels to hover over and caress, gone, my years of handprints on them, up in fire, Bible, Bacon, my dear Coke, beloved Milton I kept good company with, sweet Andrew Marvell, disputatious Freeborn Jack Lilburne, profane Greeks I had to hide and all lest they tempt my neighbors to jealousy at my learning. Mary's knittings and weavings could not be rescued; each row a minute, each blanket a winter, as the Indian women, too, spend the cold months, the years of warmth piled high. Well, it is all gone and there's nothing to be said about it, after all.

Little did the young boy that I was, praying and prattling, dream that I would end here by this river this June morning, and watch an ant climb a blade of grass. Fail and try, fail and try, fail and try, and when his journey ends, be only at the pinnacle of his world, the top of a blade of grass.

My blade of grass is here and I have tried and failed and tried and failed again, and will be forgotten. But I still am rich as Tyre and Sidon with voices and places that cannot be taken from me, my world within as great as yours or his or hers who has memories, found again in age as clear to me as when I fled from them in youth. Who among you ancient men hide not your night dreams of old loves, old desires, old terrors, and old losses you thought had released you long ago?

The sun is high. Daniel and Hiram have lost their shadows. I have been asleep. Asleep on watch. Well, like the animals, the savage men do not come at noon. I dreamed that I was . . . where? Fog. Fog from another river. Over and over in my life the time has come to bring the day of burning in London back to me. It came again when I watched my house and buildings that had sheltered so many lick the sky with their flames. My house gone that friends and I did build with our own hands and felled the trees and smoothed the floors, I who had made a courtly leg as I was taught before a spavined and drooling king. For all the years it was a welcome place and sign of love between us to those very ones who have done this deed and often as many as fifty or so wigwams graced my home field. I watched it all burned by those men with wolves' hearts I honored and so long tried to understand. Though we may for all that have been on different stars.

Before God my beloved Bartholomew appeared to me that day within the burning of my house, as tall as a great tree, only for an instant. Did he speak? Did he speak then so long ago at Smithfield when I was a boy of eight years? I kept on asking one and then another as I shouldered past their legs to go nearer that burning, for I was too small to see over their heads, but was hearing or thought I heard something. How can I ever know?

I am in that morning as if it covered this one an ocean and a time away. The mist from that far river blots out this sun, turns it to dark gray fog. There is still the smell of death from the sea coal burning, or was it he? It was a cold day in March then, too, the other time of fire. I was a child in London. I could hear through the fog the lowing of cattle brought to Smithfield market, the neighing and restless moving of many horses, and the crowing of a late-arisen rooster in the distance. It was, I know, eight of the clock. I could smell the dung of creatures and the old sweat of the crowd who still wore their clouts of winter, huddled together as if they could warm themselves by Bartholomew's fire.

I knew then that I heard the animals because there was no sound of people, only a vast breathing that mingled in little clouds with the mist, all the terrible silence and the fear. I had never heard such loud silence. It stilled even the cutpurses and the whores who earned their meager living there; it wrapped us around in some strange comfort, as if we were blessed to be part of the burning.

How could it be? It was. I remember that it was. It comes back as it has today, and always did and will. Dancer in the flames. Horror like something white and still. Nothing. Nihil. The cold smell of despair.

My father sent me there. He told me I needed the lesson of what befell those who did not obey, no, honor he said, honor their fathers and their mothers, after the commandment, because I would not listen. But I had listened and listened well, and stored it in the private parts of my small mind where no one could come and berate me.

The new Bible was printed the same year in the king's name, and put in gold upon the cover, as if he were the author of that beautiful flowering of simple words. I knew then, boy that I was, that it was wrong and blasphemous to call such a one head of the church as of the state, but I said nothing. There was no one I could trust to say it to, even Bartholomew Legate, who had made his own leg to the king and honored him with argument.

Bartholomew Legate. I learned to love with knowing him. So did others but he was to me another father. He was a comely man of black complexion in his beard and curly hair; strong, too. He could lift children high. He laughed much. He was a merry fellow even when he taught us, who would creep to him in an upstairs room that he said was like the poor rooms where Christ Jesus taught too. There were only a few people, old women, children, some brave men who had dared to come or were too old to care or were zealous to learn, and some more dangerous, who would use his words to spread their own anger. All over London there were such small rooms to hear the new Bible, for the official state church of the nation took over the churches that had been built so long ago by the Papists and then taken by the old king, Henry.

I went then because the new Bible was too costly and my father would not buy it. Bartholomew read to us from his copy, with the king's name on it in gold, the most dangerous book that has ever been released upon a people, and in those days and all this wild tumultuous century has caused more death, more life, more blood let, more hope and more despair than any other. It came as something new to those around Bartholomew, and they acted on what their attention caught and kept, no more. He planted words of fire.

My father said that common people should not read it for themselves, that they needed church ministers to guide them on what to know and what not to know, as the king the country and a father his house, not some foolish purveyor of goods like Bartholomew. He knew him from a child. I said nothing when he spoke so. Was not there. A little pitcher.

That year the Jesus I heard and saw around me was, as He had taught, not peace but a sword. My father said it was that book that caused riot and danger but it was a danger of freedom no matter how wild, the beginning, as if a lid had been taken off a muttering pease porridge. Once as I walked past a tavern, two carpenters rolled drunk at my feet and gouged each other's eyes and yelled at one another that one was more like Jesus and then that the other was more like Jesus, they being carpenters. One called the other Amos because he used a plumb bob when no good carpenter had so faulty an eye, because the word "plumb bob" was from the prophet, Amos, in the Bible.

Bartholomew said that Jesus was a man like us who lived in a far country, who walked barefoot on the sandy road and gathered a few to follow Him, a fanatic among many, but this one in God's image, a seeker after truth, not to be caught like flotsam on floodwater, clinging for safety to one word among so many. No. He told us the man Jesus became as God, he said part of God not son or begotten of God, but one who came most near to the terrible simplicity of His love.

The women and the children around me turned to one another and murmured, not understanding. They had been kept sober and docile by being told in the churches of a great judge who would come and judge their simple sins, and send them tumbling down to hell. He let them dispute together and then he said as if he answered all of them:

"No. The man Jesus walked nearer and nearer the love of God He sought until He too was love itself and that is why the gates of hell cannot prevail against us."

My father said he was mad to lose his family and a good living selling cloth, because he had left silk and damask and linen and such, to
be a fanatic and a heretic fool, though I knew already that if he was, he
was God's fool, though mistaken and half blind as we all are. My father
said he had no business with thinking himself an equal with the
preachers who had been to Oxford and Cambridge and spoke languages
not meant for common people.

Bartholomew, he said, deserved what happened, but I knew the man
too and saw because he told me the miracle of being alive each day,
even that day in that place and among those people, crowded together
against the morning and his death.

I was almost there when I heard a boom, as of small cannon, and a
vast sigh. Someone of the soldiers or the executioners had taken pity
and put gunpowder among the faggots to kill quickly, though I heard
someone say above my head that the king had forbade it.

Then I saw my friend. I saw his face. I saw the stillness of his handsome face. His eyes were open and reflected the flames. He burned
there and I thought of course of Jesus hanging. This time his name was
Legate, my own Bartholomew. Once he had placed that burning hand
upon my head and I felt blessed.

He danced behind the pale flames, made surly-colored in the fogbound morning, danced behind a veil now of fog, now of my tears. I
could not tell if it was his writhing or the writhing of the flames that
tossed his body in a dance. He smelled of meat burning and of a sudden I thought of holiday meat on a great spit.

Above me someone said in a whisper, "He is dead. It is only the
burning."

I never knew who spoke so to me; maybe it was within me, maybe
above me, maybe another who had been touched by him. Near him
women sobbed, but so quiet, so quiet that I thought I heard it in the
distance but it was my own sobbing, he who had told me my soul was
ever free and no one, even the bandy-legged king, could take it from
me or go there, where I am, now, here in this sun, an old man young
again, standing before the funeral pyre of one who said he saw in me a
fire that once kindled would not go out. He said it to all of us who listened one day, but I took it to mean me.

It takes a long time to burn a man. Late in the day, one by one they came, as silent as they had been all day, and picked at the ashes and put them in kerchiefs and little boxes they had bought at the stalls of Smithfield. I had no box, only my pencil case. I can see yet my child fingers lingering in the ashes of Bartholomew. I picked up a pinch and put into my pencil case my share of Bartholomew Legate, though it was a pagan thing to do, yet it comforted me that something of him could be touched. Deep in the night I would take it out and wait until my brothers slept, wait abed in the attic room on my pallet, for his words to come again. Sometimes they did, but mostly I could only hear the bellman below call, "Remember the clocks, look well to your locks," and whispered it with him, "Fire and your light and God give you . . ." until his voice was lost in the wind and I said the good night. And waited again.

I kept the candle going and it lit the low ceiling of bare boards, but the wind from the broken plaster between the lathes made it dance as he had danced, and I blew it out and faced the dark.

I lay there for long hours in the night in the silence of darkness which was no silence, but the breathing and chomping of my brothers, the call below of the watchman on the hour to comfort and warn and comfort again, the bellowing of one who had stayed too long in the tavern and the whimper of the wind in the rafters. I heard the faint ringing of the handbell at Newgate jail as the guard reminded those who would be turned off at Tyburn by hanging the next day to have a last atonement. I knew by that bell it was midnight.

I sought his beloved voice as if it were a jewel I could hold in my hand like his ashes, but it, too, faded, like the voice of the night watchman, and I was left alone, seeking still. As I am left here in this morning with only that one word, "seek." I am a seeker to this day. After all the disputations and prolixities, legalities, tables, types and antitypes, and all the other wasted words, I still wait, still seek that love which passeth understanding, not kinds and divisions but pure light. Sometimes I have seen it, and see it as clearly as this noon sun that shines across my eyes.

Later in the market it was rumored that the king was sore amazed that such a sinner and evil man would garner a harvest of such love as

Bartholomew Legate; he had demanded of him when he commanded him to the palace that he state his case, and when he did the king spurned him with his foot and bade them take him away and try him. But the silence in the days after his death was as great as the silence of the burning and no one dared speak but those who called him evil and devil lover, Arian, and such things, warlock and all.

But some months later men came with great wagons of cobblestones and paved the whole of Smithfield as if to bury where he had been but they said that it was to make a better place of it, so that the fine horses and the cattle would not sink in the mud there. The voices rose again and the sound of the flutes and the calls of the trumpets and the great bells of St. Sepulchre that tolled each death turned off at Tyburn away in the country beyond the city. Toll. Toll. For me they tolled for him who had been to me a father. Taught me fathers could love as well as punish.

Sometimes when my father had not drunk too much ale at supper, after he had talked to my older brother, apprenticed to a Turkey merchant and learning carpets and weavings, or to my younger, who being the youngest drew forth from him some solicitude, he would turn to me, as if he had forgotten me and suddenly remembered, called me middle son, neither most expected to follow or most loved, and did his duty by me.

He would explain each time, trying to keep his voice gentle, that the king was God's voice to him as it should be and he was God's voice in the house, being my father, and then he would pause, watching my eyes, and beg an answer and wait for my "Yes, father."

In those days I was as broke to his words as a horse is broke to the bit. Sometimes my bit was leather. More often it was iron, like the bits and the harnesses that the smiths at Smithfield made while I listened to that different tolling, the ring of their hammers, and watched the color of their fires. My father called me Little Teacher, and Little Ranter, and if he found me listening to the street preachers who vied for customers like the mummers and jonglers at Smithfield, Lord, he grabbed my collar and dragged me home and whipped me till I bled. He said it was to keep me safe because such things were frowned on by the king and the bishops and I could fare as others had. He did not use the word but we both knew I could grow up to be murdered for my thoughts.

And so I learned to keep my thoughts to myself until the time when they burst forth out of such need that I am accused of never shutting up. A bursting forth as a fountain of words, but at least, I think, they brought some who listened to a trust in their own voices. All that can be given is a chance, an arena, hope of a listener, one among many. The teacher's prayer that all would not fall among stones as prolix nature casting forth seeds.

I I

The truth is, the great Gods of this world are God-belly,
God-peace, God-wealth, God-honour, God-pleasure, etc.
These Gods must not be blasphemed, that is, evil spoken of,
no, not provoked, etc.

— ROGER WILLIAMS

I WOULD I HAD NOT GIVE UP COCUMSCUSSOC, WHERE
I kept my trading store for more than twenty years. For no place have
I found in my life that was so peaceful and blessed a home among my
friends. I, Roger Williams, once lacky in the most depraved court in
Europe, a storekeeper trading in beaver skins for London fashions, and
so, as were we all, tied to the greedy mother by the strings of her apron
of lace and fur all trimmed with gold and silver. I sold Cocumscussoc
thirty years ago and yesterday. I miss it still, and I go every month to
speak among my friends who are left. They are so few. So old. There are
neat English farms and fat cattle where once the Narragansett villages
stood.

No one ever was as rich as I was then; as rich as only one can be who
has space and silence and all outdoors to think and write in. Silence I
learned to cherish as the best gift to me of the Father of Lights. From
my small rise of hill, I could watch the Narragansett villagers going to
and fro upon their business, see the lights like fallen stars at night
when they lit their fires within their houses of branch and bark and
animal skins as snug as the beavers they learned from. Beyond them

was Narragansett Bay, where their canoes slid forth to fish or on their voyages among the tribes.

They saw me as a sachem, for I spoke their own language and was useful to them in their diplomacies, an arbiter who saved many lives. I did. I did so for all. Sometimes they saw me as one of their gods, but I railed at being called Manitoo. No, I said so often. Netop. Friend. I traded skins for cloth and blankets, pots and pans, sugar and all, but never guns and never strong waters but to aid in their sicknesses.

I groan and grumble over my aches and pains, but they were stoic and never admitted pain, even in childbirth, except for one thing. No Indian I ever knew could stand a toothache. It made them as sick and noisy as any babe.

They are gone, that great nation, and those I meet are made servile by their hunger and their treatment. But once, oh once I had a blessed retreat among them where my heart and brain could flourish, and was their friend and they mine, for the years before we pushed them to the insanity of suicide in King Philip's War. Only that makes me glad that I sold Cocumscussoc. I had to do it, for the other colonies, like the wolves and the Indians they despised, bayed at our borders to overtake the one place in the new world, truly I think in the known world, with liberty to worship as we would, and choose our own laws to live by. That was what was hated here at what we call Rhode Island, island of roses, that the mind had escaped its holy chains.

It may be that after all the quarreling and the noise and all the begging for a charter that would protect our liberty of conscience and our lives, something will come of all this in time, aye, but men ever love their chains as well as their liberty. It is always a choice. Once, there at Cocumscussoc, I did write down all that came about to make us into a colony of our own. But my notes burned with all the rest and now so much is only in my mind, the deeds, the debates, three charters, the final one a caprice of a king, the letters from my dear John Milton, from Harry and Lady Vane, who opened their hearts to me as I to them. So many others, bales of words in love and hate and law and disputation, Winthrop letters, Endicott letters, and those damnable letters from John Cotton that were more like whips.

All burned. All dead as late afternoon, or such smiles as light on others, forgotten or not meant. Why this morning anger brought on me by dreams I have forgot? I would flog it out from my mind as Mary flogs a rug. It cannot be of the devil for John Milton has convinced me beyond a reasonable doubt that the devil is within me and not a painted scarecrow. It cannot be witchcraft for there are no witches in Providence, nor no heretics, for there is no law against them. Except that there are times when as the Father of Lights is my witness, I cannot explain it other. More quarreling in my home meadow, for now the house is burned they have made of it a cockpit. More drunkenness in the street as more ships come into our port. More my God your God, my way your way.

Oh I would be delivered of this. And yet I too went along those paths and before God was as noisome about it as any naked Quaker!

That was long ago, and yesterday within my soul. For we destroyed them for a little land, a little passel to die in, or live a savage loneliness after the dirty comfort of our birth. I think I was never alone until I came here.

God gave me my birth in Cow Lane over against Smithfield in St. Sepulchre parish of Farrenden Without beyond the old walls of the city. Though it was but a ten-minute walk even with dawdling to Paul's Cross before the cathedral right in the middle of London. It was the year of the old queen's death. There was plague in the city. The new king, James, who they said was as poor as a church mouse, came down from Edinburgh and was so impatient to see his new wealth that he slipped into London with a kerchief around his face and a posy of medicine flowers at his nose to keep the plague away so he could play with the crown jewels.

Later, after the plague had passed, he rode into London in procession with such a rabble of hangers-on and poor Scots courtiers in their skirts that the children of London chanted, "Hark hark the dogs do bark; the beggars have come to town; some in rags and some in tags and some in velvet gowns."

I grew to boyhood in Long Lane, where my parents had gone up in the world. It was a tall narrow gabled house that I still see, although like so much of London it is only in my mind, for the city was burned in the Great Fire they said was started by the Jesuits in the year of our Lord 1666, only ten years before this burning of Providence. Truly, though, it was not enemies as it was here, though many hoped so for the politics of it. A baker left his oven lit, the fear of every housewife when she walks abroad. Our house was lath with wooden beams, very old, and would have made good tinder.

It was four stories high, counting its attic, the tallest the law allowed, and the ceilings lowered and lowered as I climbed up the steep stairs. On the ground floor was my father's tailor's shop, only he pointed out always that he was a *merchant* tailor, not a simple cutter or sewer, and, as he said so often in his cups, a member of the Merchant Tailor Company and I must never forget it. Across the street my mother owned the Harrow, the finest tavern, she said, in all of Farrenden. Money was their God, and land the church where they worshiped.

Farrenden was my playground, where I trained a good arm for games by throwing mud with the other small fry at the felons of Newgate. It was not in a dull school I learned my languages, but there, playing from the time I was in skirts with Dutch and French and all. I found it easy, without knowing it was an art; my father said I was a magpie, picking up their words as I did, so he found a use for me when the strange men came with their wares, and their talents. I could speak with them. He became rich from the foreigners who worked for him, but he still hated them, and refused even to learn God Bless You in their language.

He sent me often to Paul's walk, the very center of the cathedral, where the high ancient vaulting of the ceiling sheltered the fashionable from the rain and dirt as they walked to and fro in their fine clothes with an eye out for one kind of preferment or another, or to escape their creditors by staying on holy ground. He told me to eavesdrop for him, for many spoke Latin and French as affectations and I had that ear to pick up languages as a dog picks up commands. He bade me take my slate to draw for him the fashions of the gentlemen who strolled there so that he could copy them.

On the other side of Smithfield, only steps beyond the market, were country meadows. Those acres were my joy, had been since my mother sent me for milk from the dairyman each morning rain or shine over the bridge beyond the Fleet. The green meadows were so peaceful there that I dawdled and let my eyes wander across the lovely country of open fields, so near to my home. That was my pleasure, Smithfield my school, my university the mingle mangle of farriers, apprentices, farmers and whores and jackanapes and rogues and knights. It is where I picked up the speech of many countries, Dutch and German and French and Turk, for those who had fled their own countries flocked there outside the walls of the city where the law was easier and the living and dying cheaper.

Oh I knew the language of sin and degradation and survival, too. But I learned another thing, that among those turnings and twistings of streets and alleys there was kindness, and good merriment as much as anyplace. There was what I grew to see as love, its gestures, as when Kate, the pretty light-fingered pickpocket, lifted me up when I had been thrown into the dung of the market by apprentices who bullied children barely younger than themselves. She cleaned me off with her kerchief, took me to the horse trough, washed me and the kerchief, then hugged me and said, "There. The world's a place of shit so why not fall into it?"

You see love where you find it but you must know it when and where you see that gift. I learned to trust, which is its open gate. It has been slammed in my face and opened again and slammed again, but by God's grace I have never learned cynical discretion, and have stayed a fool all my life.

Farrenden was a fine place to grow toward late boyhood; it contained all. I knew those streets, Gold and Chicken and Cock and Fleet, Pye Corner, Gilt Spur Street where the usurers gathered, Fetter Lane named for the lazy drifting men who lounged there, and when I listened, seemed to know the answers to everything, what the king should do, and the Parliament, and all. My own Long Lane was the home of apothecaries and doctors, and was known as Quack Lane.

Cheek by jowl with them, the great houses were half hidden by their gardens and parks as huge as country estates, only overgroomed like foist dogs with rows of espaliered trees after the French manner that lined their roads like soldiers. Statues of fauns and nymphs showed ways of oyster shells to the distant doors.

The finest of all was Hatton House. It was etched by light against the sky above us, uphill in the distance; its brooding spires and towers looked down on us, as aloof as judgement. Once it had been Ely House, built by the Bishop of Ely like a castle. All I knew of Ely was that its bishops were traitorous but little else. But, oh, the fine neighbors when it was Hatton House and the carriages of kings and queens and all rolled with their cantering retinues up that long way between the trees to feast there. Those who lived there when I was a child were familiar as neighbors too high and mighty to do more than stare at and to provide a neighborhood show, and gossip from those who pretended to know them better than they did.

Lady Hatton was a shrew, they said, who led her second husband a merry chase. It was whispered that when they married she was already with child, and that when her new husband patted her belly and said that there was a bun in the oven she parleyed with, "That is why I married a Coke!"

That was what I first heard of Sir Edward Coke, master cook of the law they called him, the Chief Justice, and said to be the finest lawyer in England. Sometimes when he went in state to the court with the mace carried before him, and his mounted trumpeters ahead, followed by a retinue of clerks in livery, I could see him in his carriage with his badge of rank, the great chain of gold links we called the esse collar, across his scarlet robes. Sometimes, though, the clop clop of his horse in the empty dark street would wake me at three or four of the morning, for he kept early hours. He would be riding to Sergeant's Inn, where he had rooms. Once or twice I saw him that early when I had to be abroad for my mother, and he wore then an old comfortable brown robe and his nightcap. I caught glimpses of him beyond my father's broad back when he came up the aisle in St. Sepulchre's church, where he came often, a very tall, proud, handsome man who strode up the aisle like a countryman walking fields he owned, looking not left or right.

For the rest, Farrenden was my garden as Hatton House was his, and I could disappear down private alley and mews as well as any boy. In this place so long since I can hear the sound of Smithfield, the loose clatter of the horses' harnesses and the lowing and the wild yells and laughter sometimes and I would watch the fighting of the sluts, and try to learn how the cutpurses worked. I knew every brothel and every tavern by the time I was breeched at five or six years old. By the time I was a schoolboy with my satchel on my back I was surprised at nothing. How can one born to Smithfield not be so from the time he is let

loose in those streets and alleys where the life surged and played and
teased and shouted?

Smithfield. No one can say I chose my path to this tree out of ignorance or innocence. I knew the whores, the thieves, the cutthroats, the
usurers, the buyers and sellers of anything and everything, even so my
father with his God Money. I should, all my life, have growed used to
that, but I never did. I was blessed with forgiveness, and I pray for
understanding but the balm of forgetfulness is denied me.

Being the middle son between Sydrach and Robert, I did have the
grace of being watched less, so I wandered through the city of London,
although the near and royal city of Westminster was forbidden me. I
watched the ships in the Thames harbor waiting at anchor, settled as
great birds on the river, breathing as the water breathed. I was already
a seeker of some place to be at home as I had been with Bartholomew
for that small time I knew him.

Often I dreamed of a Smithfield that no longer was, but had been
before the houses and the taverns and among them the grand palaces
that had been where the black friars and the white friars and the Bishop of Ely had lived before reform, or what was called reform. Even as a
child I knew stealing when I saw it.

Then I walked in the open fields of Farrenden as in the ancient days
when the king and all the court came to watch the jousting, and the
clanging I heard then was not of the smithies but the softer sound of
the golden jingle of the horses' harnesses, not the heavy tread of the
draft horses drawing their huge heavy drays across the paving and the
cursing of their drivers, but the silver-shod steeds of dreams, with their
ladies in fine silk and the silken banners, when the knights had rode to
Smithfield to the jousting, gold-caparisoned, with ladies leading their
mounts on gold tethers. That was long gone except in my mind in the
days of my childhood. To find a lie of land where the young sirs, and
lords and rioters, still rode and gathered and practiced jousting with
one another, I would wander uphill and across the fields to a country
then as free and empty as this one and dream, not of Jesus, but of those
golden days of knights in armor as boys do, for I was, after all, a boy
like any other.

What a dream that was in a world that had grown so gross, the buying and the selling and the laughter in the taverns when they spoke of

the Scots king and imitated his broad speech. And aped the riot of a masque for the queen's brother, the king of Denmark, that was acted before the court, and how when Faith and Hope entered in their silken gowns, they burst with giggles and forgot their lines for they were as drunk as the lords and ladies who watched them. How they were led out to the marble hall where they both vomited up pools of wine, Faith leaning on Hope and Hope on Faith. How then when Charity staggered in bearing gifts of food on a golden tray she stumbled against the king of Denmark and christened him with meat and sauce and grapes that sat upon his pate, and when he rose to acknowledge the fair gifts that dribbled down his velvet and gold lace, he staggered and fell headlong and was took off to bed. That was a far cry from boy dreams.

Later I knew them and watched such goings-on from among the pages. Oh I did know them, as a boy knows who is forgotten in the room while the men spar with words, king and lords, judges and councillors, all in their fine robes with the smell of age and winter upon them. I was young and comely then and ambitious as Lucifer although I knew it not, but thought myself so pure a soul with thinkings of my own that I saw later were not my own.

I must hide all this and always have had to. I have lived for so long among neighbors and friends as well whose ignorance of the ways of the world I knew censored and censured me. Sometimes by those who fought me tooth and nail over land and land and land said that I bragged when I spoke of that time. Sometimes when I forget and say such as the king was a swearer from his youth, or the king was bandy-legged, and had patted my cheek too long, a stare comes to their eyes as if I had been caught in a lie. I must keep silence lest my colonial neighbors take an envious way against me when I let drop before my thinking shuts my mouth that I moved so among the powerful and would again were I in England. It is sinful of me to scratch their envy so.

But I did know them all and saw the evil ways of that poor dwindled king after so great Elizabeth. He tried always to step into shoes too large for him. As a boy I knew two kings, one fat, riding past in procession high above me, all decked in hunting green but trimmed with gold and flashing jewels, followed by glorious colors of knights and lords and ladies in velvet and silk and fur. He was surrounded by a guard of pretty soldiers, handpicked they said, laughing in the taverns. They were oft clad in red silk and velvet with shining breastplates and the silken banners of St. George and of Scotland waving and snapping above them in the wind from the Thames.

The city of London was then and still is a public village where all is known or thought to be known. The court was as open as Fleet ditch, as foul of humans and evil-smelling. When the king was within the walls of Whitehall he was a thin man with little reedy spindled legs, for what was thought fat was only many layers of wadding to deflect the knife or the bullet that he had feared. Poor wee bairn as his courtiers called him behind his back was as cowardly as any rat-tailed cur.

When I think that it was he who had the Holy Bible named for him, and who argued with Bartholomew Legate and spurned him with his foot and had him burned like meat on a spit at Smithfield as he had had so many burned in Scotland while he and the queen watched and ate and watched.

I am supposed they say to remember my school, but I hear little but the tired repeating of boys' voices mine too amo amas amat over and over hic haec hoc. I think I was too old for school when I was born, so that is hard to bring back. It was for me easy and unimportant. I do not remember going or learning but being there in the dark time of winter, my little body shivering like a dog shitting bones. My father let me stay to school until I was fourteen and thought to apprentice me to a scrivener to harness, he said, all I could do since I was not good enough in his eyes to buy and sell and too impatient to learn to be a cutter. He said I would dream away the profits and my mother laughed and they fell to talking of what mattered, God profits and God rents and God tavern, and how she owned and ran the finest tavern, at least she said it was, in all of Farrenden.

So there in the street, I see me in the street always or alone in my own soul, a boy my brother teased, my father whipped as any boy; but that was only the surface, growing out of my clouts, awkward, at least I thought so, but the lasses thought me pretty.

Oh my pretty child wandering with a soul as big as all outdoors as all men's are if they would open them. Not one other soul ever searched for me beyond my eyes after him that was burned until at church one fatal Sunday morn I was torn from Smithfield and set upon this path.

As was my habit, I took down the sermon at St. Sepulchre's in my short hand to take it home and translate it into Latin, to keep the secret writing I had learned to hide my thoughts and my Latin honed and ready when it might be needed, for no one around me spoke it. I had done that since I was in school when each week it was our assignment to stand before the master and answer his examination of Sunday's sermon in Latin *ex tempulo.*

I I I

———————◆———————

Well and truly ye shall serve the king and his people. And ye shall take no fee or livery of none but the King nor gift or reward of none that hath a do before you except it shall be meat or drink of small value, as long as the plea hangs before you. And ye shall do equal law and execution of Right to all the King's subjects, rich and poor, without having regard to any person. Ye shall council our Sovereign Lord the King in his need. And ye shall not deny any person of common right for the letters of the King or for any person nor for any other cause . . . So help you God.

—THE JUDGE'S OATH, TAKEN BY
SIR EDWARD COKE, 1606

IT IS THE MIDNIGHT OF THIS SHARP AND BITTER SEAson. The moon is full and white. The snow makes spindrifts in the wind as if there were a frozen ocean as far as I can see. I take comfort knowing where the other houses are, even though Providence is only ghostly shapes of snow in the distance. I am on watch again, but for the night itself and not for danger. It is too cold for that. Here at the window where we have the luxury of glass, a rare thing and only for one window, the blowing of the glass makes wonderful shapes of moon and snow, as if they had moved, erupted, split, and frozen when I turn my eyes, my head, an idle thing to play.

I have awakened deep in this night. The sweet peace of sleep was jostled out by the thousand imps of land and money and land and land and all that has followed me here. I have waited for the past to come and free me for a little from this present.

I thought that I would write. The turkey quills ready whittled, the ink mixed and the house asleep, all of them, wife and son and daughter-in-law and children, all close, all quiet. I sit within the comfort of their breathing. But as the fire retreated into its banked-up night-long embers to be ready for the morning, my ink froze in its pot.

So I can only sit here and ask the Father of Lights and the snow and the moon. Why? Why is this old man harnessed by trivial ropes of God Land and God Greed and God Money which in my innocence I thought to leave behind in old England? By Christ's soul I, who made the first colony in all the world, all the world, yes, where one can speak his mind, man or woman, without fear and worship his God in his own way without arrest whether he be Jew or Turk or Seeker or Quaker or even, God help us, Papists theirselves. And even, God my witness, the dour and petulant Puritan saints, who by their habit are ever as right as righteousness itself. Here are a free people not enslaved to the bondages and iron yokes of the great, freed in soul and body from the oppressions of the English. Yet I must admit as one admits in the depths of night that it has opened a damnable Pandora's box of passions.

For our new freedom we are the joke and censure of the other plantations, a despised and outcast colony. The Quaker women run naked in the town because the Holy Ghost has told them to strip down to Indian bare. The men fight in the street and some, out of countenance with hardship, lie drunk all day long.

Those who never owned a rod of land have fought for forty years over this bounty of God. It is the cause and root of all our present mischief. In friendship I, Roger Williams, and those who followed me here were granted the use of the meadows along the streams of Pawtucket and Pawtuxet without limits for the use of our cattle by my dear Canonicus, the sachem of the Narragansets. I loved him as a father and buried him at his request with my own hands. The words "upstream without limits" were read by the greedy as conferring some legal right to grab the land and become kings of the wilderness west all the way to sunset. Enough has been grabbed, claimed, stolen without bond or payment, and I will not have it. I will not. This is not freedom. This, as my beloved Sir Edward, God rest his litigious soul, would say, is damned and dishonest misreading of the law.

Did I follow God Light and God Hope to this new, hard, clean land to sit here in this night and chew at litigation myself like a dog a bone? Did I let loose free license and thievery where one man desires power over another, where a man beats his wife insensible for knowing herself as free by Providence's law as he? Did I take days of God's sweet time to chase a man who skipped the colony and nearly caused war between the colonies when he was arrested for buggering his heifer?

Oh, someone stirred. I must not laugh. Though laughter saves me and has many a time in all the hardship of this place. Daniel turns in his sleep and mutters come to bed. He thinks it age and sorrow that wakes me to sit at the window. I am alone as I was when all the world that I could fathom was snow. Once lived that holy loneliness recalls me sometimes. I yearn for it. I find peace in it I cannot tell a soul.

How young I was, how cur-scared when Sir Edward Coke, that great man, called me to him. I knew what he wanted, for he had sent word to my father to deliver me to speak with him, needing one who could use secret shorthand and who knew Latin, French, and Dutch. This so impressed my father that he made me a new suit that fit so that for the first time I can remember the sleeves came to my wrists. I was growing so fast my hands were thrusting out as if they wanted to grab the world.

Perhaps they did. Perhaps they reached out for that glorious ambition for preferment I dreamed about in the attic room all that night before I was sent to meet with him, that night as this one, awake and dreaming. Tatters of that ambition still cling to me as far away as here in space and time, even as I know it is as false as painted faces.

Oh my Lord Christ Jesus, how hard it is when I am bright as Lucifer to listen to the others as they fumble toward resolve, and try not to be aware of condescension. Well. That is what I have been tested by, over and over, thrust ashamed of myself into the humility I seek and do not seek, want and damn, love and hate.

Still in my soul this midnight I walk again down Long Lane as I did that strange thawed morning at the beginning, in the dark then, too, for Sir Edward woke each day at three of the clock and wanted me there

on his waking, fresh and ready to be questioned. There was not a soul
in the streets but the watchman. The bells of St. Sepulchre's church
were still. The carts for Tyburn gallows waited empty at Newgate. I
walked by Pye Corner where already the ovens lit the street, and the
glorious smell of meat pies thrust back the clinging odor of burning
sea coal in the mist. Down beyond Holburn and Paul's Cross, the
pigeons sat with their heads tucked beneath their wings and churtled
and burbled in their sleep.

At Sergeant's Inn hard by the Inner Temple, I took a deep breath,
crossed my Rubicon, and raised a trembling hand to knock at the door
of Sir Edward's chambers. I can still feel the terror of it, and hear the
voice, "Enter."

That one awful word, hollow-spoke beyond the door. I stood, frozen
in a January morning in the dark, fingered cold through my clothes
and my hair, making me shiver to join the shivering of my fear. I made
myself push open the heavy door.

He did not look up. He sat there, the first I ever saw that dear
beloved man, shrunk in his dirty fustian winter robe, a nightcap on his
head, no crimson robes of state nor golden esse collar but the haunted
relic of a man thrown into oblivion after years of service, stripped of everything. I knew from the town that such things had happened and that
he was beloved by the common people and so feared by the king, or so
they said, who spread rumor as manure for a fine harvest of gossip.

This was no man beloved by anyone, but some dry and lone soul,
grown thin, his beard untrimmed, his eyes sunk. I saw, or thought I
saw, a man dying of exile. But when he spoke in that strong voice that
I had only heard before when he called to his coachman, I knew he was
not dying, but protected by fury. He looked up, took me in whole, but
did not look into my eyes. He gestured toward my commonplace book.
"Take this down in your secret writing." It was an order. He turned
away and spoke into thin air.

"Nihil est adeo aut memoriae insitum, aut infixum animo, quin
intervallo temporis obscurari, sensimquiae sine sensu deleri possit."

"Nothing is or can be so fixed in the mind, or fastened in memory,
but in short time is or may be loosened out of the one, and by little and
little quite lost out of the other." He was wrong about that but little
else in all the time I knew and grew to love him and what he offered.

Oh no, not lost to memory but savored to this night because I, Roger Williams, became part of his great work that morning, the pride of my life.

How could I forget? "Read it to me," he said, and fingered some papers of his own that lay under his hand.

I had no voice. I could not make a sound.

He looked up. "Why do you not speak, boy, read what you have written." That voice had thundered at Essex and at Raleigh. That voice had threatened the king himself by trying to force Robert Carr, the king's bugger, the newmade Earl of Somerset, to tell that open secret under oath, while two of the king's men stood by him with a cloak to throw over Carr's head and muffle him if he spake to save his life. 'Twas said that the threatened king began the lord Coke's downfall that day.

In a little peaked voice I found I said, "My lord, your presence diminishes me."

He smiled and that smile lit his stern face so it became another, a small face with twinkle eyes, amused and pleased. "Diminish. That is a fine choice of word, a fine word, diminuere."

I had not known until he said it that I had answered him in Latin.

"Now," he said, kindlier, "you must have a place to sit, and then you must transpose your secret writing to whole words, and then translate it into English, and if you can do that you can do what I have a mind for you to do."

He stood up, and up, and up until he towered under the ceiling of the room. Only his little face up there was thin, the rest strong and supple, though he was already sixty-six years old. He was six feet four inches tall while I then was only four feet and never grew beyond five and some five inches.

He moved around the paneled room of his chamber. The Coke Reports that were already canon of the law of England lay around the room in drifts and shoals of learning. Every surface was covered with wafer-thin fine parchment, some colored by time, some new, some fallen to the floor, some showered across three heavy tables. The candles guttered and a lamp wick moved when he moved and made the room and his figure dance across the walls as he shuffled parchment that smelled of the French leather for gloves that fine people used.

He cleared a place for me at the corner of a table near the fire, and I fell to work as I would do for over four years, in the same place, the same chair when I was in the room.

His quill scratched and mine as we worked together. The rest was so silent that when the sea coal shifted in the fire it startled me. I finished, and waited, but he was so deeply sunk in the moving of his quill across the parchment that I dared not speak, and hardly dared to breathe.

Now in this night of snow I know that year was not his defeat, but could have been the greatest of his life had he not turned aside to his shame. But it was only when he was an old man that he chose the law and not preferment and he never ever after wavered until his death. He said change the law, not break it, and he labored at that change until he died.

I watched the shadow of his gaunt head move a little in the predawn dark, a man in love. That was what rumor said, that he was in love with the law. The law of the land. He would change it with the second Magna Carta. He would move England toward a split in its soul that was civil war, an end that would have cleaved his soul had he lived to see it, but by God's grace he did not. I was one of those who suffered before that love, and still I honor it as one whose life was saved by it.

He had been diminished in his own life; a terrible diminishment. No wonder that he sought out that word in what I said. Tidbits had flown a long time in the alehouses, and in Paul's walk among those who pretended to be in, how his favor with the king was very loose, how the queen and the prince defended him, how Lord Bacon despised him. I took it for the gossip of who's in and who's out among the gallants and job seekers strutting and pretending a closer ear to the court than they had.

There always seemed to me to be a silken cord that held all England to the king's whim, even the gossips and the bawds. First Coke's cord was uneasy, then loose, then he was made sport of at Cambridge in a play, and they said the king laughed.

He began to fall within the king's laughter. When the king laughed the city smiled, and when he frowned it was an absolute frown that spread across the faces of the courtiers and the would-bes and the might-have-beens. There was rumor that Sir Edward had cajoled the other high judges of England to sign a letter to the king defending their prerogative. But I knew not then what prerogative was and had no one to ask. I only knew that the man whose shadowed face I watched had had to kneel in supplication with all the judges to be forgiven for touching the king's prerogative, whatever that meant, and how when the others rose, he stayed on his knees before the Privy Council that he had been a part of for so long, and the monarchy that he had served for twenty years, the late Queen Elizabeth her Solicitor General, James his Chief Justice of England. He, who had loved the monarchy and protected the common law, did not rise when the others rose, but kneeling there, said the words that flew around London as if a carrier pigeon had taken it to all, told the king and those of the Privy Council he had served with so long, that he would fain do that which should be fit for a judge to do.

Fit for a judge to do. Later when I knew of such things I understood at last what the others in that Privy Council room knew that day. He had reminded them of his oath as a judge, "Ye shall not deny any person of common right for the letters of the king or for any person nor for any other cause, so help you God." He had upheld his oath of prerogative ordinary over prerogative absolute and so defied the king. By that he became champion to all, and sealed a fate that had left him sitting there that morning in his chamber, gaunt and bitter, amid the shoals of parchment that were his very life. They in the streets knew not causes and reasons among those they had learned so hardly were their betters, but they knew as a cat knows which way to jump that he was being thrust out.

The king even went to Star Chamber and those who pushed their way into the public court to be within hearing bruited about that the Scottish new rich king had spoken to all that kings sit in the throne of God and that they are God's judges on earth, and it was presumption and high contempt to dispute what a king could do.

So Lord Coke fell down and down. Men of the Privy Council with not a note within them of his fine tuning in the law shuffled through his private papers to find treason, and found none, read through his eleven published Reports that had already become the bastion of English common law, and the wits said they were all asleep by the fifth book. They found only what they sought, that he had ruled for the old Magna Carta rather than the king. They ordered that he should delete such "mistakes." O rule misruled as in a farce. But when Lord Coke appeared they said he had only corrected five small spelling mistakes, three in English, one in Latin, and one in French.

Those of the Privy Council where he had served so long treated him with contempt as if the banked-up fires of their jealousy of his learning and his arrogance flamed into action, until the dancing Queen Anne herself insisted, for she had ever honored Sir Edward, that King James must tell them to at least let the old man sit down.

Then there were the final days. They said in the taverns and in Paul's walk and in the public galleries of the courts that he had fallen to four Ps. Pride, praemunire, prerogative, and prohibitions; the words became as prayers to some and jokes to some, and few knew what they meant, only that he who had been in was out, and those out were in, for in and out and up and down are the true lawful directions of a courtly life.

What has all this to do with me and this cold night and snow here in New England? This false decision or that lying rumor, deaths and shames and passions not for woman as a little venal sin, or for truth as few have heart to defend, but for God Power, and that at any cost to commonwealth or the Father of Light; we have brought it all with us from old England as truly as we brought ourselves.

Rumor waxed and waned and then was no longer spoke of. The strollers of noon in Paul's walk gossiped of other men than Edward Coke. We all knew, for it had been sold for a penny in broadsheets in the marketplace, that he had been humiliated in any easy way that could be thought of, first that the new judge in his place sent a servant to buy his gold esse collar and he retorted that he would keep it for his heirs so they would know that once in England they had had a Chief Justice for their ancestor. A good phrase, they said of him, a fine phrase, as if he had been player in a play for their pleasure and contempt. One accusation, then another, to ridicule and make the people jeer at him; he was even accused of the grim crime of letting his coachman drive without a cap upon his head, a long neglected prerogative of the servants of the king!

They saw him fallen and made witty and licentious quips, as he had long been thought a cuckold, and hen-driven, for his wild contentious rich second wife made great gossip. But I saw him there, day after day, leaning like a praying mantis over his lifework in that dusty room he would not brook cleaning for he knew on which pile years of papers rested, bearing the decisive and human names and form that were to him the love letters of his abiding passion.

Below the level of court, client, and ambition his honor grew until they said of him that he was the most honest, just, and incorrupt judge that ever sat on bench in Westminster.

But reputation is as far away to a man alone as the wind outside the window; it avails nothing. The face of the man I saw that day in the candled darkness before the dawn was drawn and painted gray by sorrow. I thought that I could read his history in his face, how he would stare beyond the window at the faint beginning of day and then, wincing as if he had a body hurt, force his mind back to the legal matter on the sheet where his hand rested, as if it kicked against the prick of his discipline.

At first I took down a language I hardly understood, for the language of the law is grave and secret, a fenced language that seeks to protect its decisions from any if and or but that might be borne in the mind of an advocate. Everything said at least four times, front and back, sides and roof, and all passion leached from the event. I was gradually persuaded that it had to be so; as all argument must be armed against inroads. It has made my written words prolix and my opinions stern, arrived at over long roads, traps and clogged and muddy ways of my own.

That morning when the dawn came he seemed to remember I was there and took from me the transcript and translation as if I were again a boy in school, nodded and said, "Good." He had the power with me always to say that one word like a blessing.

Day after day I picked up crumbs of what had really happened between him, the king, and his bounden enemy, the lord Bacon, that brilliant man of talent, erudition, and the deep wound of ambition too long thwarted. I saw my lord Bacon many times, and if you can read a man in his face, I see him now in my own mind's eye as one on whom the servile humility he presented to the king and his new favorite, Villiers, sat like a children's goblin mask.

Sir Edward gave me, let drop, the meaning of prerogative read as treason in others. The poor old vicar, he called him that, and when he spoke of him his voice turned harsh. "Poor old fool," he said. Preroga-

tive then had the name of Mr. Peachem, for it was on that slippery case
called treason and punishable by death that my lord fell.

I have certain cause to remember poor Mr. Peachem, for it taught me
to write little down and what I did to write in my secret writing in
that dangerous time in that dangerous place. Poor Mr. Peachem had let
out his spleen in a secret sermon he made for his own relief against the
king and never preached to anyone. My lord Coke ruled that he had not
committed treason, since he had said nothing publicly to cause dissen-
sion; the king argued that he had, and took the case from Coke. The
Lord of Lights resolved the matter by taking the old man to His bosom
in a wet cell in a winter prison. Sir Edward's names for prohibition
were Colt and Glover, for praemunire, a Mr. Owen, and the pride he
kept for himself.

He saw always in terms of the people accused, never abstractly. But
I had to make myself listen without breath for fear of missing words
when the matter came to that which had taken Bartholomew Legate to
his grave. It took me months to have the heart to ask for fear that he,
a father to me as Bartholomew had been, had agreed with that obscene
punishment. He had not. He said simply that he had ruled that heresy
was not punishable by death, since heresy was of the mind and not
public actions, and that a man's thoughts were no crime under civil
law, except, he added, when they caused riot. He showed me then
Bartholomew's case in his sixth book of Reports.

He smiled as he did more and more and there was change, once
again, in the air of his courtly world. One morning he read aloud, as
coolly as if Bartholomew had not been burned to death but merely censured, his decision. I remember that we were eating the breakfast his
man brought with the dawn, as we had often done when I was called
before my own house woke to day, when he rose from the table corner
to find the reference.

Here in this cold night with the fire almost gone to sleep, I am
astonished that I, Roger Williams, a poor boy from a poor parish, knew
for so long and began to take for granted the powerful of the earth, saw
them fight and scratch like the whores at Smithfield. But instead of
fingernails, they fought with catclaw words, uses of the law, bowing so
often to the demanded pleasures of the king. It would have been easy
to see that the man who was the king, who had the habit of fingering

his crotch, who when he drank, dribbled out both sides of his mouth down his doublet, was contemptible, but my master said over and over that he was no fool. He counted him a worthy contender.

When Hilary term began on the twenty-third of January, 1617, in Star Chamber, I found then why he had taken a fourteen-year-old unknown boy in his service. It was because of that, that I was fourteen, small, and unknown, and could shift and sidle among the crowds that pressed forward in the law courts, find a seat unnoticed and take down in my secret shorthand every legal case that he had marked on the docket, for he had been exiled from the Star Chamber and the Privy Council, those beloved places he had served for so long.

Sir Edward Coke was not letting grim and vulgar circumstance get in the way of his life's work. It was Star Chamber he cared most for, because it was there that treasons were accused of men, an easy accusation since then a word, a shrug, could land a man into deep water. Most of those whose records he demanded of me were accused of criticizing the king, for it was prerogative he and the king had locked their horns on, and my master resolved to seek out cases where the king had claimed prerogative that Magna Carta had not allowed.

But even then, he, who was royalist, excused his king by saying he was a Scot and knew not the ways of England, and never learned. God's earthly shape he may have been in the wilds of Scotland, but in England he was only a poor man grown newly rich and spending the treasury as if every day were New Year's. But always he was a man changeable as a figure seen through this midnight window, behind it, simplicity, often kindness, deep cruelty, a varying intelligence. My lord Coke said he was an honor to spar with, so for that, boy that I was, I watched and tried to honor him. Had I not I could have lost my new station. It was the way the world worked, all the way from the king down to me, fourteen, on the way in the dark by barge from London to Westminster the first day of Hilary term.

IV

---✦◆✦---

*It is a woeful privilege attending all great states and per-
sonages that they seldom hear any other music but what is
known to please them. . . . Of which power, upon a grudge
(as 'tis said) about his wife, King Henry despoiled the
pope, and with the consent and act of Parliament, sat
down himself in the pope's chair in England, as since his
successors have done.*

— ROGER WILLIAMS TO PARLIAMENT

HOW WELL THE YEAR DIES, AND WITH WHAT
holy grandness and pomp! On yonder hill beyond the river the frost has
painted the tops of the maples bright red. The virgin tree beside the
water is decked with yellow leaves, and I will go down to it from Foxes
Hill slowly, with my stick with the wolf's head on it. How smooth it
has grown under my hand. Well, I too have grown smoother with age,
under the weight of Providence, and Providence. I promise myself this
fine morning no railing at circumstance, no judgement, no decision, no
quarreling with Papists, Presbyterians, Quakers, Baptists, Boston
saints, drunken sinners, land grabs, land deals, money, power, Mr. Harris, Mr. Whipple, or any other of the thousand things that goad me. I
will simply take my morning walk along the woods, skirting the
meadows lest one ear of grain be lost to my foot.

I have walked by the waterfront before the new houses that still after
a winter have the smell of pine resin where the sun rests on the log
walls. We have tilled more fields, girdled more trees with more inva-

sions of that primeval barrier of forest that stretches uphill behind us all the way to forever.

Only one year, and a few months over, and some have gone to what they think of as safer places, as if that were fact and not some painted fancy. Most of us have stayed, and now benign smoke spirals toward the sky from busy chimneys that all survived the burning, and were a map of Providence so that we could begin again, each family at its own fireside.

We have had two harvests in some over a year, after the time of pain and fury and fire. It all grows again, and we are more wary, sometimes more contentious, as two women fight over the borders of their gardens as if there were not enough for all. All winter the good wives have made new quilts, woven blankets, for they scorn to sleep on skins as the natives do, though I do not. A bearskin is all we need to keep us from the winter, one over, one under, once the smell is leached out.

The ships from England have brought new porringers, and plates and spoons and all the things the women have longed for have joined what we culled from the ashes of the old town. To remind us, some spoons and plates are scorch-branded by their past and burial, some lines along the faces of men and women that were not there before, but even those begin to disappear. I can hear it behind me in Providence—the season of the axe fall, the rhythm of the looms, the calls of women to their children to help fill the cellars with dried food for the winter. Uphill behind the settlement the men are making corn shocks that stand like wigwams in the gleaned fields. The hay pyramids lean against the center poles of the tree trunks within that hold them in place.

I, Roger Williams, standing on this hill, vow to keep my thoughts to myself, which I, according to my friends, my family, my neighbors, and my critics, have seldom done in all my life. None but myself can know the old man's peace that I have this morning, not that after riot, but a void, a soul cave within, allowing color, senses, vision, space to enter into my soul for a little while, forgetting all pains, bruises, and indemnities, only standing here pleasing the Father of Lights and myself.

No man constructed nor no woman wove so fine a garment as New England wears in autumn! Tree red and tree yellow make the dark solemn evergreens stand as kings within their trains of color.

From this hill meadow there is a slope where the cattle still graze before their winter barn life, and the river flows below before it turns to a highway of ice. All summer I watched while the boys of Providence swam there with an abandon their parents could never have known, what with shame and religion and cold keeping their clouts about them as they did in old England. The boys were like small white Indians, as savage, as innocent, and as full of grace before the weight of beginning adulthood fell upon them and having been innocent on a Wednesday they sinned on a Thursday with the same acts.

I see what now for me is called a second childhood when having admitted to myself and all that I am lower than a dead dog, and having found a way through the fog of sins, judgements, righteousness that the Lord Jesus said He came to rid the world of, I am here again, no more, standing on a hill looking on a river. Oh please Christ a few minutes more before words and thoughts and memory take me back into the moving of the world away from its stillness.

Again last night I tried to give speech to that dear youth who crowds into my memory. I must learn to love this child who was myself, forgo shame and denying of his small hopes and fears and sins, and simply go there in my mind's eye and take him by the hand. The relived vision was there last night but not the words, the sounds but not the way to tell them, the color, oh dear Father of Lights the color, man-made then, not like this.

Regal power has a color and I saw it then and will never forget it, that first morning so long a time ago, though I am not able to put it down so that my New England children and grandchildren will know how the fountain of their civil being, which they do and should take for granted, was once a fight to the death for so many loved ones. We did bring little of it here. Myself without, my soul within, the face of God, and my bitter and haunting private memory was my lasting baggage.

I thought of it again last night in the hour I have taken as my own. It has become for me a habit of peace after the others have gone to their beds. Old letters spread out before me then received no new words. But I did go into my memory and brought out a morning stowed away where I can always go again even though I cannot tell it.

And even if I told it, who among the new children of this land would believe it? They would think of it as only a story told by an old man of olden times, half forgotten and half made up, like a woman's pretty quilt of saved scraps that mean much to her and nothing to anyone else. But that morning is not scrap of memory but a full vision as clear to me as this vision of the morning and the river.

Who could forget such a thing? I must cross a gulf of sixty years and a sea change deeper in the soul of Englishmen than any time since Christ. Would they believe in this new year of 1680 that so short a time ago in 1617 when I began my journey out of Smithfield there once was a king whose sneeze could shake the world I knew? They live on the far bank of civil war in England that killed the "prerogative absolute" of a king by cutting off his head. A radical solution to say the least, to cut that one word, "absolute," from the laws and minds of Englishmen!

Now beyond terrible civil war, the change of spirit that came with it is the only proof I know that revolution has happened to the mind. After an avalanche of action and a flood of words it is like a shining pebble left in my hand. What is taken for granted by the young was treason in the time I seek, though there were rumblings, and not least by Sir Edward himself.

Early in the morning of the opening of Hilary term in Star Chamber, he sent me upriver in the public wherry he had taken for over thirty years from the Inner Temple. On January twenty-third it was still near dark on the river with only the promise of day and the swinging lights of the rivermen in their boats going upstream and down. I was afeared, I confess, but thrilled as well to be going at eight of the morning up the sweep and force of the Thames past the great houses. The flambeaus on their docks danced in the cold river wind. We passed York House where Lord Bacon lived, who had designed the fictions that brought my lord Coke down so low.

The light from flambeaus streaked the darkness as the servants moved back and forth preparing for the waking of the king. Their hurrying and pausing marked the vastness of the Palace of Whitehall, but the palace itself was only deep shadows and hints of high solemn buildings that I would grow to know so well.

I remember that morning and my innocence of that morning and my wide-mouthed boy's surprise as the wherry slid alongside the water gate at Westminster where the judges and the guilty, the innocent and the quarrelsome, landed to go into the great courts of Chancery and Common Pleas and King's Court and all that took their places in Westminster Hall. Mountain-high above me the steep-gabled Star Chamber cleft the dark sky. Faint lights of flambeaus darted and swam beyond its great windows. It was the first building of all, nearest the river, my second home for over four years, from boy to young man. It was the most public and most feared court in England, the Star Chamber, where the king's Privy Council sat twice a week in the winter term of Hilary, the spring of Paschal, the summer of Trinity, and the autumn of Michelmas, year in year out never changing, the fathers of the land being stern with their wayward children, judging the world and eating like pigs.

I stumbled as I climbed ashore and nearly fell into the river. The rowers laughed. I walked the long stone quay with Sir Edward's letter clutched in my hand as if I feared the wind itself would steal it from me. The grandest of the Star days, the beginning of term, drew all of London to its colors and its pomp. I twisted and turned through the crowds trying to find a place within.

It took until nearly nine of the clock and the full sun-splashed day of the January thaw before I reached the huge doors where the doorman held court and for that little while was the most important man in London. He took more money on opening day than anytime after except when the cases smacked of court or royalty, and then the curious and the gossips gathered like mayflies feeding on the private errors and sins of those they saw as their betters.

At the moment he read the short note, I found with what awe and honor my lord Coke was held in Star Chamber. He dropped the courtly arrogance he assumed for that day and smiled. "How is he?" he whispered. "Tell me of him." So while the crowd stomped and nuzzled behind us like cows to the barn, I told him half-lies, knowing they would pass from his ears to those behind him to those behind them to Paul's walk, to the taverns, and I yearned to protect my new friend.

"He is well and full of plans for his books, and he makes jokes and eats sparing and we walk together every day through the Temple Gardens and all along the river to London Bridge. Early in the morning," I added, not wanting to be found out, and knowing how empty the city was at so early an hour.

"How does he with his lady?" He leaned close and whispered and may as well have shouted his question for the ears behind us pitched even closer to my lying tongue.

"Well, I thank you, most felicious and intimate," I lied. The whispers swept away until they joined the wind.

"They say . . ." the porter began, but the crowd saved me and my lord by pressing forward.

Sir Edward had told me to sit where the law students of the Inns of Court sat, and to take down what they took down as well as those cases he had marked. When I got within the chamber, I stopped, no matter that the crowd behind me surged at my back, for it was near time for the procession to come from the inner chamber. There above me was a room so vast and so high that it seemed a part of all outdoors but roofed against the rain by a rich deep blue sky of its own, sprinkled with gold stars. I saw many a great chamber after but that was the first and most remembered.

Where my lord had told me they were, the members of the Inns of Court sat, leaned, bantered, called to one another over the noise of the crowd settling for the show. I knew them by their youth and their commonplace books, some opened, some still clutched in hands that waved one to another. They were boys, older than I, but they had all the relish and the noise of apprentices or Roaring Boys, some handsome, some lithe, some heavy toward their becoming men. They greeted me as if they had been already told that I would be there among them, for news seemed to travel before tongue in that huge room.

They made a place for me, and even vied with one another about where I should sit. I was surprised that they knew me or seemed to. They honored and loved my lord and had waited to see how he would indeed deal with being and not being in his second home.

They leaned around me and whispered, for the room was becoming quiet as when a play is about to begin. Their breath formed clouds of cold; they asked of my lord and I told them he was well, and that he had sent them a message to take their notes as if he were still there. He had been used to nodding toward them when an important point of law was about to be argued, so that they could, as he had told me, wake up and pay attention. He had marked for me and for them the parts of the docket they were to mind, for he was a natural teacher and had been so with them for thirty years. So I, small and scared and new to the grandest room I had ever seen, was their lifeline to their teacher, and they watched my hand all day.

By the whispers of "How doth he?" and "Is it true . . . ?" and so on, they were sending their curiosity and care for him as if I were some messenger that ran from them to him they so revered. So I spun a gauzy net of white lies to protect my besieged master. I was only trying to present him as he would wish. I whispered that he and his lady were happy together, that he worked well, and was grateful for the time to do his work, and so on and on.

The clock struck nine.

What did he call, that one at the door of the inner chamber? I do not remember, although I heard it so many times that it acted only as a demand that the great crowd calm and quiet itself. Oh I hear it again, "Oyez" said as "Oyea" for it was French from the old time. "Oyea oyea," from the depths of legal time the call went forth.

They entered within to all standing and a great silence, such a parade of the grand and the powerful, such color of red and gold and purple, such Orders of the Garter, and jewels and satin and silk and furs and robes that swept the floor. The only sound was of their rustling, leaves of taffeta and satin in the morning. First came the presiding judge, one Lord Ellesmere, a sworn enemy of my lord. That I knew well. Gossip and Rumor, those half-blind peeping-tom twins, had sung it about. He was said to have been the handsomest man in England by those who had never left the font of London. I had long forgot the man until this lovely morning where the profane colors of my memory matched the sacred colors the riot across this river.

He followed the Great Seal and the Mace that was the king when the king was not present, which he seldom was, but when he did come, as my lord Coke would complain every time, he shot himself in his foot.

The youths around me were a different breed to me. I sat there stunned by their careless loose-limbed tall bodies, which made me see myself as one pinched and cold. They lounged on their shoulders, owning the earth and all that in it was, while I sat huddled on the edge of my seat, smaller, shorter, embarrassed, and cold as charity, for I did not, like most of the others, wear a broadcloth coat against the cold, much less the fine ermine and miniver collars that warmed their faces. They wore their riches to keep them warm and show who they were. I wore the clothes my father made me, that only weeks before I had strutted in with such pride. As the day divided into the causes and pleas of the troubled, the angry, the vengeful, the fearful poor and the arrogant rich, the Privy Council sat above them with their robes close around them and tucked under their feet, hugging their warmth. They looked like hooded hawks.

Those first days in Star Chamber were an unhappy time for me, for I was the butt of their whispered jokes, the pet names clerklet, bumboy, girl-cheek, for I was delicate of color and my hair curled then. They fell to practical jokes, as wetting my seat under their cloaks with their piss, and whispering that they would cut my purse and my pretty hair if I ventured forth into the dark without my keeper. All this in whispered riot while I sat hunched over my own commonplace book like a pinched clerk indeed, or one of the starved and wretched solicitors that hung about the doors of the courts to pick up crumbs of business. I took down the docket my lord had marked with pencil after pencil in my secret writing, until my hand was filthy with black lead.

Within two terms I suffered there alone, through the winter Hilary and the spring Paschal, taking down words that meant no more to me than the sounds of them, and transcribing them when I went back to Sergeant's Inn. Often my lord Coke did not abide there but went to the great Hatton House, and in such short time his most intimate business was so well known among the gossips that my protecting lies fell on their laughter. But many times and then all together, I slept on a pallet in the corner in his chamber, too tired to go forth, and in truth, terrified for my purse and my hair in which I took such pride.

Sometimes, half asleep, and often hungry, I heard the riot without. It had a joyful tone of playing boys, let loose their youth and energy in the night, as when the apprentices wilded their ways through the streets at holidays. Sometimes the clash of steel, for they were allowed two weapons within the confines of the Inns, one dagger and one knife, to use for eating.

I remember little of the cases but I was learning a thing about the law that astonished and pleased me. That turgid language seemed cut to cover passions. Anger and hurt were calmed as a fractious horse is calmed by patience and delay. I learned too that it was good to be born well then in England and I suppose now although I still have hopes that someday what is real will match what is thought to be real, and all will be equal before the barre of justice.

There were sweep-ins of ladies in fury with each other, for the court was known to be awash with the spat insults of a troop of the most belligerent and fractious court ladies in London. The favorite's mother, Lady Sutton, and the lady Suffolk, rich with public bribery, were said to be the worst of the noisy witches who beleaguered the poor, frightened king. I fear my lord's wife, Lady Hatton, was of their gaggle. She was so proud and so arrogant with land and money that she refused even to wear his name and kept her widow's name so that she would be Lady Hatton, a better connection with that bawdy court.

To this day I can hear the echo of their shrill voices from other rooms of my memory. That hallowed parade of the insulted or greedy, bad-tempered Lady This and Lady That, brought their malicious spit to spray Star Chamber, albeit in a different language and a colder fury, but in temper much like the whores and cutpurse girls at Smithfield. They stood glaring on either side of the great floor of the court, each surrounded by her coteries of silk and satin, and accused of slander and malice like the gold porringer calling the silver teapot dented. The pot and the kettle were the providence of lesser mortals, who made Star Chamber matters of who threw hot slops in the face of another to settle an argument, carried all the way through the lower courts and usually thrown out, being no Star Chamber matter. What beating, what tossing into plashes of water, what riots where farm wives and farmers pitchforked intruders who were there with the excuse of improvements on the land, as dikes and canals to drain the water for their masters' use. Park land for the new gentry against age-privilege of common land grazing was brought to Star Chamber over and over, that which was to become, away beyond religion, the greatest cause of coming to this new land that ever I knew. Then, over and over, roaring at one another about hunting rights, and rights of speech, and scurrilous verses suppressed long after they had become commonplace jokes on everyone's lips. All of these swim together in my memory as what was interesting enough in the days of Star Chamber to prick my ears to listen to import and not only to words.

Laughter cut short by the solemn judge would wake the boy within the clerk, so would the horrors, to me, of much punishment, never given to lords and ladies, the face brandings, the whippings, the stocks and the splitting of noses and the bloody loss of ears nailed to the stocks and then cut off. There was one difference I remember that split those in the court by birth, breeding, size, and arrogance from the poor and troubled. Only gentlemen of equal class were punished for dueling, for the king hated violence of any kind. It was considered that if there were words or swords unsheathed between a superior and an inferior, a servant, or a tradesman, there was no punishment, since the gentleman, no matter his reputation for brutality, was, under precedent, considered to be correcting the mistakes of his inferiors.

Star Chamber tried cases that did not fit the laws heard in Chancery and Common Pleas. Well, after a time I wondered what other quarrels among men and woman there were, for all hurts and angers, even stunned by legal language, were paraded before me. Riot and libel and treason and all matters of the voice, insults, satiric verses, trespass, property, and untrammeled tongues were punished there. The punishments for the poor were terrible in their carrying out, whipping, the stocks, the Fleet prison they called fleeting, all given for crimes that were decided to be crimes as the evidence was brought forth. I knew then more and more why my lord needed to codify those decisions, for he yearned to set down for legal precedent a way of harnessing that dread place where laws were made up for the day, and no protections were given to those who had no connection of birth or influence with the bright-robed council who sat in judgement over them.

I had, of course, been familiar with the marks of punishment all my life. Dolly, young girl of thirteen, a child whore proud of her talent for leading those who liked little girls into alleyways where her gang stripped and robbed them, wore her branded cheeks with a difference. If one or another wore longer hair than was then in fashion it was taken for granted that one ear or both had been lost to the law, often for the speaking of their minds in the wrong company. So many had such long hair that it was to become a jeering fashion among the courtiers. London was a garden of fine trees and pretty gardens and gibbets where dried and leathern bodies creaked in the wind and where children starved to death and froze in the streets and were swept up in the morning long after I had passed by on my way to keep my lord's hours.

There were so often heads piked on public buildings, and parts of bodies from the quartering rotting on high stakes, their humanity long since lost to us who passed by, They ceased even to be a warning any more than garbage in the Fleet river or animals drowned in Houndsditch. Why hearing the punishments meted out by those powerful robed men was worse to me than seeing the flotsam of their results I know not. Oh I do know, it was the coldness—the protections of those who sat aloft from the guilty and the shamed and decreed stocks and scars and brandings and whippings for those whose crimes were so often done in passion or for survival. I truly did not know how terrible a place that lovely city was until I left it. We grow used to the perils of our own time, and safely keep our judgements for the past, for the future, or for other sinners.

V

·————◆————·

*Kings are properly judges and judgement properly belongs
to them from God: for Kings sit in the throne of God, and
thence all judgement is derived. It is aetheism and blasphemy to dispute what God can do; so it is presumptions
and high contempt in a subject to dispute what a King can
do, or say that a King cannot do this or that. . . . I remember Christ's saying, "My sheep hear my voice," and so I
assure myself, my people will most willingly hear the voice
of me, their own Shepherd and King.*

— KING JAMES I,
JUNE 20, 1616 — STAR CHAMBER

I HAD DREAMS LAST NIGHT FROM THINKING YESTER-
day about the child of London that I was. How many evils do we face
in sleep until our waking frees us . . . must I protect this child I was
even from my dreams? For in the night I stood before the Judge of all
sins. I was in a darkness that I knew was forever. But I heard thunder
and understood its words. In the dream I was as I am today, myself, old
man, and with me was a boy, and both were myself, and I argued
against eternal damnation because the boy lied. Father of Lights and
Truth, I pled that my boy-sins would be forgiven. Still, now awake, I
argue at the barre of eternity.

Poor man. Of course I lied about my lord. And I would lie again as
I did then, and tell it to the dawn that streaks the bay with fire and the

sky with clouds so red they warn as I was warned in the dream; red sky at morning, sailors take warning.

The wind from the sea all the way across the water to England calms my troubled soul. What grace and meet there is to be alive in the early morning. No, I could not tell what I observed, for I only half understood it, and too, the places and the people and the newness and the true astonishment that this I saw and this I became a part of was not less than the power and pulse of England—the law, the court, the grand deceivers, rulers of the roost, the weight and thrust of decisions over all the unknown people I had grown with for fourteen years, knowing no other.

I had, in one walk past Paul's Cross and the leathern bodies swinging in the wind and the sleeping birds, left behind my friends and neighbors who went about their daily tasks and sins and pleasures trusting that they were overwatched by their betters.

I loved much and at once and kept my judgements to myself, for he, my lord Coke, had rescued me, and set me on my course. I was thrust forth into a fine, gracious, rich, dangerous, tormenting, powerful, polite, hell I thought then was heaven, but not, oh Lord, for long.

My lord was as a child, so deep was he into the pits and perils of the time and the decadence, the choices both evil, the roads not strait nor narrow their gates, both taunting to one as he was, sick with ambition he thought was health, who had been taught and formed from his youth to follow the road to power as if it were his duty. I never knew him to succumb to the obscene obsequies of that disgraced court as others did. He scorned that, but when he could stand exile no longer he let circumstances flush him like a quail, and he fell to the guns of his own ambition and so turned away from his one protection, his pride.

I saw it all with the eyes of that boy, and my thought was that my lord Coke may know more of the law than any man in England as they said, but he knew not how to protect himself in a dirty fight. No matter how much he tried to fool himself to cut his life more to the pattern and style of service to the state, he could not fool a fourteen-year-old boy. Remember that.

Lord of Love, who am I convincing here in the first light of morning but myself? Can that man in the canoa throwing his nets, black against the wild red sky, hear me? Can God hear me? Can the boy?

Oh little Roger Williams, you knew and did not speak. You, too, had succumbed to a new ambition. You were a boy among many men and riot and throngs of actions. You thrust aside such thoughts as judgement of the actions of those who you had been trained to the halter of seeing as your betters. But it was there, the clear eye given me as a grace and burden by my dear Christ. Sometimes my own voice pricked and offended me, sometimes Bartholomew's. As late as now, this morning in the red dawn, I the old man will listen at last to what I was.

Dear Lord of Lights, it was a fine new world then. Take the food. I had never seen such food, although my parents were not poor. It was thrown away in the court and in the Star Chamber when the Privy Council stuffed themselves while the starving gathered without and prayed for scraps, and the English sailors starved to death in his majesty's ships.

And the color, what of the color? The dazzled boy I was saw and kept the pictures in my mind's eye to bring out this morning and confess before my Father that the color blinded me. They were fine sights and all in the dirt of power and London. That year, or part of it, I saw power working in the corridors, in the corners, whispered behind regal hands, courtiers, favorites, hopeful seducers. My lord instructed me what I must know about the strangeness of the court but say ought about now I was legally a man but a boy withall. The strangest secret, though much suspected in London, was that the king loved, as any man loves, dotes, gives gifts, fawns in the public eye on the other on whom he dotes. In the king's case, having, as he explained so carefully, done his duty by his realm by producing three heirs, his doting eyes fell on men not women.

The factions of the court combed England for handsome boys on whom to pin their hopes for preferment. They formed businesses, pooled money for dress, French lessons, and travel to make their property attractive to the king, one going so far as having the cheeks of a hopeful courtier paddled with posset curds each day for his pretty skin.

But by then the king had fallen in love with the handsomest man in England, thrust in his path by his moneyed backers and the Archbishop of Canterbury. George Villiers, an unknown pretty boy, would in a few short years rise to knight and baron and earl and viscount as if they were steps to heaven, until in the latter years he was the Duke of Buckingham, the first duke ever in England, called the uncrowned king. He was the youngest ever in the Privy Council.

He was so handsome that one looked away, dazzled, on seeing him for the first time. That lovely-looking man had a face and skin as delicate as a young girl's, a face bewitched and bewitching. He was of that, to me, most rare breed of tall slim men, straight-legged, unricketed, unblemished, unstarved, unbeaten, uncropped, unbranded, unscarred, untrained to fear. Within a year the king did fawn on him in public as in private and pinch his cheeks and call him his Steeny after a painting of St. Stephen, and let him and his family gather riches where they list. He so doted on him that he quite openly said that he, James, had his George, as Jesus had His John.

George Villiers was to rule England to its cost for years, but until the day the king died he signed his ill-educated notes to him "your dog, Steeny."

The word of my being called his bumboy had reached my lord Coke's ears, and, furious, he spoke. Such judgements and rumors were in the air of the time around us. Within a week all taunting ceased together as I sat among the Roaring Boys. I knew how the word had got to him, for nothing ever was secret in that time, words had wings and settled like ravens on the shoulders of the victims of gossip large and even as small as me. My lord Coke had spoken in one of those thundering whispers of his; the corridors and fine great rooms of the Inns of Court echoed with it, for he was as always their mentor.

One day on walking back down the Thames side from Westminster to London, I was so cold that when I put my hands to the fire in his chamber, I could not stop the tears of pain coming to my shamed eyes. That was why, my lord explained, he bought for me a long cape to wrap around me in the cold Star Chamber as the others did. He chose a dim dung-colored broadcloth. He cut my pretty hair with the great shears he used to cut parchments, making me as plain a boy as he could, fussing like an auntie. He saw to it that in that strange weather no one would take me for his bumboy.

As for the lies I told of him, what could I ever do? I was treated as

a path to him, and I never let it happen. My mother had took to mentioning my lord's name whenever she could to her customers in her
inn, quite heavy with portent, her connection through me to Sir
Edward, and through him to Hatton House, and through Hatton
House to the court and through the court to the king, to which she
always added, his gracious majesty. Which was, of course, the road that
the world took, a friend of a friend of a cousin of a friend and so on to
the king of England, which was, then, the font of being.

So when I went to my parents to sup with them at my old place at
the table, they seemed to know more of Sir Edward than I did myself,
although whatever they asked me I denied, half truthfully, for never
did he mention to me during the whole time what I still see as his
shame. His chambers at Sergeant's Inn were his haven and mine.

So I was late in knowing and all by other paths what a fool that
proud man had made of himself. When Trinity term was over in June,
he set forth, leaving me behind. Then was when I would trudge back
to my home at late bright evening of summer on the path I had taken
that first morning, along Fetter Lane with its gaggles of ne'er-do-wells
in their borrowed or stolen ragged finery, by St. Bartholomew's to Long
Lane, and be a boy again under my mother's questioning and my
father's thumb. Oh it was hard being boy and man at the same time,
never knowing which was called forth.

And that is what I did, innocent, deaf, and mute. While he charged
flying into scandal I sat day after day in that chamber of his as cut off
from charges and countercharges and disgraces as a monk in a cell,
transcribing the sea of shorthand notes I had made through Hilary and
then through Paschal and Trinity terms, while outside the long vacation was another world.

He said not a word, nor changed his way of study through that
summer. What I was stopped and asked of never entered where we
were. There it was as quiet as breathing, as a turn of crisp parchment,
and pen scratch and fire fall, that only. Sometimes I watched him and
thought he could not be the man they speak of, but he was. Oh, he was,
and when I saw the change in him when it was over, for he wore the
cost in his face, I lied for him as one would lie for angels accused of
thievery.

He kept it from me that the older brother of the favorite, one Sir

John Villiers, had taken a fancy to his daughter and his money and with the aid of his ravenous mother, who worshiped God Gold, offered marriage. My lord kept his council for a long time and then, when he could stand exile no longer, fell to offering his daughter and his fortune for preferment. He did not take me with him to Newmarket to meet the king and bow before him and kiss his soft hand. Then I was disappointed for I did not know as I do now that something within him was ashamed at having to toe the line. So he went to Newmarket for the king and the favorite's return from their triumphant tour of Scotland. At least triumph was the word, for no man nor even the powerful awful women of that court dared call it otherwise.

So my poor lord, one of the richest men in England, made his obeisance and kissed hands of the king. The king's smile reached London by the black raven of rumor that the great Sir Edward Coke was once again in favor. He simply could not bear to be exiled from power, and he told himself and let me listen, as was often his habit, that his poor country needed him too much for him to stand so arrogantly on pride.

I had not seen his wife except in the distance, high above her neighbors in every way. She was the daughter of the Earl of Essex, a landowner in her own right, beautiful and arrogant, as rich in debt as in money, and as selfish as a pig. She rode rough shod over the court, the world, and my lord himself. He, so feared by so many, was treated by her that year and ever after as a contentious nuisance. If he moved she parried. If he stayed still, as he tried to do, she acted with such force that he, poor man, riposted. Oh my dear that man who had downed Essex, condemned Raleigh, defeated Somerset and his faction, shaken and cleansed the laws of England, was a victim of the shrill rancor of a vixen wife.

The first time ever I heard her—she was a woman you remember as hearing more than seeing—was a voice shrill and vexed, screaming within the heavy oak door and her words piercing through it as if it were carved of paper. I thought it was my mother, but then I knew it was not, for she knew not where my lord Coke's chambers were, and said so with some pride, sniffed, and she sniffed well, as if that were a credit to her, that his chambers were somewhere in the world beneath her ken.

Then I knew it must be a mistress, a whore's voice, and by Christ's body I had heard enough of them in my time from the day I could understand. I was afraid to open the door.

"Betrayed! Robbed of my goods and chattels! Thou art a servant and no husband of mine, thou common *cook*!" the woman yelled and flung the door open. She did not deign to look at me, but I saw her. She was a beautiful woman, cased in satin and noisome taffety, clanking jewels about her stomacher. And a king's ransom dripped from her ears. She had used to her own husband and my dear better "thou" instead of the new and fashionable "you." "Thou" remained among the great to be used for servants.

He never said a word when I went into the chamber with our meat pies from Pye Corner, for I had broke him of eating from Mrs. Grumms, who cooked with so terrible a smell and taste for the riotous boys in the Inns of Court.

He never said anything in the whole time he went through such a public quarrel, although of course I knew at my own father's table in the seldom times I went there how, out of pique since she had not been courted for decision about the marriage, his wife had kidnapped their own daughter in the night from Hatton Garden while he slept.

It was told me as if they were there and part of it, how, when he woke, he took horse and road through the night, cantering in fury along the road with mounted men, armed with swords and pistols like a knight errant in a bad play, waving a warrant to redeem his daughter, how he had thundered at the great oak door of their retreat, broke it down, roared and rampaged through the country house of his wife's cousins where she had taken refuge, grabbed his daughter and thrown her crying and wailing over the back of his horse behind her half brother Fighting Clem Coke, and carried her off to Stoke House.

And then how his wife had followed with her own retainers, how her coach overturned in the mud and she was thrown into a puddle. How she went mud and all to the great house of Sir Francis Bacon, the new holder of the Great Seal, and demanded that he get her back her daughter, whom she saw herself as owning as surely as the jewels that clanked around her muddy throat. How she marched into his sickroom, for he was often ill, and knew that he would honor her since he and my lord had been rivals not only for preferment but for her hand.

Oh it did make a comedy for the stage or a joke or a derision.

My parents and my brother, Sydrach, tried to question me for tid-bits, pigeon-pecking at any words I let drop, but I pretended to know even less than I did. I did know that the king had taken my lord's side and put my lady Hatton to shame for kicking against the royal pricks, for he knew that Villiers wanted Sir Edward's money, even though she had more and tried to stop the marriage out of spite at not being in its charge.

Sir Edward was then a landlord of sixty estates all over England that he rented out, it was said, to pay his sons' debts or gave to his children and grandchildren when they married, for it was well known that even the highest judge in England earned so little that he must needs make his fortune in other ways. I had not ever seen the fourteen-year-old girl, my own age then, who was tossed back and forth between them like a ball in that royal game of tennis not played by common people. Though I had known many a time when a girl at Smithfield was beat for not obeying her father about the man she married, for marriage was a business arrangement, as usual and as approved as the sale of land or goods, planned amid sighs of disappointment at the cradle that it was a girl, so only a chattel bought and paid for after much bargaining and pinching of legs as a filly, if indeed filly she was.

'Twas said that even the great Sir Thomas More, who lost his Papist head for defying the king, had taken a suitor to his daughters' cham-ber and throwed the cover back, presented the naked girls, and told the suitor to take his pick. For a suitable price. That went without words.

All that was certain for me was that while I was still working at my notes on the Paschal term cases, he came from Hatton House to his chambers to live again in the long vacation, and that he went much abroad to court when the king was at Whitehall or at Theobalds. I would watch him then sometimes and wonder how that still, contained man, working at his papers like a monk, could be the same that they said had taken horse and cavaliered through the night like a wild high-wayman.

I may then as well have been a machine, a thing wound up like a watch, and finally, like a watch, I ran down and put my head upon the parchments and went to sleep. He heard the new crackle of the parch-ment and looked up and said, "Dear Master Williams, I have drove you to a halt."

So it was then that he took me with him to Stoke Poges. I drove with him in the carriage I had seen him in even when I was little more than a babe. It was the first time in my life I had been so far abroad from London and I fell in love with all that I saw. The luxuriant Thames I remember to this day as flowing through country woods and meadows to the sound only of the horses' footfall and once in a while the clatter of a stone under their hooves. We went for miles that were time suspended until his coachman turned the carriage into a long narrow road between trees as old as the hand of God, and walked the horses deep and deeper into the country, and drew them to a stop before the first tall iron gate. There were two gates to this Eden, at least I thought at first it was that, the second deeper into the lane. I had seen his family coat of arms often on his seal, only on the scrolled wrought iron of the gates it was large, an ostrich of argent silver holding in its beak a horseshoe. What that meant I waited for him to tell me, but he had not said a word since London; he was deep in his work. He seemed never to stop.

We went on at walking pace below bowers of vines, past country flowers I did not know deeper and deeper into enchantment, the trembling posed silence of a doe, scawmed twin fauns asucking her, a royal stag not deigning to do more than raise his head to review us. The horses were walked slowly between ancient trees where there was nothing man-made until we came to Stoke Poges church deep in the woods and vines and scent of summer. It was so still there in a holy country silence that I feared my very breathing would disturb. One of the horses snorted and broke the spell.

My lord looked up at the sound and handed his book to me to carry. He began to tell me then, for he was forever teaching as he breathed, that the gates controlled the movement of the sheep and cattle grazing so that nothing would be overgrazed and destroy the fine green carpet of the meadows that were beginning to open around us. He told me that the ancient church was built there by the monks, and later, many a time, it was my sin of ignorance to worship there below the heavy Norman arches.

Beyond a curve, down the last line of trees, glimpsed, lost in the leaves, then glimpsed again, a huge stone house, with many eyes of windows that the sun caught and etched with fire, spread out its fine brick wings along a massy park. I forgot that I was to be a serving man of dignity before my lord, and bounced to one side and then the other of the carriage, over his feet, the great man! The old man's feet! He laughed at me, and he said, "Oh how meet it is to see it with new eyes."

We drove in a circle around the great house so that it seemed to me to be turning to show itself. In the distance he pointed out the tower above the roof where he said we would see all the way to Windsor Castle and the curves of the Thames on fine days. We passed the stone barn, a fine elegant stable with a clock, a pretty round dovecote where I would spend many an afternoon, thinking and praying and listening to the doves, a little lake stocked with fish, a river flowing from it with an ornamental bridge. Beside the bridge a man stood so still I thought he was a statue, and when I looked again he was a statue, wearing green lichen.

My lord spoke on behind me as one proud of his favorite property, pleased to show off a little, telling me of yields and creatures' births and all such farm things that I knew nothing of.

Lined up before the huge studded door the servants and his tenants had gathered to welcome him. It was a fine sight that he seemed to take for granted. He waved them back so that we entered alone into the great hall of that sad cold graceful house, with a ceiling so high that the house of my family could have fitted, all four stories of it, under the carved wood ceiling in the distance. It was so empty that our footsteps echoed. He stopped within the room where wide panels of tapestry covered the stone walls with Rameses II and the Children of Israel marching forever around the room. The sun through the high windows caught their faces and the mountains of Sinai; Rameses and his charioteers seemed to move as the sun moved behind a cloud and then again to free itself to light the plunging horses.

Turkey rugs and velvet covers and satin cushions with blanched silver and all were flung about the room on sofas and Turkey ottomans and chairs and tables. Over the distant fireplace I could have stood in and left much over were the Hatton arms of stone, guarded by rampant lions that I had seen on the gates of Hatton House since my childhood. There were figures carved of fine dark wood all shining in many colors of nature on both sides of the fireplace. They stood as big as life against deep carved wood columns as if they were waiting to play for us, two musicians face to face with me, a woman with a harp, a man with a recorder.

I think knowing myself a child that moment, I took my lord's hand. I did. I feel it now. I was so overwhelmed by what I saw there, and never did I get so used to it through the years, never lost sight of its grandness in my eyes. He stood stock still. He let my hand go. He stared at the dead fireplace. He turned slowly, an old man, past the children of Israel and the wild horses of the Pharaoh, past the chimney stone carving. He stopped at a damasked chair, its seat worn with age. He lowered himself into it as if he were in pain and he began to cry.

Tears make a child of a man and I know it now and knew it then and so I, older for the moment, went up to him as I would to anyone in pain and took his hand again and held it saying nothing so that he could feel my prayer for him and my sorrow for him through my fingers without sound and without words. It was what I had done to stanch hot tears from my friends who were beaten or hungry or despised since ever I remembered, as simple and right to me then as it had been and still is today, skinned knee to grief for the dead. A touch. A yearning to stop the flow of sorrow with my hand.

We stayed that way until I thought he was asleep and when he spoke at last I saw that he had been taking his own voyage through his summer of pain and shame to come at last to the safe cove of that old chair in his own house. His voice was so soft that I leaned forward to hear him. He spoke as a man come from a long journey.

"It was my bounden duty," he said, and then, "Do you see? I must needs do it. There was no other road for me to take. They say I did it from ambition," then he held my hand hard when anger poured into his, but his voice was still soft, faraway, "'twas not ambition for preferment. It was my duty to grow close to him and try to steer him off the rocks."

That was all he ever said about what he had done, a man explaining to a boy his trial and verdict. I am certain he never spoke about it to another soul. There was, for him, no one else to say it to. He was too proud, too sure, too private a man for all his anger and his condemnations to do other.

Who that one was who needed a helmsman he never said, but I

knew it was the king, for strangely, he was fond of the king and had not yet given up his hope of him.

From that day he honored me by calling me his son. Through four years of my growing and learning, from astonishment at all I saw to judgement to learning of his demands upon himself, I stayed by his side, there at the font of England's gaudy court until it came down around us like a banquet tent left up too long and tattered by the wind.

He let himself be a laughingstock. He bore the condemnation of what he called his peers, though to me he had none. It was only when he saw that his decision had been to no avail that he changed, but that was another time and I was not part of it.

So through a court so rude, humiliation so public, and rumor so evil and powerful a tool for jealous, ambitious men, we sat there in his chamber in term time, in Stoke Poges in holiday, working, working, walking, he talking, I listening. Those were the times I cherish as a gift of Light. The others, the days at court, the roads to Theobalds, to Greenwich, to Windsor, to Whitehall, dragged chained to the king's caprices, I, Roger Williams, poor, clever, ambitious boy, went with him, drinking it all like a fine wine I had yet to learn was poison.

We saw little of his large family, they had their own riots, families, devises among theirselves; I think they forgot him a little. His life was the most public and his days the most lonely, that ever I was to know.

VI

━━━◆━━━

*All this have I done myself until the Father of Spirits
mercifully persuaded mine to swallow down no longer
without Chewing: to chew no longer without Tasting, to
taste no longer without begging the Holy Spirit of God to
enliven mine, against the fear of Men, Tradition of the
Fathers, or the favor or custom of any Men or Times.*

— ROGER WILLIAMS

HERE I AM, LYING AWAKE WITHIN THE BREATH-ing of my dear yoke mate and the family we have spawned. How trusting is the sleeping human, whether new as the new western land, or savage or depraved, forgiven for the night, an arm flung out, a body softened, a secret smile, a snore.

This is old man's time, unmeasured in hours or days, but only by the movement of the moon, a time to piss, listen to that holy music which is age and silence, think, see again other smoke and other fires and other beds in my mind's eye. And ruminate like an old cow.

It is three of the clock in the morning, the time old men face with the clear eyes of children. And sometimes pray that they may forget. Or remember. In the recesses of smoke and night I am again within the soft silence of wild roundhouses that smell of the branches and grass of their making, where my savage friends who saved me lie on their wood benches in a circle around the fire, so innocent in sleep, as soft as ferns, anger and zeal gone from their naked bodies.

Oft when I went among the Indians and stayed in their houses, I would wait until all slept and then the Father of Lights would give leave to me to read my Bible and to ponder and oft to scratch thoughts upon the mean commonplace books I carried. There by the light of the fire and my sleeping hosts in their bareness on their furs, the word of God would fall from my lap and I would dream. Dream, half dream, and sometimes I would start awake and wonder where I was and how I came there among them.

Now I must again atone for old foolishness of younger self, and as I do I am blessed. Instead of that perpetual punishment we seek in our sickness of being human, here I am lying, granted instead gifts and spaces, a passing ecstasy, a state not wished for but given, oasis of my soul, always unlooked for, always an astonishing, a candle lit and then blown out.

Once at Stoke House in the dovecote where the doves sighed and churtled, sometimes within the firelight of the Indian smoke holes when I was abandoned, and so too in the white waste of empty winter, I have stumbled into saving grace, the gift of that holy refreshment that comes, and goes, as a glimpse in the corner of my eye, a sigh in the trees, a blessed memory.

But I must warn myself lest I see myself as chosen of all men, question that mystic pride within that tells me I am Right and must teach what I have found to be True. Oh Truth oh Right oh save me from such a trap. Poor old man, do you not know yet that ecstasy is a gift to be received, and not a state to be sought or taught or earned? You bring from that lofty cloud of mist not a judgement of Right or Wrong, but a guide for yourself and no man or woman other.

Yet there was a time I wanted to train, to lead, to argue and demand that others see through my eyes and hear through my ears, and all for nothing. A firebrand in a pepper pot. Oh old man, old man, as the Quakers shouted in derision, how often you sinned so, blind as a worm and noisy as a barnyard dog.

And so did he, by Christ's wounds, so did Sir Edward, but with what fine trappings and what style he did it! No barnyard there, but a capitol and a court to pace in, parry and thrust within the law, gored for his pains, and back into the fight, that dear pious man. He who saved the laws of England and made a new Magna Carta, was Right, and so he said and the law said and the past said, lest men destroy each other without amity. He built a structure of legality for the state as a sure and stolid building. Father of Light, how proud I was of him!

My lord's small and beautiful daughter was forced to plight her troth before God to a man she knew not who was known to be tender in his mind. She was sold to that mild and half-insane brother of Villiers, as surely as if she had been a horse or cow in Smithfield market. Those two who knew each other not at all damned themselves by taking marriage vows in God's name which was the fashion, and the lawful privilege of her father, and all fathers from Smithfield to the palace at Whitehall. They married in great pomp at Michaelmas at Hampton Court, blessed not by God but by the king, who did them the great honor of visiting them in the morning in their marriage bed, for he loved to look on what he saw as bliss.

By then of course, the poor mild bridegroom had been dubbed Sir John to honor the favorite's dull and greedy family, and after that, Lord Purbeck, to please the unpleasable and inescapable Lady Hatton into granting her daughter and new son-in-law Corfe castle on the island of Purbeck. But she, still sulking, would not give down her milk, not to the king, her daughter, or her besieged husband. Too often on those early mornings I knew he had not slept. He escaped silently into his work, looking sometimes as thin in his face as the fox his enemies called him. Hardly a week passed that Lady Hatton did not draw him into land quarrels and money quarrels and even quarrels over domestic plate and such.

I watched my lord grow weaker in his body and stronger in his mind so that I feared a palsy would take him away. I thought I knew why. His lady was trying in her legal way to rid herself of him and any hope of his preferments, and while she succeeded not at all, it was a constant burr under his saddle lest she ruin him. I did not see greater hatred of him in all the time I served him, became so close to him that he called me son, unthinking, and walked with his hand often upon my head beside him, for I was the length of a cane for that tall straight man.

She set out to destroy him. Being too wise to have him killed she did it legally, by plea after plea, dragging her powerful family along with her, rumor after rumor floated as paper boats upon the waters of the court.

Sometimes in court he seemed as awkward as the albatross who sailors say is the world's most graceful and noble in the air but an ungainly fool upon the ground. So people saw him in the court, where he was loath to be. As the fall of the year went, I saw him shrink and grow older, and once he fell to the floor during a levee at court and his friends said that she had finally found the way within the law to murder a man and marry her lover. I knelt beside him until servants came with a litter.

The king called, "Take him to my privy chamber," and I heard him say to Buckingham, "Before God that woman must leave him alone. He is the only man I know who can add."

She would have known had she not so blindly hated that he would never lose his knowledge and his honesty to her beguiling. He won, over and over. But at what cost. I feared for him. But what could a fourteen-year-old boy say to such a mentor, so old and honored a father as he had become to me?

There were two places though where he was himself again, unburdened as if he were a road-traveling peddler who had left his heavy pack at the door. One was Stoke House, where she never came. We walked and rode and played at bowls, only the two of us, for he needed quiet, and asked no company other.

Sometimes, at peace again, he would give himself the luxury of sageness with me, laced with wit. He never mentioned the folly of his second marriage but in such terms as "Marry wisely, and you will live in the sun." Or "He who marries for love has good nights and terrible days." And sometimes from far within his mind, poised to roll the ball toward the ninepins on the bowling green, he would say, almost to himself, such as "I had a fine marriage with Bridget, I was fool enough and lonely enough to dream of another such."

And in an inner fury let fly the bowl and fling down the ninepins as if he did attack a person, and I knew who it was. He hated her but never said, hated her beauty, her witchcraft, and her riches, hated her lover Holles, who he never admitted to a soul on earth was putting horns upon his proud head.

But oh the other man, the one who walked in an arrogance that protected him from any slight to his face. No one dared. He was a wonder. He threw off all trammels, rose to his height, found his stride, and was himself again. It was the Star Chamber on Star days that he came into his own. By late September when Michaelmas term began he came in procession into the house of his proud lawful heart, his robes sometimes of green sometimes of fine purple, sometimes in the rich black robe of the Privy Council, with his sergeant's coif once more upon his head, following the royal regalia shining on its satin pillow, held high to represent the king. There were once again the judges in red, the Garter knights with their diamond stars, and there my lord striding in a triumph as sure as any Roman. He strolled with that arrogant ease of the country man he was, as if he had never been dishonored.

His presence there to me as I sat once again among the Roaring Boys was as a light after the terms of twilight where voices had mourned on about their troubles and put us half to sleep. When he entered that first morning, restored to the Privy Council, the Roaring Boys around me sat up from their shoulders to their butts, flung back their capes, leaned forward and listened as if the Holy Ghost spoke.

Adoration was theirs and so the public's, too. They had not forgot that he had faced the king. The king hated that love to my lord from the common people but for a time he was so besotted himself with the young and beautiful Villiers that he was disinterested and dissembled friendship with my lord to save himself trouble. The king simply did not want to be interrupted in his daily life by what he saw as turmoil.

There my lord was, slow-paced below us, and I see him still, once the last of the Privy Council to give opinion, now first. He was not allowed to take his old place but was treated as the newest and least member, though not by those around me. He stood in the distance under the light of the morning as the lowering sun of autumn threw prisms of bright color on his black robes, and when he spoke, he nodded as he always had, almost imperceptibly, towards me when he wished me to take down a case. He hid me among the wild ones, and all around me when he nodded there was the sound of pencils scratching scratching in a waking and concentrated morning.

I had seen him reel to blows and trembling with anger; at last I saw him as I had hoped he would be again, in flight, honored and loved by his true peers and by the Roaring Boys around me in the Star Chamber.

At eleven o'clock the judges and the council went in to the famous

and infamous dinner in the inner Star Chamber where they stuffed on
great joints of mutton and beef and veal and lamb, often marrow bones,
usually tongue or bacon, always at least three kinds of poultry and
eight of game with oysters, pastry, oranges—that was the first time in
my life I tasted an orange—to say nothing of gallon on gallon of beer
and ale and many wines. He ate little, for we ate sparingly at Stoke
House and in his rooms at Sergeant's Inn. He believed that sparse diet
was the way to health. But many of the others sat among the damask
napkins in the scented air and, with their knives of silver plunged into
the gilt plates, guzzled and slopped like pigs at a trough. That inner
room was, in truth, the grandest trough in England.

I stood behind my lord's chair, for he was wont to pass me my dinner bite by bite upon a fork; he fed me like a child or dog, while I listened to affairs of the state and the bed. The other pages who stood
behind their lords were sons and grandsons of the exalted at the table.
I was the only one, I think, who was not there by the preferment of
birth. When we were sent beyond the room into a waiting chamber,
they never in five years spoke one word to me, but played among themselves as if the dark paneled chamber were their games field. They did
not even honor me with dislike or censure. I was simply to them not
there. Here I am remembering as if I had not escaped that cold indif-
ference. Well, so long as it still chills my old tired body, I have not
escaped, and will not, without grace. No matter that I have suffered
here through all these years as they come, gain spirit, expand into their
bodies, stand tall, and spit in my face.

The Star Chamber was my lord's mare nostrum as sure as he had set
sail upon passion and anger against the awful righteousness of those
who thought themselves undone unjustly. He ruled upon the unprotected and the lordly. It was all the same to him.

I wish I could remember days as themselves but after this long time
it seems only a changing vision like a dream. A day in winter when all
the torches were lit against the gloom and around the chamber there
were coughs and the clearing of throats against the damp and smoke.
A day in summer when the chamber and all within it gleamed gold
and blue and crimson with the flash of jewels that threw prisms on the
walls and faces of the crowd listening as someone called out, paced,
turned in argument.

I listened with another ear than understanding, wrote and wrote and surprised myself over and over that I had caught voices I had not seemed to hear, puer cum machina, but the machine was my hand that traveled over so many miles of toing and froing, clouds of witnesses, the fair in body and in mind, the unfair in mind and beautiful in jewels and satin, the wretched poor, oh the wretched poor.

The pleas run together, the accusations, who pushed who into a plash of water, whose wheat fields were rode over by the fine and graceful hunters, who had wrote the false wills, who had cheated, who had fathered the child, who had been suborned, lied to, who forged, who fought, who rioted, blasphemed, made slanderous verses. It was all grist to the endless mill of the Star Chamber on Star days.

VII

*But oh, poor dust and ashes, like stones once rolling down
the Alps, like the Indian canoas or English boats loose and
adrift, where stop we until infinite mercy stop us, especially when a false fire of Zeal and Confidence drives us . . .*

— ROGER WILLIAMS

MY BELOVED YOKE MATE HAS PUT ME LIKE A BABE
into this cave. She woke last night to my crying in my sleep and knew
the pain, old man as tender as a babe, and so she treated me, for she
understands my weakness. It is the mark of her holiness, and yet if I
told her she would say get on with you. I cannot see her for the skin
curtain is down to keep the steam within, but I know she stands akimbo before it and she dares one or another to say I am in this cave con-
sorting with the devil.

This is my sanctum sanctorum, long since copied from my Indian
friends. Once their hot room saved my life and now this melts the
aches and pains of my age and the rough passage I have taken my
wretched used old body. Now the Father of Lights grants me ease, for
a little time, only for that. How I hate the demands of this lower self
when I would be on my Father's business. But even the Lord Jesus
feasted with His friends, and I know He laughed. I know that as if I
had been there among them.

Drift and float. Drift and float. It is my luxury and my gift. Thank
God she demanded long since that I dig it, and line the walls with pine
logs, cut in half. Word flew among my Indian friends of what I was

doing and they came and stood stock still and told me what to do. It is behind my house that was before it was burned in that hatred, and never have we put it back again for my family decided . . . I had naught to do with it . . . that we were too old to start again and must live with the children, treated as children ourselves who once treated them so.

Now I can lean against smooth wood grown soft in the years of my being, and move only to toss a little water from a ladle I brought from old England on my last duty there. Oh how the winter in London fought my bones and sinews. Oh.

I can barely see through the steam the pile of soapstone that holds the heat of the fire long after the fire has gone out. She did this for me. She built the fire and kept it lit and then let it die, brought me staggering and stumbling, poured the first water on the stones and said, "There, you old fool. Steam out the wet weather from yourself. I told you. . . ." And her voice faded as she went without. I called after her, "Call not Raca, a fool, for fear of hellfire," and she went away down the hill through the kitchen garden she comes every day to tend, calling back, "Raca raca raca!" and laughing fit to kill.

So here I sit as naked as the day I was born, well more so for my mother said I was born with a caul. Sweat and sweat. The body that was once, if I am honest, longed for by some ladies, though it be a sin to dwell on things of the flesh. I was a pretty boy. I was. There is no reason to deny that, for that would be a lie even if thinking it is a sin of lust. Now I am wrinkled as an old tossed-out paper, my sweet hands gnarled, my muscles that once could paddle all day without question release the pain that must have made me cry. And regard my feet! Were they ever straight as an Indian boy's?

I am old and tired of sin, repentance, and redemption and happier than I have ever allowed myself to be. I am not the dead dog I called myself, rejecting God's gift of a strong body and mind in the fleshly house he gave me to whine and repent again and again. For the language of religion has fashions, and ours has been a groveling one, to our shame. I wonder sometimes if the Father of Lights grows bored at our self-flagellation and holy whining. But I have at last learned beyond that. Now I can live minute by minute as if all were my God's gift to me, even the pain that puts me here.

Ah. All the argument, all the storms. I set myself toward peace and found a constant war. I set myself no less than that I live like Christ Jesus, here in this wilderness. I thought it my duty and my love. Yet must needs question, and that too is a holy gift, the questioning, and when I stare too long at the heap of hot stones I see through the mist so many faces of those I have known and loved and fought. By the bowels of Christ Jesus I was long of words and words and words, and too oft barked them like a lady's feist dog. I hear now my lord, his voice, within my own at disputations, his training in polemics that I called holy and he called the law.

Sometimes I hear Bartholomew, this long since, and follow my memory to a room, and see ahead the sandy path he spoke of. How passing strange that "sandy" should have become a word these days for the shifting floor of half-baked thinking, as "He is sandy in his opinions," as was said of me, meaning "He is a Raca raca raca!"

So for the moment my sandy path seems to end here in this old man's body with a soul as young and as sweet with passion for God as ever it was, but one learned at last that the ways of God are unlearnable.

It has been a sandy path indeed for all my trying. Here am I sweat-slopped in a time of ease that never even the king felt. The king. The puir wee king. He comes to take me from my tread on my beloved holy desert and to a place so proud-loved and then so lowly-hated in King James's days. It is always King James. My lord taught me to see within him more than there was without, and I grew to, not love, but pity him. There I was, an unknown boy who pitied the king of England France and Ireland and thought not then of its rarity. I still do, and if it were my way to have the gall to pray for the released dead I would pray for him. For he is part of my burden of the past; though I cannot say so for his son, who cost so many lives.

I never liked King Charles. He was a timid dour boy, a bad judge of men, and too easily led, though he took most seriously his training to be king and sat in the House of Lords to hear debate day after day when he was but a boy. He said little for his stammer was so bad and it embarrassed him, but the others were tender toward him for his trying.

I followed my lord Coke then, not the lord Jesus, but a wise proud arrogant beloved mistaken man who I did not know was mistaken at first, and was ashamed to bring it into the sun of my mind for so long after.

He went often to court. I followed and carried his papers and his books. We took a boat upriver from the Inner Temple. How I loved that time along the water, for the river even with its traffic of boats and calls of Eastward Ho and Westward Ho by the boatmen was peaceful. I could see the trouble released from his face as we were rowed along the river to London Bridge and then walked to the bank above it where we called another boat to us, for no waterman would try to row upriver through the roaring current under the bridge then. It was a morning and evening ritual for both of us, between trouble and trouble. On bright mornings he seemed as happy for that little while as he was so often at Stoke. He had walked from shame to pomp and color and the thousands of candles and rush of people to find his place to sit in one small rowboat or another for the little time of peace between the Temple and Whitehall.

It is always the first day you remember. Once again, for a second, I walk within it. After that even heaven I am sure becomes so familiar it is hardly noticed, except at times when the awareness of it lights the mind.

That morning we docked at the Queen's Steps, and he motioned me to follow. We took our way along an open corridor, blank walls on both sides with one entrance up stone stairs that turned into stone gloom above us. They were guarded by a soldier, lance akimbo, and then another and another. We pushed our way through the Great Court. I thought then that everyone in London who wanted this or that of the king or whatever Privy Council eye they could catch and force papers, pleas, and weeping wives on was standing ham to ham in that vast space. Though it was opened to the sky, it was hard to breathe there. I only remember bodies and bodies, and hands thrusting pleas at my lord and some saying thanks be to God thee hast come back, for in the Great Court was the language of more common people. How it smelled.

My lord had took me that way, he said, that I might know the land ways to enter Whitehall Palace when he sent me there alone, for it wandered over many acres. We came out of the Great Court and stood below the Holbein Gate that I had passed so many times as one passes monuments and public spectacles as if they had grown there, as unregarded as trees. It rose, a fine carved stone like a house with a passage below it. We dodged carriages and soldiers and here and there a ven-

dor crying his wares, to a small door, too casual for the entrance to a
palace I thought. It too was guarded. The guard let my lord pass, and
he nodded me onto the narrow stairs. We went up and up, over the
street below. We could look down and see the tops of carriages and the
tangle of horses and harnesses, a living stream below us. On our right
side as we paused the wide stone corridor led to the tilt yard, the bowling green, the tennis courts, the cockfighting circle, and beyond a
never-ending great park with soft grassland under the trees where the
king rode out with his hawk upon his wrist. But that morning it was
as empty as midnight. When I asked of it my lord laughed and told
me that the rising time for courtiers was at least ten of the clock, that
it took them much time to stretch and dress, so I would see no one
there until noon. Later I walked the park so often to carry papers for
my lord to St. James's Palace that it became as my own garden.

We walked together toward the river through arch after arch, past
guard after guard, quite still that morning, all quite still. The stone
corridor turned to fine paneling, with many a unicorn and lion, carved
Great Seal and all along the walls. He called it the Portrait Gallery, for
it was indeed filled to its coffered ceiling with paintings of the dead
grown stiffer and stiffer as if they had aged upon the walls. The wood
of the floor was creaky and warm-colored, and the gallery was as wide
as a highway.

At the last door he walked into the chamber for the Privy Council,
met there on days that were not Star days, for from that place and in
that room the matters of state were tossed and argued. I waited without and watched the great ones trundle, sweep, God my witness, some
ran at the end when the great clock was already striking ten, I think
ten. He had motioned me to walk behind him. Around us tall men
were drawn toward that single door, bishops and councillors. I noticed
then and never forgot that they were a different breed from the pretty
courtiers, for each breed and each status differed to me in their looks,
their walks, and before God their fine clothes. I began, after he had
gone within, to play a game of separation, that one older and frowning
was for the Privy Council, that one limping and flourishing a cane with
gold and ivory head, that one hooded, one with the coif of a sergeant
at law, one younger with hair below his shoulders that was the color
and thickness of massy gold.

And then, surrounded with his own small court, a man so beautiful I bent my head and stared at the floor for fear of being caught staring at him. That was when I first saw him, who would become the great Duke of Buckingham, that year a marquis for his rise was so fast that one year he was master of horse and the next the youngest in the Privy Council. I say for him still he did not then seem arrogant; he even smiled at me, but I saw that as practice of one who knew that to smile paved the way and broadened the road to the perdition that he courted.

I was surprised at there being so few to watch them enter the chamber, for my lord had said there were forty at least in the Privy Council. It was the greatest honor in the kingdom to be of that party. Among the watchers were courtiers who stunned my eyes with their ways, their fancy dressing and their faces. Some were painted so that I could see the white powder and the eye black and the red smiles, for they too smiled at one another, but looked beyond in case, I knew later, they could catch the eye of the king or Buckingham. They scanned the gallery like soldiers on watch. Some lingered and watched toward the king's chambers, some still yawned who had walked from the stone gallery where the courtiers lived who had the privilege of apartments in the palace.

Then there were the servants darting as small fish dart among whales, so strictly stairstepped in their duties that one who lit three wall tapers with his pitchpine torch lit not the others, for that was the task for another, jealous of his prerogative as lamp lighter, for even though it was September still and the St. James's Park was green, it was one of the misty days that promised the darkness of a London winter.

In the distance upriver the courts of Westminster seemed to float in cloud. I wandered in the corridor and in the gallery, for my lord had told me to be on hand, and watched as the morning gloomed toward rain. I looked down on a garden and an orchard beyond, where there were strollers, little knots of people, woman in their farthingales, men with their feathered hats doffing and donning, doffing and donning as they passed one another along the formal walks, round and round what I learned later was the Privy Garden. Beyond them gardeners picked apples among the trees. It all looked as if it had gone on forever.

Until the rain. Such scurrying and lifting of skirts, such rushing and splashing and bumping into one another! One, tardier than the others,

ran with his wet hat and feather drooped over his face and his long wet
hair made rattails down his wet back. In a few minutes the great spaces
of garden and orchard were as deserted as I would see them so often
from that same window that became my habit window when my lord
was in council.

When the council met at Theobalds or Hampton Court or Windsor,
all that crowd, some fifteen hundred people, followed like a pack of
hounds, rain or shine, cold or warm, cart after cart, coach after coach,
the riders high on their mounts, some caparisoned to catch the eyes of
women, some slumped upon their mules. My lord went by the carriage
that had been my magic way to Stoke, but even such a fine ride became
too familiar to notice.

For me now my bringing to mind the place is in idle moments only,
tangled in memory as which came first in the early days, or toward the
last when the place became so familiar that I noticed not such things
as that morning, but events small and great instead.

It was in the Presence Chamber that I saw him most, the king,
sometimes grumpy as an old woman whose feet hurt, sometimes fawning on Buckingham. Sometimes it pleased him to be held on both sides
between him and one of his brothers. King and lover whispered to one
another and the whole great crowd leaned slightly forwards as if they
were a magnet to try to overhear those words and smiles that they read
as weather vanes.

Now the steam rises, now my body hurts no longer and I am at
peace. Where was I in my mind? Oh yes. The king. The poor bedev-
iled king. Whitehall was the largest court in Europe, they said, though
I had no way to tell if it was so, there was much exaggeration there. It
was the fashion, much frills and flourishes to make legs, curtsies, peek,
lie, so much truth hid by fashion as the bodies were hid by satin, lace,
frills and feathers and jewelry owed for. So with it all the king was less
alone than any man on earth except when he went into his water closet but even there God Protocol decided who handed him the rag to
wipe his royal bottom, and a doctor stood by to examine his stool. It
was said that there was one room, a tiny closet in that place of twenty-
five acres of buildings and such, where only the king had the key, and
he could retreat there like a refugee from his own life and make the
world wait.

But that first morning I saw none of that nor heard the gossip that was like bee buzz in the court. I was between court and park, suspended up in the Gallery beyond Holbein Gate to await my lord, who was much encumbered with the exchequer since the king had said, joking, that as damned tetchy as my lord was, he was the most honest man in the Privy Council and the only one who knew figures.

Still I stand there and the hours grow long and blot out time. I watch the pigeons at the Abbey of Westminster, and the small church beside it dedicated to St. Margaret and try to remember who St. Margaret was and why a saint, but mind drifts and I shift on one foot and then the other, and stare once more at the abbey and the little church like a hen and chick.

For four years of minutes I spent Sunday morning waiting in that gallery until the paintings and the escutcheons were drilled to my brain so that I can see them to this day, as if they hung there the same way in my mind. Edwards and Henrys and Isabellas and all and even the Queen of the Scots, the king's mother who had lost her head, truly, not like a guileless girl in love with a highwayman, but lost, as to be severed from her body and fall into a basket.

Sometimes when the council was entangled I could hear voices raised and fists pound not at each other but upon innocent tables. I would know when there was trouble within when my lord stomped out and ignored my being and head thrust forward like a fighting bear stumped down the stairs, through the public Great Court pushing his own gallery of entreaties out of his angry way. He marched through them, parting them like high weeds, me in his wake, down Whitehall Stairs, into a boat. Sometimes his concentration turned to sound, half words when he seemed to be arguing with one within his mind. He would be silent except for those murmurs, all the way to the Temple, not so much as a lift of his head when the waterman bumped and jostled to land at the Temple pier.

Later I was to see the king and all the court around me in the Presence Chamber, a room so large that it reached the ceiling of fine oak beams almost out of sight on fogbound days there. All eyes were on the king then. He moved through the crowd, picking this one and that to honor by his sometimes genial pause, their doff, the deep making of a leg, sweep of hat feather on the floor, and then the group around them paying them attention because the king had paused and honored so. That was how I met the king. He paused, a fleeting pause, and looked through me and spoke to my lord, so, "How are thee, Eddie, and who this?" And my lord did his still dance of making a leg, and I too like his shadow. It made the king smile to see so small a boy aping so tall a man, or he smiled at something of his own, or he grimaced at a little pain in his belly. Who would know? But a cat may look at a king, and so I did.

There is a way that a man made so important by his birth and stance can look politely through you as you bend the leg and doff and don your hat as I was taught, so that you know the eyes have not allowed you into the privacy of the mind, that you are looked at but not seen, that he speaks but says nothing. But I when I first saw him so close, I took him into my mind as he stands now even if long dead, impatient I think to get away from all the demands for notice, the tittering, the endless play for attention that went on around us. It lasted for half a minute at the most, and all my life. That is the power of kings.

His face was sometimes as pale as death, sometimes red with anger, for he was quick to anger, not towering as my lord sometimes, righteous and right, but impatient, petulant. He was the king of petulance. As he progressed around the Presence Chamber, all eyes followed him, mine own too, so that he seemed to me sometimes to be the spoon that stirred the pot of England, round and round a room as public as a street. He would pause, and the eyes paused. He would speed and the eyes would speed. I played a game of knowing where he was by watching some near eyes of a courtier, greedy or praying for the attention of that royal pause. Sometimes it was hard to see him since he, like me, was smaller than the rest of those tall animals. They seemed to have been bred to commanding bodies and minds of security of tenure and of purpose. I have not seen such splendid creatures since except among the Indian sachems, the princes of the wilderness.

When one man has the power of life and death over another, courtship is survival. Unless, as my lord was beginning to do, one accepts from the Father of Lights His greatest gift of all, the right to question, finally begins to lose the patience of obedience, and stands at first alone.

So I began to see change in my lord, not of demeanor, no, that too.

It began as a preoccupation. His mind seemed to go into secret places, behind a shut door. I saw it in his treatment of the king, a deliberate ease that I had not seen so clearly since I was a child and watched my Bartholomew when he walked the streets of Smithfield. My lord had within himself a holy gallantry, not those aping, foolish gestures men set store by as who they are, but a something sweet toward his enemies, and toward the king and all, even toward his wife. He was never more dangerous. It was a terrible revenge on them that he neither meant nor planned.

I saw his wife silly in his eyes, and the king so weak and furtive and painted and sad, the giving in to one tainted model of beauty, one who by the studied parody of obeisance that I saw demanded the world as his due. I saw it. I watched the sadness of love play out, the pity of it, and that in a king.

My lord did his duty, day after day, month after month, thought for himself and finally began to speak as if the doubts within his mind and heart had at last found words, and that I was privy to for I heard him speak so for no man.

While I? I ate among the pages, ignored so that the wound of that loneliness among them still hurts in my soul when it is touched. No one who has been so alone can ever forget it. It is the solitary confinement of place of which we are innocent, and not of wrong action or anger or despair which are our bounden sins, and those once faced, leave no such scars behind within the soul. I am shamed when such sins take my soul, but when those scars of another's making wrack so small and take my mind again, I am more ashamed, more impotent, for it is not my sin but others, as the banishment has been, as of those days in a cold caul, sitting there among the pages.

They spun connections among themselves, webs of kinship, and I had none. But I had one friend, one older, who found me alone staring at a painting in the Portrait Gallery willing it to speak, and then it spoke through his voice. He said, "You make it alive by watching it. Paintings not watched die." What was his name; I have half forgot and must wait. Nathaniel. That was it.

There was no return for my lord to the bench, no preferment beyond a Privy Council the king paid mind to less and less. He used my lord as a lackey when he needed honesty, and wanted not to speak of it himself, but set my lord on their greed and usury and stealing so that he became as a gaoler for the weak and simpering harshness of their lies. So he was hated, and behind his back made a figure of fun. But the courtiers feared him, and he treated them with a patient kindness in return that seemed to me to be beyond control, meant, a little sad, some inviolate sweet ease. He did as the king bid him. I see now that he who was not born with the gift of patience waited like Job.

It was Mayday—just over a month after the death of the poor neglected queen, she who had been once so pretty and so the dancer had finally wasted away into the pit of rottenness. We started early in the morning at Somerset House, at least my lord called it that, he was stubborn about changes of names. Others, keeping within the fashion of the court, called it Denmark House. It was the queen's official residence, though she had died in Hampton Court in March. She had been moved back to Denmark House away from the king's fear and displeasure for he ever hated death. She had been lying in her catafalque in state ever since in the great hall of Denmark House, for the king was arguing for public money for her funeral since he did not want to spend his own privy purse.

That is what I will never understand, that a man may call himself poor because money is in one pocket and not in another in the same pair of breeks. The unthought-of, unmourned queen was only forty-four years old when she died, and those few who saw her in her latter years said she was still beautiful but dressed in a parody of what she had once been when she had tripped as one young and lithe, the dancing lady.

There ahead of us were the carts piled high with the queen's treasures, being took to her palace of Placentia at Greenwich, for the king would not go near the dead, and his majesty had decided to meet her ghost at Greenwich and ordered my lord to bring her fortune there. He said my lord was the only man in his Privy Council that he trusted not to steal, not because he was honest but because he was too damned proud. So all her treasure was loaded into the carts and she was left behind at Denmark House, poor cadaver, as unburied as those starved in the street I saw every morning.

That was the way the world was that morning as we cut through the crowds in the Strand, high above the ordinary and the poor. How we strutted. Even the horses strutted along the path made for us by the soldiers who shoved humanity out of our way as one cutting weeds. We rode, guarding with the soldiers, my lord's followers, and all, on both sides of that line of slow and ponderous carts, so heavy that their wheels ground down the muddy street and made great ruts that by evening dried into place and left a history of our going.

I owned the ground my pretty pony paced. I would if I could but cannot regret that morning even now, though I know that much of dreaming and most of memory is confession of sin. And yet, what sin was there in a sixteen-year-old boy all dressed in his master's fine livery, a feathered hat upon his head, silver spurs holding leathern shoes, and all so fine? That morning I was in love with my city. That is rare. We take our streets and our land for granted until one day, as that day for me, we move through old haunts as if they were new built, new shining, even, I confess, new stinking. The apprentices who had once kicked me and buffed my ears doffed their caps. I know now that it was to my lord who rode before me on his fine steed, but I took it to be me.

I would honor the city as I rode through a street of illusion. Down the Strand, past the great houses, York Place and the Savoy and all that I was used to seeing from a boat in the river with their fine lawns and their gardens and the strength of their trees. God of Lights, you made a fine city.

For a few miles only. Slow as a procession we moved through Temple Bar with its griffon, and we were out of Westminster and back into London, my true city. Then Fleet Street where the stink of Fleet sewer broadcast itself long before our coming. We passed the Palace of Bridwell, no longer a palace, but of late a prison, palace and prison. From what I saw in those years the difference was only in the food, the feathers, the fine jewelry, one as much a dungeon as the other.

The carts were too wide and the escort too many for the mean little streets beyond St. Paul's. We turned into Paternoster Row—then and yet I wonder how those places have kept their Papist names—beyond Cheapside and then Corn Hill, where we turned toward the river and Fish Street, and that stretch of the river where the fishing boats were tied to the wharfs, and the smell of their catch so great we might have been at sea.

And why should I not think with pride of London Bridge? It was so fine a place, a little city of its own, houses and shops clustered on both sides of the bridge street. The soldiers shooed the people into the shops like chickens toward the roost, and we had the bridge to ourselves. The horses' hooves and the cart wheels made a new hollow sound over the water. We saw the river below us only where the boats rowed down-river and shot the rapids made by the rushing current between the central stone arches. Shouts from the watermen who saw us up above them, respecting nothing, caring nothing that we might even, yes, even be the king himself, riding there beside the high-filled carts.

And so we passed into Southwark by St. Mary Overies, and in the distance upriver the sinful Globe and the Bear Pit. How was it then that it was not a sin to go to the Bear Pit and watch our poor fellow creature bears taunted and torn to death by hounds, and yet a sin to see players? But I never went. Never. That was one sin the boy I was did not commit. I yet wish I had, once or twice. When I told John Milton years later he said I was a fool, but it was too late by then for the government had outlawed players and plays.

Past St. Olaf's and beyond, in the river, lay the moored ships that plied the known world. I have crossed five times in them and know how small they are, and as frail in the great sea as eggshells before the wind, but then, that morning in the May sun, they caught such splendor of light upon their drying sails. I wondered then if ever in my life I would take ship and see the world.

We passed the waste pits, the dead animals, the human shit, the horse manure, all took from the streets before dawn to feed the fields of Pimlico where there were great blankets of herbs and vegetables and flowers. My lord sniffed and said it was a wonder of God that down-river stank so and upriver was so perfumed from the same source.

The houses were smaller, and then smaller, and then far apart in villages and we were in country lanes with people going a-Maying. The hedges were sweet with hawthorn that we knew not to bring into the houses lest we bring bad luck upon ourselves. I have long rejected such false beliefs and yet I would not bring hawthorn into the house.

I rode in quiet after the noise and shuffle of the city. I could still hear it far away, a dim moan, softer than the clop of my pony's hooves on the land. All the hedgerows were abloom, and the sun was sweet. How could I feel sinful then? I think often but do not say for fear of misleading the weaker ones around me that if there is sin in joy it is in not seeing it as a gift from the Father of Lights to remind us of the blessing that has no name.

Ahead, where so many ships were moored in midstream, I saw the towers of Placentia, the queen her country palace. It seemed so small in the great space of its park. Behind it a high hill rose. It was the first time I had been to Greenwich. It seemed, that morning, as if it were dedicated to the far sea, for the Thames widened and widened into a great lake toward Tilbury. Hundreds of ships lay tiny in the distance, grew larger and larger covering the water, for this was the roadstead where the royal fleet lay.

Greenwich that morning was a lone place where the satellite mansions that had once held courtiers for the queen had been abandoned when power moved hence, following the king, who had not lived with her for many years. Even the palace that was stretched along the waterside had caught neglect. It seemed long unnoticed, without echoes or voices, hollow-sounding as we rode into the first courtyard. The carts clattered across the stones and left their signs in mud.

All of this, for me astride my pony with the jongling spurs and the pretty reins of leather, was only a hint of loneliness that surprised me, for there were indeed people there though they seemed careless, moved slowly when they showed us to the great hall with my lord's lists and boxes, all that the queen had left. The dusty tapestries that lined the walls were ghostly, faded by the sun, stained where streaks of damp had dried. The chairs were empty, the fireplaces unfilled. It was one of the saddest places that ever I saw.

The servants unloaded the trunks and bales and boxes so that they nearly covered the fine marble floor. It took all of the morning to get them ready and the king did not come. The sun dipped toward afternoon and the king did not come. My lord told me to go without and watch from the hill.

I was again a boy on a May afternoon; I stood like a soldier doing my duty, then sat, then lay upon the meadow ground and watched the ships far away below the hill. Between the near waterside and the Isle of Dogs on the other side of the Thames God had made a basin to protect the ships. There were hundreds roosting there like gulls. Upriver in the distance, St. Paul's church was a toy, and the fifty spires of churches in the city but a field of spears, so small they could be held in my hand. I forgot the king and my task and all, for I was king myself, there on the hill above Placentia, and I knew why it was called that, a place of felicity and kindness and pleasure, and I commanding it from where I lay in the sun.

But nothing was still; the ships rocked in the water, the comings and goings and slidings and movings of barges and wherries loading, unloading, afar the hulks no longer fit for sea where prisoners were kept. There were Turkey merchants the size my brother Sydrach took upon his comings and goings to the Levant, to the Turks, to all the places I envied him. There were bigger galleons where the sailors, it was said, starved from neglect except their wives and sweethearts came to them where they lay and succored them. All of them seemed that May afternoon to be gathered there, a fleet of ships, a gaggle of geese, a flock of gulls, and one much like the other to a boy half asleep.

In the distance I heard, then saw the king's retinue cantering along the road below. I ran back downhill, past a little unfinished building, a folly the workmen were covering with thatch to keep the rain out, through the formal park, and I burst into the great hall where the bales and bundles lay.

There it was, all arranged for the king to see. Silks and satins swathed across the tops of boxes, clothes fit for a queen, furs, the soft shine of gold here and there among the piercing color of jewels; it was the Aladdin's dream Sydrach had told me of, a cave of captured sun and riches from beneath the earth. The queen's ransom.

They rode, forty or so, clattering and clamoring into the courtyard below. We ran down the stairs to bow and make all the gestures the king expected. He motioned his entourage to stay as he would a dog, and dismounted into the arms of an attendant. When my lord presented the list, the king waved it aside to one of his guard. He trusted my lord with baubles.

He clung to Buckingham's arm up the stairs to the great hall. He stopped at the door, his arms festooned by then across the shoulders of Buckingham and another pretty boy. He was not in mourning clothes. He was an old man dressed as a young blade himself, all in pale blue satin with an osprey feather in his hat that curled around his neck. They were all laughing at some quip made without that we could not know. They paid us not a nod, nor a gesture, nor a greeting. My lord made his leg and I with him, as fine a flourish as I could, being so short. Then he stood, as abandoned as the rest of us who watched there as at a masque.

They pranced among the jewels. The king would drape one stomacher of diamonds upon Buckingham, then toss it aside, and choose one of emeralds instead. They played like children until Buckingham was festooned with blue sapphires, white diamonds, green emeralds, ropes of pearls and rubies. He was as some May queen herself, only bound with those glittering treasures instead of ropes of roses and leaves and bluebells and early daisies. When I glanced at my lord he was studying the marble floor.

Oh it is hard not to see that past day through my old glasses of today, for of course it was shameful, of course it was cold-blooded to treat the queen's treasures so, but in truth I did not see it so then but stood bewitched by all the color and the play. I had not seen so open happy affection between the king and Buckingham, for they had been more formal in public before. This time the king tweaked his smooth cheek and kissed his mouth long and hard, as he decorated him, not with Orders, but with jewels rich enough, hanging on that one man, to feed the fleet without upon the distant water, to save the starving, treat the sick and wounded, and strengthen all within the city.

But that was then and this is now, this morning, in this sun and not that, this old man, and not the boy I was, staring so that my lord had to jog my shoulder to motion me to follow him.

That was the most intimate I ever saw the king, who could joggle our lives in his hands as carelessly as he tossed and played with the dead queen's fortune. It was only a small part of what I had to learn, the thousand rules unwritten, the thousand gestures and unspoken policies, so much not worth learning, but could damn. Those with the wrong stockings, the wrong length of hair, the wrong cut of clothes, and those who, fearful of doing wrong in meeting the king, did wrong by accident and were cast into some outer darkness, as in touching the royal hand with the lips instead of kissing the air a half inch above his sacred skin. Outer darkness. I have seen the king wipe his hands upon his breeks and turn away, so casting one or another beyond the pale, for he took pride in his pretty hands that he never washed for fear of hurting their softness.

Little was give to poor Prince Charles as the queen had intended but not wrote down, for she had not believed she was going to die. The poor bandy-legged boy seemed always those days in some shadow, first of his handsome, much-loved older brother who had died at eighteen, then pushed apart by Buckingham from the king's notice.

The king and retinue moved back into Placentia, for Buckingham liked to sail. The courtiers' houses came alive again with banqueting and riot and playing. I waited so often, stretched upon that hill, dreaming myself at sea in the ships below me, that it is hard for me to take out that one day and remember a place that had been so haunted and sad. The little white folly they called the queen's house remained unfinished for years.

The king was ever moving. He lived and died unsatisfied with where he was. So I followed with the half-mile-long retinue of courtiers, servants, women, royal family, and all who were in his train as surely as they and my lord and I had been a cloth-of-gold train pinned upon his back. Through those years I saw, lived in sometimes, and became so used to those high corridors, those ghosts of kings and queens past, dead and live courtiers, shadows upon the surface of things, as the wind moved the tapestries and the candles flickered and the torches flared, while the nervous king of all that folly simply could not sit still, except when he was tied with rope upon his horse.

He was often so drunk he would have fell off, and even then an honored gentleman attendant rode beside him always to fill his cup with the strongest Greek wine which was his favorite. Once my lord was ordered to hunt with him and ride beside him which was thought by others to be such a mark of favor that it was rumored that he would be made treasurer, but it was only a caprice. The king plied my lord with wine and later he told me it was the strongest he ever drank.

VIII

*It is not a suit of crimson satin that will make a dead man
live, take off and change his crimson into white he is dead
still, off with that, and shift him into cloth of gold, and
from that to cloth of diamonds, he is but a dead man still
for it is not a form, nor the change of one form into another, a finer and a finer, and a yet more fine, that makes a
man acceptable to God.*

— ROGER WILLIAMS

I CAN NEVER KNOW WHEN I WILL STUMBLE INTO
that place within where memory keeps its court and its sins. As I
walked abroad this cold day to see Mr. Tribble on some errand, memory, that imp, blotted out the reason for my visit and took over so that
I have to stand in the middle of the road maundering like an old fool
and try to remember why I came out at all in such pert and blowing
weather.

By the blood it comes, the same and not the same, filling my mind
instead of my errand. It happens oft these days. Sometimes I am at
Stoke, sometimes at the Star Chamber, sometimes alone with my lord
Coke, and sometimes it is so vivid that it haunts the day as it does in
this quiet afternoon where nothing is happening.

I am at the finest display of color and noise and the sense of importance I have ever had or hope to have; then as always the memory
changes and the color disappears and as I pass the last of these houses
that straggle toward the meadows, I try to find my way back to the

color, so beautiful, so grand as at the first of the vision, but it fades in
my head. Sometimes, I see it in a distance undefined and cannot reach
it, it or them, I never know and wander still, thinking that once I was
loved by the mighty and now I am alone.

Oh Roger Williams for shame of you. Want you to lose your immortal soul by going back? Take strength from what you have learned and
paid so for, and see that child's hope for what it truly is, as a real place
among the real.

So, as I have done for years when the memory comes, sometimes I
see it coming from the devil, sometimes from God, for we all know
thoughts are messages and until I know which it is this time, I will go
on, at my age, tasting the sweetness of its bright beginning and its
love, and then the emptiness, the long road where there is only the
searching in this life, no beginning, no end. I must think why this
time it haunts me and makes me stumble.

Last night my dream was so strong of days of show and power that
when I woke I was in a less real world than that where God or the devil
sent me to in the night, and I, old man, old funny crippled man, who
was laughed to scorn, am a boy again in this old body and cannot shake
it from me. There was so great color and heavenly music then. At least
I thought it so, being of those who take all from the Father of Lights,
either thanking or blaming as the case may be.

I have wrote much of this to exorcise the haunting. But all of that
was taken up by fire, with my letters and my papers, and I have them
only in my mind still, and must, one day, write them again to warn my
great-grandchildren of the faces of the devil if for no other reason but
that I like, and I must confess it, to think of it, not often, but once in
a while, to remember what I was then.

It all perished and all I have left are letters I wrote to my brother
from the days of the Quaker wars, for wars they were, wars of words
and loud-flung insults in the name of one sweet and simple Jesus, for
I did not know yet how simple it is. How simple. How awful—as in
the awe of it and the sweet vast honor. But it matters not for the road
is so strait and narrow and beautiful that every poor deceived and
taunted human must needs find it for himself, or herself, as Mary says
when I say "men" meaning mankind. She has a great way of sighing.
Her sighs are fathoms deep, more eloquent than my poor words.

And I know by now by God and by holy Jesus and all the saints that I am where I belong. Goaded here and pricked and spurred there when I balked.

But yesternight I rode in triumph to the opening of a Parliament that not the king nor the members wanted. On my livery was the ostrich of my lord. My lord had so oft told me what the ostrich meant, not to the College of Arms, which he said was as corrupt as all the rest of the government, where all was for sale there for a fee to make gentry, but to him whose family had had it long, to tell him that it was a sin to bury one's head in the sand and wot not what was gone wild in the kingdom. He had let that fall as we walked at Christmastide at Stoke. How could I forget that walk? He looked at me as if for the first time, and away, and said nothing for so long I thought he had forgot me, as he did sometimes when we walked together, mile after mile across the meadows and along the river.

It was a day in the chasm of winter. The king, who had so oft cursed the people as he rode by them, for he hated and feared crowds, was a different man that day. Once he had shouted at those who looked on him as God on earth, "Do you want me to take down my trews so you can see my ass?" Oh but that day he shouted God bless ye, over and over in the distance as his entourage led the progress, and they said he even reached for hands in the crowd and was altogether a new man. I was ashamed of myself for thinking, "He wants something of us." I called the seats of power "us" then. It was my sin of innocence.

He was tied fast to his horse and escorted by an hundred mounted men, all crimson and gold. Their pennants snapped in the coldest wind of the year. That was a year the Thames froze twice over and as we passed I could see great ogres and angels of ice and high ice palaces sculpted by the wind. It was, they said around me, a bad omen. But I did not listen.

Behind him rode old earls and many more new earls for titles were for sale in those days, as all else. Leading them all in pride of place, beside the favorite, and his close friend, Buckingham, at last at last, rode Lord Veralum, Francis Bacon, the Lord Chancellor in glory made up of color and silks and furs and long long dreams he trailed. Only a month before, my lord Bacon still groveled before power, as my lord Coke saw it. He had seen it in the late queen's time when she, canny and mistrusting, ignored Bacon as a toady. Finally he reached the pitch of preferment. He had been made the Earl of Veralum, his own choice of title, after Albans and all the other honors he had collected. There was for him a fantasy of celebration for his dubbing, great feasting and a masque and dancing, but for the others, new, too, who rode behind, only the parchment patent for all their money.

My lord, when he heard of the name, laughed and said, "He would cling to truth as his title who knows it not in politics, and clings to it in his fancy writings. Beware, son, beware of bright minds and cold hearts together. They make a bad marriage. And ware those who speak of truth too much. Their hand is in your pocket."

What he felt for Bacon was deeper than hatred, which would have, in its evil way, honored his existence. He felt contempt, which blots the other from even an image.

Oh Father of Lights I was so proud of myself, ariding there as if I were riding through the sky and the cold clouds from the horses' and the men's breath. I still have it in my body as I did that day, a straight back, a fine carriage, and my lord riding ahead looking so grand he could have been the age of his son, Fighting Clem Coke, who rode beside him, his favorite son who caused him so much trouble and sorrow.

I rode as one in a boyhood dream of knights going forth, for in boy dreams knights ever go forth and never backward. It made me smile, I remember, to think that, and then a shiver caught my body under the jerkin and I thought it was the wind from the frozen river and then no, it was that I knew that they rode the same proud way, the soldiers of Rome, toward the slaughter of the innocents. If there was a dark shadow that day it was then, shivering in the wind above my head, or in my soul, I forget which now.

That is the way visions come, a whisper, a shiver, a sudden seeing, the gleam of love, then gone as sudden, a candle blown. My mother would have said it was someone walking on my grave. When it came to me so then, when I was young and thought myself handsome and full of wit and learning, and chose for preferment, I wanted no such folly.

My lord had let himself be put up for the Parliament to please his majesty, or so he said, and I did not understand. But I thought I did, for he had after all fallen within the bounds of preferment when he sold his daughter, but when those thoughts came I felt disloyal, and pushed them out of my soul where they lodged, deep below my mind, but they would not be gone, there in the wind and the shouting. He did not brag, for my lord was contemptuous of braggarts, but he did let know that he had not asked or courted for a single vote, take it or leave it. As men of the king's council said, the worst insult to their rivals was "He is popular."

I thought he had, at last, become a king's man, what the Lord Chancellor Bacon, now Veralum, called a lion under the throne. It troubled me when I would let it for it was never what he had stood for all of the time I knew him and walked with him and took down his very thoughts. But he was elected to represent the king with sundry others, from a Privy Council the king had paid no attention to for months for it interfered with his hunting and his drinking. That is cruel to think. But that is true to think, too, though no one said such words aloud then, and God knows never wrote them to be found by anyone, not after Mr. Peachem.

He had let the king choose him to run for the Commons to spy for him. The king wished to use my lord's popularity with the people, which was great, even though popularity with some common herd beyond their ken was a joke in the court. I think even now that my lord was honest in his obeying the king for he did not yet know the awful blows of truth that would fling him back into the passions of his youth in his last years. And I think the king, as shortsighted as my lord in the matter, was simply using him again as he had done since my lord had rejoined the Privy Council, as his errand boy.

The people did not return most of those put up by the king's party, but only those they could trust, for it was a shaken time in England, that month, full of cold and fear that the pomp of royalty could not hide. Under all that color and delight it was the worst year for trade that anyone could remember. They said within the safe confines of the room of the Pharaoh and the Children of Israel at Stoke that the money had literally been flung away for fripperies. I forgot who said the word, but I never forgot it. Fripperies. Those who cheered him that cold morning still trusted that the king, like the father he said himself to be, would fix the evil brew, not knowing that it was he who had cooked it.

We could tell where his majesty was by the scream of joy from thousands in one vast note that followed him away ahead in the distance and was quieter when we passed, but some in the crowd knew my lord and called out "What cheer?" to Sir Edward, for he was much loved by the people who saw him as their champion. God forgive me, I thought that day when I could not push it away and love the part I played, that he had chosen against them and become indeed a king's man.

The shouts ahead grew to frenzy as the king was lifted from his horse to a chair to be carried into St. Margaret's church for God's blessing on the new Parliament, for the London crowd has ever loved a king. The grooms behind us ran forward to help us dismount and we went as fine with color as the knights of old I had once dreamed about to hear a long and boring sermon by one chose by the king, and pray and be blessed by prelates and bishops, and I loved it all, the holy entertainment.

And so I walked among the others, the pages and the secretaries who followed after their members of the House of Lords and the House of Commons as they loitered and lounged across the lawn of Westminster toward their separate chambers. The Lords sat in a fine great chamber. The Commons met in little St. Stephen's chapel where it was said they would have had to sit upon one another's shoulders had they all appeared at once for sessions. Which they never did. There was a tradition that it was infra dignitatum to hang about the Commons day after day. My lord Coke heeded this not at all. He attended every day that spring. I should have known then. I should have known.

St. Stephen's chapel had been given to the Commons long since and they took much pride in it. I thought it would never hold all the members who stretched ahead of me, released from prayers, across the fine lawns of the Parliament Square between the Minster and the Old Palace Yard where I had been at home for four years, and where, now, people said it was haunted by the great Sir Walter Raleigh who was beheaded there. Even I, who scorned, or tried to, such maunderings, walked too quickly through the Palace Yard at night when my lord supped there.

Many times through that winter and the beginning of spring, what plans they made were under the cloak of visiting Mr. Cotton to discuss his historic collections, some said the finest in the world. I would sit in those days late in his tumbled library poring over manuscripts my lord and his committee friends never touched. They were making history then, not reading it.

WE PROCESSED FIRST into the House of Lords, where the king spoke on and on and on until he had lulled the Parliament and the visitors into a daze. He wanted money. That was the gist of his hour-long rambling. In eighteen years of his rule he had bankrupted a rich country. He had give it away to favorites, thrown it, dropped it among the beseechers who surrounded him. He had a lazy habit of generosity. He could not refuse. With the power he had he choked trade with patents that went into the pockets of the court and the favorites. Buckingham and his grasping family had milked the realm of all its cream. I knew all this for I had heard much at Stoke, too much. I was afloat with half-thought sureties in those days. And in these? I know not.

I loved knowing things, if only gossip, beyond the common knowledge, as when the king quipped that his chancellor's book, Lord Bacon's, was like the peace of God, it passed all understanding. I loved the conversings there had been at Stoke that winter when men who had been new elected to the Parliament came and talked in riddles which I, usually mistaken, thought I understood. It was where I first met Sir Francis Barrington, who would be the people's hero, and Pym, and Digby and the blessed father of one who would be my dearest friend for life, Sir Henry Vane. I loved knowing them, the leaders of the Parliament, the county faction, so called, led by my lord, who planned much and argued much with them all in the great hall of Stoke. I loved my clothes and my learning and my place in the world. And over all I loved my lord Coke, who had give me all of that and treated me as a son he took joy in teaching.

Raleigh had of late become a hero once again for he ever hated the Spaniard, and Spanish hate was being new nurtured by the opposition since the heavy sword of the king's prerogative hung over the heads of all. The king was negotiating with the king of Spain to marry Prince Charles to the infanta.

Already there were murmurings and mutterings, as much as anyone dared, against marriage to a Papist, for the fears left by the Armada and Guy Fawkes's attempt to kill the royal family and the government still smoldered. The Armada had been defeated and Guy Fawkes killed, but they had left a surly undertow of hate.

Wars that would last for thirty years had bursted Europe asunder. Spanish armies had overrun Protestant Bohemia and thrust out those two lost children that the Jesuits joked and called the Winter King and the Winter Queen. The Winter Queen was James's daughter and much beloved. So there were loves and hates and the war was turning into a Papist-Protestant wrestling for Europe. Religion had become politics and the dying went on and on while our king had been offered as the infanta's dowry gold beyond his dreams of paying all his debts in one fine day.

While the armies of Spain and the Holy Roman Empire were ranging Europe like wild beasts, the Protestant Huguenots of France were murdered in a bloodbath one terrible night. Those were the facts we rode through that morning of color and cold. The Recusants were another new and then so familiar word for the Papists who had refused to take the oath to the king as head of the church. The king's and Buckingham's courtship for money with Spain, and Gondomar, the Spanish ambassador, holding crowded masses in the very chapel that had been once the private chapel of Hatton House were the gossip and fear of the town. Lady Hatton had rented Hatton House to Spain. It was a tangled time.

I stood that winter and that early spring in the reflected light of my lord Coke, and often in my arrogance I forgot it was reflected. I sat in the narrow visitor's gallery, leaning over to look down on the heads of the heads of the state or I saw them as such: young Pym whose round face glowed with zeal; one elegant Sackville who was famous for having killed a man in a duel for the love of the beautiful Venetia Stanley; Calvert, not yet a lord, who was making a charter for the colony he partly owned they called Virginia after the virgin queen. It was where tobacco came from. There was one Inigo Jones, and my lord said, "Watch for him, he is a man of talent for building but out of place in the Commons."

Every time he let down such a remark I used it to brag to the others in the gallery. Some of them saw argument as too full of words and words. Bored boys dozed in the galleries. Oh, I nodded too until the brabble below us began to form a pattern.

I was much made of since I represented for the other attendants around me Sir Edward Coke, who had rose all at once on his entry into St. Steven's chapel, to the leader he had intended to be. All around me they hung on his words for they called him the bellwether of the flock, the first of the first, et cetera, and so, sometimes, they hung even on my nonsense. Oh I was a fine and sinful sight for the sore eyes of ambition.

I watched power and politics in a dance to rule the country, and was astonished but should not have been at my lord Coke's performance, for that was what it was. It was, as I had to remind myself, an old part he played, long before I was born, representing the late queen as Speaker of the House of Commons. He strode into the chapel as at home, or when I had first seen him, in St. Sepulchre's before it was possible that he would ever know I was on earth. He was easy with his words, and he told stories that made safe laughter sweep as a relief from the droning of some others. Prince Charles, who sat each day in the House of Lords, told him how he followed his words, the wise and the comic, and how he was a relief from the usual blather, or some such words. They were repeated to me by ones who half heard what he said and then mistold it to those behind them, as happens when royalty opens its mouth.

There were times even at the beginning when something within me wanted to shout, "Watch out! Ho there! We will be cast upon the rocks!" For I had seen all this before and knew to beware of my lord's quietness and his jovial times for too often they portended a change in the flow of his mind which I swear before the Father of Lights was never sleeping.

I watched and took down notes as he had told me, and there began to be a pattern in his acts and his speech, ever easy and homely, ever seductive. He knew, they all knew, we all knew, that the king had called Parliament as his money bank to give him subsidies. It began well. My lord, softly, led the Parliament into granting the subsidies that his majesty saw himself needing for his follies of state. He was happy, everyone at the court was happy at a flow of money that hardly existed, for that year there was a shortage of coinage in the realm since they at the court had spent it all in riot. That was how his majesty saw the Parliament, as a milk cow, so long as he kept his temper and his mouth in check. It had been so long since he had paid any attention to it for he hated the nuisance of governing, although he did like to appear and remind everybody of himself.

Still my lord said of him, "He is misunderstood. He is no fool." But I thought his voice weaker. He would add, every time, an afterthought that demanded to be said, "He is sick of body and easily led."

My lord Coke had waited to act, with a terrifying patience that no one, even myself so close to him, knew. There we were, my lord below in the arguments and the brabbling of the overcrowded chamber. There were times that I looked down upon their heads and thought them ever boys in a schoolyard. Or more, the fathers who had once been the Roaring Boys who had oft lolled in the Star Chamber, their fine-shod feet thrust out, owning with their shoulders and their asses the world they sat on. There it was below me, the same and not the same, what they were being prepared for at the Inns of Court, the familiar stance, the lazy voices, the hidden passions, that waited cool-ly to be released like well-trained dogs.

As for those whose intelligence and passions champed at the bit, they too knew to hide behind a cloak of insouciance like a dagger in its scabbard. There was a sobering rein upon their tongues and their opin-ions, led by my lord and a few others. I would say I began to see a plan, but I was young and that was not true. Not then. Not for a long time. I took the path of the way of the world without thought and without judgement. It was so bright with promise if I questioned not.

Gradually, subtly, my lord Coke, like a good fly-cast angler, began to jolly those friends of the county party he had planned with at Stoke toward cleaning the Augean stables. I should have seen but did not, being too naive then, that it had been planned not only long since at Stoke, but in his chambers, and in his heart. It saddened him, what he knew at last he had to do. But no one saw the sadness; he moved gal-lantly through the early days of the session in St. Stephen's chapel, and I darted back and forth with the other pages, all of us basking in reflected importance. It made us take our busyness out in darts and runs and bodies tense and hurried.

Down below us in the chamber, Sergeant Richardson sat sadly in the

Speaker's chair which he treated as a prison stool, and he chained there. It was said he so disliked and feared the task he had as Speaker that he wept when he had to take it.

At first the men below in that crowded pen of opinions thrown back and forth across the center aisle waved in unanimous votes to rid themselves of thinking. Sometimes they spun arguments that turned toward quarreling. Fighting Clem had to kneel before the bar like a truant schoolboy and apologize for hitting one of the members in the back for passing before him, or for making a remark against his father, I forget which that time. He had a pride as tender as a boil on his neck and was oft in such trouble.

All around me I began to sense something that seemed like bright fear, taken out in movement and toing and froing, arguing and interrupting each other, while they did the task the king had called them to do, give him more money, and more money. My lord Coke led them into easy alms to kingship; the king's so-called needs came first and foremost or so he told them all. Even the Speaker relaxed in his prison chair when all had bowed to royal wishes and nobody would be led thence to the Tower or worse.

As January turned so politely and with such calm, led by my lord, into February, I slept or dozed no longer but hung upon his light words. Oh I missed much then, but there were clues. He spoke of grievances, and pointed to four sorts of men who had milked the country dry. No names, but descriptions. Almost as lightly as a jest, he pointed out the waste of gold bullion in the making of gold thread. His words perched birdlike, but I still only half know why I jotted it down so carefully, as I usually did only when my lord nodded toward me in the gallery as he had been wont to do in the Star Chamber. After long argument as to the shortage of gold bullion, he added, "The patent for gold and silver lace, which only consumes our bullion and coin . . ." and the word "patent" hung more heavy in the air than gold itself. I, and I know the others leaning with me over the gallery balustrades, would think of the acres and veils of gold and silver that the courtiers vied with each other to spread over themselves.

Then, one fine day, as they say in the folktales of the rustics, my lord Coke made his first move so subtly that it took much thinking on my part later to fathom the beginning, like tracing the source of a stream.

One of the terrible drains on the country's crops and goods was the ever easy granting by the besotted king of patents and monopolies. It was his way of buying, not love, I will say that for him, but the luxury of being left alone a little to hunt and love and be a fool like ordinary men, poor child of his own lusts as he was, wanting only peace.

It was the beginning of the cleaning of the Augean stables and my lord Coke roused the Commons to do what was needed. What was the name of the man it hung on? I remember the acts better than the names this far from it all. Monpesson? Monpisson, anyhow that would be a fine name for him, had held the patent for the inns and had squeezed the life out of poor common men who ran them. He had made a scandalous fortune even for that thieves' kitchen of a court. He was the loose string that was pulled until the whole great scandal began to ravel and run. Somehow Monpisson eluded the sergeant who had him in custody and escaped abroad.

He escaped suffering the ridicule of one Sir-Something-or-other who was stripped of his knighthood, renamed aleknight, and made to walk in a white gown from Westminster to the Tower, where he was jailed. The street crowd ever celebrated when a knight was disgraced. There was drinking and dancing and some say fornication to celebrate his march.

The king was reaping what he had sown, and before God it was a hateful harvest for him. The questing hound followed the scent of corruption nearer and nearer the favorite, for three of the accused, although there was yet no word for what they were accused of, were members of the Commons and Buckingham's kin by marriage, for the vast cat's cradle of his connections could have been placed over the vast cat's cradle of bribery, and matched to the last string.

I sat above, leaning with the others, I had many friends by then in my reflected glory, and we smiled and nudged one another to see one downfall after the other while their once friends betrayed them with such solemn faces we hid our mouths alaughing.

One after another, the monopoly of gold and silver thread, the monopoly of corn and wine and muniments, all of them came before the House at my lord's coaxing, a pricking of conscience of the rest they hardly felt but even so acted upon while he sat more silent than I had ever seen him, leaning back on his shoulders as the others did, in the accepted bored lounging. I saw gradually how he worked, how they all worked, weaving and arguing, standing and compromising, in that gentleman's way of ease and gesture that was, I began to see, as tight as a drum and in its silence, as noisy.

My lord was as a general with the order hold your fire until the impatient were ready to scream their speeches, but he held them back. He was, I see now, lulling the kings' party into as innocent a sleep as the pages in the gallery. All but Francis Bacon. My lord watched his bounden enemy and when he was ready, he acted.

It began with a question, brought up so casually it was hardly noted. No, not a question, a report from the committee chairman Sir Something, was it Gilbert, was it Phillips? I know it was so close and drowsy that March morning as if nothing was ever going to happen, and I was watching below, half dreaming. I remember Sir Francis Vane, who was of my lord's party, speaking in whispers just below me to one other, and I was lulled by their nodding heads as they agreed. All over the house there was toing and froing and soft voices, it was yet too early for argument. They paid little attention at first at the report. Then the chairman said words I cannot forget ever, and the House of Commons went as silent as a tomb.

I think now that silence was the faint seed, beginning to come from earth to the sun of the civil wars. First a whisper, a simple accusation, hearsay—that the Lord Chancellor had taken a bribe, which was common gossip, but never before spoke by those in office, for it was so common a breach of trust among the king's men.

Once the sluice gate opened, accusations poured out, too many to prosecute to stop mouths, then more, and more, until a way of life piled high with bribes and gifts and bequestings live and dead, and that cold man who lived so famously and gloriously in his own castles in his own slow-gathered kingdom of power was finally, officially, and by the book, and by the House of Commons, accused of taking bribes far beyond the common habit. That was the first I ever saw of how the law worked between the houses, for the Commons accused and the Lords judged.

I have never seen a downfall start so quietly. Then it began to mount and mount again, and Francis Bacon, the man who had clawed his way through years of servility and flattery to the Great Seal itself, fell headlong, and not even his friends in high places could save him. His tangle of debt and profligacy, his sex, his mountebank show, were all exposed for the mere and lowly to pun on, laugh and wink at and parody in the taverns. Those who would not have dared to speak his name in public except to praise him gathered to peck. It all came out on the floor of the House of Commons, then to the House of Lords, thence to Lord Bacon's mansion.

He had, as he was wont to do in times of crisis, as loss of power, love affairs, and some such, taken to his bed to pull the covers over his head like a child, his first act on hearing his fine walls crack and crumble. He lay, down in his back, frozen with what had ever froze him, I see it as disappointment, and they came and took the Great Seal from his bedchamber. Even so, he spoke to be remembered as he did as easily as breathing, "If the Great Seal were left lying in a field no one would pick it up." I must needs sympathize this far afield from that bed, for my own back has ever betrayed me. I did the same in crisis. Mine has always been at coming to the blank high wall of injustice.

My lord of Buckingham opened his pretty mouth and elegantly and gracefully betrayed them all, his brothers, his cousins, and Bacon himself, his closest friend, playmate, and bumboy. Although it was said, or rather whispered, for not one person dared speak publicly of the king's favorite unless he was prepared to lose his head, that there was more in money and planning between them than friendship and habits. They conferred secretly, and not a soul dared guess why. But in this field I can tell the dead cornstalks that those brilliant catamites had in six damned and greedy years helped the besotted king ruin the state. It took much time but in its unreeling it was as inevitable as winter.

Nothing more happened. Not then, in that session. The king's party saw that most of the accusations were turned aside. Tabled. Later. Always later. February drew into March and once the king had been granted all the money he was like to get, he dissolved the Parliament, and my lord not only defended the move, but gave it legal sanction. He had taken his first redoubt, and he retired to rest at Stoke.

So the king and the king's party saw themselves as winning all they wanted; the Parliament gave down its milk, the more embarrassing patents and briberies were tabled, or pushed under it, more like.

What sentence the Parliament gave the brilliant and cold-blooded

Francis Bacon I have long forgot, for it was commuted by his friends.
In high places there are no payments. He promised the king a history
of the world, no less, and went back into his luxury and his questioning. Before the Father of Lights I heard he died from exposure as he
tried to freeze a chicken.

But the country was rid of Bacon, and all the grievances waited for
the Parliament to be returned after a long vacation from May to
November ordered by a frightened king who saw his friends stripped
naked of the loot he said was his own prerogative to give as he
pleased.

The king went back to Theobalds, to his habits and his flatterers,
crippled and older than his years, treated and dressed as always, like a
young gallant. With him always in that spring was the Spanish ambassador, Gondomar, he who common people thought, but dared not say,
was the devil.

And before God I drank it in, all the intrigue, the shuffling, the vast
games as if England were a chessboard, and the king to be checkmated.

But that dear place Stoke for four years was private for me, for my
lord did not, as others did, place his country houses, although there
were many, within the king's orbit, like the stars that some say move
around the sun. He made a true retreat at Stoke and lived, I with him,
quietly among his true friends and his grown children who came and
went. His colleagues in the law came to consult with him, and more
and more members of the county faction in Parliament. There I knew
them as I grew toward manhood and manners and learnings, and the
polish of a gentleman. My lord saw to that, and never let me off.

Most of the men were of the eastern counties, the home counties,
and a few of the western counties. It was not so much intrigue for
power as it was the nodding of heads and the meeting of minds and
complaints as they thrust their boots to the fire after a day's riding or
hawking or following hounds and discussed freely there what any
courtier would have shook in his boots to even think, how the court
had bankrupted the country, how preferments had gone mad, how the
favorite and his family had scunned the country for riches. Why, by
then the king had made Buckingham the Lord High Admiral, in
charge of the fleet that had sometime been England's pride.

IX

———◆———

Wits full of invention, are by the Tuscanes called goatish,
for the likeness which they have with a goate, in their
demeanure and proceeding. They never take pleasure in the
plains, but ever delight to walk alone thorow dangerous
and high places, and to approach neere steepe downfals, for
they will not follow any beaten path, nor go in companie.
A propertie like this, is found in the reasonable soule when
it possesseth a brain well instrumentalized and tempered,
for it never resteth settled in any contemplation, but fareth
forthwith unquiet, seeking to know and understand new
matters. Of such a soule is verefied the saying of Hip-
pocrates, The going of the soul is the thought of men.

—DR. JUAN HUARTE DE SAN JUAN,
The Examination of Men's Wits

J AM FAR UPRIVER FROM OUR TOWN OF PROVIDENCE,
far enough to push from my mind all the land-grabbing greed along
the damnable opposite bank of the Pawtuxet. It took forty years, a
royal commission, sent seasick across the Atlantic Ocean to this little
river, to settle a border in the wilderness, to keep the greedy of Massachusetts, Connecticut, and Rhode Island colonies from gouging out
each other's eyes over these endless tracts of virgin land. Before God, it
became a way of life. Dead or alive, Mr. Harris, Mr. Whipple, Mr.
Throckmorton, Mr. Gorton, old friends, old enemies, you have not

been invited here. It is, for the time, my place in the world which grows again lovely as I lie here, tethered to the bank, my canoa breathing as the water breathes reminding me of the way the ships in Tilbury breathed and sighed by creaking their wood hulls as they waited to go across the world.

I have brought one friend, a book give me long since by my dear beloved young John Winthrop, closer to me through my life than his father, who saved my life and helped convict me all at once, a balance as pretty as a jongler upon a tightrope at Bartholomew Fair, which the dear old man sustained all through his life. The tree that leans at the bank lets its branches make a covering green tent where I can draw my boat and be as incorporeal as the breeze that finds its way under the canopy of leaves, and caresses the water and my old body. Before the Father of Lights if every man had for himself the luxury of such a place, a canoa, calm water, sweet silence, the greatest luxury of the world, I think there would be no troubles. I think at Eden with our first parents there were so many such places.

And time to shut the book, which I have opened and read only my favorite words about the goat. I paddled here to seek the comfort, the cum fortis I came for this morning, to bring before the Lord my maker, and ask the one question where there seems to be no answer. Why?

I may as well put down Don Juan de Huertes with all his wisdom for my mind is yet too crowded to invite him in. If ever there posed such a goat upon a crag it was my lord in those days and yet none saw it for he kept his counsel, even from me. I cannot think why I did not read the signs. Now looking back they were as obvious as the milestones along the highways. He was so loved by his admirers that they missed, as I did, his deep preoccupying silence, and even, for he did not so before, and the Father of Lights knows he did not suffer fools who did, he had begun to make little mistakes in the Commons that spring, so rare and so unlike his fine-honed wit.

I cannot believe that the glamour, as the Irish call magic, of the place, the voices, the color, the clothes, the admiration I was given as a reflection of him, and my silly pride of place made the mirror so dark I could not see where he was leading his faction. Not then. Even so, now, here under the hiding tree branches in this new raw place, a twinge of young pain remains in this old body that I was such a fool

and judged so with all the arrogant surety of the young showing compassion for the old.

I was a dazzled boy who thought himself a man. I had such pride
then, and all the other younger more passionate men had it. It was a
fine spur and my lord recognized it so and played us as he did the rest
like an old man's fiddle. It was we who misjudged his turning away
from us, sometimes for a minute, sometimes for an hour, often when
we walked abroad at Stoke, or rode there, through hours and miles of
silence.

I know now because I go far afield in such a way my own self. It is
not lack of remembering that takes the old so, for I am old now and go
where those who wait for me to return cannot go. They know not the
way and they know not the far fields of the soul where we are led.

But for the last few weeks of that Parliament, before the king
demanded it go into recess, he had so drawn apart from all of us that
it was whispered that he in his age was drifting in his mind, and we all
helped. The helping must have driven him mad within, but, unlike
himself who was not a patient man, he withdrew, saving both himself
and us. He was somewhere, I know now, where his soul rode a wild
horse of seeing, clearly, fatally to him, where he must go and what he
must do and how he must take the cloak of decision upon his shoulders, and lead on as he had begun that session. He was brutally patient
with us, as if we were fractious horses that could be spooked by fear in
midstream. He knew when the despair that follows hope has to be used
to goad the mare.

I was wrong and so were they, the men who flocked to Stoke, where
the great house was all awhisper with conference. Pym came there and
Warwick, Rich and Sir Francis Barrington, bringing his son-in-law Sir
William Masham. I saw Sir William for the first time there. He stood
below an Egyptian soldier of the Pharaoh.

So many of them, so unnatural in that quietness, as if they dared not
even trust one another. They talked long into the nights of May; they
walked apart two by two. It was all so intimate, so soft, so fretful and
unsure. What I picked up in their company was more than fear; it was
self-demand as if they were about to face decisions that might land
them all in thrall to a sick England that wanted daily and nightly care.
A whining place that spring. A place where I, a young fool, saw them

timid, where the expectations of what they had seen as a saving Parliament had disappointed them. The people called it a do-nothing Parliament. I called it an if only, if only they had sat longer. If only they had faced the king. If only they had not disappointed the people by delaying the lifting of patents and monopolies that were drawing off the cream down to blue milk, bankrupting England, Scotland, Virginia, the Bermudas. Never in the pasts of English kings had there been so greedy a massive sow, dressed in velvet, satin, and fur, feeding on England.

All the while the king was dickering, for I could only call it that, with the king of Spain, the bounden enemy of all we shared then, to sell his son and England's heir to the Spanish infanta for a dowry to pay his debts and relieve him of having to go hat in hand to the obnoxious men who had sunk his dear Lord Chancellor and all but sunk his friends' fortunes in the patents and monopolies that he saw as his gift and the country saw as two blood-sucking leeches. Not even we ourselves knew, all the way to knowing, that the Parliament of spring had been the first shot across the king's bows.

My lord Coke knew, more than any man in England, for he had designed and loaded the gun. But he seemed all that spring as if he thought not, cared not; I saw him as sunk into that preoccupation of bitterness as I had seen him the first morning I walked into his chambers at the Temple, mistook him rather, as defeated again.

Even his clothes bore out the farce. He wore the same old fustian robe that dragged behind him. He had lost some weight on that already gaunt tall frame. He looked ever down as if he were trying to find an answer on the ground as he went slipshod through May, the sweetest time of all in England. He walked as if he were trying to cover his land step by step, and I walked, when he shut me out by his silence, a little behind him, watching him carefully as if he might fall into a dropsy as he had that time at court, seeing him old, seeing him frail, mistaking every quiet time he let me share with him.

And all the time there were visitors at Stoke, some from the king, who I see now pretended to be his friends as if naught had happened, and for the most of us, naught had. Sometimes I thought the Father of Lights had deserted us in the house when we needed to be shepherded. And all the time that was what my lord was doing, as wise and faithful as an old sheepdog. He was spied on, leaned on, wondered at by those who had trusted him and so admired him, watching to see which way the cat would jump.

The stillness of Stoke that spring had not ease in it; the house a carapace only of a man making up his mind while honest men waited and grumbled. He, knowing all this, refusing to be prodded. The oxen had lain down in the field, and we all knew better than to prod for they are animals that will die alying rather than move in the face of impatience.

The king and Buckingham were such fools, the king too preoccupied with his saving graces of hunting, drinking, paddling his catamites acheek, Buckingham led by the nose by my lord Bacon, whose power had only moved from public to a more dangerous privacy.

Once when the king was drunk he kissed Lord Warwick on his lips, and when Warwick turned away and wiped his mouth and spat in disgust he was banished from the court beyond the verge—eight miles, or was it twelve? Yes. It was twelve. My God in heaven I am maundering as we accused my lord of doing. To think it would be the Earl of Warwick who would be my friend and save my hopes.

Buckingham was blinded by his greed, his family, and his friends, but, clever as a fawning bitch, he ever persuaded the king, the poor old man. That was much of why my lord Coke lingered in his decisions, not only that the king could take his head whenever he wished, but that he felt sorry for his peaked dangerous majesty.

But all that I would see later. For then, there were the walks and the visitors, and the voices deep into the night in the great hall while the fire died and the candles guttered and the torches shot forth smoke when the doors opened and shut and still they talked on, while I and the others of their sons and pages were sent to bed to listen to the voices far into the night as faint echoes against the lofty ceiling.

One day in summer we walked together at Stoke. My lord had his hawk upon his wrist and he crooned to it sometimes, and stroked its feathers. Why did I know there was somewhat strange about the walk? But I did. I knew before he told me.

We stood together in the field beyond Stoke Poges church and he crooned again to the hawk, wishum wishum wishum, drew off its blind hood and tossed it toward the sky. The hawk took us with him, it seemed, riding the currents of air above us, but still my lord said nothing, and I waited, knowing not to prattle. Finally he said, offhand, almost as if it were an afterthought that had little to do with my life, that he was sending me to Charterhouse school at Mr. Sutton's hospital over against Long Lane where I had been born and raised, the very place that so long ago I had shook from my courtly heels. In the first days of the school, when the boys marched past us in their black robes with their white frills, we threw mud and shit at them. To go back to that and be one of them for me was a shame I could never explain to him.

"There is something I must . . ." But he told that to the air and not to me.

Then, again, "Something." He who was a master of words seemed at a loss.

Tiring of the hawk's flight, or released into what he was loath to say, he whistled the bird to him and reset its hood. And it set its talons to his leathern wrist cover and we turned to go back to the house.

We went our way along the path among the deer so tame we could pet them like dogs. He said that he had given it much thought and for a long time, and then he explained what I already knew but was loath to hear it from his lips that since my father was a tradesman and not a gentleman I could not be prepared at the Inns of Court since those who studied the law had to be gentlemen's sons. But with going to the school at Charterhouse where he had interests, he put it so, I could be prepared for examinations to Cambridge, and there I could be trained to take holy orders and so be set for preferment as well as any lawyer. Not knowing that he hurt me, he went on to explain that many a bishop was once a baker's boy, and so and so, convincing more himself than me.

Finally I found words. I knelt in the path before him and said, "How have I failed you, my lord?" I hear even now my young voice. "How have I failed you?"

It angered him to a fury. He was wont to do so when he was crossed. He cried at me, "Want you to be a timid fawning clerk for all your days? I have trained you for four years for the preferment I see for you. I have given it thought and some tears for you are like a son to me, the bright soul I never sired. You know my boys, one dim, one a fighter, one shit-covered farmer who never says a word, but none to share my mind. I love them all, but for you, I see something better."

None to share my mind. What a cry it was. Now that I am an old man with sons I cannot speak with from my inner soul, and who can, who indeed can? Few are so blessed. I think that after the accidents of spawning, we must choose, as he did. He had chosen me, and I saw then he meant to form me into a vessel for his dreams. I resented it at the time. I did so. No man has a right to try to form another like a stat- ue of wood beside the chimney piece. Only God can do that. But I did not know that then. I only knew that he was sending me away to be trained, and I knew too from his face he did not care to do so, but that was all.

That day we walked back to the great house that loomed so high it blotted out the sky's brightness. I thought, I am being exiled from this house. I saw myself trapped somewhere beyond all the color, the excite- ment, and the seduction of being near the center of things as if we lived over a volcano, or walked where lightning followed and flirted.

Indeed, it was so. He was not putting me away. He told me long months and years later when danger had passed, that he was hiding me to save my life as Thetis had hid Achilles among the women. But on that sad day, I felt as no Achilles, no warrier, no budding statesman, but simply and hopelessly, an abandoned boy.

X

David was holy and precious to God still (though like a
jewel fallen into the dirt) whereas King Ahab, though acting his fasting and humiliation, was but Ahab still. . . .

— ROGER WILLIAMS

I T IS SO DARK AND FULL OF RAIN THIS MORNING THAT
it is hard to breathe in it. It saddens me. I am like a man in a great fog;
I know not how to steer. On such mornings I run quite backward, for
I am here alone and waiting. Before my sweet Lord I have been so many
a time, but never again as it was when the doors of Charterhouse shut
behind me and I was put away, turned back, stopped, pinned down,
and caught as flotsam in a stream.

In that place, knowing in my mind but not my heart why I was
there, I learned again, and yet again, as I do here in this winter of my
life, that the sin of the world is that one hath absolute power over
another through weal or woe. How long it took. How long it still
takes, for as they trudge uphill toward me this cold and rain-drenched
morning, the children walk toward their own misunderstanding that
I, schoolmaster to them for this day, am such a tyrant.

Learning is not a necessary here in Providence. Here a necessary
means only a privy to shit within. Over and over I have taught the children, once my children, then my grandchildren, now the little great-
grandchildren of my life. They come, sent by their elders, only on rainy
days as this one is, when they are not needed in the fields or by their
dams to do the true necessaries—little hands to string beans, sweep,

mend the plow, sew the harness. Here we must be prepared to live through the winter more than to learn to read and write.

How many will trudge through that door I know not, but I will wait, for it is my turn to teach them. I can see them afar, lingering for a few more minutes of grace before the door shuts behind them, as it did me, and does to all who have entered there if they would but remember. Those among us in Providence who can read and write take our turns to teach the children, but in truth there are not many of us here. So many sign only with their crosses, and count that enough to get along.

So there have been a few, a very few, and I know them and they know me and we have together a simplicity that wipes out age. I want to read Latin with Whipple's boy, a bright one who quests and reminds me of myself when I would go abroad finding something that I know now was evil—the power that comes with learning. I ever wanted to find out more, not for preferment's sake, but for that holy curiosity that they teach killed the cat. For most of the children, if we few can hold them long enough to get them through their first pettyes and punies, we have before God done a miracle. Even so we have, I think, the most who can sign their names and read in all New England, and not confined only to gentry and such.

But they do think the English language enough and expect the world to learn it. I am a lover of language and count it as the greatest gift of God to us poor, misguided men, so I have sought out always those with whom I can speak Latin and Greek and French and Dutch. I write to my dear Harry Vane in French, and for Dutch to the minister in New Amsterdam. I speak French to the traders and the sailors who come through, and for Greek, oh God my witness a gift for Greek and Latin and Hebrew, my loving contentious friend, now arguing with God in heaven, Mr. William Blakeston.

When he was lonely for language, company, and a glass of cider, he would come abroad to find me where I was. It was not often he came, for he found his own company enough for much of the time. He lived in a good house he built with two servants, He had many animals, the first orchard of fine yellow sweetings in Providence Plantation, and the best library in New England, I am sure, one that saved my own life and reason many a time.

He rode to town upon his bull, Ajax, who was as tame as a kitten. He was the proof of freedom of conscience here in Providence, a minister of the Church of England, an Arminian who would don his surplice and all his holy clothes and hold services with the prayer book which I still consider Papist, for anyone who cared to come the three miles to his house on Sunday morning.

He would come riding, calling in Latin to me to come abroad, and we would jest and quip in Latin or Greek or Hebrew, as pleasing to ourselves as when we were both at Cambridge. We spent ourselves in laughter making sport of the Visible Saints of Boston, for he had lived on Beacon Hill when they came first, and was a friend to some of them. When they first landed, he had took them into his house, but he soon tired of what he called their damnable cant, so he sold them what is now the city of Boston, and came here for the very freedom of Providence. He said he had come to New England to escape the Lords Bishop of the time, and he was damned to hell before he would submit to the Lords Brethren. I miss him so. From heaven he has lifted from me my melancholy of the morning.

My sons and my grandsons built this room that is now so old it no longer smells of wood sap, a little schoolroom at the corner of my home meadow for even I know better than to take too much land that can yield food only for learning. They come nearer up the hill, my sweet children. The door is open. The rain streaks down the sky beyond it, rain and rain and silence.

The schoolroom has a little ground to play, a little gate, a criss-cross log fence we have copied from our sometime neighbors, the Narragansetts who I miss so as well. It keeps the creatures out and then the creatures in. The mist lies on my school field. Only the Father of Lights can burn it away. Here I sit, old man with a stick to use upon the knuckles of little hands when the devil drives.

Once I did, too, linger and drag my small self to school as that little knot of babes in the distance are doing now. These old gnarled hands cover and hide the little hands of a child. The lettering I do now was once forced out stroke by stroke with a feather clutched in little fingers that would not obey me. Sometimes I think I have learned nothing in all the years between the gnarled hands that serve me now and the small frail hands within but that the world is two worlds all at once, a terrible place of shipwreck of mankind, and withal a holy place of the Father of Lights, and I can see them in the same meadow. I must remember my little fist and the hope I had once had and what it was that Martin Luther said in his age to his followers, "Tell me what I used to believe."

At first Charterhouse was a place for me to fear. It had been a place of concealment, a closed door that had spewed forth arrogance and power, and sin, oh terrible sin, a Papal whoredom. At least I had known it that way from my childhood. But I had to keep silent as we walked that last summer, still measured by the term times of Star Chamber, and we within the long vacation after Paschal, on the walks at Stoke that had become habit, and he discoursed upon my life.

My lord told me that he had planned for me, repeated it so that it burned within my mind, the ministry, since preferment lay that way. "These things I have considered for you. I see you as a prelate, a bishop if you keep your mouth shut. It is an open door for one with as bright a mind and soul as thee." Sometimes he used the intimate "thee" and I loved him for it, even though I silently rejected, I see now, much of what he was saying, as "You see, you have not the parchment of learning, though you have the learning." Or "There is a way of patience to use the world to overcome the world." Or "I will not have your mind lost or your body hurt. I will not."

All this meant nothing in the last summer, and when the purple daisies of St. Michael bloomed, Michaelmas term in the Star Chamber, I was mewed up within Charterhouse. I was too old and too young, and as laggard as any schoolboy. "Laggard," the word forever written across the shoulders of schoolboys. It returned to my shoulders as it had been before the world opened to me and I saw and smelled and feasted on preferment dangled before me in the alien seats of power.

My lord had sent me packing back to boyhood and a Smithfield I thought I had left forever. I was shut out from all I had grown used to, the court aglitter, the color and the language of all that power. I was set aside, even before I had used my manhood, as all around me seemed to take for granted. I had been wronged. I had done nothing to deserve exile. I excused my lord as one who knew no better, innocent through an ignorance. I thought, he means it not and one day will realize, as a revelation, how much he needs me. Oh with what fancies we arm ourselves in time of trouble!

As the sun straggles out from the clouds, I wait and watch a little longer. The children have stopped to examine a leaf, a worm within a puddle, a little creature. Anything to put off the moment. How great a burden for a little laggard boy. It is a burden that the little girls among us will not be forced to bear. To read and write gives power to hurt. But now here comes late behind the others one small and quiet Matthew Whipple, who slips away to come here. Maybe he will let me teach him Latin.

That place so long called holy, Charterhouse, had been in my babyhood a palace belonging to the Howards. It stood across Smithfield from Hatton House, but so different it could have been in another country, for Hatton House had not had such terrors, though it stood for pride and riches. So it was, too, at Charterhouse. But Charterhouse had so long been so soaked in blood that it never for me lost its smell, dried blood in the colonnades where the monks had walked, dried blood in the rafters where once I carved my initials to show that there had been one alive, huddled below the rooftree. It was, and may still be, a hateful place, hateful of stone, and brick and wood, and oak. The Howards fell from power at last. It was bought by one Mr. Sutton.

Under its surface was layer after layer of the past. There had been the lost years after its dissolution, when it was half forgotten, except when there was jousting. Then it held King Henry's silken banners and pavilions, when he invited kings from other lands to joust with his knights, making a sport of what they had died for in the past, as those who once hunted men in the woods behind Charterhouse hunted then deer when I was there and a boy.

Charterhouse was a monastery for the Carthusians, that proud Papist order for the gentry, at least it was seen so, where the monks had cells of their own that we were told were like stone houses, austere but better than most the always poor lived within, when there was a within at all and not an alley or a field to lie in with a bundle of little tender belongings. There were fireplaces in the cells, with fires built each morning by servant lay brothers. They called this luxury Christian austerity, while the forever poor lined up without for food at what the monks called the dole window as they passed out charity to win heaven for themselves as if there were a score kept by the Father of Lights.

The great oak door of Charterhouse had been a tomb and to small boys was yet blood-soaked for it was there that the late King Henry had had the arm of the abbot, John Houghton, nailed until two lay brothers had been brave enough to steal it in the night, bury at least a part of one they loved, whisper the burial mass, and run for their lives and hide among the poor.

It had been a quarrel away above the heads of common people, between two warring powers, king and Pope, and we had been bathed until our skin had soaked in hatred of Pope and Popery and honor for the king, any king, even the father of our late queen, who had died as any man, finally of the pox, the French disease, after all the killing that he had done, always through others, always justified, as we learned, and said, and for so long, I, too, believed.

What an insult to God that easy belief is. At least I have learned that. The damned diminishment of the great Light into a single human brain. I have thought I glimpsed God sometimes, never to know the unknowable, only the glimpses. I know, as St. Augustine said, or was it another? I am damned sometimes without my books. "He who thinks he knows God; it is not God he knows."

Below the Charterhouse of the Carthusians, fifty thousand people lay buried, thrown into huge pits, the victims of the Black Plague, and with them and later, up to the time of the building of the monastery, Pardon Field, where hanged felons and suicides were thrust to be prayed for by the Carthusian monks.

To go back. Or to be condemned to go within the terrible gates of what you have feared all your life: I knew that horror then. How harsh it is for my neighbors who have known only the power of those who could read, could write, could lord it over them with their knowledge and their privilege. No wonder they distrust and hate learning. It is, to some of them, an alien power, free of the dirt and fear that had been frozen for most into a way of seeing. No wonder my children here are laggard. I must needs remember always my own small fist within my hand, and how hard it was sometimes to be so young, so tender, and so afeared.

I never in my life had been so as when I was eighteen at night in

Charterhouse. To call it stupid or unmanly is to beg one's past self to do what one could not, be unafraid, or be somewhere else, and both were impossible. Sometimes, often in winter when the trees in the orchard were bare, I would try to stay awake to keep from dreaming. It was not hard since we rested two to a bed, forty boys and twenty beds, with the usher, one Turner, who later became my friend, but not yet that first Michaelmas term, resting, alert, at the end of the room. I hear yet snoring and sometimes crying and later when the very walls made us shiver with their cold, the sneezings and the coughing, and the calls from boy to boy, "Die, damn you, die," a choral joke amongst us.

For when I slept there was a dream, that the skeletons of the trees rose out of the skeletons below, the thousands upon thousands, and the trees moved like an army of the condemned and the condemning, marched always toward us, and I would wake shivering at eighteen years old, one who had kissed the air above the king's smooth dirty hand, and had made a leg and even, I confess, though not in some Papist way, had flirtings and winkings and wantoness among the youngest of the court ladies.

There were months as I gradually knew that I was trapped, that I used the time to reread much that I had read at Stoke in the long vacation when my lord had oft left me there on my own and I was at peace in his library among his books. In the small retiring hall at the end of the house where the windows looked out upon a quiet lawn were all the books I knew, and more. Once opening a book I was back there in spirit and remembering and with new curiosity found that at Charterhouse, there were, and it made me laugh to find them gone, books in my dear Latin, with all the parts took out that might enflame the hearts and bodies of boys. So I learned by what was censored what I had never seen as evil and still do not.

They were taught and I was taught to hate my body, that poor questing worm that shamed us, the sad longings we took as sin. There we were two to a bed, as stiff with sin as boards, froze with fear of the pits of rottenness that haunted the place as trees staggering and begging toward us, for we compared dreams and even those who had not had the hauntings said they did. Side by side we yearned for closeness we had nor nor dared not toward one another in the cold and sorrow of that place.

Often in daylight I walked in the walled orchard. It drew me as in my boyhood it had before, for then, upon a dare I had to take or be ashamed forever, I did climb that wall, and tumbled over and ran to the first tree, as sinful as Eve, to pick an apple. Two large arms grabbed me and without a word, hoisted me back over the stone wall, apple and all. I had won the dare. I ate the apple, and for a little while until I saw that I was guilty of the sin of stealing, was king on our little tiny mountain.

Now there I was, on the other side of the stone wall between us and the rest of the world. Then, in that ruff and in that gownboy's livery, I was not allowed beyond it. But since all the gownboys used the orchard only to frighten one another and never went there, I took it as my own, to be alone, even though I knew myself to be walking over the greatest massy pit of rottenness in London, and could, even beyond dreams, see the tree roots twined around skulls and femurs, and threading pretty tendrils though ancient ribs. It was a fancy by day and a fear by night.

Oh when was it? The first year or the second, those long years like lifetimes? I think the first, when one day, the truest of all my memories of Charterhouse, I saw a strange old man among the trees. I had seen him first standing in the shadow of an arch to the cloister where we were sometimes let out to walk. He was like a shadow. To tell the truth he scared me, and then he turned and went away. After that I saw him often as he leaned against a hoe, or turned the earth around the trees, and sometimes rested against one of the old trunks, familiar, as if he had rested there off and on for many years.

Then one day he, leaning there, spoke, and before my lovely Christ I had been there long enough to be blooded with the training enough to ignore him since he was but a servant, a gardener and cleaner of the ground around the trees. So does our training get beneath our skin and form a carapace of pride.

"I have seen thee oft, Roger Williams." His voice, his skin, his eyes were to me then as old as the bark of the tree, I was too astonished to do ought to stand and wait. "Oh oft from the time thee was a schoolboy and once thee took the dare and climbed the fence and stole. It was I who throwed thee over yon fence." Then I thought, I must needs stay still or he will see me, one devil or imp who taunts me with old pranks.

"Never fear, boy, I know thy father, and my father knowed thy grandfather, and all and all."

He walked toward me having had his rest, as I was to see him do for all the rest of the time I was jailed in Charterhouse. He became for me my friend, my sweet hand to hand to hand to the world outside and the legends of the past. We walked among the apple trees, and there were true ghosts of those who had gone before us there.

I can still hear his voice as I sit here now as old as he and know at last that it is lonely to be old and have no child to speak with and to watch grow and wax into the man or woman they will be. He told me he had watched me oft of late for I was more alone than the other boys, being both too young and too old. "Thee were a young colt," he said, "as I was once. That day when thee climbed the stone wall, I called out and thee ran, jumped and tumbled backward, thee was so afeared, and I only wished to talk, for I and my father and my grandfather and my great-grandfather have been sextons here when it was a graveyard that fills a ground the size of the Tower of London.

"We had pride in our work and passed it from father to son, and its way of doing, and by the Father of us all, its stories, how it was. But 'twas a lonesome way of being, though we took our pride as well as any family in what we did. But when I walked into your mother's tavern, the others moved apart a little, not so as to be noticed, except by me, for I was the man from the plague pit."

He sighed and sat himself down upon one of the carved stone benches that were along the orchard walks. "These here," he said, and patted a lion's head, "come with the Howards, who never did know what they sat upon, and no right good it did them. They should indeed have come here and said a prayer for the souls of the dead, it would have helped them in their trouble. Oh, I never can remember now which says thee must pray for the dead and which says thee must not. Which is it now?"

I told him, instructing, still with a whiff of pride left over, "It is Protestant, the state church now. And we are not allowed to pray for the dead." The "now" stuck in my throat, and I sat down beside him and asked him to remember for me when it was not so.

"Let me see. Well, now it is the king's church, and before that, the late queens, who I have saw many a time and once she grinned at me. She had a stride as if she wanted to measure the earth with her feet. Now before her, in my grandfather's time, it was the Pope's church and there was much burning at Smithfield for them as got it wrong, or so he told me, and so it come down through the family. His grandfather had told him how the monks were here. That was a time sent down through father to son as being Godly, but we were trained to say naught, either in the time of the king or the time of the queen or the time of the Pope and all. We had long learned to keep within ourselves as most wise men do, when them above you switch and change so as the wind blows. Way above. No, we have ever been a silent family, learned to be, all through the years that we was sextons and then gardeners but sextons within ourselves, knowing what was here hid under the orchard trees if you know what I mean."

Sometimes in my soul's memory we sit at May Day when the orchard is all bridal with blossom, and sometimes we sit there in the cold of winter, that time in February when it never gets quite light in London, lingers as if the world itself were in a sorrowful time, sometimes, or once, we sat there on that selfsame bench when we had brushed the snow from the stone, for by then he had begun to bring me news of the world across the stone wall.

But the story he told was always the same, and if he had been a countryman, it would have been the same with other scenes and other reasons. What he was telling me, when he had found one who would listen, after so long awaiting, was why he and his father and his grandfather and his great-grandfather were on the earth then and in that place. To remember the dead and look after the trees. For him it was a dear and urgent place and work.

In his great-great-grandfather's time, the first Nathan that was, he called him, he remembered not as a small boy. But he did remember the second Nathan, an old man in his smock, with a long beard. Just as he was for me.

That had been the time of the old king, Henry Eight, he called him, and he said he was told that one need not question the king. He, the king, understood not, nor cared any for the monks there for they sat upon what he saw as fine property, not knowing or letting himself remember it was a charnel house. It was one of the last houses for the monks in London to go, for there were many powerful people attached to it.

"The lord Thomas More hisself," he said, "had shared the prayers there when he was a young man before he was in chambers. He had been a devout boy, and of course, he, and the king too, had knowed many of the monks before they repented, for they were of the families of power, most of them, in the land, not from the poor, as we are."

"We," he said, for it was known of course that Sutton's hospital was for poor boys, but he stopped to explain, maundering down that side lane when I longed for him to stay on the high road of his story. "Well," he told me, "it is like this. There be two poors. They is the forever poor and the sometime poor; the forever poor is like these here below us in their pit of rottenness. Then there is the sometime poor, them as had run upon hard times, or chose, some chose that way, being of a Godly nature. Those are the boys, the sometime poor for one reason or another."

He laughed. "You see that way thee can be poor and still be gentry, gentry poor. And thou hast thy pride not took away, being of that way of being poor. My great-great-grandfather was one of they, a lay brother, yes, he was a lay brother in his youth, but when the king came with his soldiers, he with many lay brothers was turned out upon the town to shift for theirselves. So he did marry like an ordinary man, married my great-great-grandmother," and here the old man murmured and muttered on and on about who she was and what her father did and by Christ's blessed soul I have forgot that part, for he was coming to the gist of the matter.

He said, "The king demanded that the monks and their abbot, the saint, for my great-grandfather and my grandfather too said it come down in the family from the first Nathan that if any man was a saint it was John Houghton, who had been a gentleman and gone to Cambridge and all before he gave hisself to Christ or howsomever they said it in those days. The king demanded that they take the oath that he, an ordinary man when he was not being a king in all glory, was the head of the church in England and not the Pope, for the Pope was Antichrist, or some such.

"Well, John Houghton would not have it and he spake back to the king, having known him since they were playmates together when they were small, and most of the other monks having known him in his youth; some of the monks had even been at the court in all their finery and frills and such. Charterhouse was the place where the gentry and the noblemen went to retreat and confess their sins. Sometimes they stayed days, sometimes weeks, depending on how much they had sinned or who they were hiding from. So be that.

"So do thee not see that of all the monks in their praying idleness, so the king said, they were the most familiar and most proud and most stuck in the king's craw, to be broke upon the wheel? So they were, some starved to death, some hanged. John Houghton never recanted though he was took to Tyburn, hanged, cut down alive; those who saw it said he still was calm, still prayed when they cut him to death and then they took the pieces of the man he had been and spiked them on the walls of London except for his arm and that they brought back to Charterhouse and nailed it to the door, the same door there yet, the very same.

"My great-great-grandfather and his brother went and took down the arm for it was all there was left of him to give him Christian burial in the night, some of him anyway, and that was a brave thing to do for they too could have been hung, drawn, and quartered for it. They buried it right here in the plague pit of rottenness under one of the trees to mark the place; it lay with a little skeleton of a child, and an old locket and a bit of a shirt from the old days, for whenever thee dig in this place that is the kind of thing thee turn up." He pointed vaguely out through the trees. Yes, it was winter when he first told me for the trees hung in a dirty mist from the sea coal in the city.

"Now for a time they remembered which tree it was, and then the ground went back to being as the rest of the field, and they were old and forgot which tree in time or had arguments and said first one and then another, so they tended all the field, and then the Howards made a fine palace of the place where the old queen came when she was eighteen years on her way to be queen, and where the king that is today, the one from Scotland they says speaks not English like we do, held court here in the great hall that was once the monks' refectory, and made a passel of knights, thee know, dubbed they while they knelt and said their names and all.

"That was in my time. I went on tending until they thought I was one of the servants and made me one and so it is. They come and go. We stay and tend the orchard. It runs in the family."

He had reached the end of his story for that day or another day but I needed more. To drag him back to what he knew and I did not, I asked him if the building we slept in as gownboys was part of the old monastery, and was going to tell him of the haunting and the dreams, but he laughed and said, "Bless me, no. That was one of them fine tennis courts it was the fashion to build. They had to have a tennis court or they would not be gentry, you see. Then it was something else, a library. All had to have a library. That's the way it goes, from fields to buildings to tell who thou art. For my family, we have the orchard. It is all the same when thee think of it."

XI

———— ✦ ————

Every person is bound to go so far as lies in his power for the preventing and redressing of evil; and where it stops in any, and runs not clear, there the guilt, like filth or mud, will lie.

— ROGER WILLIAMS

*N*OW IT IS THE SPRING OF THE YEAR AGAIN, NEARLY fifty years since I was sent by the Father of Lights and the malice of man into this sometime Eden. Eden it is when the arguments and the fights and the opinions pause to let in blessed silence. They do, the apple trees, it is true, look bridal for the days when they bloom so, and there is aways the memory of the sixth Nathan, as he called himself, who walks beside me here in my own orchard, no, not my own, God's orchard of pippins and rubies and all he taught me of in those days and those walks in the charnel orchard of Charterhouse. By God's grace sometimes then it was lovely, too.

Now, without books, and without ones who knew me always, for they are all among the angels, there is no one to write to the way I did once, telling all, arguing, at home upon the page. Now there seem to be only two passions that hold the attention of those who are left, God Politics and, as always and forever, I fear, God Land. But with the Father of Lights to guide me, maybe, who knows, I will find silence and live long enough to write about all this and how I was and how they were in the times that made us as we are today.

To wander alone is to wander within the mind and there find angels, tigers, what's hidden, what's plain, and what you thought you had rid yourself of long ago. All is true with the eyes of sleep upon us, even what is hid by masks. By the Lord Jesus Christ's love, I must admit sometimes I wander there in fear for my soul. But then, oh then and often of late, one of the gates that lock my past away swings open and I can walk among those I have loved, or live again how it was, and is, to be shut away from them by law, or exile, or death, or hard, sweet choice when they intrude so welcome upon me.

My father bragged of me at last, for he had not had a hook in his own life to hang my going to Sir Edward, except to seem to know more than those he informed. But when I came forth from Charterhouse in my fine feathers, he swelled like a turkey cock with pride and explained to all who would stand and listen that I was among the poor boys at Sutton's, he still called it that, but they were not poor as poor but poor as sons of gentry down on their luck, for none else could go there and although, he said, he could have paid, they asked him not for I was so clever.

Well. I listened and was prone to silent laughter, and saw all England sometimes not as horizontal where all men could walk in peace, but vertical as a window, with flies climbing ever and falling ever and climbing again. Outside in the shipwreck of the city, the direction was not as I had long learned at the court, as who's in who's out, but up and down and once down down again, like a terrible child's game, or all the way up to the feet of the king who sat on top of some pinnacle and drooled his wine down both sides of his mouth. None seemed satisfied with his lot in those days, or God knows now, but the sixth Nathan. I had seen one courtly page lie and say his father was an earl, because he was ashamed that his father was only a viscount. I saw them ever looking up, and seldom down to where they might fall.

I had been so shut away in the same city behind the great stone walls and the discipline and the rules of Charterhouse that I knew nothing of the Parliament or of my lord until the Christmastide. The Parliament had reconvened again on the twentieth of November in a crisis. Most of the prattle at the table as my father dived deeper into his ale, it being Christmas, was of the Palatinate that some called Bohemia. No one quite knew where it was, but they knew that the hated Spanish had invaded it and that its queen, Elizabeth, the one they called the Winter Queen, was the much-loved daughter of King James. My father was much exercised about what he would do and not do. He would tell the Parliament, who were all thieves and liars anyhow, not to piddle about the Palatinate and take note of the country of England which was poorer than it had ever been in his lifetime.

"Piddling and prattling about the Palatinate, that is a phrase to catch meddlers, eh?" he laughed into the froth of his ale.

He said naught that was new; it was the talk of the taverns and Fetter Lane. There was none talked of more than my lord Coke, who was near worshiped in the city. Even my father who spoke as full of knowledge of all that went on as the men of Fetter Lane did, and could not be moved by facts, even to him, my lord and Mr. Pym and all had hung the moon in place. Prerogative Absolute was the word for what was wrong with the country. It was much talked of but little understood; the wits said most men thought it was a horse.

There was no hope of my slipping out of the house in clothes borrowed from my brother Robert who had grown like a weed, and seeking my lord at St. Stephen's chapel. Parliament had adjourned on the twentieth of December, leaving, they said, some kind of protestation as a record in the Commons Journal. It was not even a grievance which would have been stronger but weaker than a bill. When I tried for a little while to explain no one listened. But I filtered gossip and it only told me what I knew. I had to be satisfied with that.

Lord Coke had said, and it was on all tongues, that he offered himself as a sacrifice if they were brave enough to pass even so tame a protest for their rights. So there was rumor that my lord was once again, as he had been so long before, in danger of falling headlong. He led the Parliament into standing for the ancient rights that had come all the way from Magna Carta, for once lost, he said, their rights could never be regained, and England would be a tyranny under an absolute king as it was in France and Spain. So, buoyed by his courage they refused to pass laws the king demanded until their rights of free speech in the House of Commons without fear of being arrested were clear. The king had bragged that he could jail men as he wished, and that he was God's representative and that he could not be judged. My lord had often excused him when he spoke thus, and said he was a Scottish king and knew no better.

All that Christmastide I tried to overhear in the streets and Paul's walk and Fetter Lane and my father's table who knew quite what those rights were. Such a thing as free speech without fear was as alien to them as the road to China. I had learned "Watch your mouth" with my weaning, and I had learned my shorthand to put down my secret thoughts in safety, even as a boy.

Such a fool idea had simply arrived as naked as a newborn babe, a stranger to their brains. Even now so long later I sometimes want to charge into the one street here in Providence, the first place in all the world that I know of where such a right is part of the common law, jump over the hogs and the puddles and call out, "By Christ's bowels, do you not know what you have? Do you not know?"

I never in those days felt more an exile, only a few miles away, in a world of those who knew nothing but said it anyway. Oh how proud my anger was. I saw my lord needing me when it was I, unwanted and forgotten as I thought, laid away like some no longer fashionable cloak, who needed him, my place, my boy pride. I was a fool, but still it rankles that I was not there, yet what could I have done but stand aside?

I tried to gather papers thrown in the street, new or old, papers that wrapped fish, papers thrown in the garbage of the gutter, floating in Houndsditch. In that Christmas cold some were frozen. But no paper with a date and a bit of news was too dirty, too blood-soaked, too gross. All together, with those and the rumors and lies in the taverns and in the news sheets and tracts thrown out from many a printer's cell with some garbled and slanted hint of the news. I began to sort out the mess and garbage from what sounded true, of what had happened to my lord, what he had said and done.

My attic room was like a mockery of my lord's cell of parchment thrown across the tables I was so used to. My brother Robert touched not the gathered garbage for I had threatened the dire punishment that older brothers have ever used to play the tyrant for their youngers. Then, faint as first breeze I began to see what he had planned, and why he had kept all to himself. It was no less than to net the king and teach him English manners.

Christmastide was made blessed by my brother Sydrach, who came from among the Turks at Constantinople, and brought me the most beautiful book I ever saw. He said it was in Persian and very old, from the days when the Turkish capital was at Iconium, and Persian was the court language. It was by one Turkish man, Rumi, a sort of saint in their religion. Of course I could not read a word of it, but I loved the colors and the drawings. I carried it with me whenever I thought there might be a chance to find another to read it for me. I carried it to and fro from England in those years when I returned, and by God's grace, my dear friend, John Milton, who collected languages as I did, found one from Persia who spoke and read the language. He had come to London with rugs and cloth, and spoke some awkward English.

It was only for one afternoon at John's house, and we both listened well, but much is gone from my mind. I do remember one saying of Rumi, that what is wine to the pilgrim is poison to his follower. For years it was a burr under my saddle, until I grew old enough, or one day, it was vouchsafed unto me, that he meant that one man should not take another's word without searching for its truth for himself, whether in the church or in the state, but then, perhaps I fitted it to my own brain.

Sydrach and I had grown closer than we had ever been when it was my turn to be younger brother and be lorded over. As ones in the family who went more abroad from Farrenden, we spoke with one another of a world they knew not, and it was resented by my parents. So that holiday we spent much time in the tavern. He told me of the Sublime Porte which was what the ambassadors called the sultan's palace, though the Turks called it Topkapi. He said the sultans had many wives they called a harem, and how no man could ever go among them, for danger of his life, except those who were eunuchs. He said the black eunuchs, huge men from Africa, were the guards of the harem, the Seraglio, he called it, and how they formed a powerful inner governing of their own, and were feared by all.

Sydrach had seen for himself the splendid tombs of Topkapi. Vines of jewels climbed up the walls, and every coffin had a jeweled turban worth a king's ransom at its head to show the ranks of the dead. I asked him how such an infidel as he could do that and he said he disguised himself and paid one of the guards and stood with others bobbing and praying as they did. I asked him if he were not in fear of hellfire for worshiping among the infidels. He laughed and said he feared more the scimitars of the Janissaries, for he could have lost his head.

He said the sultan was near death from melancholy. So it is in all the world, that one rules over another to his own hurt as it says in the Bible.

Nathan, who sat with us that day, said no such things could happen in England it being Christian and the other being barbarian, and Sydrach and I changed glances thinking of the luxury and culture he had found without the confines of Topkapi, for the Mohammedans had ever led us in mathematics and the sciences.

Sydrach spoke a language which he said was Turkish of the pazar; he learned it for business. It was like no language I ever heard and I tried to find the places where it met somewhere in the Latin or Greek as the English and French and yet the Dutch and German did somewhat, but I could find no place for the language came from the great spaces of Mongolia. I have ever loved languages and the words of people. The way they spoke to one another and what they believed, like the Turks who believed in Mohammed and the Indians who had many gods, and some Chinese who learned from their Buddha, and others who followed Lao Tze who said that if one found something called the Dow or some such, he could lie in the bottom of a pool all day to get over being drunk. And to think that the people around me thought most of the world was Christendom.

I think it was St. Steven's day, after Christmas, when my father announced that my lord Coke and Sir Edward Phillips had become martyrs and lay in the Tower to have their heads cut off. I heard him say somewhere beyond the cold horror in my brain that Sir Edward Coke had been arrested for a traitor, though every man in London knew it was because my lord had been the first to bring down the king's friend, Bacon.

Overwhelming evil like a storm engulfed me and I ran away from the table. I think my mother called after me. But I only ran and ran as a panicked animal in a shambles. I ran down Fetter Lane toward the rooms in Sergeant's Inn where I had gone so often as if when I fell against his door there would be some answer. There was no thinking nor direction, only panting and dread.

There upon the door was the great royal seal. There came Bartholomew, the porter of the same name as my earliest friend, as if one Bartholomew had sent the other from Paradise, and he found me huddled against Sir Edward's door and picked me up and led me to the fire within the sentry room. He gave me a hot posset to drink and said, I remember he said, then or later, "Until thee calm thyself I cannot tell thee."

There in that small warm room, for the Temple servants ever prided themselves on knowing what was afoot, he told me of Sir Edward. He told how by candlelight, late in the night before the Commons dissolved for the holidays on the king's command, they put forth their Petition of Rights, wrote down in the Commons Journal, every word weighed and argued among their selves, as lawyers do, precedent and prerogative and all that, how the king was not allowed by ancient law all the way back to Magna Carta to arrest any member of Parliament for what he said or did within the walls of the House of Commons.

Then they all went to their homes for Christmas and waited to see which way the cat would jump. The king demanded the Commons Journal and tore out the petition with his own hands and threw the pieces on the floor and in the faces of his Privy Council, and said the words were traitorous.

All the time I never moved, afraid to stop any words from him that were like food to one starving. I sat there against the stone of the wall and wanted its cold to come through my scant robe to show I was alive and could shiver. I dared not even ask a question for fear of losing one or other of the facts as he knew them that he let down slow.

His voice murmured on above me while I drank the hot posset. "We heard here at the Temple that many miles away from Windsor and Stoke, I reckon fifteen minutes after they laid hands on him for we have our grapevine way of knowing things and depend not on slow and ponderous officialdom, oh long before, I know it was long before, for the news was brought to us by a horseman at least an hour later. He announced that Sir Edward had been picked up at Stoke and brung away to the Tower by the soldiers, and they were coming to search his rooms for traitorous material and he was to put the royal seal on his chamber door."

The soldiers took him to the Tower and they put that old man in a damp stone room cold as charity that had once been a kitchen, and there he sat without a book or a quill or anything. Someone had put a sign on the door of his stone cell, "This place hath long wanted a cook."

"And all that did happen today; the world ends for some and begins for some in a day," I think I heard him say. Did I? Are there words for that?

He roused me by shaking my shoulder. "I said he was questioned by members of the Privy Council but he being of the gentry they would not rack him. He knew that for he had racked others in his time."

I had not known I dozed off and that it was dark of the winter afternoon until he shook my shoulder. He told me to come again and he would glean and harrow from all the ways he had of finding out, a friend here, a wink there, "You never mind," he told me, "I have ways to find out." So I went to my parents' house in the dark with the sounds of merriment around me from the houses and the taverns as they celebrated St. Steven's day with riot and joy.

I stayed waking long into the night and did not sleep until gray dawn crept through the cracks in the lathing. So schooled I was to capricious death by that of Bartholomew Legate that I thought, I must know no one too close ever again in my life. They die. As if that thought stretched through the whole night, that is all I remember.

BACK AT CHARTERHOUSE I waited, and when I found Nathan, for he had took a long Christmas, it being what he called the dead of winter, and the time to let the orchard sleep, I never needed him more. When he finally returned I made him my ears and my messenger, for I had told him much of what my life had been before the Charterhouse, reliving it as surely as he relived his family history, each of us honoring the other's need to speak. My lord lingered on in the cold Tower without decision. He had been stowed away may be to think what to do with him.

Once, Nathan heard tell that the king had sent a message saying he would send to my lord the greatest legal minds in England, eight of them I think, to advise him on the legalities of the matter, whatever the matter was, but my lord sent back a message to say he already had the best legal mind in England, his own, and needed no such help.

It was said he thanked the king and said, "You have the power to take my head, so let be, do it or not do it." He sailed so close to the wind out of sheer bravado that I prayed for him to shut up. He told me later that after a few weeks he was allowed his papers and his writing tools.

But then I heard nothing, saw nothing, waited through the spring until Easter when I could get back across the city to Sergeant's Inn and glean from Bartholomew what was being said, I then as avid for gossip as the most eavesdropping courtier in the land. Oh God, to know, not know, guess, hope while my lord lingered there.

When I got to Bartholomew he said he had long looked for me for there had been a message from my lord, not to me by name, for he was afeared to use it, "Tell the boy," he said in his message or something like it for it had come from mouth to ear to ear, so fallible, all the way from a cell in the Tower to me, "Tell the boy to stay away. Stay away. I want him not in my sight."

I thought it a slight to break my heart, but Bartholomew saw my tears and told me my lord had meant that I would be in danger, though I only half believed it until the new dreams came, dreams that saw me armored with courage in the face of torture since I knew so much of his business and had long put it down in shorthand that only I could read. I think I waited days for the hands of the soldiers to grasp my shoulders and take me, white ruff, black robe, and all, to the Tower. I prayed in the night to be brave and silent, but no one came. No one ever came to find me. He had hid me too well. I began to live within what had happened, while I waited, and waited, and waited for the hands upon my shoulders.

And at no time, in the courtyard, in the refectory, in the lessons and the debates and the work and play of boys, did I hear mentioned what was going forth beyond those walls. Even today in this soft spring New England morning I can hear faintly the call of boys whose lives are led apart from everything I care for.

Spring came and still I waited. I sat again upon the stone bench that had become our domain and watched the white-veiled trees, softly drifting their petals in the breeze, and thought right in the midst of all my worry, is there a spring anywhere of more promise than here in England? I walked among the blossoms and could hear the birds nesting and their tiny domestic quarrels, and the bees had made their pilgrimage to the blossoms, so that the orchard was never silent in spring as it had been in winter. I thought it spoke so, growing out of the limbs and hopes and fears of the long dead.

Finally Nathan came back from the city where he had taken to going each morning to glean news, and sat down with an old man's sigh. I begged him speak for his look was portentous with news like a pregnant cow. I knew he would say my lord, at last, had been beheaded on Tower Green, which was his privilege, being of the Privy Council of the realm. Such were the fine privileges of high life then and in England, and now. Even now.

"Let me see." He thought for a minute and a breeze tossed blossoms on his sparse white hair and made a little halo. "He hath been allowed his books but that was a long time ago, I told you that. Let me see," and he kept me for a river long minute before giving me his news, which was that my lord's oldest son and his daughter by his first wife, one Mrs. Sadlier, had permission to dine with him. He answered then the question I had not asked. "No. Nobody else can see him."

Oh my dear and holy Father of Lights, how I longed to go and stand below his window like Blondel, King Richard the Lion Hearted's troubador, at the king's prison window, for none in England had a heart so like a lion as my lord.

Later, in the hot August of the year, after seven months of the Tower, my lord was released and sent to house arrest at Stoke with permission to travel only six miles from his house. The long vacation from Charterhouse had started and I spent the time as I had long since, running errands in several languages for my father, until one day there was a message come from Stoke. My heart wilded. I still hold the missive in my hand and see his ordered writing upon it.

So I went back in vacations to work with him and do his bidding for he knew that the king had pulled back at the brink of killing him for fear of the people and that he could work in some kind of shaky safety.

Finally on one of those walks we had that go on forever in my mind, I found courage to ask him of the Tower.

"A good place to work," he said after a time. "Nobody bothers you. I spent that time working on my comments on Littleton's land law."

He never mentioned it again except once when he muttered, "These are the mornings I do love, as quiet and untrammeled as when I was in the Tower."

XII

You will find the business at bottom to be, first, a depraved appetite after the great vanities, dreams and shadows of this vanishing life, great portions of land, land in this wilderness, as if men were in as great necessity and danger for want of great portions of land as poor, hungry, thirsty seamen have, after a sick and stormy, a long and starving passage. This is one of the gods of New England . . .

— ROGER WILLIAMS

YOU WOULD THINK IT ENOUGH. I AM EIGHTY-ONE years old. This morning like a mooning calf I trudged along through the fields, which as all know is my habit to get away to contemplation, which I admit often ends up with a fight within myself, a silent railing. I am too burdened sometimes, a grumbling mother hen with too many chicks. And yet, this complaining about it is a sinful habit that makes the bright day dark for me and spreads to all who need me. It oft makes heavy a light task.

My friends know me as a happy man, they call me a sweet man, a man who is ever ready to help, to succor, and, face it Roger Williams, to stick his oar in with a ream of good advice. Which nobody takes. I should not tax my neighbors so within my mind. It is un-Christian. But I have to admit that when they ask my help and grumble at it at the same time it makes me growl and snap.

This early morning some neighbors sprang from their doors as if they had awaited my passing to ask, mind you, if I would arbitrate for them a rod of ground they had used for their arguing and quarreling to my knowledge for twenty years. The two neighbors had long since spilled blood and bruises in the form of black eyes, some to one, some to the other, and I found myself wondering what they would do without the fire of their disagreement that had warmed them for so long. I tried and failed once again to get them to agree, and all this at dawn when a man should by natural rights have a little of the still sleeping world to himself. This little passel of land too small and rocky to feed a goat upon has been an argument they have both worn like the armor of God, each one right and righteous.

All they have done in truth is to rouse my long-banked fires of anger with the true reason for their stopping me, for they wanted to be the first to see me go up in flames. They watched my face to read as they told me, hoping to find some hint to brighten the day with gossip. Well. I gave them none. It is not their affair if I cannot rid myself of a longtime burden upon my back.

I have tried loving, forgetting, forgiving, long-viewing, all the palliatives, and yet the embers can be roused to life at the turn of a word, a gesture, an argument over land no matter how small, as this morning. This ruined morning.

What in the devil's name do people want, each over the other? I had my warnings of men and ambitions long ago and should have learned my lesson. It was in that very Parliament of 1621, before I was put into Charterhouse like an unwanted bundle in an attic, and I a boy alight with ambition myself as any other sinner, new-learned elegant manners, and deep love for my lord Coke who took me to raise in his way.

I do not forget his words for they have guided me when I will allow them. He told me of six kinds of men who would never thrive or prosper. What he did not say but may be he intended is that they allow not others to prosper, for God knows they seem, not do, but seem, to prosper themselves with their foot on the head of another child of God in that terrible Jacob's ladder made of men and their rising.

First he warned against the alchemists for he said they were liars, but good came of their experiments at last. They have been dispossessed of power except among the gullible but the learning has led to true discovery since men use the knowledge of how one element acts upon another for understanding, and alas, for destruction, too. For it is never the knowledge but the evil use of it that stings. Then he cursed the monopolizers who want all in their own power that should be free for all, then there was . . . oh my dear Lord Jesus I have been murmuring and muttering aloud without knowing for the children playing in this field have stared at me and giggled.

Where was I? Having an argument within myself, an argument I was enjoying, with voice and gestures, speaking to the ground and the trees, who at least will not interrupt! Where was I? Oh yes. My lord spoke of the promoter who lives on the spoil of poor men, the concealment monger, that was one of his most damned though he used concealment himself when it suited him.

Then the one who rouses all my ire and banks my fires and cannot be stopped, the one who is so land-greedy that he must needs have thousands of acres to himself where instead of God's hungry children he keeps none upon his land kingdom but a shepherd and his dog. That man, the one who encloses and strips the others of their homes, was, to my lord, the worst of men.

And his name in my book of sorrows, of stumbling blocks, of fury, is Mr. William Harris! They have said he was a man of good business, I see him as a man of loud mouth who used his own beaten and brutalized past to beat and brutalize and grab land and land and land until it grew to some three hundred thousand acres, got here and there by fraud from Indians he has made drunk, and I should love him?

I know it is my duty to love the damned man. But I cannot and will not excuse what he has done, and all in the name of every dumb jack religion that has been washed ashore in this Rhode Island since we harbor those who God knows yearn for freedom of conscience as I did. Quakers, Ranters, Familists, Antinomians, Baptists, quaking and ranting and roaring and quarreling, we have them all. And what dangerous pleasure they take in it, the old cry of I am right and you are wrong. They make my sighs long.

Take you, Mr. William Harris, you have cozened them all, joining first one and then another for your own purpose. For forty years you have tested my Christian love, damn you for a jackal. You are so the mold of that man who can only feel safe if he is standing on the head of his brother, you and that witch you have worshiped with her brew of fear and greed known as good business.

You have called me a fool, an ass, a dunce, a knave, a liar, a thief, a cheater and hypocrite, a drunkard, a traitor, a regicide, a whoremonger with Indian women. You stroll into my mind, as insolent as ever, mountebank, liar, and sit and grin and ape me and will not go away. I tell myself that since our Lord was called in his time on earth blasphemer, whoremonger, deciever, madman, drunkard, glutton, to be called the same is a blessing, but not by Mr. Harris.

He haunts my steps when I expect it not, a Morris dancer ringing his bells under my nose. Only love can rid me of him and before the Father of Lights I have tried for fifty years to love that sly, grinning ape so he will leave my brain with his whirling and his bells and his jeering. For so I see him, still the street rogue and dancer to pick up pennies he was once in old England.

Even so this morning he stands mocking in the way of my thought and will not go, no, not for all the land in the Americas will he go. He was one who begged and wheedled me and used the name of God and charity, was full of easy tears, a destitute, cringing, shriveled soul beaten by the world, begged to come to me in exile, he and a few others. Though I longed then only to find a place where Mary and I and the children could build and be at peace, I welcomed them as a sign from the Father of Lights as my duty. I did. Even, God my witness, that mountebank and liar William Harris.

Sometimes I lose the temper of what he has done and has tried to do. My beloved Indian father, the sachem Canonicus, whose eyes I closed in his death and who was another who treated me as a son, offered me grazing rights without limits in the meadows upriver from our purchase to drive our beasts to grass and bring them home at evening. It was a gift for me, for he was shy and mistrusting of other English, and so he should have been. How right he was. A damnable rapacious breed we are, as fierce to rule in our polite way as Attila.

And what of Mr. Harris in all this? He turned the words "upstream without limits" into an invitation to own it in the English way. So he made some minor sachems drunk and "bought" the land outright. He persuaded them to sign thousands of acres away for the wampum they hold so dear and is only shell beads upon a string. It might as well be paper.

Mine, mine, mine, has been his canticle and his prayer, one man one dog all the way to the sunset. It is like the Papists who murder for the belief that a piece of bread should turn into the real and bleeding body and blood of Christ who gave such bread to His disciples and said as a man would say this flower is the color of my soul, this wine is the color of my blood, this bread is of my body, this rock my steady pulpit. In Spain if you do not swear to believe as they do, they burn you in a cleansing fire of Inquisition as we did to my beloved Bartholomew. They took a metaphor to be the thing itself but I think innocently, misreading mistranslations of the Bible which they knew so little. But not Mr. William Harris! He took advantage of a metaphor so kindly meant and so "upstream without limits" seems to have give Mr. Harris the right to fence in the sunset itself as far as man can walk or paddle or see or dream or think. It is a way about owning land the savages have never fathomed, for they use the land when they need it, and turn it back to God to lie fallow when they do not.

Let my soul go, Mr. Harris, for they told me this morning that you are dead, and still you sit there grinning and taunting my mind, uninvited, unwanted. Did you know that? Did you yearn for understanding like all men? Did you strut within my mind to hide the deadly fear left to haunt you from some evil childhood?

Where by the bowels of Christ is my compassion? You died so brutally. Had you been a dumb animal caught in a thicket and gored to death I would have mourned or even wept for I have done that. But I only see the punishment of God upon a man I hate. There. I have said it and stove my stick into the ground to make the point. Hate. I hate the ghost of Mr. Harris who died they say in England, after such tribulation as few men have to endure. Am I to weaken? Am I to forgive the ghost of Mr. Harris? I know I must, if he will only do me the honor of getting out of my brain.

He was on his way to England to make more trouble for this colony, more demands, more claims to his little plot of some three hundred thousand acres of the natives' land. Oh, I see him as he clung to the mast and dreamed to the horizon that he saw as his border of ownership. Only this time it was water, not land, he measured with his crafty eye, yes, crafty, I may try to forgive but I cannot sin by lying. He had, God forgive me, a crafty eye for measurement.

As he watched there hove into view from below the horizon a pirate ship from Barbary. They boarded the unprotected vessel, captured him and others, stove the ship, carried them to the Barbary coast, and demanded ransom. He, Mr. Harris, was so unloved that it took a year to raise his ransom, even from those who called themselves his business partners. All that time he languished they say, chained to the oar of a pirate ship. When finally he got himself to England he was still as intent on trouble as he had ever been, but died in a tavern three days after he landed.

Well, Mr. Harris, compassion will blot you from my brain, but I am scarce ready for that. After all we have been enemies for so long, God rest your soul. There I have said it. But I will not miss you, Mr. Harris, no matter how your spirit begs and whines as you did in life.

Dear God, it makes me long for that false peace I once fled from, hallowed and idle and soft, those years at Pembroke College, Cambridge, where I was sent after Charterhouse. I was there for five years that passed as five days or five centuries depending on the weather. Even though I know it a mirage I long sometimes to stroll along the Backs at Cambridge through the filtered light of the old trees with some companion or another, all long dead, and I left here too far away to tell a living soul what we did there as we argued mighty propositions, as boys do. We spoke in Latin for it was against the rules of Pembroke to speak in English though we did it sometimes with the wicked grace of small boys playing at sin.

Idle and self-important, we took the days for granted as our ownership, for we were the chosen ones for something. I try to forget what. Oh yes, to preach the gospel while our souls were trained for climbing as agile as squirrels toward bishop. As if bishop were at the top of some great tree, the final nut for winter.

It was for me a place where nothing happened. Oh it had. There was much tradition of brave scholars who stood for truth and died for it, but that was part of the legend as boys dream of being brave if they come to the shock of battle. The days turned into months and then years and nothing happened. It was the only place I have ever been that I was cosseted and saved from daily life simply by the granting of a fine scholarship because I had a nimble brain trained by my lord and circumstance and my great pleasure of learning. And of arguing, which was then, and is still, and until the last dog falls into the Cam and drowns, ever will be the be all and end all of our talk. To don the gown, follow rules when it was meet to do so, shine with learning before the tiny tiny mighty seemed to be all asked of me. I wish I could remember happenings, events, but I do not.

They flow together in that hallowed idleness, the excitement and the argument of who should bow and who should not and who should speak before the king and who should this and who should that, as they climbed ever upward, thinking they were on the ground. A visit of the court provided meat for days and weeks of scurry, but usually there was the nod and drift of lectures spoke too often, the soft voices and slow procession under the lovely trees of men to whom nothing was ever going to happen, even in that dangerous time.

Oh there was the secret bathing in the Cam; even that river was so quiet as it flowed behind the fine buildings that reached for the heavens from meadows where the cattle and the sheep grazed. The water was a still surface where we dipped the oars lightly, or drove the punt into the riverbed, discursive talk, discursive paddling, discursive punting along the Cam forever.

Or we walked slowly slowly behind two walking slowly slowly, their robes flapping behind them, seeming to speak of scholarly abstractions but it was as always the language of gossip, be it gossip about Erasmus or another eminent scholar, or who was set for preferment and how they could stop it.

Why even to think of it tells me why I downed the tools I was taught to need there, and left, as naked as Dick Whittington, not to seek my fortune, but to seek my life. Left men who never knelt beside a friend fallen in the field, a favorite animal gored and dying, never saw the glow of life leave a beloved body as if the soul had blown out a candle and left a room, never felt life come into one's hands, screaming and wet, human or animal, much the same, never been so in the moment that it was and is a miracle to be alive, to be dead, to be witness of God's work on this earth, to be part of it. For a little wandering among safe trees, would I give forth a moment of those blessings?

Even when the facts of life seeped into the stone buildings, they scarce made a moan, except to those whose ears were trained to listen, or those who had fallen into factions that I must needs struggle to remember, though then they were life's milestones, as we tell our children.

Without them, though, I would not be here on this hill in this morning, cursing and whining to my shame. Closing in upon us in those days were the ever-growing stone walls of religion that were, I know now, but two ways to power and not to God. In five years of favor I found the drift toward an abyss gave me moments of terror as of falling.

My lord in his plan for me had chose Pembroke, the college called the College of Bishops for it had made more bishops than all the others. The patron who watched over their forms of gossip and hope was the great Lancelot Andrewes. My lord loved him as a brother. He saw me mitered when he looked at me, and said, many times, "Thank the Lord Jesus for your brains and your manners for you are set for high church bishop as the sparks fly upward."

Sweet charity and forgiveness there were times, even then, that I would wake and yearn to fly into the midnight courtyard naked as I was born and shout, "How dare you? How dare you use Almighty God and His Blessed Son as pawns in a game?" But that was only a shameful half-dream until I was forced to shout by day.

I had nothing to say to this for my dear lord Coke dreamed aloud above me and asked me not what my own hopes were. He planned for me as his father had planned for him with the imprimature of prerogative absolute from father to son that went from my own family table to the House of Commons, to Cambridge, and on, and stopped before the king, father to all before God as we were told.

My lord said, letting me hear, "We need a bishop close to the king's party." But the true reason he gave me over to Pembroke College was his admiration and love for Bishop Andrewes. God my soul witness Lancelot Andrewes was a man to convert a saint to his way. I knew him, too, with my lord at the Parliament. I had revered him always for it was he who led the scholars in the new translation of the Bible, and it was his style, his elegance, as my lord called it, his sure images, his passion, that kept the words clear and clean of one faction or another, although through all the time of the translation, preference had to be watched as a sin against God's word. There was much talk of sin

against God's word, even though it was years later and I a Watts scholar, as he had been, that my own foot was placed precisely on the first
rung of the ladder he had trod upwards, for Pembroke College was
Lancelot Andrewes's "College of Bishops" as surely as if it had charter.

Lancelot Andrewes was the most worldly minister I ever knew and
yet never did he let the world, as my lord said, grow weeds in his pure
garden. I was, my lord said, to look to him in time of trouble within
my soul, yes, to Lancelot Andrewes, believer in the king's divine right
to be head of the English church, as familiar with the teeth of power as
a woman at her loom. So I looked toward Bishop Andrewes and not the
simple Lord Jesus for my succor and my hope.

I am thinking of course about politics, the politics of God as it was
in England when I was twenty-two and liable for every breeze of controversy that blew toward me. By the Father of Lights, it is hard to go
back beyond the painful rejections that I have had to face in order to
learn to use a dung fork in the Augean stables of my mind and my
training. As if. What? As if we must learn all to reject all. To go back
through that brambled and winding blind path of the mind is to admit
that I was as passionate a part of it as any other toady, as passionate then
as now, for I am a man of passion, which is to be ever young. Thanks
be to God, I can go back and be the same yearning mind that I was.

I loved Pembroke and what it stood for, and was there one of the
elect as sure as any Puritan minister among the Calvinists or the Presbyters, I knew myself chosen, and reveled in all of it. It was not the ladder that charged my mind. I forgot that for the learning, the pure and
lovely learning, untrammeled by time and decision, pure meeting of
minds back beyond Aristotle, and Plato, and the ancient fathers, and
all the way through paths of righteousness and sin in all the languages
given me to see and understand. It was and is a pure feast of joy to me
who ever loved learning and languages as one loves play, another
women, another God.

Oh I thought myself a lover of God even then, but I know now that
it was not so, for God then had many faces and one was my lord and
one was Lancelot Andrewes. Since they knew my sponsor, for my lord
Coke was then vice chancellor of Cambridge and came often there and
always, in those days, stopped to see how I did, I was petted by the fellows who saw me on the way to becoming one of them, I, older, more

worldly, but not knowing it. How they yearned to hear my way to the court, the court of kings, the be-all and end-all of ambition and I the proud and sinful carrier of all that. What rich food for a questing boy in monkish robes, strolling along under the trees and holding forth in Latin, or in Greek or in Hebrew, by Christ's holy wounds I miss that, that nimble play of the mind.

So I sat among the pensioners around the great hall where we ate bad food, while the sons of peers sat at the high table with the more timid fellows and threw bread at one another. Sometimes, but very seldom, Lancelot Andrewes himself dined there, and the bread pelting stopped, for even the sons of peers could be impressed by his presence if little else.

A peeping chick will begin to break forth almost unheard, so faint the sound of breakage, and the crack widens in the safe egg, until the lovely shell falls and steps out the wet and frightened chick into the world. And so it was with me. By the third year the crack had happened and by the fourth of that lifeless life I saw it unredeemed and knew I was going to begin a path not chosen for me except by God. And yet I was discreet, for I had learned discretion as part of manners.

Even the calm of Pembroke was shattered by far events and far passions, and we began to split into factions, as the world outside our stone walls split, we the safe imitators of those who were to set their lives at the shock as forlorn troops begin battles. It all began for me with the cleaning of a wall. There had been for days more and more prelates going through the carved doors into the quiet of Pembroke. Matthew Wren, Pembroke's president, had been with the prince on his journey to Madrid for the hated Spanish marriage. But the people, the Parliament, feared it and loathed it. The Spanish king was even then fighting in that long brutal war of power that called itself religion on the continent of Europe, and Gustavus Adolphus of Sweden, who had raised the Protestant banner, was becoming as familiar a name on the streets of London as our own surly king. One Protestant kingdom after another fell and still the king did nothing, for he saw himself a man of peace, and he needed the Spanish money.

But the king had been duped by Gondomar, the Spanish ambassador. The Spanish had never meant the marriage to happen, but, Gondomar used the hope of it to slow the king's decision to raise a

Protestant banner. When it failed, the people were so ecstatic that it was said they lit more bonfires throughout the country than they had for the king's coronation so long ago.

But what did come of it was that Wren reported to Bishop Andrewes and his protégé, one unknown William Laud, that the prince had become more solid and dependable in his orthodoxy than his father. So from a little college at Cambridge, the politics of God was being played out as high church orthodox prelates in their robes followed by their hungry retinues swept into Pembroke courtyard and dominated the high table. The silk of their Arminian robes made a lovely whispering and flow of color in and out, up and down, all among the college rooms, where they ever sat and planned, as I see now, the takeover of the English church from the hated reformers, who they called low and plain, and the reinstitution of all the Catholic ways. Except of course that it was the king and not the Pope who reigned over the mass.

They appointed bishops, and insisted on ceremonies that had long been exiled from the English church. Politics in the bowing of the knee, politics in the taking of the bread of communion that once again, and by the law, became Christ's body, the real presence, the real blood, the real power of the king's party.

And the king, that now old man who had kept the balance between factions in the church, who had kept England out of Europe for so long, who had demanded peace, the one love of his life besides Lord Buckingham, that same king we had cursed, and whispered of, and laughed at, died. He lay in his own foulness on his royal bed, his mouth hung open, mute at last, and could not even give his blessing to his son and his lover, except with his eyes as the light withdrew from them.

Within half a year we missed and longed for him, for Charles knew nothing of balance ever in his life. He had learned too well from one of the chief intriguers, our own Wren of Pembroke as his chaplain, who ever led the weak and pliant boy, for ever boy he was, into the Catholic ways. Lancelot Andrewes, once of Pembroke, once Watts scholar, high in the Privy Council, drew the shuttle through the loom to the day of his death.

I, Watts scholar too, chosen one, set for preferment by my lord Coke's guiding, felt more and more like a sheep in the shambles to give wool for whatever was being wove. Day after day the signs were felt, as a man tests the wind with his finger. I remember the one time Bishop Andrewes stopped me in the great court and said, "Thou art a Watts scholar. So was I. Do you still dispute in Latin, Greek, and Hebrew?" I muttered yes from my bowed head and he placed his hand upon it and passed by. I saw him once again at the high table when the faction had formed, much of it at Pembroke, sometime its seedbed as a good-wife keeps the babies of her garden under shelter to wait for summer. Much was made of me by the questing fellows, their noses ever high for who was in and who was out in that tiny court.

But the second time Bishop Andrewes did not glance my way, for he and my lord had disagreed, and were no longer friends, and so all the way down to the porter, I was out of reflected favor. I cannot now, in this meadow under this sweet sky, believe that once it mattered, and still there is a twinge where once there was a wound. A year swept over us and we could hear change like the whistling of wind in the rigging. I did not then know how much I cared, but soon I had to.

I could not get rid of Bartholomew Legate. He laughed at me in dreams and saw me I know now as a scrambling toady as bad as those around me, thinking I dwelt in Christ Jesus when yet I dwelt in the tents of the Philistines where religion was politics and politics was religion and both strove mightily for advantage. It was the beginning of a nasty brutal time and grew more brutal, but as yet the brutalities were tiny pinpricks and not as they were later to the cost of all of us who chose the reformed way and not the old way, even my lord. It was to become damnably dangerous as the clipping off of ears, the burning, the floggings and yet the killings on the highway at night, the little war we fought at the beginning, I was drawn deeper and deeper into it. Over what? We thought, no I, poor fool, thought it was over the placing of a table and the naming of it an altar in the old Catholic way, the kneeling, the genuflecting, the this, the that, the facing east, the bowing and the scraping.

Think not we were mad. Men died for it.

Through it all Bartholomew taunted me and saved me by his merry face though sometimes I cursed the day I had ever listened to what I had been trained as a horse to the bit to call heresy. Oh Lord Jesus

Christ forgive me that I turned my back even for an hour on that love-ly human man. But he would not leave me, not in the night, not in my ear when I argued as I had been taught so carefully. The worst was not that his ghost berated me. No. In my memory I saw him smiling, and tossing some child into the air to play with him.

And so, then, perhaps he led me, perhaps it had been growing with-in me all the time, for I had ever taken the low church way, but quiet-ly, a sneaking, ladder-minded young man as all the rest who wandered the Backs and planned their political future, thinking by all that is holy that we took God's path and not the path to power. How we fooled ourselves!

But then, there was the wall.

For years the walls of the chapel had been whitewashed, and we took for granted that they had been built so, for the chapel was Catholic in the sense we were taught was good, the altar was an altar, the com-munion was served each morning at five for all of us shivering in our black and smelly robes, and we coughed and our stomachs rumbled through it, all on the way to breakfast. Rumble and murmur. And believe me, a holy quiet that could not be touched.

The word came down among us huddled students, whispering in corners, of the king's orders. Men came to clean the whitewash that had covered the Popish wall paintings in the chapel at Pembroke since King Henry's time. With that act it became the seat of the court's reli-gious power. For it was power, not God, all of it, Andrewes and Wren and Laud and myself and all, yet we knew it not and saw ourselves as acting before God. I faced at last that my paths were those that had always been, that that damnable word "prerogative" was the key to the matter, for the followers of Bishop Andrewes, and Wren, and already that little beastie Laud, not yet even a bishop, were the strength and spokesmen for the king's party.

My lord Coke was as Catholic as Laud in ceremony but never in pol-itics. He was not a tyrant of holiness, not even in his own home, although he held always to the old ways, and I knew at last, instead of guessing, that he had chosen his paintings of Thomas More, and Bish-op Fisher, and Bishop Foxe, because they had stood as martyrs upon their own certainties. I who thought I had learned so much had yet too much to learn. And still do. And there is little time. I still steer through a storm sometimes where the waves are high and the ship within my mind pitches and changes course.

On the wall of that chapel when it was white I saw as clearly as if it were written there "prerogative ordinary," for one praying then could see his own visions. When the medieval knights and kings and their train were uncovered to bow before the gold-spangled hanging body of Jesus, there should have been written "prerogative absolute." For it was not my God and not my Christ in that chapel.

He wore a gilded swath over His loins, and His body was stiff and formal and without pain. He looked calm and vapid. There was no blood. The wounds were small, the face clean of the scars of His beating and the bloodstains left by the crown of thorns. I had seen too much contemptible death to punish one man by another from when I was a child to be fooled. I knew that My Lord Christ Jesus had hung humiliated, naked in front of a gaping throng. The lance had made no clean wound but, as in the drawing that happened day after day at Tyburn, had ripped His stomach and the blood and guts dripped out as in a slaughterhouse. His mouth, as all the mouths of those drawn and then quartered while they lived, froze in an O of agony, and His face was streaked with blood from the piercing of the thorns. Such extremis of suffering makes all men look alike. I stood there before the gold-clad figure alone and cried my heart out because I saw it was a lie.

That day in the holy dimness of the empty chapel with the candles for the dead flickering and casting shadows, my horror led me to become ever more involved in controversy at Pembroke. Of course I leaned to what they called in contempt the Puritan side, the reformers we thought ourselves to be, and if we were not prepared to die for it, we were, God knows, prepared to argue for it. And argue. And argue.

But even in the monkish idleness of Cambridge where there was more time to brabble in than ever I knew before or since, for we were fed by others, and taught by others, and kept as safe as the ancient monks from the perils of the world's hunger and homelessness and pain, we saw ourselves as swords of change. We gathered in our brilliance to change the color of the sky over the heads of those whose troubles lie closer to the earth.

Pembroke veered as a ship caught by the wind, nearer and nearer

what I saw and others of my thinking saw as the rocks of Arminianism.
To think that we argued such all the night sometimes, not knowing
that what we were arguing was politics not God. The politics that won
came down from Lancelot Andrewes, from the king, and from the
Duke of Buckingham into our so-called holy cells of learning and
threw us into fogs where we knew not how to steer except with passion
and agreements among friends.

Why, the same one Lancelot Andrewes even went with the king to
Scotland and dressed the growling Presbyters in cassocks and made
them bow and recite written prayers they muttered out, having not the
courage to stand before so great power. And in the night, as one after
another of the reform strongholds fell, and the news became worse and
worse, finally it reached pitch point with the accession of Bishop Laud.

After five years of bowing I found a way to go nearer what I thought
was holy decision. Why in the blessed name of Jesus, that towering
man who walked the sands, and was so simple in his earthly life as my
beloved Bartholomew taught me, do I seek comfort in a past where
then there was no comfort. Cum fortis cum fortis. If it is indeed to give
courage I find it here and now, under this tree where I am resting my
aged and gnarled body so my soul can fly. It is my secret and it can be
every man's, that never did it age but remains today a questing boy as
ever was.

XIII

———◆———

He that makes a trade of preaching . . . a maintenance, a
living, explicitly makes a bargain . . . no longer penny no
longer paternoster, no longer pay no longer pray no longer
preach no longer fast . . . Such notions are not from the liv-
ing and voluntary spring of the holy spirit of God but for
the artificial and worldly respects, money maintenance, etc.

— ROGER WILLIAMS

SOMETIMES I WAIT FOR THE NIGHT AS FOR A FRIEND.
It is the first of August. These hot late summer days tire my worn body
and old mind and only with the night cool from the sea comes the
flowering of my soul that grows young again and lifts me forth to skip
the blue waters as the flat stone a child throws. Without weight. Without gall. Where the very turning of the night earth is part of my
prayer. In old England on this day we would, in school and court, Star
Chamber and Westminster Hall, begin the long vacation.

I remember alone. For here are no such matters. It has been a day of
strength, and a night of clarity so pellucid that I know I am blessed, a
night when the stars and the fireflies are the same size. I lean my head
against my son's wall of logs, now seven years old from the great burning; they have lost their sweet pitch-pine smell, but have become for
us who cling for life along the edge of the river with the fields behind
us and the great darkness behind them, uphill and far away, a stabili-
ty, a success, at what cost I dare not, yes, I dare, pay here and now and
to the sea before me.

It was at the beginning of the long vacation of 1627. I remember that date for it was at the end of July robed and capped and all that I sanctimoniously slid down the aisle at my name, and received my sheepskin prize, Bachelor of Divinity.

We few who stood out for reform in those days thought ourselves brave. So we were. Such Puritan humility, curate's courtliness, I called it, had become, especially at Cambridge and at Pembroke, a dangerous affectation. The master and what bishops came and stayed too long with their whole retinues, eating Pembroke out of house, larder, and barn, looked at us sometimes with near loathing, depending on how much wine they had drunk at dinner. They spent much time sailing like fat gold-laden Spanish galleons across the court to the new gaudy chapel, and followed by my classmates all bowing and scraping in a dance of servility that matched our own. Oh such silks and satins, such lawn sleeves, such copes and embroidery, color and solemnity.

I felt rebellious, and pure. Oh I must wash out that picture with the laughter it deserves. But no one else laughed. It was serious. It was mighty dangerous and growing more so. I took my part as led as a lamb in protest, for protest was our exercise of the right in those days, but our ways were small, pathetic, and afraid, as ones are who fear to lose their livelihood.

Even Cambridge was roused to some weak furor when King Charles forced the largest public loan in English history. He wanted subsidies to run the state and live the way he list without calling the Parliament, which he had begun to despise. Sir Francis Barrington, my lord's friend I remembered from Stoke, had been the first to stand against collecting in his county for the forced, illegal loan. His son-in-law, Sir William Masham, had refused with him. He would become my much-loved friend in later years, a shy man I remembered standing under the tapestry at Stoke one summer. They had both been sent to prison as Refusers, the people called them. It had caused much riot that still went on and had grown ever stronger through the winter, into spring, and then that summer for they still lay in prison nearly a year later when the long vacation came.

I took Hobson's cart to London in the rain. It was wet and cold. The hay rotted in the fields. All seemed cursed by God that summer. I had planned to help my mother in her inn that year, for my father had died and she said, for the first time in her life, that she needed me, Robert and the girls being married and Sydrach ever in the Levant. So I set myself up to study in the attic I had had as a child, my Greek and my Hebrew for examinations and disputations, the very heart of training at Cambridge. It was to be an austere vacation, which I welcomed with the pleasure of feeling sorry for myself as I served up ale in my mother's taproom and picked up and sorted gossip as one sorts bills or money for the good and the bad.

And in its midst did come the letter from my lord, summoning me to Stoke for the long vacation for he needed me to work. His letter fell upon the boredom that had made me dispute, protest, march, and all the things that boys do when they have decided they are men, like new sunshine after rain. Stoke at my lord's command after my degree in the long vacation of 1627! I could not believe my joy and then I thanked God, calmed down, and girded my loins with courage to go and tell my mother. She said, over her shoulder, for she was as usual, very busy, "Well, get along then." And no more.

I walked thence along the Thames first on the towpath and then on the highway until one stopped for me in a hay wagon and I sat among the hay and lost myself in pleasure, forgetting at last how important I thought myself. Every plod of the horses' hooves was a freeing and a forgetting in the sun of that sweet August.

My lord then was seventy-five years old and he would not let himself move more slowly. He was still as straight as a soldier, and rode each day longer than he had ever rode before. It was a thumb bite at fate and exhaustion for oft he had to be took down from his horse at the end of those long long rambles that sometimes, I beside him that summer, went as far as Windsor, where he would rein in and sit for an hour sometimes watching the castle in the distance and saying nothing.

I cannot think how childlike it all was as I see it now. I ever loved him, and young fool that I was, thought him old, and finished with the world, and one needing help so that he had to shake my hand too often from his arm when I forgot how annoyed he was at being propped up, as he called it, like a great dolly. By his own family, and I confess, by me that vacation, he was treated as any old man is treated, surrounded by his spawn and his courtiers. The little hall off the great hall he made into his domain, all that he wanted to call his own, strewn with parchments, dirty cups, spent candles as his chambers had been, with nobody allowed to move or clean or straighten. It was as if he had moved all from Sergeant's Inn, his habits, his plans, as hopeful as if he were twenty-five with the world before him, not fifty years older. We treated him with that mixture of deference and condescension that was ever the way with the very old.

He was no longer in the Privy Council after the Tower but he seemed not to care. The silk and taffety and gold chain he wore was as the sheriff of Buckinghamshire, for the young king on the advice, or order, as some said, of his Sejanus, the Duke of Buckingham, had made my lord sheriff to keep him from the Parliament of 1626, for it was against the law to serve both. He said it was a light and gaudy chain around his wrists. So there was, that summer, much toing and froing of officials, the judges at their assizes, and always members of the county party who depended upon my lord for guidance. They came soberdressed, not in the extremes of Puritan black we who were young flaunted, but rich brown and green rustling silk, trimmed that gloomy summer with miniver and stoat. I was much enamored of the way men dressed, seeing it as banners and badges, not breeks and doublets, and indeed it was.

Many of the county party came to Stoke. Many had joined the Refusers and were in prisons all over the country. My lord sat at Stoke and advised in the law, but as yet there was no way to protect anyone from being sent to prison without cause.

I was sorry to see my lord like a spider in his web, advising and ruling the decisions of the county party, just as the so-called disgraced Bacon had sat in his web at Verulam, the gaudy house he had built, and posed with suggestions of massy gold, what the king's party should do. I remember how my lord would come back from all the company and argument into his domain, the little kingdom he had made for himself in the privy hall, throw off his gaudy and his trinkets, as he called them, step back into his fustian robe, and into himself, to work. For work had become, more than ever if that were possible, the very center of his being. Work and Parliament—he ever said it was our only hope of justice, and justice was his God.

All the long vacation I sat beside him while he worked on his Insti-

tutes, as he called them, wrote in his hand, to be many more great volumes, while I took down thoughts for him and transposed them into
his words. As we had always done, we fell into our old habits, and at
night, or in the late afternoon when he had fell asleep in his chair, I
took to reading in the dovecote, for there was much summer reading
to do, that in Latin and Greek and Hebrew, assigned comparisons and
disputations of the King James translation, for that was my task before
I went to study for the higher degree that was somehow to make me a
more polished minister and more ready for preferment.

"I am waiting," he told me once early in my stay, "for God to tell
me, not what to do, for I know that, but the way to do it." It was true
he prayed in his chamber in that year for two hours each day, and once
again as we stood watching and not watching the fish in the little river
as they surfaced at evening to feed. "The poor little gray king," he said
then, "is as one of these meddler minnows with a layover net to catch
him." The layover, I knew was Buckingham but even in his own home
watching his own river, my lord dared not speak his name.

Fear had begun to permeate the air that summer, everywhere. It
seemed that England spoke in whispers. I had been used to such hiding of one's spirit at Pembroke among the robes of the bishops toing
and froing, but there, at Stoke, when I began to sense it I thought it
must be everyplace, for if my lord himself dared not speak, then all the
world I knew must need look over its shoulder and speak not but in
the metaphors we hid behind in those days, hoping to be understood.

Stoke was much changed. So was my lord. He seemed when he was
alone or with me, which to him was as alone, to mourn without words.
There was, I thought, no hope of his coming back into any public life
for he had been exiled by a trick from the last Parliament, and put into
the Tower after the one before.

There was much new company there, too. Great ladies wantonly, pretty courtiers, for his daughter Frances ever kept by her a crowd she chose
to amuse her. Sometimes there was riot in the great hall and the sounds
of flute and dulcimer floated out late into the night. I would wander
in the garden, and watch the shadows of dancing, the flinging of bodies high into the air in old-fashioned dances as the Volta and the reel,
which as a reformer I had been schooled to despise. Yet, there in the
dark, there were times I thought I might like to try it if any asked me.

Of all his children it was the one most led into trouble by him that had come home to roost, and it was her, Frances, scandal-ridden, saucy, unrepentant and excommunicate, he loved most among his daughters. Two of his children came oft to visit him, the lady Sadlier, his oldest daughter, who would sweep past Frances across the lawns as if she did not exist, on her way to tell her old father what to do from time to time for she had succored him, as she thought, in prison, and felt she owned him. His first son, Robert, came, too, who thought that love and acreage were the same thing and spoke of little else. My lord drew pleasure from his grandchildren, the children of his son Henry, who farmed the home farm and was the most down to earth and contented of them all.

His favorite son, Clem, Fighting Clem, he cared for beyond the others and he hid it not. For Clem was ever in trouble and never in all the time I knew them did my lord censure him. Never with his money, or words, or with that most terrible of parental weapons, silent disapproval. I think that Clem, of all the boys, was most like my lord's secret self, for he had been a handsome, turbulent man, but with words and not with sword. It was that in him he gave to Clem with his blood.

But it was Frances, that sweet ironic child, the one most like him, his secret wit and tenderness, on whom the old man doted. With the others it was a duty to love, but it was Frances, who teased and hugged, and made witty gossip for him, who drew his smiles.

She of all of them, near to me in age, took my friendship with my love for granted. She had known me long, and I think was fond of me. She set out to make me, too, smile when I was taking myself more seriously than ever a young man should, by calling me her Puritan and herself abandoned sinner, all in merry teasing.

He loved her and I loved her as my secret dear bawd sister. It was she I watched, as innocently as if I were a child not invited to a birthday party, when she was flung high among the dancers. She had already gone far beyond the pale and stayed there happily, and adored her father.

The terrible marriage to the Duke of Buckingham's brother that my lord forced on her to buy his way back into court was a trouble waiting at the altar. Her poor husband was as gentle as a baby lamb when he was sane, violent only when he had fits of madness they called melancholy, but even then he only harmed himself. He adored her, and stayed beside her bed when she was ill of the spotted fever and thought not to live. He watched over her like an old and faithful dog, while she was pregnant with her lover's child. Long before she ran away to live with her lover, he had already brooded into bloody and rage-ridden madness, broke the glass of windows and tried to kill himself, and screamed to the laughing crowd without who watched, for the crowd ever loved a madman as entertainment, that he had committed the unforgivable sin against the Church of Rome and slit his wrists with the window glass and writ the name of Christ Jesus in blood while the crowd cheered.

Long after her lover's exile, long after all the horror, Frances and her son, a pretty boy of six or seven with all her wit and beauty in him almost as a curse, came again to her father and he treated her as ever the prodigal had been treated, as his most loving daughter. She was, as near as I knew my own, of my age, then twenty-four, as much a lover of tricks and jokes as a child.

Once that summer, I woke in my small room I loved so, where I could leave my treasures, and go and come as I pleased, to find that all my clothing was gone, my shirt, my clout, my stockings, my black suit, the last my father made me before he died. There I was, stark naked, as robbed as one on Hampstead Heath, caught by the footpads.

It was noon before a knock came at my door. I sat in the buff I had slept in, translating Origen, for I knew it a sin to waste time. I leapt back into my bed and pulled the coverlid tight around me, presenting only my head like the head of John the Baptist, to whatever enemy approached me there.

It was Frances. Over her arm, for she had scorned to send them by her maid, were all my clothes. God help me, I thought from her reputation that she meant to defile me. She said, "My little Puritan coney, my pretty boy, thou hast naught but these and they wanted cleaning, so here they are, and before you go back to Cambridge I will do this again, but next time I will warn you."

Such kindnesses were hers, fine wanton kindnesses.

For the rest, it was not all labor for every day for our health's sake, my lord and I mounted and rode to take the air and as he called it let the wind blow the cobwebs from our minds. I rode the little filly, Chloe. She was a cool horse, tender to the bit and evasive as a nymph.

Sometimes we played at bowls, the whole family together, and I remember those days and will always, the balls rolling across the cropped grass, and Frances calling to her half brother, "Clem, you cheat!"

For the rest, in that long vacation, I bided with my lord in the wing of the house where he had retired among his books, and his three most beloved paintings, More, Fisher, and Foxe. We sat before the privy fireplace with its carved musicians, as were in the great hall, only smaller, watched the fire on cold days in August, and talked of God in Latin and often in Greek for he ever wanted to keep his languages polished, as he called it.

One night before the fire, for although it had been a sweet day the rain had come and the air was damp, he spoke for the first time of what had been on his mind, he said, ever since I had become a Bachelor of Divinity, using the title almost as a joke.

"The man to watch is Laud," he said, as if I and the whole of the country had not already had whiffs of his growing power. "The man is dangerous." And then he fell into the protection of abstraction. "Authority without consensus is brutality, no," he added as if he were writing it and changing the words in his mind, "not consensus for consensus can come out of fear, without concommitment. Without concommitment from the people, authority is brutality, and concommitment without any authority is anarchy." He was still for along time as if those words had satisfied him.

But they had not. "I have watched that crawling climbing weasel for years, and he has grown apace in righteousness. God protect me from the righteousness of those who are convinced that they are right, as righteous and as cold as stones. In the name of some God he has, we must all worship as if he had private knowledge of the unknowable."

A log dropped in the fire and sent out sparks. I remember that.

"Now," he said, settling back into the old chair he had ever used, the same one he had cried in so long ago, "I have had word oft that you have took yourself into extremes, and made yourself known as a fanatic Puritan. Damn I do hate them both for they destroy the balance that is the soul of the law."

The soul of the law, he said, not of religion, not of Christ, for he saw all as a balance as delicate as a dancer. And I realized then that all in silence, for I had seen him only at the rare times he came among us at Cambridge as the vice chancellor when the audit days came, he had watched me, not over me, letting me grow and flourish among the monkish and idle scholars.

"I cannot blame you, for I did the same when I was at Trinity," he said. I said nothing. How could I speak? There was nothing, I was certain, he did not know of me. He said that it had made me less useful for I would not be trusted in the court and among the Arminians in the growing gulf that threatened to split the country.

"Religion has become politics, and my beloved Lancelot Andrewes did innocently foment it. Laud and Wren and all the rest. Damn them," he said again to the logs that had settled back to dim embers. "Damn them. I ever have hated extremes." It was all he ever said on that subject, for many of his country friends were known as of the king's party.

One night he said, "I was mistaken to send you among the high churchmen, for I knew as well as any man how the Arminians were set to take over Pembroke. It is of course the end of your chance to become a fellow. Ho, that is no matter, you would be wasted there. I think you need disputation as I do, and action as much as any man." We spoke in Greek that night as we did oft when we did not speak in Latin for he ever enjoyed it, there being nobody in his household to accompany him in that pleasure but myself.

"Now that you are a gentleman," and I smiled and would have laughed at such a conceit but he was serious. He saw no irony in it, being of his age and time as one in a cage of expectations and ways of living within that fence of possibility. But I, alas for him, was beginning dimly to see beyond the gates of his life. "Now that you are a gentleman, since you have earned your first university degree, I suppose you must needs go on to the higher degree while we wait for this political unbalance to right itself. But there are rocks ahead. That damned weasel, Laud, hates me for I ever fought the bishops on praemunire. They have no business trying to judge civil matters, any more than the state should judge in religion. The damned business of the church is not the damned business of the state, nor of the damned state the damned church! It is against the law!"

There it was, that night in the cool of the dying fire, while it was still light without, it being midsummer, the words that to this dark night have guided me. He went on to speak of what was the place of religion, what of Parliament, what of the Lords, what of the king. He saw it as a tender balance, only fearing, not yet knowing, that the balance would be toppled and he would be a part of it so soon.

So we rode together and walked much in silence as we always had; the trees, some young then, that we passed, the places we paused, fragments of what he said to me, a wild flower, a faun, sometimes a feral cat stalking in a tiny jungle of a garden, the sound of the doves churtling, I can call to mind all these pictures, as clear to me as if it were yesterday or today.

How we sat within the little hall while the music came from the great hall and the tromping of feet and calling, while he planned much for me, but most of all, how we shared silence. It is an art that few men have.

"I am heavy tired," he said, and he got up and mounted the stairs to his chamber tall and gaunt as a grasshopper.

My lord was much maligned in his time, and much loved, too. I see now things I could not have seen then, how before I knew him he was made to become Lord Chief Justice of England away from Common Pleas because the people had took to admiring him more than they did the king and all the silly court, how he walked the length of Westminster Hall, kicked up the stairs of the law, crying, with most of the officers of the courts crying with him, a weeping multitude of legal minds. It would be a comic memory were it not so sad of what I never saw, for I knew him not until three years after, and I a boy.

At Christmastide I went back to Stoke. The great hall smelled of green branches, steaming hot possets scented with strong water, apples and cinnamon, much fruit, the cooking of the boar, the sweet cakes baking, the waxing and waning of the beeswax candles and the pitch-pine torches, even the mistletoe that had ever been hung up at the winter solstice all the way back to the dawn of England.

That New Year's when the county visited there was much hospitality, wassail, and all. Friends, courtiers to him for he had his own followers who sued ever for his time, all brought presents for the New Year, but there were less than before from his Parliament friends, for by New Year's there were so many in jail and more going every day for the refusal to pay the forced loan since it was considered unlawful, and that of course straight from the mouth of my lord Coke.

There, that day, in the midst of the partridges, the buck, the slaughtered piglet, the tuns of wine, the gloves, the cloaks, and I know not now whatall, were my own New Year's presents.

Frances had took my last clothes made by my father, my one black doublet and breeks, to measure them for copying in two suits of clothes that were the finest ever I had upon my back. One was of brown, one of green, elegant but not saucy she called the colors, and she grinned with her father. He said, "I had to stop her making them of silk for she ever would."

He stood that cold day in the great hall, leaning upon the arm of Frances, all of them together at the end of Christmas, and when I think of that day it comes back so vividly I still hear the huge Yule log that had been burning since Christmas eve, groaning and shifting. And still smell all around the hall the festoons of ivy and holly until it seemed the scent of summer had crept within the hall to give us hope.

Bluff John, timid Robert, fighting Clem, silent Henry, and a tumble and rush of grandchildren moved around my lord. The refectory table in the great hall was laden with so many presents that they half hid the Turkey carpet that covered it, what I could see of its dark rich colors catching and throwing back their own light. While all around and forever, and I suppose this late in the century, though I will never see it, the Children of Israel still marched round and round the hall followed by the chariot of the Pharaoh, his whip held high.

For my lord's New Year's present he gave me Chloe to get me back and forth from Cambridge when he would call me, and the first volume of his Institutes, a book with gold letters. I kept it by me, with his two letters within as bookmarks, until it was burned with all the rest. Did God burn me? Did the Father of Lights take away my last treasure of memories and guidance and leave me with nothing but that within my mind which grows more vivid and sweet every day? How much we blame on our Father of Lights when we have lit the petards of our troubles our own selves.

After the banquet I watched him fall sweetly asleep in the privy hall before the fire, that great flawed man. There he was, old grasshopper, snoring quietly. His mug of hot posset still steamed on the floor beside him, staining some parchment he had thrown there. I watched him for a long time as he slept, but when I moved a little in my chair, to get up and go to my bed, for the riot had long ceased in the great hall, and the sound of good nights and happy new years faded into the night, he opened his eyes, and said, "I was not asleep," as if I had accused him, and fell to talking of Marcus Aurelius and Commodus, how it was a mistake that could rot the realm to let family fealty and profane love triumph over sense. I was so tired I hardly followed, and when I moved again he said and his voice was sharp, "I have not finished. I cannot go until I have done what I must."

And I thought, poor fool that I was, that he was not giving me leave to retire.

So that night of New Year's we sat on late into the night like truant schoolboys, my lord seventy-five years old, and I, twenty-four, newly a gentleman, newly a minister, taking thought for the morrow, as if we had not learned to seek not what the gentiles seek.

Next morning at the late dawn, I crept into his chamber where he was still abed to make my goodbyes and have his blessing. But he still lay, his face exposed in sleep, and I dared not disturb him, for I thought then, knew, as we know nothing, that he was old, and in his dear retirement writing his last admonitions to the law, he had grown tired with all the play around him at the Christmastide. It was the last sweet time I ever saw my lord.

There I was on my new mount, Chloe, a well-trained man easy to the bit of ambition, to the world looking as any young minister in black, my cloak around me and my wool hat drooping, my fine clothes in my saddle bags, Chloe's hooves making no sound along the snow-laden roads. Under the drooping hat, my mind whirled and fought within itself, for somewhat great and pregnant within me without my knowing, was ready to speak out and harrow me.

XIV

We count the Universities the Fountains, the Seminaries,
the Seed-pods of all Pietie; but have not these Fountains
ever sent what streams the Times have liked? And ever
changed their taste and colour to the Prince's eye and
Palate?

— ROGER WILLIAMS

EBRUARY IS EVER FOR ME THE MONTH OF OLD
England, when this new England reminds us of who we are and where
we sprang from, and the Father of Lights knows what baggage within
and without we brought here. Habit. Memory. Ways of knitting and
weaving and dispositions and taboos away back before the Saxons. Here
am I, a great-grandfather, still yearning as the boy I was when I
thought the Millennium upon us with all its glory and its terrible justice. Why even thought is as much habit and past as that chicken
growing in its egg, as it always has, and always will. How frail we are,
how kindly we should be with one another, we who can be swept away
so neutrally as quickly as the stepping on of an ant.

These are not good thoughts for my new room. Robert and his sons
have made it for me, pleasing the old man they call great-grandfather,
but not one of them I love so and take such pride in have any dream of
what they have put in this room: I, Roger Williams, disputatious as
ever, as my lord was, God's blood as he was.

That old man retired into the corner of one of his many mansions,
and this old man has retired into the log room set against my son's

house. It is eight by eight feet, the size of the monks their cells at Charterhouse in ancient days. There is, as there was for them, a fireplace to
warm me and a table and a chair my sons have carved for me with a
stool to put my bad feet upon before the fire. Well, it has not a vault-
ed ceiling, and a fine chimneypiece, as my lord had in his privy parlor
in his last years, but it is more the same than not the same, for we have
brought within it our minds, our memories, and our ever young and
urgent duty to finish what we started before we go to our Maker with
all our sins upon us. Or be empty to rot away like an animal in the
woods. Or fly on angel's or eagle's wings we ourselves envision to bear
the unbearable to an unknown place. How arrogant we are in the face
of our Maker to pretend to ourselves that we know.

My sons have decided that I wish to write sermons. So I have made
a list of thirty of them that I would like to expound as, God forgive me,
a legacy for those who have not asked for it. And so I sit here in candlelight and the smell of melting tallow, my fire banked, waiting for a
sermon to visit me.

But I think not of my Maker in His glory, but of Chloe in her grace,
for her many greats of granddaughter has foaled early and stands dripping before my little window, her head down, and her filly nursing.
She is as pretty as Chloe herself who all have forgotten except for me.

It is in February days when New England is as gray as old England,
and the wind blows from the sea as if its fingers sought out the dis-
comfort and depression of man, that I think back to that terrible year
and I am still as ever clopping along betwixt and between, questioning, hoping, and pining, a sniveling boy within at my age, for that is
the path the Father of Lights has give to me, forever seeking, never
finding, except in glimpses, through a glass darkly, but never in February.

On that cold morning along the London road I saw only before me
a choice I could not yet make for I already knew that in that hateful
time there was little to choose between the quarreling factions. The
center where I longed to be did not exist. It was, or I saw it as such, an
abyss where there was nothing but depth without motion, as mysteri-
ous as the deep sea itself. And no one there.

But in the meantime, or be that as it may, I had to get to Cambridge
for my studies for I was, after all, on some kind of path even had I not

chose it, of preferment of one sort or another. There was none to advise me in Cambridge where I felt as much in prison as ever I had committed a crime, and knew not what it was.

It was hard to keep awake, for I had spent my last night at Stoke with my dreams sailing in the mist of the new year, followed by Furies, some in motley and some in bishop's scarlet and some in white lawn flipping and flapping as they ran. I was, by necessity, riding along to the wrong place at the wrong time. I flew against it in my soul as a moth upon a window.

Chloe went along under me as patient as an old mare. Often on that ride to London I would be so deep in my thoughts that I would wake to find her foraging along the roadside, her head down, the reins loose. I decided to leave her in my mother's field up beyond Charterhouse in the country between the village of Islington and Farrenden, the field I had crossed so often when a dreaming boy, for I had heard that Mr. Hobson's livery stable was unsafe. He would let out our own horses by the day without so much as a by your leave, and anyone could ride her, whip her, saw her mouth with an iron bit. Besides, to stable her cost money and I had none for that, so thought myself that I would come by Hobson's cart to London and pick her up there when I needed her to get back to Stoke when my lord called me. All of this planning drew my mind away from dark thoughts, thoughts of being led by the nose as surely as a young bull, balls new dropped and knowing not what to do.

In the half dark of early evening, as I was leading her past the stone wall of Charterhouse orchard, I heard his dear voice: "Master Roger Williams, know thee not thy old friends?" Nathan sat upon the wall, grinning and calling Merry Christmas to me. He sat with his great white beard like some imp or what they call gargoyles that they say sit above the cathedral in Paris and spit down rain upon the people below.

I jumped up on the stone wall beside him and we had much pleasure in each other's company. He talked as usual, and he reminded me once again of how his grandfather told his father and his father told him that the gentry and gentlemen all did change their religion as they would change sails before a veering wind, from King Henry VII's days, Catholic, and then in King Henry VIII's days, he who died of the French pox, Protestant, and then Queen Mary's days, Catholic, and the

Inquisitors came to England and they burned many, and then Queen Elizabeth's days, how they all were Protestant again, the same people.

"'Tis no matter to us. We do our task give us," he ended as he always did, and chewed his toothless mouth, and added, "No matter. 'Tis happening all again and will and will not and will and will not. Oh I forgot, Master Roger Williams, thy father died, God rest his soul, and thee are astudying to be a gentleman. Well. Well. Well." And he maunched again awhile. The winter mist rose around us and through the bare apple trees, and into our bones.

Before I jumped down from the wall he told me he would look to my lovely Chloe. Odd, so late to remember that little meeting aperched upon a wall. It was a happy small time in an unhappy year.

So as dragging as a schoolboy I went back to Cambridge. King Charles was more a slave to Buckingham than his father had been. He made that light, tripping man, who could hardly read and write, no less than chancellor of the University of Cambridge.

He was already whispered of as the uncrowned king of England, so powerful in the young king's eyes that no one dared speak his name. In the earlier Parliament in 1624, when my lord was kept away from his seat by the high and doubtful honor of being named sheriff of Buckingham, they had passed Articles of Impeachment against the duke, but the king and the court simply ignored it. The duke quipped that no Parliament could touch him. He was, he said, Parliament-proof. It became a bon mot at court, which was by then that empty of wit. My lord had said of the king that he remembered laughter when the boy was young and sat in the House of Lords to learn his trade, but when he became king his smiles ceased and he was pulled hither and thither like a puppet on a string. He, who had always been a shy, stammering, halting child, became in his fear of doing wrong as stubborn as a rock. He loved the Duke of Buckingham, not as his father had, but as a shy young boy a hero.

Laud had already climbed to Bishop of London; the duke spoke at the bishop's bidding. Laud had made himself his dear friend and confessor ever since as a young man he had been chosen as King James's favorite. All were to blame for the troubles of the kingdom and the church. Long-ago Abbot, the Archbishop of Canterbury himself, had thrust Villiers into the old king's presence to get rid of Robert Carr, the favorite all disliked. No one's hands were clean of the Duke of Buck-ingham. Laud, they said, dreamed of him much, and in his diabolic self-deception, took the dreams to be holy portents.

It had already much touched Cambridge. Laud had advised the duke to forbid the teaching of John Calvin and even Ridley and Latimer, the martyrs. I doubt that the beautiful duke had ever heard of John Calvin or even Latimar and Ridley. It was all at Cambridge as it is at univer-sities, a reflection or a parody of what was being argued and punished and causing dangerous schism in the real world, or what I saw as real. And I was not there. By my soul it haunted me.

It was the darkest dampest coldest February I could remember, both in and out of my soul. The cutting wind was from the fens and the North Sea. Chapel each morning was changed into a mass, and only the night sweat and dirt on the bodies around me at five of the morning as we fumbled our sleeping way into the service, trying not to yawn, unfarted and unwashed, was ever the same. In the candlelight the newly uncovered Jesus flickered to and fro on his gold cross as if He too sought bodily comfort.

It was somewhat a pleasure at first to see the overweening obedience of those among my fellow students who thought their way to prefer-ment was to dance that pavane and dress themselves as actors on a stage, oh such flounces and taffeties, such lawn sleeves and embroi-dered surplices sent by their mothers. The language of the Papists was took out of old trunks and flung all across the body of mother church, as if there had been not reformation in men's minds, no burning of Bartholomew or the Oxford martyrs, as if there had been nothing except the replacement of a papa with a papa, a Pope with a king, and all the rest swept out like rushes that had been dirtied by many feet.

It was the return of the icons, and it of course tipped the scales so violently to one cliff that the other nearly sank beneath the waves. It was the wiping out of a past and all its blood to the first whispers of such as John of Leyden or the old Lollards in their time. At least it seemed so to us who as students were forever seeing in extremes of our own.

So we learned or pretended to learn, for if we had not voices we had eyes and shrugs to trade, to bow and scrape and face east for redemp-tion and face west for sin and face south for what I have forgot. Oh it would have been a comic time was it not to cause so many deaths, for a bow, and the bending of the knee, and the gold crosses that returned from whence they had been kept. I would have had much pleasure in the patens and the cups and the candlesticks and all the pretty luggage, for I have ever been drawn to color and shine, had they not been used so diligently as cudgels.

In early January a Parliament had been called and most of the Refusers let out of jail, my lord's friends, ran for seats. I could see in my impatient mind's eye so many gathered at Stoke to see my lord and hear him, for the king had called the opening for March, and they would be hustling to decide who would run and who not of the county party. I heard nothing from him. He ran for the Parliament with all the Refusers, and I knew, or hoped I knew, that he much needed me, if he stumbled, or if he fell asleep. I worried that he at his age might be foolish in front of those who trusted him as their bellwether, and there would be cruel teasing of him I so honored and loved. I wanted to care for him as one would care for a father too old, too fretful, too private in his ways.

He was elected by a large majority to the most astonishing Parliament that had ever walked into St. Stephen's chapel. I heard that one lord in the House of Lords said that the Commons could buy the Lords three times over, for they were the rich landowners of the counties, the local gentry and in England in the country then the local gentry stood as mouthpiece for their neighbors, their fiefs, their servants, their tenants in a way they have not since. By my impatient soul, here in this morning over fifty years hence, I still hear like a knell, as I heard myself whisper in my mind that winter at Cambridge, "I am not there."

I searched for solace wherever I could find it, but I fear there was small hope in much I found among the early church fathers whom I was reading to prepare for disputation by memory in Greek on Tertullian, that harsh old man. I sat within the library or my chambers, reading or trying to read while Tertullian swam like a fish before my eyes and my soul walked the paths of Stoke and then of London.

I thought it was at least new within two centuries, this fight of ours, until I read of the martyrdom at Lyons, when Tertullian praised the orthodox that they mingled not with the heterodox as they went into the arenas to be killed and eaten by lions. It made the tears spurt that it had always been the schism, Christ and the Pharisees, all the way from the beginning, and I went to the window and watched the garden below to calm my soul. It was there I saw the first cuckoo of spring, mincing and hopping from branch to branch to see whose nest he would overlay.

My fine new clothes were the disguise that my dear Frances had intended, being, God knows, wiser in the ways of the world than I would ever be or am today. So I walked the streets of Cambridge with my lace upon my collar, and liked the way I looked. Some of the pensioners, poorer than the lords of the valley of the Cam, the gentleman scholars of Cambridge, all of the king's party, had to wear their black abroad for it had not been long since that such clothes were a badge of honor and reform. If they were caught they were tossed into the Cam, in that cold water of winter, and had to skulk home dripping and forlorn as chickens abandoned in the rain, their collegiate robes soaked and freezing on their boy bodies.

Daniel has come to take in the foal from the weather. He is wonderful with the animals and awkward with people, trusting one more than the other, and I cannot blame him for he has heard the loud voices of disputation all his life, all the fighting of new-freed men who shouted politics and religion in the meadow in a way they had not been allowed before in their lives.

Since the law at Cambridge, hardly honored, but a safety all the same, was that we should take the air two by two, I was able to walk with the few close friends I could trust. We could speak our anger softly to one another.

But even that was took from me, for I was called before the master, one Beale. I hated him. Yes, old Christian man, you hated him, his lordliness, his boot-licking of Bishop Laud and that one William Wren, all of them I had been warned of by my lord. So I kept silent for my lord's voice was ever there when I threatened to balk and speak my mind, "It is not yet time." Not yet time has drawn the life from many a pure gesture.

My lord Beale kept me standing, of course, I expected that, and then he delivered his oration upon my sins. I cannot forget for my heart hurt from knowing that I had been betrayed by one I trusted. It is a sad fact that in the minds of the old, small hurts long buried come back to haunt the night.

He had arrived at the center of his complaint. His face swelled with anger; his voice held hysteria, and being a tall man he spat words down at me. "You, sir, are a Watts scholar and we expect more from you than from the others. Remember, sir, that your model is Bishop Andrewes always. You have been heard expounding on *predestination* and *grace* which is against the laws of this university. Thank your God if you have one that you have already been granted your degree, or else I would stop it."

I thought I caught a saving whiff of sadness in his voice when he said, "I, too, am obligated . . ." and seemed to forget what he had been about to say. When he remembered he forbade my saving walks away from the college.

It was not only the way of the world that I was shut away from, but I had to wrestle with impure thoughts. Cambridge I saw as a cesspool of lust and wantonness and such evil ways invaded my dreams. The gentleman scholars were more gentleman than scholar by their habits of playing at games, drinking and whoring, and pushing from the walks any scholar they had decided was one of that strange ilk, intelligence. So they who traveled in packs like highbred dogs would see us coming and call, "Lady Lady," as we passed, and "Hast dipped thy wick yet?" and such rude insults.

Waking it bothered me not, but sleeping was a different matter. I was then young, Puritan, and virginal. I had not yet mastered those lascivious sinful dreams that sometimes left the bed wet, for I was in the flower of manly youth and yet unpicked. I had always gone for long walks and swum in the Cam when I was out of sight of anyone, but that was denied me by the master and so the only way I had that spring to harness my disgusting wishes was prayer and much reading of St. Augustine. And when it was too strong, the terrible sin of what I see now as simply being alive, I would take a willow branch and beat myself around the legs and bare body in imitation of the old monks.

What I was seeing around me was as always in the universities a parody and farce of what was going through the country as they gathered for the Parliament. And I was not there. Instead I joined in remonstrances at Cambridge. They seemed to me but riotings and wildings of the old Roaring Boys who would use any news for argument, noise, bonfires, and fighting.

Sometimes in these late days when I wake from dreams I know I have been in St. Stephen's chapel and heard my lord and Eliot and Pym and Digges and all the others speak out in danger of their lives, or sometimes I have been in Sir Robert Cotton's library in his house in Old Palace Yard where my lord and his friends met to discuss the history of the realm, for Sir Robert had the finest library of old manuscripts and books in all of England and many came there to study. I spent many an evening nodding over old texts when my lord went there to confer with those he trusted behind the safety of the old parchments.

Long afterwards Sir William Masham told me he had been there with my lord, and Sir Thomas Wentworth who had been in prison, and Sir John Eliot. I knew them all, and honored them, for what that was worth in an ill time, as my lord called it. He said once that he had cleaned the House of a devil as in the Bible in the old Parliament and after in the Tower, but he ran for the new Parliament because seven devils had entered the House where one was before.

When February was over the master remembered himself of my punishment and called me in again. He told me that he had rescinded my confinement for my health. But I was not to walk with others since I had spoke so against the church, and might affect others vulnerable to my persuasions for he told me with a sneer, a real sneer that was almost comic but not quite, that I was too popular, for to be popular was ever a condemning word, as "Puritan," that vile and pernicious slur that was used for anyone who disagreed with the court party.

My master at Pembroke said I must walk alone for one hour each day and if I needed more to request it through my tutor. My heart leapt with joy that I would be alone for it was a luxury at Cambridge, but I put on a suitable face. I thanked the Father of Lights that so high an ant hill was made of my little grain of sin, and I broke out of the great door of Pembroke as a cat among the pigeons.

I rushed to wherever I could find news, and it was glorious. Everyone who had been jailed by the king for refusing the forced loan as illegal, who had been been let out of jail and then run for Parliament was elected, Sir Francis Barrington, Sir William Masham who had begun the protestation, four of the five knights who had sued for false arrest. One lost his nerve and could see himself head parted from body resting atop a gate of London.

The king had always taken it as granted that he could depend on a good number of Privy Council members to speak for him in the Commons, but with the new Parliament only three of all who ran were returned to plead the king's cause and they from rotten boroughs. My lord Coke was elected from two constituences, and I heard that he bragged that he did not ask for a single vote from any man. All the Refusers, twenty-seven of them with the pallor of prison still upon them, took their seats in St. Stephen's chapel. The young king had like a curious child stirred a hornet's nest.

I ran on to my private and hidden place under the new green of my willow tree and stripped and jumped into the Cam. The cold water dashed the winter from me, and I lay afterwards upon the floor of the sky looking up at that blue that never ends, on a soft bed of new spring grass and betook myself to the Parliament, for it was as familiar to me as the ground I lay upon.

In that Parliament that would point the way as none had done since Magna Carta, I am there but as one is there in hope and not in body. That lay naked as the day I was born in the sweet grass of spring in a place so quiet that I could hear the movement and the chaumping of the sheep and lambs around me. Two of the lambs spronged high, turned in the air, and landed on me, folded their front legs and sat on my stomach, so I stayed until they were ready to leap again, not wanting to disturb them or myself or any living thing that day.

XV

My much honored friend, that man of honor and wisdom
and piety, you dear father, was often pleased to call me his
son. . . . How many thousand times since have I had the
honorable and precious rememberance of his person, and the
life of writings, the speeches, and examples of that glorious
light? And I may truly say that beside my natural incli-
nation to study and activity, his example, instruction, and
encouragement have spurred me on to a more than ordinary
industrious and patient course.

— ROGER WILLIAMS

I HEARD NOTHING FROM MY LORD. I WAS ONLY AS
close to the workings of the Parliament as the news and rumor that
came to the Fens and blew over Cambridge. Time and I slowed to a
crawl and waited and waited for the summer, when I would go to Stoke
House and take up my work for him in the long vacation again.

Then one day, sent by an angel, came Sir William Masham to Cambridge, he who with his father-in-law, Sir Francis Barrington, had been
the first to be imprisoned for their refusal of the forced loan to the
king. Dear Sir Francis had died of sickness caught in the Marshalsea
prison, but only, they said, after staying alive long enough to take his
seat in the Parliament to be part of the prayed-for triumph.

When I was sent for and came down from the library, I could hear
Sir William's voice in the gateway. It was loud as if he were announc-
ing to the world his visit. He was telling anyone who might hear that

he had come to see his dear young friend Master Roger Williams, gent. He announced that he had come to Cambridge to straighten some difficulties with his widowed mother-in-law, her endowments with Trinity College, for she had took over Sir Francis Barrington's business there. I took his loudness to be his way, since he was a countryman. But when he threw arms about me and kissed me on both cheeks as if he counted me his nearest and dearest I knew then something was amiss.

He said, "Come, Roger! Dear boy, thou lookst pale from study. Walk awhile with me. I love Cambridge and there are buildings I have not seen." I knew at once that it was his way to get me beyond the ears of Pembroke for some reason. There were no fine buildings in Cambridge that had not been there long since. All around us as he drew me to him as if we were close kin, and kissed my cheeks, students and fellows who were passing drew closer, sneaking and dissembling to listen to what he said, for not only were there spies lurking everywhere on what they thought was God's chosen work, but curiosity for any stranger and especially one titled was as seductive as an open gate to a herd of goats.

I told him that I must ask permission of the master for I was still under restraint. But the word of an important visitor had got to Master Beale and he was already flapping across the court in his robes to greet Sir William with all the curiosity and manners due his station. He gave permission with a flourish and said he knew of that family's gracious gifts to Cambridge. Even though they were of the county party and not Arminians, he still smelled power and money and bowed before it, and said how proud they were to be entrusted with Sir Edward Coke's ward, and how I had done so well in my studies, my languages, and my disputations. He spoke as if I were a calf he had raised and was selling at Smithfield. I thought at any moment he would slap my flank. He ended with, "Of course, dear boy, your confinement is lifted," and explained that I had broken so small a rule that it mattered not.

So we were allowed to walk along the Backs, the first time in many days I had had company, and Sir William gave me news at last of my dear lord Coke. We strolled across the narrow river from the colleges and stopped oft to gaze at them for they are the finest row of buildings, I think, in all England. The ancient buildings were clear reflections in the still mirror of the water, and through the leafy ceiling of June, the sun sifted lines of light through the trees. Away in the distance across the fields beyond the river the spires of King's College chapel rose as out of the earth itself, and on its home meadow cows grazed. I wished that I did not remember that the wits of Cambridge said the chapel looked like a sow lying on its back, for to me it was beautiful. Though pagan in its way.

The path was empty before and behind us. The river ran smooth. It was so quiet that day. We turned beyond Trinity, and walked back slowly toward the fields to Grantchester. For half an hour Sir William had not said another word.

I was surprised that he moved with such grace, for he was not a young man. He was hard country fat, and his face showed long hours of weather. Finally, in the middle of the meadow on the way to Grantchester, he flung himself down upon the grass, first looking carefully for cow dirt. For a little while he rambled about how he had read law at the Inner Temple, and how Sir Edward would come to them at their moots sometimes and terrify them all. I asked what moots were. I knew the Inns of Court as well as any man, but he seemed to be waiting for me to ask. I was becoming more and more confused, and wanted him to stop talking of such and tell me of the Parliament and my lord, but he seemed to need to explain slowly, somehow to take the whole path of memory of how we had got there in the grass, all the way from his youth at the Inner Temple, so we played a game.

I pretended ignorance; he avoided his reason for coming to Cambridge. He told that moots were an exercise in the Inns where a subject was chose arguable in law, and those who would be lawyers planned its attack and defense, and then play-acted each side of the question with arguments and such. Then, here he laughed, he said they all went to the tavern. Those who lost the argument, the case, he explained, must buy for all.

I thought he would never get to why he was there until his voice went down, and he looked not at me, but began at last to tell me about Sir Edward and what he had chosen him to do, and added that it was a great honor yes a great honor. The first thing he told me was that I was, being in the service of Sir Edward, noticed and on the list for censure by the court party in the church for having spoke Puritan sentiments. Even to me, who was nobody, the tentacles of Bishop Laud groped so far afield. I could see a vast net of reports, all with his thoroughness, names put down as O for Orthodox and P, using the pejorative term "Puritan" for us of the lower church. Bishop Laud was efficient, more efficient than any man in England, and he was rooting out enemies in the church as weeding a garden of noxious weeds. I, a noxious weed, was being pulled up by my roots. I was not surprised except that I wondered why he would bother with one so unknown as I.

Sir William said that Sir Edward expected any day to be took back to the Tower and that I was to stay away from Stoke for fear the king's men would find me and use, he said, extreme methods to find out anything I might know about my lord, meaning of course the rack. He sent the word that day under the trees that he was to seem to abandon me for the danger was too great and he believed and was to prove right that the victory that had been celebrated was hollow.

Then, at last, letting me question him, Sir William gently parted for me rumor from fact, for he had been every day in the Parliament. I knew the import. We at Cambridge had lusted for news and sent some of our friends to creep into the visitors' gallery which was as open as a public fair, and listen and report. What I had not understood or fitted by rumor on rumor, report on report, Sir William told me at last.

So it was, finally, through his eyes that I saw the members at that opening of the Parliament, saw them marching afeared, according to Sir William, which straightened their backs, and lengthened their strides. There was much fine dressing of the body to hide the mind, as he said, all the courtlike frills, some long hair, and pretty roses on their shoes, though there was not a man near him, he said, who was of the court party which had got smaller and ever smaller. He said they knew, all of them, that they had reached a place where the laws of the land and the power of Parliament was for sale for a penny. He said it so, "For a penny," he said. Then his face glowed with one of those smiles he had but seldom like the sun coming out across his face, he, a shy man usually, laughed as if he was fit to kill with jollity.

"All," he said, "but Sir Edward Coke, that old devil, why he shuffled into Parliament that first day in his slippers, ha ha, and his old robe and his nightcap upon his head, which he did not remove, saying that the March winds were bad for his aged pate, shuffle and snuffle, he went, and even when he rose the first time they all thought he had

lost what will he had had through age. He started so mildly that we
gossiped behind his back that he must be watched lest he forget his
way to the door."

I knew the act for I had seen it often, and he had told me the whys
and wherefores of it. "It stops," he always said, "nonsense. There is not
even a fool who will not pause in his flow before a drowsing man."

Sir William lay back upon his elbows in the grass. He said Sir
Edward hunched like an old dog by the fire for the beginning of the
Parliament, how he never raised his eyes when King Charles, that
unwary boy, opening his third Parliament before the Lords and Commons with much state, said what he had been told to say by the upstart
duke and his cronies, and terrible Bishop Laud who had put the words
into his willing mouth. He announced that he had not called Parliament to threaten them but to tell them his needs to run the war he had
stumbled toward in the Low Countries, how he wanted no waste of
time for unnecessary debate and argument. He ordered speed and
banned less important matters and grievances.

Then he added the fatal words "I scorn to threaten any but my
equals," and ignored the whispers of shock that swept through St.
Stephen's. Those fatal words were never forgot for a king's words live
longer than he does.

It was almost a habit as unwary and took for granted as breathing to
apologize for the young king, and Sir William added, "Poor fellow. I
know he is a religious king, God save him for it, and free from vice as
much as any man in England, but he dealt then and does now with
other men's hands and sees with other men's eyes. Sir Edward says he
needs a little more vice and a little more backbone."

He told how the old dog snuffled and yawned as if he had hardly
heard the king's words. Two weeks passed. The subsidies were granted
without a date for their payment, which was a way for Parliament to
hold the king's ever rash feet to the fire. Everyone but himself launched
into long-winded speeches and much Latin and some Greek, and Sir
William would yawn and maunch.

"We who had depended on him thought he would never speak
again. By God's holy hand the old man seemed to sleep through everything and so we took for granted he would not take part, being so old
and full of his past."

I knew already better than Sir William that my lord was coiled to spring. It was a trick, a layover to catch meddlers, he called it. I could see him there as clearly as if he were in the meadow on the way to Grantchester, my lord slumped there in the hot chamber of St. Stephen's, watchful and dormant-seeming as an animal in winter, at his most dangerous.

"Finally, finally, in the grievance debates against the billeting of the soldiers on families and such rambles and rumblings and rapes and licentiousness and horrors to the common people from the soldiers as we never heard, we longed like hounds ourselves for any small tidbit of red meat that he would drop. Someone interrupted with a plea to include unlawful imprisonment in the grievance.

"By Christ's bowels and body the old man lumbered to his feet and spoke the first time, as I remember, and he said, 'Jailing of men without cause shown, is restraint. No restraint, be it ever so little, but is imprisonment,' and from then he seemed to grow younger, and bit and snapped at any waywardness of the law against the straight and narrow path of Magna Carta."

Sir William was, at last, back in the Parliament and he sat up from the grass to free his arms to gesture and beat the air in his excitement. "I remember once he was in full cry, and we had begun to mind what he said, it seemed a straight path he was cutting through all the high grass of so many voices, as, when the speaker brought, over and over, the same words back from the king. After every separate grievance had been presented to the king much against his will and his command, he sent back messages that by his grace he would promise to honor the Parliament's wishes, citing 'his royal word and promise.'

"Those words brought Sir Edward to his feet, and he snapped at his majesty's heels. 'I honor the king but I cannot take his trust but in a Parliamentary way,' that's what he said. The house was stunned at such defiance! Every time such a message came he was on his feet shouting that the royal word and promise was no law. By all that loves that old man was himself again."

I could see it as if I were there for I had seen him do the same in many a court case and many a debate. Of the verbiage that grew like weeds in the court, he always said, "Tares, my boy, tares. Cut 'em!"

Sir William told me then that when the king threatened to adjourn the Commons until he got his money, my lord said quietly, "This house adjourns itself. It is the law." At first there was dead silence at what he mumbled, and then recognition, and then a cheer that grew to a roar in St. Stephen's.

The leaders of the county party had sat together at Sir Robert Cotton's table in Old Palace Yard until almost dawn sometimes, arguing, thinking what to do. Sir William remembered how my lord Coke grumbled, "If there were one of that damned canting brood who knew the law we could cut this to what matters. I see the duke's mind, what there is of it, stirring it up, but worse, I see that legal fool Coventry getting it all a bit wrong," and he would drink the fine wine Sir Robert always served in case the king's men would come snuffling and listening at the doors and windows, so that it ever seemed a simple supper for friends.

Sir William told me how my lord had first brought in a mild bill that disappointed them; he recited precedent all the way back to the Exodus from Egypt. "It was all to soften us of the county party, and more to soften the king's party for he was even then as wily as a snake, and it was all an act, the maundering, the maunching. It worked as well. He led us as gently as a shepherd coaxes his flock into the shambles, into what we had to do and the path we had to take to do it. And then he waited, hunched as one husbanding his energy to spring, only we knew it not.

"I tell you, Roger, it is not too much to say that the Duke of Buckingham, who ever spoke for the little king, took the bait. So did Bishop Laud. He lulled them so that they put words into the king's mouth to treat the Parliament like naughty children. And then what was it he said? Something about trusting his prerogative to care for them, as if the leading minds of England, many old enough to be his grandfather, were children to be cosseted.

"By God's holy tears, on the fifth of May—who can forget it?— Edward Coke set us on so dangerous a path as we have ever run. Having prepared us deftly to lose our damned polite timidity, he got to his feet and seemed to grow back into the vital man he had been. That day he wore fine clothes and was once again handsome Sir Edward Coke, and it was then his voice rolled out across the silent house, and he said, for I cannot forget it, and have read it much since, 'Of late there hath been public violation of the laws and the subjects' liberties by some of your majesty's ministers.' God my witness, here he came close to the man traps of the king's hunters. His voice softened so we had to lean forward to hear him. 'No less than public remedy will raise the dejected hearts of your loving subjects to a cheerful supply of your majesty.'

"He stood so resolute that he put iron in our backbones. And when the king answered with another Letter of Grace, he thundered to the close-packed members of St. Stephen's, who had of late been cynical and now crowded the House to see what he would do. 'The people will only like what is done in a Parliamentary way,' he told the king in answer. And oh by Christ's blood, I will not forget it!"

Sir William's voice rose from the grass as if he did not care a tinker's damn who heard. The cows looked up, and down again to their feeding.

"'Let us put up a Petition of Rights! This threatens Magna Carta, and Magna Carta is such a fellow that he will have no sovereign.'" And he stomped out of the house after bowing and grinning at the speaker. Then he went away. I know not where."

But I thought I knew. I could see him in his chambers, bent over his parchment like the man I had first seen on that January morning. I like to think that he said his prayers, and smiled, and began to read what he had long since written, and had drawn the Commons after him to be ready for it, the Petition of Rights that is known as the second Magna Carta. I think he rolled it under his arm, took the public wherry to Westminster as was his habit, and walked into St. Stephen's. They made a seat for him, for that was one Parliament that nobody missed, all four hundred sat cheek by jowl, ham to ham, squashed into the little chamber.

Sir William said he was ashamed to tell how when Sir Edward rose to speak the whispering and the jostling hardly stopped, for they yet expected little from him. Then he told me that my lord sprang up as young as a schoolboy and shouted in the voice they had long been used to and thought was gone, which was of course what my lord intended in the first place for I had seen him do it, the lull before the whip or the carrot or the stick he intended.

"By God," Sir William said, and clutched my arm. "By God! The thunder of that mind rang through St. Stephen's as if he had never grown old. There it was, the wit, the country humor, the legal erudi-

tion back to the Flood, and then, one by one, the grievances. In language untrammeled with any flourishes, the ban on the billeting of
soldiers in private homes without leave, the arresting of men without
knowing cause, the illegal forcing of loans. He had left nothing out. It
was simple and barracaded legally against courtly or wild interpreta-
tion as if, as he always had, he heard the arguments against it and
replied long before they had been thought of."

Sir William said the tall old man sat down again and folded himself
in the dashing red velvet cloak he wore that day, and seemed to drowse.

I knew that my lord had led, as he always had when he was in Parliament, the presentation to the House of Lords. When they, less brave
than the Commons and more wily, added a phrase to protect the king's
sovereign power, he rose again and called out the words that rang
through London, how there was no such thing as "sovereign power" in
English law, that it was against Magna Carta. His words flew all the
way to Cambridge by that island whisper that travels as fast as one man
putting his mouth to the ear of another that I had seen all my life.

And how King Charles had answered the bill through the clerk for
he ever stammered so that when he needed to be precise and powerful,
he had the words read for him. They set the flame to the House of
Commons that my lord had waited for. How those holding of the
king's hand had written his answer, "The king willeth that right be
done. He holds himself in conscience as well obliged as of his prerogative." It was a pretty phrase, a polite phrase, but a phrase as dissembling as a whore. The wrong words. Seven words and the law hung on
them. Three words, "the king willeth," instead of "Let right be done as
is desired." Soit droit fait comme il est désiré. The legal words that had
ever been used as approving of bills.

I asked Sir William how the Commons had took such royal inso-
lence, for it could not be called other. He said that they sat silent for
they thought they had failed. The king had not sent the correct words
to make a law of the petition. They waited for Sir Edward to speak.
"'This weakens Magna Carta,'" he told the Commons.

"Then, making it as vibrant as a person, he brought Magna Carta
into the house and spoke for it as for a man. He led us into representing the bill again although those of us who had tasted prison felt the
cold of it on our tongues again.

"Finally last week, by Jesus' bowels and blood, the king came into the House of Lords and we, the Commons, were called to the barre to hear his message. He was dressed in the robes and the jewels of his calling. The clerk read the words that will ever make thoughts into laws in England, 'Soit droit fait comme il est désiré.'"

Sir William added in a kindly voice, "Let right be done as is desired," and patted me on the back, for I had turned during his opening of that greatest day of my lord Coke's life, what he had worked for and waited for, and what I know had kept him alive through all the errors of that harsh time. I had buried my nose in the sweet grass of the meadow, and I truly think that Sir William thought I was asleep.

When the news had come of what had happened in London, Cambridge went as mad as it could under the watchful eyes of the clergy, fellows, masters, and all their breed. Bishop Laud's hirelings, Wren's bowers and scrapers, our own Beale watching like a terrier at a rat hole. The bonfires of triumph in the Cambridge streets were reflected in the Cam. They made the colleges seem graced with fire themselves, not fearsomely but with wild joy. It was so, I heard, in every town and village after the Parliament had won. Some of the scholars spread the word that the Duke of Buckingham had been arrested, drawn, quartered, and hung in bits on London Bridge.

"The joy," Sir William said, having punched me harder to be sure I heard, "spread out of St. Stephen's chapel, into the street, into the river, everyplace, spread and moved from town to town, and I never in all my born days heard such a roar. The bonfires were lit and all London through the night celebrated what they already called the new Magna Carta, and Sir Edward. Most of them thought the duke had fallen, and boys even took down the scaffold on Tower Hill to make a new one for Buckingham to drop his head upon the grass below.

I turned. "It was so here in Cambridge," I told him, "within an hour of the words spoken. I have oft seen it, that news flies in England more birdlike than the slow official roads. By that evening there were bonfires here and riot, and yes, I joined in them all, only half believing, for as in the child's game of whispering, one to another, by the time the news gets to the last whisper, it is much changed. By midnight here in Cambridge the duke, Coventry, and the bishop had all lost their heads."

We were still, lying there, watching the birds. There seemed more to say but no words for it. Then, that man who was ever gentle with animals, including boys alying on the grass, subtle with the bit, gentle with the prod as I would see, began to tell me what I had waited all the afternoon to hear, as if it were a story for bedtime. As if I had asked him he almost whispered over my head. "My lord Coke says you are not to come to Stoke this long vacation."

I could not move. "He came to me at the prorogation of the Parliament and drew me with him into Sir Robert Cotton's house for it was a safe haven for us all. He said that he had found that you were indeed in the bishop's black book, for they were trying to punish without a public account anyone who sat too near him. 'I expected it,' he said. 'Tell him,' and here he paused as if he waited for God himself to tell him what to say. There were tears in his voice. 'I love the boy and expect much of him for the state. It has been so planned,' and he told me of sending you to Charterhouse and after your fine work that earned you a Watts scholarship, which, of course, he said, drew their eyes to you even more than knowing you were his ward, his son, he called you, his Roman son, as after the emperors who found the best in the Roman Empire and adopted them as their heirs.

"'I am going to Stoke to await my arrest,' Sir Edward told me as calmly as if he and I too did not know the cold misery of the Tower, 'and I must make a public matter for the gossips that I have rejected him for his Puritan ways.' He found a little laughter then and said, 'I do, by God's holy Son I do, dislike you damned reformers for you are without joy which for me is the greatest of all sins against our Maker, who made us for laughter as well as tears. Tell him that.' And he sat down and began to cry. Through his tears though he went on planning. 'I have spoke to the Bishop of Lincoln, my old friend John Williams. He is the only one rich enough and brave enough to stand for balance against this radical and terrible split in my church where I have worshiped since a babe. Damn you. Damn you all, you are too young William Masham for your dour Puritan ways,' and he rose and hugged me and dripped tears down my back.

"'He will ordain the boy. Take him to Otes. That will not surprise them and he might be safe there, if any of you are safe. God knows I am not and will never be.' And right there in Sir Robert's library, he threw back his head and laughed long and said, 'Come, enough of this. Let us drink to the boy, and tell him I love him ever and will write to him when I know it to be safe.'"

I too was sobbing, sobbing into the ground, for I had turned again and lay in my own arms for comfort.

XVI

Being by God's ordinance, according to our just title, Defender of the Faith and Supreme Governor of the Church . . . We have . . . thought fit to make this declaration following . . . that if any public reader in either of our Universities, or any Head or Master of a College, or any other person respectively in either of them shall affix any new sense to any Article, or if any Divine in the Universities should preach or print anything either way, other than is already established in Convocation with our royal assent; he, or they the offenders, shall be liable to our displeasure, and the Church's censure in our Commission Ecclesiastical, as well as any other; and we shall see that there shall be due execution upon them.

— ROYAL PROCLAMATION,
NOVEMBER 1628

J CAN STILL REPEAT IT, HERE WHERE THE SUN drifts among trees as huge as they were in the Garden of Eden, before men felled and cut them for his uses. I am, this morning, yes, this old man, disobeying all of them, Mary my dear one, my children, what friends who have not been so drowned in disputations over land and religion that they have shut their hearts. Welladay, all have forbid me this forest for they fear that if God took my soul here they would not find me where the trees are and the animals and the light and where and always I, crying in the wilderness, have found the Father of Lights I sought.

I think they fear that my bones will not be found for the Resurrection that is expected by some any day. And always has been. And always will be. For myself, I cannot think a finer fate for my old broke body than to be food for my brother animals.

There is that in me which must needs come here to meet. I thirst after silence and the ways of the Father of Lights. Let them for all their love and care take not the private reaches of my soul that is released by light and silence, God Light and God Silence. Whatever sickness of soul there be, the living silence of the earth assuages it for me, and what for long years broke my heart, being exiled from what I saw as my brothers, I welcome now and thank them in God's name for they sent me not to death but to life. Here in the forest the first green of spring exalts me, and the wise indifferent life of the earth flows through me as through the trees with their new sap rising.

Think how I suffered and most of it needless if I had only accepted it as my path and not my punishment. If I stumbled where it was rocky and bellowed like an unbreeched child at the noisome toing and froing and climbing and falling of cities and power and land and righteousness, the awful seeking of it, it was, at the time, all I knew.

Then so be it.

I was an excellent good fighter. It makes a pleasant memory for an old man and I thank the Father of Lights my witness that I will not ever have to do it again. Think how after the events in the years between that proclamation, took for granted then to shut the mouth and freeze the soul, and today it is only an ancient fable of old times.

It was the very day it was put up on the wall of Pembroke that Sir William came again to Cambridge. I remember how desolate I was when he left and took his jolly kind large face upon the road to home. He had left me standing in the door of Pembroke that November day with the rain lashing my face. He had took the time, bless that loving man, to promise me safety, on his way home from London.

He told me of a plan of the richer reforming religious men to hide young clergy who showed promise in private houses as chaplains until the times were less sullen. The prisons yawned and the branding iron was being heated to be used for whosomever the power of the land, which was Bishop Laud, chose to call heretic, which meant often that they—we—did not tread the fine line of his rules. It was better though than in the days of such fires as sent Bartholomew to Paradise for they had long since been stopped by a public murmuring that was, if they liked it or not, strong enough finally to move the state.

We were not surprised by this royal declaration for it had been long coming and had waited only until Laud had climbed high enough to take the reins of power, while the king ever nodded and did, like a good boy, what he was advised, in short told to do. It was an awful and wonderful year when the king's declaration shut all of our mouths, but not, by the Father of Lights, our minds. This long since I can still repeat it, for it was yet another of those milestones that sent me on my way among these trees, so old, so huge, but, as I am, too, new with the leaves of a baby in this springtime.

I can still see the parchment pinned to the wall of Pembroke so that none could miss it, a large fine-looking scroll with the king's seal. One corner had been caught by the wind and it was trying to tear it off the wall. It flapped behind me as Sir William rode away into mist and cold. I was alone and afeared. We all were, afeared of each other, too, for none knew then who would peach on the others. I had already suffered so, and knew I would again.

Within a few days, as fast as the wind and the birds that fought it, came his letter that I was to come straight to Otes, his manor house, as the chaplain there and he and my lord had arranged for me to be ordained, but I was to say nothing. Before my dear God, I examined the letter and its seal with the tenacity of a spy myself to see that it had not been tampered withall. That was the way the world was then and will be over and over, if we cease our vigilance against those who would enslave us, either minds or bodies.

So I did take my few belongings and ride Hobson's cart to London to gather my dear Chloe from my friend who had sleeked her and cosseted her, being a man who took his promises as things of gold, as the caring for all of the trees in the orchard so he would be sure to care for the apple tree wherein the arm of the martyred abbot was buried in his great-grandfather's time. Before God, who knows this, I was more loath to leave Nathan than any other in London. He was the only one

I told where I was going, for I dared not trust my mother lest her brag betray me.

I set my path toward Essex as Sir William had told me. And I left behind any further study in that monkish world that had sheltered and fettered me for five years. That the king's declaration had changed the course of my life I hardly paid my mind to. I did not see myself on the road that day bounden on that path I had been led like an ox with a ring in my nose. Lord Christ Jesus knows that I myself knew not yet that the road of both gold cassock and fine cross with the genitalia of Jesus politely covered, and the suits of solemn black that we sported in our ideal white-walled churches, led to the same abysmal swamp.

So up the London road to Essex at first until the road was empty both before and behind me, and then set forth across the stubbled fields and the hidden paths with the compass my lord had give me the last New Year's I saw him. I have carried it ever since. It is here, as always, in my pocket, as I keep telling Mary who does not trust such machines. It has many a time, from his hand to mine, kept me from being lost long after I could read the north by the moss gathered on tree trunks, and a hundred other ways my Indian friends have taught me. It was a way to Otes I took many a time after, until I knew its twists, its turns, its dangerous places, in rain, snow, ice, and then the exalted trembling beauty of England in spring.

I stayed one night at Otes before Sir William sent me off to Lincoln to be ordained by Bishop John Williams. I had seen him many a time when he was Lord Keeper in the days of the old King James. To tell the truth, we were beginning to miss the old king as my lord had foretold. We were beginning to see him as a favorite flawed but kindly uncle instead of the head of God His church on earth when he was not drinking, hunting, paddling his fingers on the cheeks of pretty men, or showing off his polyglot learning like little treasures he squirreled away and loved to take out and use to astonish.

Of the ordination I remember little, at least little solemn enough to think about. I must have seen it as important at the time, hem, as the curate clears his throat of borrowed wine, hem, I mean of course my little place then in history as one affected by the great power of the establishment within the church that brushed over me. So I went to Lincoln. I was ordained a deacon of the Church of England, and give a pretty dinner by the bishop who took delight in besting his enemy, Laud, in such small ways as one ordained unknown deacon slipped under Laud's nose.

Bishop John Williams, dear friend of my lord Coke, was also cousin german to Sir William Masham's wife or mother, I have long forgot which, so far away it is now. Anyway it was one of those veins and arteries of kinship that made the eastern counties so strong a weapon for the reform. It was at that dinner with the bishop that I first heard the name of Oliver Cromwell, for he, speaking of all his relatives at Otes and beyond, lit upon the name as a poor relation who lived in the fens at Ely, and had just been elected to the Parliament. "Lord of the Fens they call him, for he stands against the draining of the fens and the enclosures of the common land. Good power to him I say for it is all for money hiding behind noble excuses. He carries a chip upon his shoulder and has since he was breeched dared the world to knock it off. That makes nine relations, no ten, I have there," he said. "So think of that, Will Laud, you canting meddling little backstairs hocus pocus." He laughed and poured more wine for us. He and Laud seemed then as familiar with one another as boys in a schoolyard.

"We have kept an eye upon you for the road to bishop when the time is ripe," he said, smiling at me as if the smile itself were a laying on of hands. "My lord Coke has told me why he sent you to Pembroke. A very good move, I think, for you can always put upon yourself the pretty garments of Arminia. It means little."

He was an honest, pleasant, corrupted man. I have found in my life those more tolerable than holy reformers who whine about God the Punisher, and dream about God Money and God Land. He had joy within and he shared it, casual with the gift, unthought.

"By the bye," he went on, "how are those holy play actors?"

I knew not what to answer.

"Advice to a future bishop." He drank again. "Lay a little silk about your neck. Those lawn garments and gold thread scratch and cause a rash."

A boy let out of school, a fine young man, to be took seriously by those who were older because hands had been laid upon my head. I look on that now as blasphemy, but then, oh then, I was the sacred cock of the holy walk and saw myself so, chosen of God, a new-made mystical merchant. I was that foolish and knew it not, that arrogant and knew it not, that useful and ambitious for them who trusted me and understood no better.

Otes. It was a huge house built around the refectory of an ancient monastery, as so many houses, Stoke and all, had been in the days of the late queen's father. There was a moat and a sunken garden, dovecotes and stables and pretty paths and fields to the horizon. There were sixty people there at any time, and I, though some twenty-four years old and ready to take my place as a man of gravity, had no idea what to do. Even so, I was in charge of the souls of all.

The grandeur of Otes was only facts, sixty-nine rooms, and I can call them forth in my mind's sight from attic to great hall to basement wine cellars, but when I go there in my soul it is evening, cool in summer as shadows fall in the late sun, dark in winter with the candles and the torches guttering in their sconces and throwing shafts of light upon the ceiling, as far away as the sky, for the great hall was the height of the house itself.

I stand uncertain but trying to show some weak authority while the whole family of Otes is on their knees for evening prayer, day in day out. They kneel in ranks of their stations in life, their duties, and their blood: the family, Sir William, his wife, Lady Elizabeth, her daughter, called Jug, Jug's maid companion, the daughter of the vicar of Worksop, who basked in the favor of the Earl of Manchester for his living. She had been chosen for her background, higher than the housemaids, a little lower than the gentry, for even in prayer, this mattered. It was as formal as a Chinese puzzle or a court dance.

Behind them knelt the menservants in their ordered ranks, first the head butler and the head gardener, then the wine steward, the bailiff whose nose ran in winter and whose name was oft forgotten, one born trembling, a stealer of little mean sips from the decanter; behind them row on row of housemaids and houseboys, with their domains and jealous of their places, seeing only what was lower to order about, seeing only what was higher in that domestic tree for them to fear.

They knelt there in their simple clothes of black, their white collars, their chaste caps, while the family knelt before them in black, too, but of velvet and satin, the coverings for the gentry.

But what I hear is below this sight, and I still hear it when I go back

in my soul to Otes. It is like the fall of water in a brook, the soft murmur of the little maids, whispering in their time of silence and peace
for the only time that they, trained on hellfire if they broke a plate or
disobeyed an order for whatever reason.

"Now lettest thou thy servant depart in peace according to thy
word." I hear them still, under the boom of Sir William, the chaste trill
of Lady Elizabeth, the slight grumble of Jug, as ready to rise and run
as a restive filly, the sweet murmur of little maids.

For the rest it was my duty to hear their sins and so the little ones
made them up to get me to come to their attic where the rooms were
so low that I, who was never a tall man, had to bend my head. They
would confess whatever sins they could think of, for they were all, the
giggling crew, convinced they were in love with me and contrived
together to draw me thither. I could hear them giggling and prating
in whispers as I went again down the stairs when I had relieved their
souls of sins they had not committed.

These were my parish and some of my duty, though I had others, for
the Parliament had been recalled and sat in London and by February it
was my task to wander London and take soundings of opinion. It was
the most disordered and distressed Parliament in many a year. No one
knew when the lion of state would claw their backs for passing the Bill
of Rights, and for refusing to give down milk for the king his debts.
Even so, the king had had the first version of the petition, the illegal
one, published, with "the king willeth" instead of the lawful words.

My lord Coke did not attend and no amount of trundling back and
forth to Stoke could draw him from his lair. "Let the lads do it. It is
time for young men. Listen to Pym, and be watchful for John Hampden though he says little, and Holles, though he be a hot-headed brat."

All of this went back to the Parliament and caused much laughter
and wit. But I knew why he stayed away as surely as if he had told me
of it. He was waiting to be sent to the Tower again and he wanted no
one to be took with him. More than that, he had seen a new Magna
Carta passed into law, his whole life's work against prerogative
absolute, and I knew he once again leaned over his parchments like the
praying mantis, taking every precious day he had left to finish the
Reports and the Commentaries that were to guide English law for so
long after.

But even the Duke of Buckingham, whose picture of himself with-in his own pretty head was invincible, knew better than to jail a man of seventy-seven years, who for that short while was the most beloved man in England by the leaps and flows of the county men that the court, the prelates, and Academe viewed only with contempt. As my lord foretold, the triumph had been empty; it had only scotched for a pause the terrible revenge that Laud was taking on the land, for the one he loved with all his heart had been murdered at last, and he, whose diary was full of his dreams of him, mourned with his hatred the Duke of Buckingham. Laud had had to listen, and the king, too, as the people cheered and built bonfires of celebration, for the duke had been the most hated man in England. I should have pitied Laud for a love he could not recognize himself, but then I did not, for I knew not that pain.

So I was eyes and ears for Sir William and his brother-in-law, Sir Thomas Barrington, and all the kin and party of the eastern counties. For no simple man would speak within the hearing of those powerful gentry in the silks and furs of Parliament. God Politics that year was for reform but it was as feared by the common people as the arrogant court party flashing by and sweeping the dung of the road under their gaudy heavy satin. I love the word "gaudy" for it tells all.

So once again I was a welcome guest at Sir Robert Cotton his house in Palace Yard and the garden that ran down to the river. He was an old man by then, and glad to see me, for he loved who loved his books, and I had devoured his library in the old days when I awaited my lord and his inner circle who planned the road of their county party. My lord had always been pleased to use Sir Robert his house to take his rest when the Parliament went on too long by candlelight and tired him. And also to use the jakes.

Why is that library of Sir Robert more real to me now than all the prating of politics and opinions that I, too, thought so important then? It was there I held ancient texts in my own hands, the Bible in Hebrew, in Latin, made by the monks in the old days, the word of God from many voices and many dead hands. I read as well as I could in the dim candlelight the words of Tertullian in faded brown Latin so early I could hardly fathom it; I held the earliest parchment rescued from some monastery in Ireland of the *Confessions* of St. Augustine, that pas-sionate man, and I saw for myself the innermost parts of my own body in the drawings of Vesalius that he made from the bodies of the dead, and was astonished that I, Roger Williams, like the beggar in the street, was planned of the same bones and muscles, liver and lights.

It is so meet and whole to my wandering soul this morning so late in life and so far away to come again upon the colored drawings in a folio of Michelangelo's blasphemous paintings on the walls and ceiling of the chapel in the very center of the house of the Great Whore. All in secret I lived with them night after night then, the image of God flung across the ceiling, the beautiful bodies that embarrassed me in those days for I knew no better than to accept some gifts of God and reject others, as the way we are made and how the blood flows, and the bodies of the dead and those wise faces on the ceiling.

Once a man who had come to see Sir Robert had been put within the library to wait. I was waiting, too, for Sir William and Sir Thomas to finish letters to send to their mother at Hatfield. He saw what I studied and said that he had broached the very center of the Great Whore and would have fell, he said, upon his knees for the beauty of the place, but could not, it being Papist. Oh God Pure and Blessed Eye what fools we are and have been, and I fear, will be, when what is real demands too much of us.

I never knew who he was. May be he was an angel come to still my embarrassment at being caught looking at naked bodies, and my judgemental eyes, for he took the book from my hands gently.

"I brought this folio to Sir Robert," he said, and he smoothed his hand across the parchment cover with its beautiful scrolls. "I bought it of a poor artist in Florence who made his living copying. I want you to see another thing. This from Florence." He turned the pages of the folio and handed it back to me.

I looked at it for so long that when I looked up again he had gone without a word, long or short gone I knew not. All I know is that there before me was the image of our lives upon this earth, a marble man struggling out of a block of marble as God carves us with the same blows, the same shaping, throughout our lives, while we resist as stone. I sat and sobbed, and turned the pages to escape so painful an image, and there was, at the end, a rough staff of marble with the mark of the chisel upon it, and wrote beneath it in Latin, the last work of Michelangelo in his eighty-ninth year.

I did not know until then that a word could be cast in stone. It was my Lord Jesus took down from the cross, and held by His mother, all as primitive as a child's attempt at carving, but it was the opposite. It was pure grief in stone.

That was where Sir William found me that night and said we must needs get along to bed at his brother's house. He was so full of what had happened in the Parliament that day, and so insistent on my telling him the opinion of the street and what the far-flung tracts and daily tattle had said, for it was my task to distill them for him. He never noticed that I had been crying. I was grateful, for I could not have shared that image of God with a living soul, then or now.

The Parliament without my lord was, to me, a pack of hounds without a lead dog, baying up an empty tree. They argued and murmured and sometimes they shouted, toing and froing below me, for I sat sometimes again in the place where I had been so diligent for my lord in the days of the old Parliament in 1621. So I was there when they locked the doors against the king's messenger, when he came from the king to knock upon the door of the Commons with the Black Rod as tradition demanded, to announce the close of Parliament.

Led by young Holles, they held the speaker by force in his seat so he could not rise to dissolve the session, and they voted, sweating and yelling in the evening gloom. They knew, every man of them, that the next home they might have would be the Tower or the Marshalsea or the Clink or one other of so many loathsome cages the king had at his command to set them in and leave them there. They had had at last a victory of a kind over Laud, for they outlawed by force his Arminian policies. Oh, they called it that and saw it so, but it was truly his hands around their necks that they were trying to loose.

That night by candlelight behind the locked door with the Black Rod and king's troops pounding on it the Parliament tried to protect the country from the court's drain on the taxes levied without the order of Parliament. Of course the leaders were sent to prison later—Holles and Eliot and all. Some died. And none of it, none of it then was more than the wisp of a dream.

When Black Rod was finally let into St. Stephen's with the king's orders to dissolve Parliament, it was not to be called again for eleven years of absolute rule. Every night in the same white heat of fury I tried to write down in my shorthand what I had seen and heard for I knew it as a momentous time. How I wish I had wrote instead of the sad faces of the people in the street when they knew better than the Parliament that it was pissing against the wind of very powerful stupidity, the most frightening combination on earth. For with it comes always the growing daily fear, the lowered voices, the glance over the shoulder, the distrust in a friend's eyes. We had plunged ourselves, we purists, into a Gehenna, the silence of the beast and not the lamb.

How I wish I had wrote of all this in a quiet time when I was not forced into words by the white heat of controversy. I seem to be put on earth to fight, and yet, sometime I have wrote more tenderly and wisely, part I think of my dictionary for the Indian language so that our settlers could, and I truly thought so at the time, be friends and neighbors. Then, once, I wrote to my Mary for she was sick and troubled in her faith. I wrote it in the woods, thinking of her and how I loved her and how she asked for help.

Of course, being an educated and eloquent man, except for those two times, I weaned it was urgent to trace, as I had been taught, with the usual paints and flourishes to brag my education, the history of every argument I touched. I wrote, alas, not of so unimportant things as the sun on my back. Or wild flowers on a bank. I was far away from such fripperies as that. I used much quoting to prove my points and larded the story as one would a joint turning on the spit, with Bible proof of everything from such policies as whether one bowed to the left or to the right or wore a robe or a cassock or this or that. Oh God help me for my foolishness that I added to blood hate.

But by God after that I did speak and do and will against persecution of anyone for what they think or what they worship. And that protection for black robes or white lawn sleeves that scratch, or however the Pharisees think to dress themselves in from time to time, even their bare skin like the besotted Quakers. It was all there but it was half hidden for I made sure, even so, as my lord Coke had taught me, to write as it were a Christian legal brief, plugging up all holes in the disputation, using God's ordinance and fury against those who were trying to shut my mouth and many mouths. God my soul, now at eighty I wonder at all the words when it can be simple and true and I can let the sun shine on me, and remember, as any man remembers, within his own soul and heard only by his God.

I remember most of the March ride back toward Otes, from wet day into fogged night with the shadows of Sir William, Sir Thomas, and seven of their cousins who were members of Parliament. It was the first time for John Hampden and Oliver Cromwell, who were younger. Their cousin Whalley, who would have a regiment later, had joined them to ride forth, and one young man, Oliver St. John. It was the first time I ever saw him, and then only his sopped back. They all rode with their heads down as the horses' heads drooped in the rain, and they spoke little. Parliament had been dissolved for a week and there were many secret meetings to agree on what to do. At first there had been more members along the north road, all in mourning for what had happened. Gradually there were less as some said goodbyes with a hint of tears as they turned toward their own estates.

So the barriers had not moved but had been strengthened and there was hopelessness in the shoulders of the men from the House of Commons, all except for me, who had, out of politeness, to hide my bright joy at going home.

XVII

— ◆◆◆ —

*I desire to be more thankfull for a reproof for aught I
affirm, than for applause and commendation. I have been
oft glad in the wilderness of America to have been reproved
for going on a wrong path and to be directed by a naked
Indian Boy in my travels. How much more should we
rejoice in the wounds of such as we hope love us in Christ
Jesus, than in the deceitful kisses of soule destroying and
soule killing friends.*

— ROGER WILLIAMS

MARY HAS THROWN ME ABROAD THIS SUN-DRIVEN
morning with the rest of the winter sweepings through the door for
she turns out the house of our loving daughter-in-law as she once did
her own and that for near fifty years on every April Fool's day, rain or
shine, daughter or no daughter, and woe to him who gets before the
besom. She turns witch that day and drives before her besom all the
winter out of Robert's door. I know she used a heavier stroke on the
back of my poor legs this morning for she knew, she always knows, that
I had been dreaming by the look in my eyes. Sometimes she says,
"Gone soft again, you saw your pretty ghost yesternight," or only
smiles.

Here we live on the edge of the water, and when I wake I remind
myself where we are, and how endless forest paths long we have loved
each other with daily love, Christ love, never ending. It was not Mary
who led me to it, but the one in the dream.

Mary knows that and it makes her laugh. I love her laughter. It warms my soul and opens me to the Father of Lights as none else. Oh Christ Jesus' heart my Mary, you know at night when I dream so, old man young again and innocent as a puppy. She knows and touches me with her tender hand. She knows where I have been as if she dreamed with me, watching me in the garden from her dream window. Even sometimes when I have forgot the dream, I know from her face and her "Get along old man" and her grin that I have been there and she has been there and knows where I was. As this very morning, April Fool's day, by the nudge of her arm as I went from the door with her laughter following me, "April Fool!" she called after and then behind me there was the sound of the besom and I was let loose in another morning upon this new raw world. But of what comes on mornings like this one after dreaming, I have not wrote nor told nor would not. Sometimes, turning a corner in my walks or in my mind, I come against the miracle and am at home, as I was then.

My shadow drifts over another sunlit day so long since but only yesterday in my mind. And there I am, a young boy, an April Fool. To see oneself silly is to see oneself naked. And the Father of Lights knows I was then naked and innocent. What a happy mystical merchant I was then, knowing no better, riding Chloe along the path to Hatfield.

I thought I had stuck in my thumb and pulled out a plum and I was, as the rhyme says, a good boy, well kept as any animal, but knew it not in that way. For God my holy witness it was a comfort to any man to be so cosseted, so admired, so petted, so loved, so honored, so innocently used.

I watched my shadow flow across the April flowers beside the road. The shadow of Chloe's ears laid back, head up, her nose lifted into the breeze. Happy the horse with the breeze up its nose. I rode her toward disaster, lulled by the clip clop comfort of her hoofs. That morning I lived in love as warm to my singing spirit as the sun itself.

Sometimes, as now, my shadow on a wild hedge on the rim of a dark wild forest in a wild country turns me back of a sudden and it is with my heart and the first learning of my soul to hear without judgement and smell and taste without guilt that always new morning. This old April Fool was as alight with happiness to live at Otes as one mistaken and trusting could be.

It was a fine day and I was going where love was. Six miles to go to love for I thought then it was a girl in a place who held that warmth and light to give to me. Then, as now when I dream, she ran toward me from beneath a tree where she waited, that lovely created being who had trapped my soul.

I was, still am, still young, still a part of morning and she turns and sees me forever and does run toward me, hardly touching the meadow grass, and we are alight together as we hold one another. Why for the same love I learned then and for the Father of Lights and His Son, my Christ, do I have to explain like a conjurer's assistant that there was no lust in this? No lust, no way of telling in other terms, as poetry, flowing streams, et cetera, none of that. It was, as awkwardly as I can put it into words, that we were found in each other, and never again with any human being, even my beloved Mary, would it be so again.

Oh, to have the world darkened, to judge where there was naught to judge, to sin where there was no sin, to stand back and be righteous where there was no need but that was what the world around us saw. But it was not so. Chloe sniffed and ate the meadow grass, her reins lying on the ground, for she was so tractable she stayed close as a well-trained, loving dog. We stood there for the time that is no time, touching one another so lightly, so blessed, or so I took for granted as a gift of God.

I can still this long away in time smell the scent of that new meadow grass released by Chloe's grazing; the scent of Jane Whalley's skin and her hair, where the wind had moved her curls and wisps and cleansed them with the morning, the slight dampness of her cheek against mine, and the basket she carried, her excuse for coming to the meadow, and the dress she wore, new cleansed and dried in the sun it seemed to catch and hold within its weave.

No matter that she who was my beloved is now a canting old woman, and has turned to be one of those pious judges that we reformers produce when we cannot or will not let them be happy. No, they must maunder and whisper and suck their gums and judge the young and ever ever see only the ugliness of the shipwreck where we live and never the fine pebbles on what shore we have been cast upon.

No matter any of that, for in that April morning, and in my dreams, the girl she was runs toward me and enfolds me and I her as tender as babes and share the warmth as nowhere and no time else. I know the girl is gone from her, not a trace within that whining woman she became. But she is still within me. By God she is.

So whatever else I learned then under a tree within the folding of her arms and my arms and our cheeks against each other and the smell of her hair, what I learned with her toppled my life down and rebuilt it in a better way. I learned then to recognize love when it came to me, from friends, from Mary, from my Lord Christ Jesus, from God, from the world He let me live in.

Of course what I came officiously to do was to listen and advise about God, young as I was, an old and melancholy woman who had took to me as one who understood her grief and her holiness and wanted, every morning, to speak of this, and I must admit, speak and speak and speak, judging the world more strictly than ever the Father of Lights does, while I listened and nodded and earned my holy penny.

She was a widow. An ever mourning widow, a heroine, a tyrant. Lady Joan Barrington had gone with her husband to prison in the Marshalsea when he was the first of the refusers of the king's illegal forced loan. I will confess that there were times I wondered if he was disappointed when she made her brave and public gesture for it may be that he had looked upon prison as a way to rest from her insistent voice.

She was and she let me know at once the daughter of the Golden Knight of Hinchingbrook, and with a clearing of the throat each time, connected him quite closely with the late sainted Thomas Cromwell, the old king Henry's great minister. I once took for granted that he was a sainted reformer who cleared the land of Papism, but I see now that he was King Henry's hatchet man, as the Indians call them, the doers of the dirtiest work.

So I rode slowly on in the fine morning, tethered Chloe to a hitching post before the great door of Hatfield Broadoak, and walked within, on my road to bishop when the times were ripe, as Bishop Williams had said. Laggard boy, ambitious chaplain, I was what I was raised up to be by my patrons, one who like all the rest of the fearful clerks as they called clerics in those disjointed times was wont to glance at the Palace of Lambeth where Canterbury lived and wonder when, if ever, we low church English reformers would take that citadel.

She sat always in the same sunny corner of the privy parlor, her good things around her within an easy reach, her Bible, her prayer book, her needlepoint upon a stand with a message from the Bible upon it for she was a very pious woman. It was her time to have her first light wine of the morning and she explained, every time, as a habit, that she had been told to take it for her melancholy by the physician to the Bishop of Bath and Wells, not Laud, that dread man, she would hasten to add, but his predecessor. For even a glass of wine had its social explanations in those days, and, the Father of Lights knows, nowadays.

She would have a text for me to explain and prophesy upon, and I, talking of my Lord Jesus and thinking of my Jane, would comply, knowing no harm in it. She told me of her sorrow and her melancholy which she seemed to cling to as expected of her, and she spoke of the burdens that God the Father placed upon such as herself bereft and lonely. She seemed for that hour of holy chatter to forget that she was surrounded by fifty or so people ready to jump to her commands, cosset, comfort, bathe, scent, and as was my duty laid out as carefully as all the other duties of the household, to pray for her; to say nothing of the roost she ruled with every relative, son, daughter, nephew, et cetera, for she held the purse strings.

All the time she clasped her thin chest for she was a woman to whom gesture came easily; it was her gesture of piety. She had tiny hands and I have not been able to look since at women with those small paws, for like lap dogs I expect them to bite.

That morning in April, when I began to sit down before her, she cleared her throat and I thought she was skipping to her connection with Thomas Cromwell but she was not. I cannot this far since remember many of her words, but the gist of it was that she very kindly reproved me for my courtship of her niece.

"My niece," she said, not Jane's own name, as if she wished to set upon my mind that Jane was hers to dispose of. She did not mention our love but she spoke around it. She spoke of what she thought was Jane's passionate, rash, and inconstant spirit, needing as wayward children do a curb to cure her haste and indecorum. "Come always on God's work with me," she finished and was ready to dismiss me. Her hands came down from her bosom and sat in her lap, those two small animals who had done some obedient duty. "Do not keep me waiting, for the knell is ever ready to toll for me. My spiritual health is in your hands and I am, as you know, frail.

"I know," she said at last, "your care for her soul. Speak plainly of it when you come again, and think of it." She added with that small sweet voice she used to rule her world that Jane had few expectations, and that she would have to be satisfied with very little since her own dowry was in litigation. In short she put our love in terms of money and connection and sent me on my way to think upon the future and come again when she commanded it. My Lord Jesus, that morning, was never mentioned.

She was godly and pious, and gave to charity and lived by her own rules gleaned from the Bible. She chose the prayers from the fine language of the prayer book, and we prayed them together. We met every morning, even Sunday, for she felt that winter and spring too weak to attend her own church where she kept the living of the poor clerk of holy orders on a short lead. She was one who had persuaded the world around her to placate her lest she withdraw her blessing and leave them in a cold winter. I think she was the most evil woman I have ever known.

I SAT IN my room that night. God the Father knows what I suffered and all for words, the right words, the polite words, the politic and placating words for that woman. I wish I felt more kindness for the boy I was, but now I see only toady and client, deeper in fear of her rejection than ever I would be with anyone again in my life. I had no fear of my dear Jane. My dear Jane, thank God today, is safe within my dreams and not prating pious platitudes in imitation of that woman.

It is the scratching of a quill that sounds like a mouse in the wainscot that I hear when I see myself there in my cell, for cell it was. The constant sound of the night, a shuffling of reeds, a breeze, a falling of a log in the fire, reached me faintly, ghosts in that old house. The night bore on, grew heavier and heavier, and I poor fool prayed to myself and not to my God to give me the correct words for the way to Jane was through the harsh piety and sense of her station in life of my lady Joan Barrington, for she was her guardian and had her marriage in her hands to give or take away.

I wrote that letter four ungodly times, scratching away, my pen-
manship becoming smaller and more cramped as the cold night went
on. I made a list of what I thought she wanted to know, instead of telling
her the truth as I saw it, alone in my tower. I wrote what she wanted,
not what I had to offer, which was so simply love and trust. Item: one
income, two prospects, three heritage, four holiness, five much quoting of the Bible, and six my present assets. I did not linger on my
hopes or my dreams or my love. They all seemed as whiffs of dreams
beside the cold facts of what I saw as her demands. And they were.

Since she had spoken so slightingly of Jane that morning, I tried to
smooth over that first. It took three copies of the letter to change "you
said this morning" to "you said" to something like "objections have
been noted, about her spirit and her passionate rash inconstant hasty
self" which she had pointed out to me. I recognized the indecorum of
Jane's wayward descent to my low ebb. I stated that I had refused a
New England call, and had had two offers of marriage, which was
true—Mary Barnard's father, who was vicar at Worksop and who wrote
books, and the second gardener, who was the father of one of the maids.

He had caught his daughter as she ran past when I spoke with him
in the kitchen garden, lifted her skirt, slapped her bare rump, and said,
"My boy you could do worse than this fine hardy wench," while she ran
off giggling fit to kill. I listed that, too, as a proposal. Oh Father of
Lights when I think of it, of that night of lies and entreaties, I am still
bowed with shame.

I listed my pathetic assets which consisted of some clothing give to
me by Frances, my dear horse Chloe, some fine books give to me
through the years by Sir Edward, though I mentioned him not since
she had once expressed the notion that if her dear husband had not
been influenced so by Sir Edward he might not have gone to prison and
might be alive still. How her mind went questing and found that trail
of tears I knew not, nor could see it.

"Dear Madame," then "Your ladyship," then deep into the night
simply "Madame." I was buzzing with lack of sleep. At last, having
acknowledged myself unworthy and unmeet for such a proposition,
having said I was hopeful of twenty pounds a year income when my
mother died, which I hoped would be as long in coming as the litigation that had froze Jane's dowry, I sealed the letter with my simple seal,

went to my cot and lay awake all the rest of the night, and so carried on an endless dialogue to soften her heart, the lady. Much I told her that she would never hear, I kept within my soul.

All I can say is that the letter now exists only in my faulty memory. Thanks be to the Father of Lights that she in her fury would have destroyed it for I had seen her destroy other missives that displeased her, tearing with her tiny hands. Though I thought she was tearing at my soul, poor woman.

Her answer came at once, as if she had waited for the time to strike. The missive was four lines, without preamble, without politeness, without even the mercy of formality. It said, and it is burned forever upon my soul, "Sir, neither your family nor your fortune are meet in any way for the connection a marriage with my niece would warrant. Therefore I must ask you to cease your visits to my house. It is most inconvenient for me to forgo your solace for I have much need of it but I have told my own vicar at Hatfield to take your place. Yours in Christ, Lady Joan Barrington."

I have in my life been called heretic, drunkard, thief, liar, whore-monger, madman, gadfly, firebrand in the night, Indian lover, a name which for long gave me the most pride I ever had, traitor, regicide, and more all in the heat of censure of battle or land passion, but only twice have I ever received as an innocent such words written on pond ice that froze my soul. A place within me still sits upon my bed, looking down at the letter, reading no longer, shot in the white of my heart, for unlike words spoke in disputation, these were without malice, or anger, or passion. They were of a duty performed, as cleaning up the mess of a puppy.

I saw myself as one whose place was to provide Christian entertain-ment, to be taken with piety, once a day, like a pill paid for, a lover hired. Because she was of a Puritan lineage, she enjoyed Godliness as her pleasure, but it went not deeper than her once a day, as meet to her as her morning wine, which she sipped with her mouth made small and ladylike.

And I who saw myself for the first time as I had let myself be seen, worshiped with them God Politics and God Entertainment. How often I had heard criticism of a fine sermon as if it were a poem. How I had imitated Bishop Andrewes as if he led me and not my Lord Jesus. How sweet and terrible it was to know this. I froze at first and then melted as ice thrown in the fire with anger which of course I saw as judgement, for after all I had been ordained to judge—and judge—and judge.

So I wrote once again to my lady in a cold fury I took as zeal that I was forced for want of a full gale to make use of a side wind and salute her ladyship by another letter, being for a time shut out myself. What I wrote then, with as always many references from the holy Bible, since it is a fine book to threaten the Puritan rich withal, that her Lord with whom we all deal regardeth not the rich more than the poor, that the Lord owed her no mercy, that she should strive not to turn away from those sharp files of melancholy and duty, which mostly consisted of dictating the way the world around her should go from birth to marriage and even unto death, which to them all was not a miracle of God but a large division of property to which the lady held the reins and chased the world like the Pharaoh after the Jews on my lord Coke's fine tapestry.

I remembered to her that her candle was twinkling and her glass near run and that she had but minutes in the eyes of God to repent and offer a heart softened and trembling, broken and contrite. I trow she had not had such a heart in her bosom since she was born the daughter of the Golden Knight of Hinchingbrook, where she had been fed pride of place with her wetnurse's tit.

XVIII

———————•◆•———————

*Since I have not been altogether a stranger to the learning
of the Egyptians and have trod those foolish paths to
worldly perferment which for Christ's sake I have forsak-
en. Since I know what it is to study, to preach, to be an
elder, to be applauded, and also what it is to tug at the
oar, to dig with the spade and to labor and travel day and
night amongst the English and barbarians, why should I
not be humbly bold to give my witness faithfully, to give
my council effectually and to persuade the same truly pious
and consciencious spirits to turn to law, to physic to sol-
diery to education of children, to digging and yet not cease
from profesying, rather than live under the slavery yes and
censure of Christ Jesus and his saints and others also, of
the mercenary and hireling ministry.*

— ROGER WILLIAMS

OH FATHER OF LIGHTS IF WE COULD ONLY CUT OFF
memory without pain when there is an ending but alas, we cannot, and
so this fine and brutal morning I am demanded to go the whole hog,
as I always have of remembering shame and loss. Why can I not be here
and now for the lovely part is gone and my triumphant words are gone
as if a rain or tears had washed them away.

At first I thanked God that I had taken the blow from the old lady
so well, and was even, from time to time, without despair. What I took
as manliness was my soul frozen with the shock of blind casual life, its

stunning cruelty, cruelty that had come without thought and without stint, only as a way of getting rid of petty annoyances. As to swat a fly that presumed to interfere with holy thoughts at the right time.

I prayed much but shut not my mind and my mouth long enough to hear the Father of Lights. But as for the world I kept what had happened within me, and rode sometimes in such pain that my chest hurt from the heaving of my heart. I saw myself then diminished to a puppet, an entertainment that the reformed ladies allowed themselves, light wine at ten and talk of Christ at eleven, so long as it interfered not with the rhythm of their ways of living and who they were and what they were and who I was and what I was, an upper servant who was hired to keep the souls as the under butler had been hired to keep the silver counted and polished. No child of God, but servant to the rich, the newly rich who teetered in their county places. I had had no hint of this before in my life since I walked within my lord's chambers at Sergeant's Inn, a boy who knew not of these things, not at least with the whip across the face for getting in the way.

I had, in plain English, presumed above a station I did not know was my allotted place in the little world of Otes and Hatfield Broadoak in Essex in England. God my witness, Sir William, son-in-law and on the rise himself, suspected my hurt for he saw to it that I met and was a part of all the more and more private and dangerous discussions with those who came to Otes.

One of them who would be a friend, I would love, I would hope for until his death, was the lawyer John Winthrop, who for twenty years had had a place in the Court of Wards where he had helped Jug, Lady Elizabeth's daughter by her first marriage. She had had trouble with her inheritance and that was a barrier to her marriage for who would want a woman no matter how wellborn, with the burden of the Chancery Court on her pretty back?

Even if she was gentry, which was two steps below younger sons, which was two steps below nobility which was two steps in a long line below count, below earl, below duke, below king and must needs keep a marital foot on the great golden ladder they had replaced Jacob's ladder withal. I told myself that knowing all this so sudden as a shower of snow down my poor back should never throw me into the sin of bitterness, though irony I excused as a weakness, not a sin.

A boy's broken heart shows to those who watch and Sir William was a sensitive man, though trapped as son-in-law. He and my lady did what they could to assuage my dispair. They were embarrassed and ashamed for they had backed my cause with much affection. It was then that I am sure Sir William began to see that the meetings of the eighteen relatives who would later sit in the Long Parliament, and their friends in the county party, took place at Otes and that I was always part of them.

He would call to me as he sat sometimes in his little hall, away from the family, and smoked and drank his port and rambled about the most important days of his life, or so he said, that sweet country man with his country manners and his country duties and troubles and language for he was more at home with animals than men. It was more meet for him as he saw it to care about the growth of corn than even the fine horses he raised to suit his picture of himself, the necessaries of country gentry. He too laid his hand to the plow to plow the first straight furrow, and his strong arm to the scythe to cut the first harvest. He ever loved the country and I think often in later life he envied me, for he had a simple picture of a free and easy life in the new world, and thought it was all leave behind and start again, which God of Lights knows is a delusion if ever there was one.

When he heard of the meeting at Sempringham, the seat of the Earl of Warwick, about business plans to found a commercial colony in the new world, he insisted that I go, and he wrote to John Winthrop of my coming. He explained to me, believing it, that they planned to combine money and piety, to make a success of a new Zion where reformed gentry could live without persecution, but with their servants of course.

I remember well the first time I ever saw the elder John Winthrop at Otes. He was to be my friend, beloved mentor for some years. He was a tall man, with a long thin nose, and a bitter way about his mouth, and I read that as his disappointment at being singled out by the Laud party. For after many years, comfortable as a country squire, and appointed to the Court of Wards and Liveries, an honorable and much preferred position, he had been set aside without cause. It was not only the reformed ministry itself that Laud had listed in his black book, but anyone suspected of being a fellow traveler on the road to

Parliamentary power. No one was safe from the devious tendrils that
stretched from Lambeth, across the river to the king at Whitehall, and
all the way to the victim of the day. Often no one knew why but that
the archbishop had followed a string of fact and rumor so tenuous
sometimes that it seemed to be only a pencil line of legend and gossip,
to some such a man as John Winthrop, who was very much of the county party.

There was relief to get away from the sadness within me at Otes and
go with the leaders of the reform ariding to Sempringham to meet with
others of our party, for it was indeed a party, as a political party, jock-
eying for the rail of power, but all, of course spoke in terms of Old and
New Testament.

I was more than honored to ride along beside the beloved and
besieged Thomas Hooker, one of the most famous of the reformed
divines, and one I loved all his life since. We were welcomed along the
way by a Visible Saint among the reformed church, John Cotton. Sir
William had done his work well, for I was taken as seriously as if I had
indeed become one of the voices for reform, to be listened to and honored. Pride replaced the wound of loss of pride in love, and so I trotted
and walked and jogged and prated alongside the leading lights of the
reform movement, telling them my most dangerous thoughts about
the mass book and so on and so on, but all still within the fold of the
Church of England, whose holy head, King James, had compared himself to Christ when he said, "Christ had His John and I have my
George." I cannot believe all this was took seriously, could not then,
cannot now, and wait for God's laughter, though it took the lives of
thousands on thousands.

I was listened to, and even had the honor of being argued with by
Mr. Cotton who informed me in one of those kind fat voices of surety
that he too had questions about set prayer in the mass book, the high
church's name for the Book of Common Prayer, and so he chose the
prayers he felt most suited for his parish. This was in his carriage where
the three of us rode the last few miles to Sempringham, since Master
Cotton liked not to ride ahorseback. So Master Cotton napped and
argued and napped again as we theological three clip-clopped our way
to Sempringham to discuss the business of a migration to New England, to set up a pure colony for the Saints beyond the whip of Bishop

Laud and to make money for the company in England that would back the project.

Beloved Thomas Hooker. When Master Cotton was so sweetly condescending, that dear man caught the tone as well as I, so during one of Master Cotton's naps, he softened it by saying, "Keep on thinking," and then, in a whisper, "Quis dubitas?" What do you doubt? I had found a friend to speak with without stint. I will never go back on my confession to Thomas Hooker, that true and almost only saint, that I was to know among the Visible Saints.

I who had not put it into words, even to myself, found myself whispering to that good man, "I think, but I am not ready to aver for averment closes the door of the mind."

He nodded, and whispered, "I have been there by God's heart and bowels, I have been there."

Still I could not speak, and when I did, I was surprised at what had stuck in my young and foolish craw. "We belong to the rich and the crown and not to God," I whispered, and it made the tears spurt from my eyes to say it.

Mr. Cotton moved and snorted and Thomas Hooker whispered, "We will talk of this at Sempringham. Now we must pray together," and so, quite silently, we gave ourselves together up to the Father of Lights and through it I heard the stones of the country road turning and turning. I think I drifted from prayer to dozing for the change among the stones to smooth oyster shells under the carriage woke me, and Master Hooker smiled.

Six years later we took up the confession where we had left off as we walked in the garden at Sempringham, in a far place I had not thought then ever to see. So all the years of disputation with Master Cotton and all the years of agreeing and not agreeing, blowing hot and cold with Master Hooker, began that morning in a carriage on the way to the Earl of Warwick's country seat.

A fountain brought plashes and veils of water to the window of the carriage. Two nymphs stood in marble at the foot of the great stairs, for there must ever be nymphs and satyrs at such houses, as if they laughed at any holy endeavor within and called for no endeavor at all without in the garden and among the treaded grapes.

Project. For most of them it was that, and they spoke business, having prayed together, all but two, myself and young John Winthrop, who had been brought there by his father. We walked often in the garden and talked of our dreams and hopes, mostly I remember to stay in England and fight. He above all but my sweet Harry Vane would be my dear beloved friend for life. Oh Father of Lights how I miss them.

It was almost a family meeting to plan for the greatest enterprise yet thought of for New England. Lord Saye and Seal was akin to the earl and various others of the meeting were introduced as cousin, cousin german, distant cousin, and on and on. It was at Sempringham, as he stood behind the heavy oaken library table where we had our meeting, that John Winthrop, that man of incredible tenacity and courage, placed his hands carefully upon the Turkey carpet covering the table which I had been staring at while they talked beyond my ken about money, and made his announcement.

He, a squire, a man of money and land and position, had decided to pull up stakes and go off to the wilderness. Not yet Thomas Hooker nor John Cotton, but he John Winthrop, took the first step. This was no capricious religious Roman Candle as I was oft accused of, but a solid, sensible, profit-planning decision. He laid out plans before us without papers, for he had thought much of it. His voice faded for me behind statistics, number of artisans, number of servants, horses, cattle, people, money, supplies needed for the plan. It was a brave and holy step into God's unknown for the right to worship without fear, make a thriving city of corn fields, and, here that bitter man smiled, an apple orchard. John Winthrop was carrying his bitterness and his wisdom, for he had much of that, all the way across three thousand miles of ocean so, as he said, he could breathe.

I had never until that moment known what bravery the times were calling forth. It was no less than to step from the comfort of years, by a middle-aged man of parts and means, across two or three months of sea in a cockle shell to make a city. It sounded like the travels of the nomads from Asia, who went west to seek grass for their herds and found a civilized world and conquered it. A chill ran down my spine and I wondered at illness for it was very strong, but it was cold recognition at what these men, some in their fifties, in their earned comfort, were proposing to do. They were of all shapes and sizes, it seemed to me, gentry and nobility, for Lord Saye and Seal's son, Mr. Johnson, and his wife, Lady Arabella, planned to go. There were merchants, and ministers, who glowed with plans of a new Zion. Some other faces I recognized from Parliament and the county party, some from court, and some from Star Chamber, but all under the heavy weight of Laud.

John Winthrop singled me out as a friend and introduced me to the company as the ward of Sir Edward Coke. He spoke to me of what my lord Coke had told him, thundered rather.

"Oh yes, he thundered for I wished his opinion on our movement, and he said, roared, 'Separation from the church is against the law. So long as you stay within the law you can think as you like, for it is also the law of England that no man can be prosecuted for his private opinions unless they cause riot.'"

"We will stay officially within the Church of England," John Winthrop said later to the assembly and I could hear a distant roar from my much loved Sir Edward. "We seek freedom, not discord," and he repeated all that Sir Edward had said to him word for word as if it were his very own, but lawyers do that. It is a part of their training.

Then having dealt with the church and freedom they got down to the business of planning how many masons, how many carpenters, how many servants, how many cattle, how many horses, and above all how much money. I lost much of it in dreaming, for I had much to dream of, but woke myself to be cordial and polite when one by one they came to me, and flattered me with hopes that I would join them. It was so far from my mind then.

There were long discursive dinners, and plans spilled along the table. One, I think Master Pym, was asked not to down the flying thoughts, for he was ever warning of disaster. So good wine and thoughts flowed and there was even some merriment, decorous for ones facing weighty matters. Financially, when they cleared the great refectory table and got down to business, they had a plan to raise two thousand pounds at first to begin their enterprise. I remember that it was there that they, someone, I know not who, thought it meet to call the flagship of the fleet, for there was to be a fleet, the *Arabella*, in honor of the lady who was the sister of the Earl of Warwick who was the son of . . . my attention flagged as it always did when they began to talk of bloodlines and connections.

On the way back from Sempringham, Mr. Cotton and Thomas

Hooker talked much. They thought to stay in England until the first work was done, unless of course they fell to Bishop Laud. Thomas Hooker had already been singled out, but Laud's advisors had told him to tread carefully for Hooker was much beloved, and also Cotton, who was much honored, and that, as I think of it, was the difference between them.

I sat in the corner of the carriage and then picked up Chloe at Master Cotton's stable. Thomas Hooker and I rode back to Essex together. It was a quiet happy time. I have much loved the man even with our disagreements, and I kept quiet about them. They were growing as a gross unwelcomed picture in my soul.

Where there is schism it is like a wide deep sore upon the belly of the land, but I thought in lesser, smaller terms than that. What grew within me and would not be stopped was that both sides faced each other with an abyss between, in hatred they called Christian love. They grew for me into mirror images of one another, but I did not yet know why, and tried to put the thought from my mind as I listened to that dear man's voice and hoped against my hope that he would guide me out of an unknown that threatened to engulf me.

How could any man think, for I saw myself a man, champing at my bit, that so pure a man as John Cotton, or the great Ames, both reformed divines who had had the honor of being barred from Cambridge, or even God help me, Calvin himself, could mirror the overcertain face of pinched little Bishop Laud? I was teetering on the edge of the dark abyss that was widening beyond understanding, faith, or compromise between them.

XIX

—◆—

So rid ourselves of all the beliefs that protect against the abyss, and yet be of good cheer so as not to alarm the others before God readies them for their nakedness.

— ATTRIB: ROGER WILLIAMS

J COULD NOT WAIT TO GET BACK TO OTES AND NURSE my pain. Jane was everywhere, and I even had dumb hopes that I had been mistaken, that Lady Joan meant it not, that she was the holy wise woman they all told her she was, but all the time I knew it was not so. So I floated about like the lover with a posie in his hand in the raree show at Bartholomew Fair, watched by all though I knew it not.

One night I faced the truth and began again to pray, this time by God's grace, in silence and not troubling the Almighty with ceaseless jabber. Hatred and despair dripped from my soul like vomit. I had stored up anger for so long without notice; I had chewed what was expected of me without question and swallowed without tasting and I saw my sin as a lash across my face, and worse than sin, my foolishness. I begged upon my knees, with an offering of the tears that finally ran at my cold lonely loss, that God would enlighten and enliven me about the tradition of the fathers or the favor of custom of any men or any times I found upon the path ahead. I prayed to give me leave to learn how to welcome the wounds that must come from the holy scalpel that cuts us bleeding from the stone that is our prison like the slaves of Michelangelo, to rejoice more in these than ever again in the deceitful kisses of soul-killing and soul-deceiving friends.

I fell into my own tears as one as overburdened as an overworked ox. If I sank in time I knew it not. If I spoke I knew that not. Once when I was a boy I went into a cave for I was always questioning and I wanted to find out how dark darkness could be. So I climbed within until the room of rock was lit only by my candle. I blew the candle out. A weighty shroud of blackness pressed me, and I fought to light the flint and escape it. But I cannot compare it to the blackness I entered in that room or to anything before or after or in the world. It was a chasm where I sank deeper and deeper with some notion so primitive it was a hunger to get to the bottom, get to the bottom of things, what things I knew not, for there were no things there, no dark as anything, though sometimes since I have glimpsed a darkness of soul that only reflects the place where I was.

Then one day I knew the bottom and could have stayed there forever, a damned and bitter cynic at the world. It lasted eons and a minute, an hour, a day. It was outside of time. It was not. Nihil. Nothing. Even remembering in words is false.

But time came after time. There had been a time when I had fallen to the floor of my room and had sunk into that chasm of darkness. Time began again when the feet of my soul touched steady and I stood, aware at first that I was more lost than I have ever known. I was stripped naked of knowledge as a newborn babe. All was gone from me, all of the will of God was in that darkness. It was the ladder I fell from. I see it now, the ladder I had once seen at my parents their table, with the king atop it, the old king learned in patches and drooling in streams. I saw my ambition, corrupted from God's grace as any other ambition for court or money or land or human love.

ALL MY PROUD past lay about me in the dark in shreds, broken and tattered around my bare feet. I had let myself be fooled. I could only wait there in my soul, in that dark night. I waited. And seemed to wait forever and then they began to visit me, as to pick up what was useful from the tatters at my feet. And there was at first the little wavering beam of candlelight of one coming nearer from some faraway tunnel. It was my lovely Bartholomew, and I said to him, "I thought you were dead."

He laughed, that laugh I remember as a child, as if his death had been only a door and not that funeral pyre. He helped me cover my nakedness with a garment of light for those who came to see me there, finding their way through corridors of hopeless black to help to guide me out. Some I had never seen, some I had forgot, but all of them in common held for me the memory that they had sometime someplace smiled with love upon me for a minute, a day, the length of a true friendship, and each of them brought more light, dear Frances with her tangled curls and her impious smile, Bess the young whore, and old Nathan and my brother Sydrach, and others I did not know, for my eyes were dazzled and I could see only their forms against it. There was laughter. There is always laughter and dancing at a birth or should be. The miracle.

After the vision or the dream or the reality faded, I was conscious from time to time that someone, she, my dear, reached in and touched me and with that touch made the dark of the cave into light. When I opened my eyes I was not upon the floor where I had fallen in that few minutes of my despair, but upon my bed, and her hands were washing my face with a cool wet rag. It was Jane, my beloved.

It was not Jane, but Mary Barnard, sent to tend to me, and when she saw my eyes were opened she grinned and said, "Well 'tis about time my dear," and laughed but the tears were coursing down her face. "O my holy bowels of Christ and the Lord God you have near died my coney. The sight of the fool who has been took and found it out is a sorry sight."

"Was she here?" was the first thing I asked.

"Now be not so silly," she said, and she patted my cheek with a little slap. "Thee must be done with that nonsense. Better the hands of a friend than the kiss of a fool," she said, plumping the pillow and hiding her face in it.

"No fool," I muttered.

She looked over the pillow. "It is time thee woke. Thee hast talked enough nonsense."

She busied herself womanly about the room, brushed my little library of books five or more times and hid her face from me. When she did turn at last she was full of gossip. "They have done found a husband for Jug at last," she said, "one that suits all around. Money, not much, but he has been in the Tower for his politics, so that is a fine recommendation hereabouts. He is, they say, on his way up."

I thought of the ladder and how I had fell from it, and thanked my Christ that I had, for her gossip that before my fall to the floor would have meant much, meant nothing to me. I had dropped the burden or it had been cut from my shoulders. It was gone and it seemed already to be only an amusement and an entertainment, as one watches lambs gamboling in a field, or the solemn imperious billy goat chewing his cud.

I smiled and then, God my witness, laughed and she as rosy with joy as a babe ran from the room in tears. She brought back my lord, my lady, Jug, and Oliver St. John, that fine man who I know now carried his fate already in his face. They knelt around the cot, to my embarrassment, and thanked God for my life, and it was all devoted and kind, but for one who had simply passed out on the floor and been put to bed by a dear girl, it seemed to me to be excessive.

But when I asked how many hours I had been passed out, they all talked together that I had been as they said at death's door for two weeks with a burning fever. After they had trooped out, Mary told me that I had spoke much while she tended me, but what I had spoke she remembered not, and then she grinned and I knew she would never tell me.

"That's done past and gone," was all she said, and she went from the room again to make a hot posset for me and left me alone. I knew where I had been. I had been wandering in what the Papists called the dark night of the soul, and I had been led from it by the celestial color of a fine jewel, a color that was light itself. A deep and brilliant blue. They called the passage of my sick soul a burning fever but I knew then that my Lord Jesus and my God had led me into a new birth, a new hope, a new chance, and relieved me of the burdens I thought were priviledge.

What it was I knew not then, but I looked at the fine books, the Vulgate, the King James that had turned the world upside down, the Hebrew text, all that I had studied and not studied, had learned and not learned at Cambridge, and I knew that from that morning on, for I saw that it was indeed morning outside my window, I must search within those texts to find where I had been, was going, though it took my life long.

I knew too that as with Jacob I could say Peniel. I had seen the face of God and lived.

Jane's lithe self where I had learned how to love another lay like that hidden blue and glistening jewel within my bosom to take upon my journey and lighten the way. I thought of Plato and his love of one and then the love of all fair forms, and smiled into the morning and my new and lovely cell.

When Mary came with the posset she saw that I drank it while it was hot, as one does for the sick, making the little unthought words, "Now let us see the bottom of the cup," as to a child.

Before God she treated me so as she helped me back to health for my legs were as wobbly as a new calf and sometimes I bawled like one, unable to stop myself, as she held my arm and walked me in the garden and spoke seldom as if she knew I had to be alone within myself.

But when she did speak she told me of herself and how she had growed with four fine brothers she cared for, their mother being dead God rest her soul, she said that as all one word deadgodresthersoul, and it delighted me. The way she said it. The way she was. She told of her father and how he had wrote books himself that earned him much-needed money for he was afeared that he would lose his living to Laud though his bishop was BishopWilliamsgodblesshissoul.

When I spoke of Jane at last Mary said, downright and in plain English, that she had thought much of it. Her father had told her that the most perfect knight who ever loved a lady from afar and wore her colors and won many a tournament so she could be the Queen of Love and Beauty, had a wife and eight children.

"For," she told me, "there is a saying that you know for everyone does that if you marry for love you have good nights and bad days." She blushed, not the brush of rose as with Jane, but a fine suffusion of red.

"Now I know this for I took my mother's place and raised and comforted and nursed all my brothers and my dear father who had not sense enough to come in when it rained for he would wander and think too deep to pay attention. So I know much of what daily marriage is and that is love too, and grows and is solid. These ladies like Jug and Jane want waiting on, and can do nothing but sew a fine seam and quote the Bible. They will need servants and cosseting too much in the sweats and stews of childbirth." She spoke of childbirth without shame as if it were a thing that happened every day.

"I midwifed by the time I was twelve in my father's parish for the poor need help too. All women do, if it is only a soft hand upon their forehead while they groan and scream. Why think you that men are not allowed near the birthing stool? They are not to be trusted not to carry on worse than the women theirselves," and she laughed so hearty at letting me into women's secrets that I caught it and laughed with her, which made her stop and punch my arm and say, "Get along, you know not why you laugh."

But I did know I was plain downright in plain English, too, as happy to be with her at that moment as I had ever been with anybody in my life. Thanks be to God that happiness grew into another kind of love until we knew we would marry but kept it to ourselves lest those who were our friends at Otes think me frivolous to change so quickly from one wench to another, like a bouncing tennis ball, as she put it, not I.

We had six children, not eight as the pure and perfect knight gave his wife, and before God I have known well the pains of the birthing stool and how brave she was amid the filth and bloody effusion that brought a new and squalling child into a wilderness with no fine mid-wife nearer than an hundred miles astraddle of a donkey.

She has and does look after us all as she learned of four brothers and pa who had not sense enough to come in out of the rain when he was thinking. Often she says I remind her of him. "Mooning more like," she adds, and smiles that lovely wise smile of hers, sometimes shy, sometimes as bawdy as a fishwife.

Not a soul ever knew but my dear one sent as an angel to me in my need how far into the dark I fell.

XX

———◆–◆–◆———

Let none now think that the passage to New England by
sea, nor the nature of the country, can do what only the
key of David can do—to wit, open and shut the consciences
of men.

— ROGER WILLIAMS

MARY AND I WERE GIVEN AS SWEET A WINTER
wedding as Otes could provide, in love and garlands, wine, posies, gifts
of silver, blankets, as if we were going on a long voyage instead of back
up the stairs to my room, for our nuptial night was up four flights of
stairs where we found our main wedding present. It sat there all splendid, a fine carved oak matrimonial bed, with feather beds to drown us.
We slept in that bed until the burning, forty-six years.

The household gave us a fine feast, for weddings are for the company more than the bride and groom. Mary's father and brothers came
from Worksop, from the west country, from all about and we had much
pleasure together drinking good wine from Sir William's cellar, and
answering much toasting. Sir William proposed a toast to one of the
brightest stars among the rising generation of clergy, and there were
cheers and table thumping and all and Mary beamed as if I were her
baby.

To say what Mary's father was like, I need only to remember what
he named his sons—Besekiel, Hoseel, Masakiel, and Cannavel, and for
my soul in years of idle and curious researching I never found the
source, not in Leviticus or in any other, even Gilgamesh. He was called

Reverend Richard by his children with a little chiding and amusement. They loved him without respect.

He considered himself a leading light among the literary reformers who were pouring out secret tracts like rain upon a parched land. He wrote and wrote, straight down the middle aisle of the Church of England, a conformable reformer who used enough ceremony to keep Bishop Laud from clawing his back. Even so in those days any anonymous writing was a brave thing to do, for the punishment if and when the authors were found ranged already from prison, to branding on the cheek with the letter H for heretic, cropping of ears, ruinous fines, and hours in the stocks with the apprentices, the drunkards, and the rapscallions throwing dung and garbage.

One of his books, *The Isle of Man,* was well-known enough to give him his sweet and innocent airs. I grew to love him in that year of knowing him, as one loves a precocious and tender child. He was, when we married, sixty-one years old. When at last I read his book I saw that he had sought erudition and found obscurity and resolved never to do it myself, but alas I have been told all the rest of my life that I have not succeeded.

He gave me as much advice as he could cram within the festivities, and he had a habit of repeating everything twice to give solemnity to his pronouncements, as when innocently I broached him with what he thought of separation, and he said, "Oh dear young man, I went through that in my youth as well. One outgrows it. One outgrows it. Church of England. Church of England is our shelter, though a leaking one these days. But not schism. Not schism." He turned again to me as he began to make his way toward the notice of Sir William, "Not schism, my son." For the rest he chased after Sir William, and Sir Thomas Barrington and all as nimble as a courtier in the days of my youth.

Mary and I were happy at Otes. She stayed companion to Jug Altham, and Sir William stressed his own version of equality, inviting my pleasure to learn to use a pitchfork and guide a plow thanks be to God. He said it was good for my health. He listened to my maunderings as gospel when I knew not myself what I was saying.

Gradually I began to sink into the dailiness of being handed along like wampum on a string from comfort to comfort, but all, alas, other people's hopes for the protection they expected to grant me as one "coming along," assured as ever of a place sometime. But in that spring and into summer what was growing within my soul took all my passion and love, and it included my dear Mary. I was without much thought of preferments and such for the first time since I had walked into Sir Edward Coke's chambers in the Temple, a scared and skinny boy.

Jug and Oliver St. John were married in the early summer. Their wedding was vast; a meeting of the most important reformers of the eastern counties, Sempringham three times over: Barringtons, Cromwells and Whalleys, Wallers, and Hampdens, enough to form a list of who would lead the Long Parliament and fight the war on the horizon.

John Winthrop was not there for he had sailed aboard the *Arabella,* flagship of the largest flotilla to go toward New England. I spoke with one wedding guest who had invested in the colony. He said it was a business enterprise and if John Winthrop wished it to be soul searching and God loving piddling about in the wilderness, well, as he put it to me, 'twas his own damned business, though he added, "I am sorry for him to let bitterness overwhelm him so that he in his middle age goes bounding off like a puppy, nobody to talk to, drink with, or hunt with." And he wandered off, his wedding wineglass in his hand.

For the rest St. John was the hero of the hour. He was much petted by the leaders of the county party; they had chosen him for a safe seat if Parliament ever was called again. From hearing this I was prejudiced against him; for me such a man was only a power-driven politician in a different coat.

But during the time of his formal courtship we became fast friends, and by the Father of Lights who would ever have known then that he would sit in the seat of power in England when I needed his help most. Thomas Hooker was not at the wedding for he had been chased into Holland as a refugee by Bishop Laud, but in the vast tangle of kinships, the family made a powerful county party of power of its own.

I see them now in a formal garden. They stand in twos and threes, and they are earnest together although it is a wedding. There is, for once, some color in their attire especially among the ladies. It is hard to be one of those known derisively as Puritans, when your eyes and soul yearn for color and jewels as it was before you became a symbol. Jug was demure as she had been taught, and looked a pretty child although she was old for marriage and quite homely though rich.

I am unfair to her. She was a good wife to St. John, not as Mary was to me, but good withal. She gave him four children, set a fine table, paid for his politics, and sent him on his way each day with a heartfelt blessing that her search for a husband who suited everybody was over. She even died at the right time for him, at the beginning of the Long Parliament, when his mind was alight with politics and he had not yet tired of her. Mary truly loved her. Jug had humor and kindness and she never treated her with the mixture of condescension and old clothes that a companion was oft subjected to, especially one from a clergy family.

For the rest, I remember that first year of our marriage in small scenes, some as still as drawings. I see us at morning prayers, all ranked, all kneeling, and instead of starting the prayer they expected that they could say while they were free to think of other things, I said, "Let us pray in silence and without words, for each of us can listen to the still small voice of God who spoke unto Elijah, and each of us can repent in our own words in our own thoughts and to our own joy."

I waited until first the maids and then the gardeners and then the rest began to move and scratch. I said a loud AMEN. Ahh Menn. And those who had nearly fell to dozing jumped within their skin. Then I blessed and dismissed them to their daily work as I always had.

Well. At least it was a beginning.

But later in the morning Sir William called me in and, embarrassed and apologetic, he began to point out to me what he called his duty. "We are," he said, "of the established church under the king, although as the wing of reform we do stand against the bishops, especially Bishop Laud, but I doubt . . ." Every word was unnecessary and we both knew it. He grew red in the face and I knew already that his wife, who was a godly sweet soul but close tied to the learned rightness of living by the day, and probably his mother-in-law had been on his trail. I went back then to the morning prayer as it was put within the mass book for I was his employee, although he ever and all the rest of his life made me his loving friend, that dear lumbering man.

But rumor flies and lights on ready ears as always and within a month I received the second letter I ever got from my lord. He told me that he had heard that I was showing signs of treachery, all based, I gathered, on a little silent prayer on a weekday morning. Laud's spies were everywhere; the least and simplest gesture was noted and punished. My lord wrote, "The established church is the law of the land and if you leave it or break its Articles which you signed freely when you left Cambridge you have committed treason. When you have come to your senses and are back upon the true path of your life as a responsible citizen, come to me and tell me. Until then we must sever relations, for I am ever a lover of the law." And then he put at the end of the letter as if he could not withhold it, "You will know that I have fulfilled my purpose in seeing the Bill of Rights passed into law and must now work on finishing my Reports and my Commentaries for it is what I leave to the future. I miss you, my dear. I wish you were helping me as ever."

I clasped the letter to my heart, yes, clasped it to my heart as if I expected my heart to read it for itself and made it up the stairs and to Mary's and my room before a sob rose to sound. I lay upon our bed and sobbed to the Father of Lights, I could think only of the words of Luther, "I can do no other."

I needed as a man needs water someone to talk with. It was Mary as it has been ever since. Mary hates still what her father stood for, though she has said no word against him ever. She rails at what she calls holy toadies who hang about the rich estates for their livings and their patronage and are invited to dinner once a year as a duty, and give a bonus at New Year's. It had humiliated her, for who ever knows as the children play in the great gardens, while their father bows to the king of whatever small domain they play in, how much hurt, even in the choosing of sides or catching in blind man's buff, how oft and with such brutal innocence, choices are made.

It was Mary who found me there asobbing and picked up the letter which she could not read, and said, "Get up and read this to me." A command.

When I did she said, "I know you see him as the king of the cats, poor old man. He is too old to change and you love him, is that not enough? Leave off thy arguments and prolixities and the bathing of thy face with tears. Oh men! Thou will never persuade him to love thy choices." She had used all the words I needed then, love, choice, poor. I saw him still under the never closing eye of the absolute state, still protecting me the only way he could, to denounce me, for when I left off grieving I had no doubt that he had seen that the letter was read by spies before he sent it. I could see him leave it on the damask of a table, or a chair, or the floor, no not the floor for there ever was a puppy or an old dog at his feet.

Later, in his chamber, Sir William bore it out, that the old man was under an unofficial house arrest, "though, thank God," Sir William said, "it is in his own house and unofficial which means he will not be bothered though his writings may be sequestered." Indeed that was so, for it was told me later that while he was dying in the great bed with its cloth of silver hangings, the king's men below were packing his hand-wrote life's work into carts.

AND OF CARTS, I see one hay cart, the largest at Otes for all of our belongings and gifts and tender memorials, our medicine, our copper still for strong water, shovels, pitchforks, a plow, a harrow, seed for planting, books, clothes, bolts of cloth, a huge cheese, a haunch of venison, cackling chickens in a cage who never ceased complaining for two hundred miles, nay, for over three thousand, for they could be heard over the wild wind of the north Atlantic.

We had been warned to provide any food beyond ship's fare, which was poor. There were hampers of bread and dry biscuit and dried fruit, oranges from Spain, a tun of strong waters, one of wine, lime juice, a tub of butter, conserves with the names on the bottles of who had made them, from Lady Elizabeth, to Jug, all the way to the little maid whose father had offered her healthy bottom to me. Everything in the cart, crowned by two chairs and the fine bed, was a tie to Otes for years for us. All of these things are in my soul being loaded and Mary stands beside it to see they do right.

I stood at the long graceful window of Sir William's chamber. He held on to my hand as if he would not let me go, and we shared tears. He had handed me a leathern pocket with an hundred pounds within and I knew not what to say. It was ransom, to me, for a prince.

It had been gathered by Sir William and his brother-in-law, Sir

Thomas Barrington, and many of the rest of the family who were part of a secret group to protect Godly ministers who agreed with them as to the way of Christ and the Parliament's work, one so entangled in the other that they spoke of them together always. I had been part of that hiding of what they termed the deserving, talented, and the educated in private houses and estates as tutors and chaplains to protect them from Laud until they saw the time ripe for true reform.

But the cat had tracked the mouse. The choice once again was slipped from my own self. The pros and cons and decisions Mary and I had dreamed of in our own private chamber were a bit of field chaff blown by the wind, no more. Bishop Laud had chosen to seek his enemies among the gentry, many of whom were rich, and God knows the king needed money. The little bishop was simply plugging up another rat-hole in his holy ecclesiastical barn.

So, in the fall of that year's leaves, for it had been a cold summer where we were, I think the last truly summer day had been Jug's wedding, word came that Laud was levying heavy fines on all reformers with large estates if they hid ministers in their homes. Laud knew us all. He had spent years making lists. He was a maker of lists and a keeper of books, a man full of zeal and hate he called his holy duty. So the choice for us was Holland or the new Zion, and we chose the new England. Or we were, as I said to Mary, summoned by the Lord of Hosts and prodded by the Lords of State.

The cart was ready with Jethro, the huge farm stallion, at the traces, for Sir William had refused to let us go without a draft animal. He said he was damned if he would think of Chloe in the traces of a plow. Mary and I set out, with Chloe, a cow in milk, and a bull calf tied to the back of the cart. We could not see them, for the cart was piled so high with needs, or what the whole household decided were needs in a wilderness none of us had ever seen. I hear yet the fine clatter of Chloe's hooves and the plod of the cattle behind us.

We looked back, always back, all the way down the oyster-shell carriageway of Otes, under the shade trees to the main roadway. It was as if we were still and they receding, smaller and smaller until one of the tiny figures turned to go within and the others followed after and we were alone, adrift on the cold November highway.

It was over two hundred slow, weary miles to Bristol, the most west-

ern Atlantic ocean port, for the Channel was ever open to the Dunkirk-
er pirates and the weather at that time of the year. England was gray,
gray sky, gray land, and the rain filtered down through it, not a fine
feeding rain but a dribble dribble that sought out our necks and our
napes. I can rightly say that in that late November into early December, for it took two weeks to reach Bristol, and we plodded on, we were
as unhappy together and separately for the first time since our sheltered
protected marriage, as we had ever been. It was touch and go if it
would bring us closer or drive us apart into that silence where so much
marriage exists. Thanks be to God it brought us nearer to each other's
heart.

When we passed Windsor way along the road where we could see
the spires of Stoke House where my lord was, it was as bitter as death
to me that I dared not stop and ask his blessing and acquaint him with
my conscience and my flight. He would not approve. He would not.
But neither would he withhold his blessing, putting himself into the
place of God's judgement.

I was blinded by tears. Mary took the reins in one hand and held me
close with the other while I leaned into her and sobbed. Never in all
the time I had known and loved my lord did I realize with my whole
soul that it was he who for the first time in my life had accepted, loved,
nurtured my natural inclination to study my beloved ancient and new
arts and languages and to act on my conscience though it was leading
me on paths he did not take.

When we said farewell to Mary's father, that dear and addlepated
man, it was her turn to sob and me to comfort, driving with one hand
and holding her with the other. Oh we must have been a fine sight,
pining and sorrowing together all the width of England. For it was not
only the incessant rain that year but the tears of all of us who were leaving home that damped the fires of courage. It was as if all England,
men and women, were crying their ways to the wilderness.

As we neared Bristol the road became ever more crowded and we
part of a long parade out of England. I saw us as the despised and
rejected as Jesus had been. For some reason I cannot fathom I began to
laugh for the first time since leaving Otes. Mary caught it like a new
sweetness and there we were giggling together not knowing or caring

why as we trundled on toward the busiest port in those days in all of England.

I know now why we laughed so. It was relief. The wonderful weightless ease of being noplace. All the chains of love and hate and failure and hopelessness dropped from my shoulders. I was, for that twinge of time, completely free, neither yesterday nor tomorrow to fear or remember. I was entering the totally unknown as a door. I had never been to sea before, never faced until that moment that the future is always unknown, and I sensed that all the long procession of people we went along the road with, slowly, for there were many chairs, tumbrels, farm carts, laden mules and donkeys, some carriages whose drivers seemed to fill the need to get to noplace before we did, and used the whip to show they were not of our motley crowd. The condescension of the shires had followed us all the way to Bristol.

We knew not where to go. So stopped at the top of the Clifton hill road that went down into the town and waited for the Father of Lights to guide us. I heard a voice call, "Roger! My dear Roger!"

The angel was John Winthrop, Jr., lounging on a stone fence eating an apple, his horse tethered beside him. We waded toward each other through the near roadblock of humans, horses, bray of mules, lowing of cattle as if Smithfield market itself were going to the new world.

We kissed, Mary too. He said, "I heard thee were going. Oh by God's garters I wish I were but father made me stay here to sell Groton, for he waited to put our place on the market until he inspected the coastal grounds and he says they are wonderful for the start of the new colony." Mary saw our pleasure and said she would stay with the cart while we strolled and spoke, and so we ambled through the crowds.

"And thee here?" I asked him. He said he was seeing to the loading of supplies including more people, for the Massachusetts Bay Company had lost many due to returning and to freezing and to illness and hunger in that first winter. So he had took up residence for a while in Bristol until the company released him to go his own self.

"I cannot abide it here waiting and waiting but it must be God's will for me else I would cut and run," he laughed. "Now you will need lodging and a stable for your goods and chattels. Let us go back and lead Mary to the place I know is safe for there is much thieving here.

Of course there would be after all, for what is this dunghill of people going to the new world but failures, jailbirds, and younger dissolute sons, and ones like you whose tail has been lit by Bishop Laud, and is on fire."

We laughed together for it was a time of such crowds, such new hope, such excitement that we caught it from each other. So we found Mary and John guided us to what we had not known we needed, a safe place to stay until the wind was right. We had thought to go aboard at once.

Late into the night as we sat in a tavern, and Mary was at rest, he told me much that had happened that first year in New England.

"Father writes as joyfully as he can for he does not want to disappoint us after this awful solemn move from home. But I know from those who have returned that the first summer was hot and they were gnat-crazed and had to depend on the company settlers with Endicott at Salem even for their food, for they had ate all on the way, it taking six weeks even in good summer weather. Father wrote us letters we could find pleasure in, for necessity must needs turn into adventure or we could not bear it, the leaving home, the danger.

"That first winter they lost so many to cold, for the tents from the Indians were all most of them had, though some had built log huts to live within and stay before a fire where the smoke was up a mud chimney. I know all this for I have ever been the one who set the emigrants abroad, and who questioned them when some came back, their tails between their legs."

He was so still I thought him some other place and did not call him back. He drank, and set down his tankard, and finally said, "So many died. Lady Arabella within the first month, her lord, Saye and Seal's son, within the year. And of the poor, so many, so many to be replaced with lies and hopes for that is my task, to get them to go there."

We saw each other much in that ten days in Bristol, for we had to wait for the weather and the packing of our goods. We would not have survived without him. He went among the travelers who had not come from too far away, and told them to go home again after they delivered their cargo, and advised them on what to take aboard. Though the five pounds fare included provender, he said that the voyage could last two

ck or half rotten by
the time the ship made port.

"Take cheese," he said as solemnly as if he said, "Take Bible." "Take
cheese and more cheese, and lemons. Forget not lemons, for they keep
away the scurvy. Remember the voyage is long, the way sometimes terrible with storm on storm and you are at its mercy," and then he added,
sadly, "And I would give my life to join you but I must needs stay here
for a longer time in this prison they have made of England for my
father has so ordered."

He had rented a small house at the port and we stayed with him
those ten days. I was more grateful for that than any other gifts he
showered us withal. I feared getting to the new world without money,
for I could not fool myself that the new differed from the old so much
that manna came from heaven as in the days of Moses. Mary was happy
there and made friends with others of the women who were set to go
aboard the *Lyon*. There were only a few for winter was a not a time that
most chose. She tried to comfort them for some were blind with fear of
the voyage.

XXI

———————◆———————

They that go down to the sea in ships, and occupy their business in great waters; These men see the works of the Lord, and his wonders in the deep. For at his word the stormy wind ariseth, which lifteth up the waves thereof. They are carried up to the heaven, and down again to the deep; their soul melteth away because of the trouble. They reel to and fro, and stagger like a drunken man, and are at their wit's end. So when they cry unto the Lord in their trouble, he delivereth them out of their distress. For he maketh the storm to cease, so that the waves thereof are still. Then are they glad, because they are at rest and so he bringeth them into the haven where they would be. O that men would therefore praise the Lord for his goodness; and declare the wonders that he doeth for the children of men! Exalt him also in the congregation of the people, and praise him in the seat of the elders!

— PSALM 107

*I*T IS AT THIS LOW EBB OF THE YEAR WHEN THE world itself seems weary, and there is little sound or light in this far northern day, that I am saddened as I was then for the leaving of home but dared not then or now show the low estate of my soul to Mary for she suffers too, and takes to mentioning ones long dead who sailed with us. Most of the year I forget it, but when the light goes at four of the clock and the forest is dark below the tree ceiling all day long, as

if it were midnight in a great cathedral, and the frost has give sound to
the dead leaves on the floors of the meadows and the woods, and my
soul sighs heavy, it comes back.

That first voyage of the five I would take across a beloved alien sea
was never yet faced by me without that halt of breath within, fear and
excitement and joy together as one. We were swung to and fro among
the vasty waves, dependent on grace for there was naught other that
could sustain us in that terrible and wonderful ocean. There were twenty passengers only for John explained that it was mostly cargo to take
to the new Zion for some were dying of the scurvy there and his father
begged speed when there was no speed and supplies when there was little money and that to be begged from the Bay Company's coffers for
they wanted much for little.

The company had promised a minister for every voyage to give solace and courage to the others. John had decided that Mary and I being
the youngest, and our need being more urgent, should go. He told us
how many we thought true ministers of reform had bowed to Laud's
demands for their families' and livings' sake, so with all the promise of
a new holy land, the hireling ministers were more loath to go than
those poor families who left so little. The voyagers at the other end of
the ever present ladder when we English are gathered together for
whatever cause were some of the county gentry who took to the waters
as an example and lead for the others, and to escape the shires ere the
state fell upon them to ruin. I was counted as one of them, a Cambridge graduate, ergo a gentleman, where the qualities of command
were taken for granted.

Besides John's secondhand but carefully weighed knowledge of the
new Zion, there was much else he told me. He even told me things that
I had said and forgot, some in my prophecies on Sundays at Otes, some
along the road to Sempringham, some at Cambridge.

"There are spies for both heavenly sides among us," he recalled with
a laugh. We were walking abroad among the pinnaces, the wherries,
scows, rafts tied up to the ships, with their loads of goods and needs
and people, so many goats, so many sheep, so many horses, so many
cows, so many farmers, so many masons, so many carpenters, so many
shoemakers . . . John's list went on and on while all about us the bark-
ers for their ships, some still unfilled in winter, were calling out the

promises of massy gold and much tilled land in Virginia and New England, all for the taking. Wherever their ships were going was paradise, as they bawled at the top of their lungs, although they had not been there and were never wont to go, either to America or to heaven. They promised riches, jobs, and hope like vendors at Bartholomew Fair. How much of this brought childhood to mind, for I had heard them there years before, entrancing little boys with the same shouts, when Captain Smith brought Pocahontas to London and I saw her myself in St. Sepulchre's church. I remember that she sat there all in English finery, poor thing, and I wondered if the women scalped the English or only the men.

John said that it was known that Laud was ready to as he called it stop the rat holes of East Anglia, where there were too many stubborn and unrepentant Puritans. Which now included for that passionately narrow man any member of the Church of England who did not agree with whole heart and habit with the new dispensations of lace and surplices and holy vestments and tables for communion set as altars in the right, the Laud place, and grace and not work instead of work and not grace as if they two were not married at the hip and heart and thigh. All of this holy Christian doctrine of love shouted through clenched teeth.

I see finally this late in life that the man was mad with belief in his own power and rightness and thought it God's. Oh, would the Father of Lights give me a questing mind alive, His greatest gift of all, lest I tread upon other souls. Show me question as a part of grace.

It was fifty-three or so many years ago, on the tenth of December, that Mary and I stepped aboard the ship *Lyon,* two hundred tuns, large in the port or seemed so, one hundred feet from stern to bowsprit, like a large commodious barn. She had a deck below with portholes for air and for the small guns she carried. It was where most of the passengers set up home. At its aft end there was a cookhouse for the passengers, and a dining cabin, and a jakes. Below that, the hold was give over to stalls amidships, where Jethro, Chloe, and the cow and her calf were lodged with a dozen other animals, horses, cows, two goats, and four sheep, all pregnant.

Mr. Pierce, the captain, said, "They always ship pregnant for it costs for one and taketh two," and he looked at the goats and said, "or three or sometimes God my witness four, and once five." He added proudly, "I have not yet by God's grace in all my voyages, and this is the tenth to the new world, lost a single animal." He did not, then or ever, mention humans. He was a small, hard-muscled godly man, as gentle as a captain of a ship with ruffians to sail her could be, and much trusted by Governor Winthrop.

All our worldly goods and succor for the colonists already there were our ballast and the ship's as well, for the whole of the rest of the hold was cargo, limes for John Winthrop, for scurvy, cheeses, grain, medicine, need after need, barrels and tuns and boxes and cartons. In the midst of all, as sure in its place as if there had been a lady within, a painted pretty leathern-seated carriage, carefully stowed next to our hay cart.

The *Lyon* truly was like a barn turned upside down, its top ridge the keel, its bottom floor the handsome open deck where the white sails flew, the ropes hummed, and the ready ship moved with the tide like a young restive horse. Mary and I stood in the prow as she passed down toward the mouth of the Avon, commodious and elegant, for it is a rare ship that does not look elegant with her sails aloft, to the Severn, and into the Bristol Channel. We had looked backwards in tears long enough. I stood where I had longed to stand since I was a boy yearning toward the ships in London's harbor.

When we rounded the Lizard into the open sea we turned from a ship into a cockle shell. As we dropped the land behind us, we stood with the rest as if we were all at prayer but no one said a word as we watched the last view of England slip over the horizon and disappear and there was only a gray sky over a slate-gray winter ocean that rolled and breathed its mighty breathing. The ship pitched, prow aloft over the waves' crests, then buried herself deep in the troughs between with her bowsprit underwater and her deck awash, plunging and rising to America against the prevailing western winds. Mr. Pierce sailed her straight into the huge waves as if that terror were a simple, normal thing to do.

It was my duty, and I saw it as a loving one if I could only stop vomiting, to see to all who were afraid, all who mourned, all who needed courage, I who was truly in the same boat as they. So again as I had been at Otes, I was their hireling minister, and Mary who had done it most of her life since the death of her mother became on shipboard the parish listener. For the most, so as not to upset the others, we all learned to try to be merry but there were times at the beginning when every passenger in the harsh heaving ocean heaved in rhythm with it, sick and moaning, tossed in and out of their rugs where they slept and vomited in the stinking airless gun deck, whose portholes had to be closed against the weather.

Mary and I had long gone into our tiny cabin aft the main deck beside the crew's cookhouse. There we slept and ate and worried and learned to live together for two months. We had the only private cabin, being company clergy. And still I cannot believe I sailed so. Mary made a tidy nest of it as children do with pillows and rugs and all to make a play home in the corner of a room. We had for winter fine down coverlids and pillows and rugs, all the household needs for the time at sea to keep us from the cold. We piled there our shipboard food and belongings. We were all at the mercy of God and the winds. Some ships in the summer had took only six weeks, some as many as twenty in bad weather.

Mary had spread our feather bed for us to sleep on the voyage, and she lay across it, too sick to straighten her body, retching and retching, her face white, her eyes sunk in her head as if she would die. I sponged her forehead as best I could between my own dry heaves. I found my sea legs first. Then, two days later, Mary fell into a deep sleep for fourteen hours and when I called in panic for Mr. Pierce he smiled and said no she was not adying but sleeping her way to her sea legs. It was true. She woke well again and merry.

After a few days at sea, the crew ordered us all upon the open deck where they had stretched a rope from stem to stern and bade us hold upon it though some seemed too sick to do so, and heave up, lower down, heave up, lower down, heave and lower, heave and lower, heave and lower, until tempers were restored and sickness ceased. I can still hear the calls of the seamen, heave, lower, heave, lower.

"I do it every time," Mr. Pierce told me. "Never fails to get they over the sickness." He was right. The children had begun to roam the open deck, and to play together. The mothers clung to the yards and watched the sea. The fathers smoked tobacco and talked of the future in the new Zion and where they had come from and who was kind and all. The bright winter sun broke through and colored the water an endless rolling blue not seen ever upon the land. That first day of sun was lovely and holy and thought of ever after.

Who ever thinks that it was a small thing to make oneself sail aboard a hull afloat and at the mercy of the wind in a vast ocean never seen before has not done it nor dried the tears of those who have, nor prayed with them in storms that swept the deck clean of their belongings and sometimes of their loved ones. It is a terrible and wonderful thing to take a ship that seems as small as a leaf in that vastness of ocean where porpoises the size of cattle and the leviathans are at home as we are not, such huge playfulness that could overturn our frail ship when we were cast from the tops of water mountains where all the sea world spread out to the end of sight, into the low troughs of the waves where we plunged down into darkness and flood that threatened to overwhelm our lives as it had overwhelmed our courage and already drowned it.

But if I could cross it, and learn to love it, I and all the rest can tell about it to their sorrow and their joy. It bound all who had made the voyage for the first time together as those who have been comrades at war. So in my soul the ties to home stretched, broke as they did for Mary, and we leaned closer to each other and said not a word about it.

We could hear the animals below us amidships in their close stalls in the hold. We could hear them moan and bellow when the ship rolled but we were not allowed by the ship's crew to visit them or succor them. The gun deck passengers were ordered on the open deck for air in the daytime and to eat while a crew of them in turn each day sluiced out and swabbed the great wood space of night shit and vomit. The ceiling was so low there that even a man as short as I had to bend his head to walk.

Most had no privacy. It reminded me so of sleeping in the tennis court at Charterhouse, body after body in long rows, for many had brought little to comfort themselves withal. We were profligate of room though for the ship could hold an hundred more in summer, the master told me, but for our voyage goods and food were needed more than people.

Sometimes, oh often, I lay awake and listened to those below, awake, too, for I could tell so by their breathing and turning. One or another called out in sleep or half awake, and there were snores and coughs and all. Though in the daylight after the first week the whole ship's company made themselves more hearty and gladsome and played at fine plans and hope, I wondered how many of those awake to their night thoughts already longed for home.

It was there, in the night, awakened by the sounds belowdecks of one snoring, another heaving with the seasickness, some turning in their sleep, some groaning, that I rose from no sleep and made my way below as silently as I could, thinking, I still swear, that my name was called. By the lantern light the children were as peaceful as angels in their sleep. The stench was terrible. No one had called for me.

I made my way back up to the deck and stood against the rail and let the wind and darkness swallow me, one with the night and the sea and all the depth of bright stars for it was a cold bright December night three days before Christmas.

My life to now from then was coming close though as yet I had not words for it, not like afterwards when I was as profligate with opinions, words, admonishments and Bible-haunted truths as any man alive. I was beginning to know, though, what I must do, and I knew that it would be a burden to my Mary. I faced, I know now, what so many reformers in their livings did, but thinking of their families and their lives and hesitating for that second too long to act, all those left in England who would seethe in silence and do what they were told until they burst their bonds in civil war.

I had come to my crossroad there in the darkness of the sea and the black sky and the huge bright hanging stars, where the wake was afire with a million glistening jewels and no one anywhere. But one came and stood beside me. It was Mary. She took my arm and said, "Come to bed."

"I cannot, Mary. What am I to do? We have took the company's shilling and so are as tied as ever, and all the tie is against my mind and soul. I cannot do it any more. My mind is as alight as that water, and I must speak it. The time is slipping away."

"Then do it," she whispered for there was a sailor near us on the night watch, ready to sound four bells for midnight, "for I would hate to think of thee in hell."

The next day was Sunday and we held our service upon the bright

deck, savoring the weather we knew could not last, for that morning
the sky was red with the sunrise, and the master explained that it was
a harbinger of storm. I spoke of Elijah who stood upon the cliff and
waited upon God to speak to him in all the storm and whirlwind and
earthquake. He, his small exposed self there against the sky, expected
great majesty.

"But it was not in the wind, and it was not in the earthquake, and
it was not in the fire," I called out over the waves that beat and broke
upon us, "but in a still small voice within him." There was a crash and
splinter of timbers. Darkness lowered upon us within minutes. The
passengers were ordered below and the crew ran helter skelter, clung to
the rigging, climbed the masts and brought down the sails while all I
could do was stand and pray, scared and cold and feeling a fool.

Then I saw a boy, a mischievous child who tried to climb the rigging after one of the sailors. A wave came and claimed that small body
and swept it into the raging sea. He lay atop a vast swell while the seamen tried to launch a boat to reach him. There was not a sound from
him. I watched him rock there, his spread-eagle body all luminous
with glistening sea glow. It seemed hours while they came closer, but
it could only have been a few minutes. He did not move or call out,
but lay there rocked by the water and before the boat could reach him
the water claimed and overlay him, the light around his body went out,
and he was gone.

I went below to tell his parents. But I could not say the words they
wanted to hear, that a small boy lost in a great ocean sinking down
down among the fish and flotsam and alien world of the sea and its
darkness, was the will of God as punishment for his little sins. I could
not. I could only cling and let weep, and pray with them. He was Mr.
Raye's son, but to my shame I cannot now remember his name.

Day after day after day came and went and it was as if we never
moved for the night covered the water and the morning exposed the
water, the same water with its giant heave and flow and we were bored
and sickened and long since out of merry words. As in a village, for it
was for those weeks a floating village, some made friends with those of
their ilk; some argued politics but thought it religion for they had only
religious words to use. Two aboard would be my friend and nemesis for
years to come but then they were simply two young men who came

unencumbered with much family or religious reasons, but only for adventure. One, that Morris dancer name of Harris, seemed jolly then for he would put on his knee bells on sunny days and show the children the dancing. How could I have known that dancing belltinkling man would stand for all my troubles until the day of his death?

The other, Mr. Throckmorton, was also young and less wild for he had a new wife. We became friends there and would be close for years until the Quakers, that ungodly riotous ignorant crew, came and bewitched him and he turned on me, and I on him, I must admit. Old men, the two of us sat five minutes apart in our houses and wrote violent religious letters back and forth to one another when we were near enough each other to shout out of the window. It was and ever has been my duty to point out error, I think, but lately I wonder.

One day in the silence and the boredom there was a call from the crow's nest, "Iceberg!" There it was a great high tower of whiteness in the dark water, the first sign we saw that meant we were near land.

One iceberg then another until we sailed, a tiny ship among the walls of a bright white city of ice, sometimes so close we could reach out and touch them. Oh Father of Lights it was so beautiful and so inhuman as if we belonged not there in that world, not made for us at all.

The master tacked and dodged toward the land we could not yet see, but at last could trust was there, for we smelled a new scent, the scent of land wind carrying within it the essence of pine from the great forests still out of sight down the horizon. Headwinds kept us out from the shore, but we came nearer one day and another, nearer to islands, all white with snow in water that seemed black around them, hundreds of islands, small and some so large that it took a day to sail around them and avoid the island currents. This was the master's element and his art, for he steered the *Lyon* as casually as if he walked some meadow of his own. He had been many times into the harbor at Nantasket.

So the land grew near and near and then in sight and we crowded the deck and thanked God all together with the psalm 170 taking our voices up to be lost in the new world air.

Cold. It was bitter cold, colder than any of us had known, and so still as the air around us seemed paused from time to time as if the wind, tired of blowing us off the shore, gave in and let us land.

XXII

———— ◆ ◆ ◆ ————

*I know what it is to study, to preach, to be an elder, to be
applauded, and also what it is to tug at the oar, to dig
with the spade, and plow and to labor and travel day and
night amongst the English and barbarians, why should I
not be humbly bold to give my witness faithfully?*

— ROGER WILLIAMS

THINK I AM GOING TO DIE THIS YEAR. I AM WEAR-
ing out, an old horse, lamed and tolerated. I believe from that thought
I have grown too self-pitying to live. Oh come Roger Williams, you
feel a failure on a snowy winter morning. So I did this morning what I
do when I grow testy and a nuisance to myself. I walked along the port
to count the pinnaces, the canoas, the coracles, and the blessings of a
few seagoing ships as well. Their toing and froing comforts me and
tells me the town is alive and grown so far beyond its beginning, that
little line of raw wood houses huddled at the riverbank and alive on
hope and not too much of that. It has always been small, derided, a
flotsam of a town, both in people and in goods, half forgotten by the
other colonies that flourish and brag. Oh shake off this melancholy. It
is unkind. It is untrue.

The golden treasure that we have here is far beyond their riches, for
we are still the only colony in all the world I know where it is wrote
into our charter that no person shall be molested or questioned for matters of conscience so they be loyal and keep the civil peace. So we
should give up land and what men call success before we part with such

a treasure. I remind myself on a white morning under this lowering dark sky, and I tell who will listen any more for they have so long took this jewel for granted that sometimes I fear an old man's fear that they value it no longer. Though it is hard to keep repeating the words to men and women who are looked on with contempt, who cannot eat the great gift nor sell it nor trade it for land, land, and more land, the craze of this so old a wilderness and so new that we have but scratched it, not tamed nor ever will. Or I pray not.

For nearly fifty years this great gift has been my hope, my choice, my road. Of course I wonder if it will live beyond me. How can I still convince those young ones who have not known the brutality of persecution for conscience, the prisons, the beatings, the hangings, the maimings, the exiles? Not only in our corrupted old England but in New England as well. And to this day. Why, if the Virgin Mary were in New Haven, they would hang her for adultery.

And as for Massachusetts, well! They challenge the inquisition that put Galileo into limbo for discovering that the earth moved around the sun before the Pope did. Yet they do the same. We see ourselves converting the heathen Indians to Jesus Christ the Prince of Peace and at the same time make war upon them, their women, their children to clear the land for our own taking. And call it righteousness.

When I fall into this whining sadness, I make myself go back to one evening and the words of John Winthrop thrown at me across the fire and comfort ashore for the first time in the two months it took us to sail across the wild Atlantic. Ha ha, it pleases me to remember and hear his voice again. "Roger Williams, you young fool, it is your choice to do it and your burden to bear its hardships. Thee will not last out there in the wilderness for thee have the slim muscles and the fine hands of a scholar and a gentleman."

That was late, after we had talked too long and I had been too prolix and too honest, an ever present fault. It was the day of our landing, that other snowy morning at the beginning, as our ship was took by the lighter past island after island named for the deer, the birds, the trees, and here and there the wisps of smoke from farms set out upon them. Huddled under that huge dark sky, we followed the channel marked by floating pots and floating ice. The snow blew in our faces.

We saw a raw unfinished Zion. Sheds half buried in snow. Some Indian tents with smoke coming from a hole in the center of the ceiling, at least we supposed they were Indian. The smell of wood fires and evergreens and the fresh winter air of a continent blew the salt wind behind us. All the passengers looked frightened and sad. I think they—we—had expected a town of some kind of settling. But that morning there seemed only the drifting snow with the terrible solid barrier of trees bigger than any except the trees in the royal forests blocking us out, or so it seemed, a wilderness nearly black in that winter light, no roads, no paths, no way within.

We stood beside Master Pierce as he pointed out strange white hills in the black water, strange names, and no blue ocean as we had ever known in all our lives, but black to green. The ice floes nudged the wooden sides of the hull of the poor *Lyon*. They seemed to forbid our landing.

I thought then, God my hope, we have not come to a new land but to a land as old and untouched as in the beginning when Adam and Eve were thrust forth out of their sweet garden into the wilderness to fend for themselves. I thought of Caesar and seemed to know his mind there in the mouth of the Thames, facing the dark forest and our ancestors as wild as dangerous animals. Well, it was ever this way in strange lands.

We landed first at Nantasket. There on the shore a man stood dwarfed by the wilderness. Behind him a little drift of a settlement looked as it would be blown away, a few houses, more teepee tents, a long pier of logs out into the water. It was all so rough-hewn and seemingly neglected that we thought, I thought, "They have gone and left us," but it was not so. One man came out of the tents, and then another, some like scarecrows, scurvy-ridden poor people wrapped in whatever blanket, skin, or clothing that would keep out the cold.

The first man went on standing apart, as alone as if he were the only man on earth. I knew him, John's father. I carried sheafs of letters for him. He was thinner than I remembered at Sempringham when we spoke of my lord Coke and he questioned me so. He stood much taller than the rest as he were of a different breed, longer-coupled, better bone. He was dressed in a coat of fine fur skins, his face half covered with his great collar, Governor John Winthrop, who had give up his manor house and much land and place in England for this—this sad unplanned gathering of hovels along the shore.

As we came closer, he waved like an excited child, hallow hallow to Master Pierce, and he fell upon his knees and began to pray. One and then another huddled against him on their knees and prayed against the wind. He leapt aboard as soon as the gangplank went down, before any of us could touch the pier. He hugged the master, and the children and Mary and finally me. "Dear Roger, dear Roger," he said and said again as if we were old and tender friends, which we became though it was a private thing between us and our wives, a blessing.

So he rode with us along the inner islands to the port of Charles-town, and talked as a man let out of prison, how so many had died and how they had planned a fast for two days hence to pray to God to bring the *Lyon* to save the ones alive. "There have been so many deaths in this raw world, harsh, harsh," he said, as if he talked to himself and we were not there. Scurvy, the physician's name for starvation, had broke out among the poor, and even the gentry, the company members who had give up so much, gave up their lives as well that winter. Governor Winthrop told Mr. Pierce that Mr. Johnson, Lord Saye and Sele's son, was the most missed of any man who had gone in the first flotilla. All this as we made way among the islands.

We entered the port to one of those pictures of men in hell drawed to frighten children, but John Winthrop seemed not to know it, he showed by God a pride I could not believe and he strode ashore to a wispy roar of welcome like the wind blowing leaves. There was much kissing of kin and friends and much springing of hope. For some it was too late for they had long run out of any food but half-spoiled ship's biscuits and jerky, and even the young moved like old people for the scurvy attacked their muscles and their spirit together. It was the sad-dest sight that ever I saw.

But John Winthrop walked right through it and motioned us after him. He called to us and to the crowd, "Call off the fast! We will kneel together and thank the Father of us all and have a thanksgiving instead as soon as the *Lyon* can be unloaded!"

Had we expected shouting and glee from the shore when we arrived? Had we banked our hopes on welcome? There was little for us but

much for the stores within the hold. They scrambled aboard and had
to be held off by the crew.

Master Pierce had known it would happen; he had had the sailors set
up a long table on deck with bread and beer and meat, and he warned
all before they were allowed close to the table not to eat too much too
quickly for it would kill them, and to drink each of them several sips
of the warm blood from a new-killed calf for it would succor them.

But some rushed and some died later. Mr. Pierce told us that at dinner at the governor's large but simple house for he explained that he
had to be an example to the others lest they think those who owned
shares in the company lorded it over them too readily. But John
Winthrop called it the great house there where "great" was no word to
use for anything except our little plans and little hopes to fight despair
and wilderness.

We had staggered after him toward what he pointed out as Beacon
Hill, where the better houses were. They stood away up the hill with a
view of the harbor, far above the hovels and the one-roomed thatched
building in Charlestown nearer the shore. They had already named
their separate settlement Boston, for Mr. Cotton's parish in England.

We were still at sea upon our floating legs, and he moved fast for he
was used to the frozen wallows and deep iron-iced ruts of the carts, the
noise and thin riot of voices and swearing and calling from those bun-
dled people, whipping their nags forward against the wind, and stopping to greet one another and shout news of the food, and after that
there were passengers as well, and somebody laughed and said, "Oh
they poor buggers." Another said, "Odds fuck, more to feed."

There too was our first sight of the red Indians. They were tall, taller
than we were. In fair fight I thought they would kill us as easily as flies
upon a window, but they seemed then to be friendly for I learned later
among so many other things of them that they had a law of hospitality for strangers. I saw some of our sea companions cringe when they
saw them, for there had been many a wild tale of ambush and death,
boiling alive and God knows what, and much I had had to calm and
deny aboard the ship. Though I knew little more than they did, I could
smell a tall tale when I heard it.

I told them that the wild men hidden in the wilderness were as we
had once been when we looked from our wild hiding places on the

ships of the Romans. When I tried to tell them it was a new beginning as England had been before it was tamed and made gentle and tractable by men, it stilled them not. Many never got over that first bald fearsome unwelcoming sight of such strangers, and went back rather braving the great ocean again than the wild land.

Mary, bless her soul, stopped right in the middle of the road and stared away beyond the frail houses at the great wilderness of black trees. I thought that she was resting and trying to get her land legs. I took her arm to help her, but then she pointed to the forest like a fishwife for she had been long trained never to point her finger. It was her first shedding of what she called later her burdens of training.

"Now I know why men yearn to deflower virgins," she said, looking at the trees.

"Mary!" I remember saying, aghast at her thought. For I was still, God help me, a young prude.

Each of us, Mary and I, knew the other was heartsick but we said nothing, hid from each other that first brute blow of the place where we would be, behind us our Rubicon, before us nothing but wilderness. I would fall in love with that wilderness, as I fell in love with those who hid within it, and had learned through all their generations not to conquer but to submit, as sailors learn to submit to the sea and let it float their frail ships. My soul would yearn to touch their souls. I would, thank God, spend many years among them.

Late at night after Mary and the governor's younger sons had gone to bed, John Winthrop and I sat before the fire as I had sat at Stoke with my lord Coke. I studied his face as he stared at the huge log burning, the long sharp nose, the sunken eyes, and I thought, he has been through too much. We sat in the kitchen for it was the warmest room in the house. The kitchen fireplace was a room itself, with a fine finished log as a chimney piece that reached twelve feet across the top. Two great pots hung within, warm upon their hooks.

He kept a poker and from time to time heated it in the fire and plunged it into our hot posset of strong water and molasses. He was a man beset with housekeeping, and he talked as he thought that night. The colony had to be financially successful though they said it could not since it was not good land for slave labor as Virginia. The servants and artisans the company had brought over had caught the first air of freedom in their nostrils and made to charge more than they had in England and complain and all until he had had to make an example of the worst of the complainers and slit his nose and brand his cheeks as a lesson for the others. Some hid aboard the ships going back to England. Some had to be deported, some took off for Salem where there had been a town so much longer, long before John Endicott arrived as governor of the Massachusetts Bay Colony and threw the ones already there off the land and took it for the company in King James's name.

He told it not that way but that, I learned, had been the way it was, for that was when I made fast and loving friends with Mr. Blakeston, the Anglican minister and scholar who had spent his inheritance on making a farm and library for himself on Beacon Hill. He was a high church near Papist. As for the Visible Saints he told them they could have Beacon Hill for a song and call it Boston after that damned Puritan stronghold Mr. Cotton lorded it over back in England for all he cared. All he wanted was to be left alone to be a gentleman and a minister. Finally he came to this beloved Rhode Island, where even Arminians are welcomed, poor benighted souls.

All of these bits of past and present history tumbled out toward the fire in the comfort of that warmth of the man and the kitchen. God bless him, John Winthrop. Oft times later he had to stand out against me, but never did I lose his love, though for a time I thought I had. Oh that was later, much later, not there that first night drinking by the fire in his kitchen when everything was new. It was the year of his death he wrote me a loving letter that said, "Roger Williams, we have oft tried your patience but have never conquered it." It was the only apology he ever made, being a proud man. Those words too went up in the smoke of the firing of Providence, but they are here, still here, in my heart of hearts.

My mind wanders over that long time ago, and I think of John Winthrop, rest his dear soul, for he had much to try him. That night he was comfortable though and he told me of the hopes he had and the rules of living he wanted to pass on to me in a new world, harsh, he called it harsh, but beautiful, he called it that too.

"Thee must needs not be seen to be popular for we need the discipline as if we, the gentlemen here, were fathers, strict but loving. I have put my hand to yeoman's labor to be an example to the others, but it is not good to join them in a popular way. We must needs watch for such religious rabble as Ranters and Familists and Antinomians and all of that for it has no place in the God-blessed country of New England."

He laughed then, the candle guttered. "Oh to bed. Remember, it is not for us to root hog or die as they say in Virginia of the common people, but to take our responsibility as leaders." He yawned and apologized and yawned again. "It has done my soul good to talk with thee, Roger," and he got up. Again that tall man reminded me of my dear lord Coke, so tall, so thin, so sure that he was right.

"If all else is forgot remember that democracy is the meanest and worst form of government in the world, and it is not warranted in the Bible as the right of kings and fathers and judges." He was gone. "The Old Testament," I said so quietly he heard me not. I have ever liked better the more honest way good fat John Endicott said it, "Damme, Roger, if all governs theirselves who would be left for us to govern?"

That night before the fire, alone, my brain was by then, as was said later of me in derision, a very windmill. A sense of wrong overwhelmed me that had no name, no words. I tried to push it away as the fatigue of the journey but I knew it was not. What that dear man had said in his corrupted innocence was that the Massachusetts Bay Company was a commercial enterprise expecting profit, owned by the gentry who came on the surface of their minds to do God's will, and to decide what it was, owners and proprietors as they had been in the old England of county estates, same churches, reformed, but under the cloak and crown of the king. Though they might deny it as an expediency he told me and some did, without the promise of church conformity, no matter how reformed, they would not have a charter at all.

I did not answer much of this for I had not yet found what I should say in conscience, but there within me was Bartholomew and my lord Coke who I had brought with me to the new world as surely as the clothes upon my back. "Heresy is not punishable for heresy is of the mind and not public actions, and a man's thoughts are not a crime under civil law but when they cause riot." I could hear my lord say it as I had heard him so often.

"Such denials and persecutions are against the law of England," I told the fire for John Winthrop, Lawyer, had by then been long abed, and even longer and more expedient, forgot his law. When I went to bed, Mary was asleep, but when I touched her dear cheek to say good night her face was wet with tears.

I lay awake beside her until the late New England dawn drifted to the window with the shadows of the terrifying trees. At least I thought them so then. It was later and for years that they became for me towering sentinels in what I sometimes saw as a great cathedral, with narrow beams of sun through its ceiling of leaves, touching on snow or on tiny flowers.

XXIII

When I remember the high commendations some have given
of the place, and find it inferior to the reports, I have
thought the reason thereof to be this, that they wrote sure-
ly in strawberry time. . . . The air of the country is sharp,
the rocks many, the trees innumerable, the grass little, the
winter cold, the summer hot, the gnats in summer biting,
the wolves at midnight howling, etc. Look upon it, as it
hath the means of grace, and, if you please, you may call
it Canaan.

— A GENTLEWOMAN OF BAY COLONY

MARY SLEEPS CARELESSLY. SHE CAN SHUCK OFF troubles with her day clothes and in her night dress puts on a child again. How open to the moon and the tide she is, floating there, her hands together as if she had gone to sleep apraying. Her silly little pigtail of white hair sticks out across her pillow. Once upon a time when she sat upon her nursing stool and loosed it for combing, it fell like a shining chestnut tent around her and curled upon the floor. She called it her shining glory as women do.

Oh Mary, you kept me oft afloat as you are now, peaceful when I could have fell into a darkness again those first days. I remember that one day in near summer before the fields had begun to yield, and all were hungry, we paddled in a flotilla of native canoes and fed on strawberries in a field we called Strawberry Field, a few miles from Salem.

Ever after, when it seemed we had been deserted, my Mary would say, "Let us eat the strawberries give by Lord Jesus, my dear."

And when I feared for her she would laugh, and say, "Thee know me not. I have done told thee over and over. Now hark again. To one who has become mother when my mother died, and me eleven too, and looked after Besekiel, Hoseel, Masakiel, and Cannavel, and my poor windward father, this new England is naught to me."

Mary who could raise a chicken, name it, pet it, and then wring its neck and pluck it for feasting, Mary who could lift a hay bale fussing all the while will you never learn to bind tight, what did they teach you at that fine Cambridge, Mary who bore me six children and followed my wandering ways with never a whine but often a comment and sometimes a shrug, was, when the gentry came to see us, as pliant and meek as one who had been at such a place as Otes for all a useless life. We laughed of it together.

She has ever been my companion in my choices, for she hated the toadying of her reverend father. It had been the shame of her life to watch him so, for she much loved him. She would tell me, "Whatever else, thee have not put me through that diabolic error," for she has ever had a way with words.

It was she who packed and unpacked, rode Chloe while I drove the stallion, for they had both survived the voyage, though the milk cow had died in midocean and we had all eat her sadly. So we had, to charge a good fee for, a fine bull for breeding. We tethered him with two goats, male and female as in the Ark, to the back of the heavier cart I had made.

Many a talk into the deep night we had, first in Boston and then after, in Salem and then in Plymouth among the Pilgrims there as they called themselves, a Godly people but as far too many, as right as a rigid block of ice after all. To them every sneeze was the fault of their little human idea of the God of Abraham and Isaac and Jacob.

I learned to be carpenter, farmer, stonemason, logger, and all, and those hands that John Winthrop had said were scholar's hands were made hard by long rowing in and out among the islands, in the open sea, up and down the river. Even though my feet were never right after that winter of wandering in the snow, my arms and shoulders could take me rowing anywhere. Why I thought nothing of taking off for Newport thirty miles away by sea, with only a little sail to help me when the wind bore right.

Within weeks of our arrival in Boston, more name than place then, I was asked to be the teacher of the First Church of Boston, a one-room mud hut then. John Winthrop was as pleased as a boy again that he had brought it off by leading the vote, as he said, and much relieved he was that I had, in his eyes, took up in the new England as I had left off in the old England.

It took only one night of thinking and moaning over my conscience with Mary as midwife to my decision, to send a polite letter to the church saying I dared not minister to a church that was still a part of the Church of England. We argued only on one point; she insisted that I say CORRUPT Church of England, but I would not. "Mary," I told her, "you are a greater firebrand than I will ever be."

John Winthrop was hurt, but still he had to honor my conscience. "I can do naught for you then," he said at last. "It is root hog or die, or, God help you, Salem among the ruffians."

Mary's answer to that when I told her was "When Adam delved and Eve span who was then the gentleman?" I accused her of anarchie, for the rhyme had come into the language from the old Wat Tyler rebellion near three hundred years before, and she laughed and said, "No, we will indeed root hog or die as Adam and Eve our first parents did at the beginning of the world."

I remember where she was when she said that for I often heard her voice when I was alone and thinking of her and saw where she was and what she was doing when she said a thing first. She was at her spinning wheel that day, and when I hear her voice I hear its whirr and the rhythm of the treadle.

So we went first to Salem and we were happy there among those John called ruffians. But in those days I committed one abiding sin and before the Father of Lights I still do. What I learned in my soul come out of my mouth, not in the passionate argument I was accused of, but simply, to me, a sharing. It happened that it was a sharing the Visible Saints of Massachusetts did not abide. They were in charge. They meant to stay so. They made me gadfly and many others who thought not as they did, those who they feared would shake the frail balance of their power. The Massachusetts fathers demanded of the church at Salem that they turn me out. Poor men, some I loved and still do love, in my soul, for most of them are dead. I have well outlasted them which is one way to win a battle I never cared to fight.

Social pressure, so much greater than physical pressure, the disapproving glance of a neighbor, the shunning, all the weapons used by the conforming to cut out the faulty sheep from the flock were used, and I had to leave Salem. I who had refused the fine offer of preferment from the First Church of Boston had committed an error so egregious that it had to be punished. I had complained of civil punishment for church nonconformity as against the law, and also for the taking of Indian lands without paying for them which seemed stealing to me, even though they said and honestly believed that such land was God's gift for the taking. So along the shore road toward Plymouth, shunted back and forth, no, that time we went by boat and Mary made it into a pretty journey, three lovely days in May and nights ashore beneath the stars.

Is there one ever in the world like the miracle of the first child, the astonishment of it, the shock of happiness? Our sweet babe, Mary, kept trying to fall into the sea around Cape Cod reaching for things in the water only she could see.

When I had seen Governor Bradford and was welcomed there it was a relief as one who had been from the gates of Otes in Essex through the voyage and on to Boston and then Salem, blown like one in a fog at sea, forced to steer by a side wind, all over New England. It seemed so anyway.

In a year after we came to this new world I was finding surety in some thoughts I had followed to where they led me. I had gone far in learning the Indian language as one learns the language of any country where one decides to sojourn, though others of the English saw it not that way. It was a blessing of my life. I long times forgot the mother country, the ways of the English, and in moccasins made by the squaw of a friend grew so familiar with the forest that when I yearned to be alone I could go without the naked Indian boy who Massasoit had give me to be my guide. Mostly he accompanied me, for I had half prom-

ised Mary. I still see him ahead in the mast barefooted, making not a
sound. It was only when I came behind him with my glumping civilized feet that the deer even lifted their heads.

By the Father of Lights who ever loved me, it was a wonderful thing
to be prepared by my study of languages to find this new, or old, one
to learn, to go among the savages and make peace between them and
between us, who they saw as the new tribe of the English, the Yengees.
They saw our differences as a hierarchy of power, from Visible Saint at
the top, or as one of their sachems, to simple plowmen who cleared the
land, from rich to poor, from freeman to bondservant, and then along
the edges as once I had seen the fortunetellers and the necromancers
follow the court when it moved from Theobalds to Windsor, or Whitehall, the thieves, the pickpockets, the drunkards, the layabouts and all
that make up any English town.

We stayed two years in Plymouth, but it was not my place nor ever
would be, not separated but half dependent on the power of the official
church in old England. The certainty had grown in me and in Mary,
and we discussed it long by the kitchen fire at night, sometimes with
neighbors and our new friends, that there was little to choose between
the corruption of the Jesuits and the Puritans, although I found myself
thinking sinfully within my soul that a Jesuit would be fine to talk
with in the wilderness, they being educated men. Sometimes when we
met deep in the wilderness, the priest and I would sit by a bonfire, and
talk for hours, he as lonely to converse as I.

When our beloved Mr. Skelton, the minister at Salem, persuaded us
back from Plymouth to Salem again where we were indeed more at
home, we pulled up our stakes, loaded the cart, and moved north once
more along the shore road, by that time as busy as any country road in
old England. It was a godsend to find a two-roomed house where we
could put our bed into a room by itself which was the greatest luxury.
There was a fine big loft, a fireplace that had two hearths, one for the
kitchen and one for the bedroom, hospitality from our old friends and
neighbors who still harbored, they told us, shame at having bent to the
will of the Visible Saints. It was this way we trundled ourselves back
to Salem where there was, to me, a surer commitment to that power-
lessness which is the power of God.

There were two years again of peace, time to breathe out, make friends, and for Mary to be with child, time measured by events in days that seemed always the same, seasonal and muscular with hard work. I was satisfied with it; it was meet to me and to Mary that we who followed the beaten crucified Jew we called our Lord Jesus did as His followers did, worked for our food and our shelter. I have often wondered if Christ came to London or Boston, what church He would choose— that is if any would let Him in for there would be rules to prop a hierarchy as strict as the Papists. For they all lived by rules He had not made, being One who threw down the dead laws of the Pharisees and replaced them with the most sensible and simple and world-astounding love the world had ever seen nor ever will until the Last Day. Besides, his dress would be too outlandish for simple Christian conformity, to say nothing of His nose.

Sometimes Mary and I strolled dreaming through shortcuts in the wilderness I had learned. In autumn of the year New England would be aglow. We seemed to walk through color and through light until we were part of it, the color and the light. And the days became daily as one sees them again in the mind's eye, no great matters, but will it rain on the drying hay, will so and so and so make up their quarrel, did so and so shoot the stoat that wallowed in his road, and on and on and all of that.

Around us the wind grew stronger. None of the Visible Saints had forgive me for kicking the dust of Boston from my feet but John Winthrop. He had lost his governorship to Mr. Haynes, for he was accused of not being stern enough with dissenters. So he had not the power nor the tools nor the mind to stop the quibbling, the quarreling, the reporting of my words as if I was one lawless renegade with a rapier in hand to slit their throats. And alas, in the war of words, I could never resist a quip. If I sneezed it was whispered and gossiped in Boston that I was dying. If I stumbled on the ice I was drunk.

I went more among the Indians who had become my most dependable friends, having no stake in God Colony or God Money or God Power or to be honest God Excitement of any kind since I will admit that in all the small villages grown up at the sides of the veins and arteries of the blessed waters of New England, there was little else to do but work from dawn to dusk. The Indians had no time nor pleasure in arguing religion, and what the minister said or did not say.

It was sad to me that my friends, especially that dear man Mr. Skelton, were forced to defend me, but they needed me as I them. Many a time they knocked upon my door before they knocked each other's heads in from frustration and asked me to settle this matter or that, as poor and as innocent as if they too had been the native Indians and not the lordly English.

And all this before I ever was made teacher of the church at Salem. Mary and I set hand to plow together, she leading the stallion for he ever liked women more than men.

Governor Endicott was a fine fat man whose mind had been made up at his birth and never changed. He had already bought from the Plymouth Company as cheap as dirt a sixty-mile-wide stretch of land in New England that reached in the deed to the Pacific ocean, and waited only for new settlers to pay him quitrents. It was our good cess as the Irish call it that he was born upon the side of Tolerance, though he was one of the most intolerant men I ever knew. God my strength he did many a foolish thing in the Lord's name and I was often blamed for influencing him, when it would have been easier to influence a boulder in the middle of the road.

I stood for heterodoxy. A crime. I was, to the Saints, a heretic who had escaped the name in England and found the name in New England. I simply did not agree with them. And do not. And will not. A crime. If I pointed out in some weekly lecture that there was not such a thing as Christendom since the only Christians who could call themselves such were the true followers of our Lord, in the same way as the first disciples, it was heresy. If I taught that when the Roman Empire took over the religion of our Savior, they perverted it into a powerful tool for the three Ps, this time not my lord Coke's pride, praemunire, and prerogative, but now persecution, politics, and power.

I taught, I admit it, that such was so far from that one Man upon the Galilean road that had it not broke my heart it would have made me laugh. Even this late in my life it is new, that astonishment of a boy before a true thing for the first time as it was in that time at Otes when I was stripped of all protections as the paint had been stripped from the chapel at Pembroke, to show the crucified Man of Truth. That racked body has ever since that day shone brighter for me than the sun itself.

We must ever know that our words will be twisted, rewrote, and misunderstood as our Savior's were, but must still contain a grain of the truth that cannot be changed, the pebble, the little rock held in the secret hand. My beloved Mr. Skelton died, he who had made me as one whose mind was welcome to him, and that only seldom in this world. I think it was the memory of his love that gave my friends within the church at Salem courage to ask me to be their teacher. They had gained spirit out of their love for him. It had sustained us all. It was a proud moment for me, that first step on the unknown road to the persecution that would become to me as the stone give David for his slingshot.

We had our new yielding field that we had cleared and fed and plowed ourselves. There we got our bread from grain to mill to the arms and sometimes the face of Mary to the scent of fresh baking in the small beloved house where we hoped then we would be able to stay without stint.

The stone in my hand. The waiting for what I knew not. Whatever it be was in the wind and I knew it in the night but never spoke. Mary too knew it in the night and spoke not to me of it until we each confessed to the other. The righteous were ever taking tales to Boston, for we had not been invited by all the church, and some were still afeared, and I, poor God's fool, went whirling about with the Indians I so loved, and the wilderness that was becoming a home to me that I spoke of so that the others would not fear it so. In those days the sachems came to my house as if it were their own, and set up tepees in the home field for there were twenty acres, a great fortune in land to us, that went with the church.

Still it was paid ministry and it rankled. Still it was pay and pray. The words of new thinking along the road I had taken were ashes in my mouth for want of speaking. Even innocent words, or what I deemed innocent, were reported in Boston, that I had in sermons or in passing remarks one morning to so and so or one evening to so and so, said such things as that I deemed it wrong to imagine that a king so far away could think he owned the new land and could charter it while those, the barbarians, were ignored and not paid a decent money for it.

I was called to Boston, I remember, to explain that when I hardly remembered I had spoke it. What comes back to me in that journey that was to end on this far shore of Narragansett Bay was the sad face of John Winthrop, who said then, "Do you know how you have let down your friends?" and I told him I had to follow my conscience where it led. He said he understood but hated it and ever after as he had done for two years, honored me and treated with me. But in private. For he found later that he in good conscience must go with the General Court of Massachusetts Bay, whose decisions were as final as death or redemption.

XXIV

———◆◆◆———

Mr. Williams holds forth these particulars: That we have not our land by Patent from the King but that the Natives are the true owners of it and that we ought to repent of such a receiving it by Patent. That it is not lawful to call a wicked person to swear, to pray, as being actions of God's worship. That it is not lawful to hear any of the ministers of the parish assemblies in England. That the civil magistrate's power extends only to the bodies and goods and outward state of man, etc.

— GOVERNOR HAYNES,
    MASSACHUSETTS BAY COLONY,
    THE GENERAL COURT, NEWTOWN,
    FRIDAY, OCTOBER 9, 1635

*T*HE WORDS, BEING SHORT, AND TO THE POINT AS legal words are, were, of course, misleading, far too prolix, and left much unsaid, as, for instance, I do not believe that the state should do the work of the church nor the church that of the state, neither speak for each other, condemn for each other, nor punish for each other. Damme, why did they not say so?

My Star Chamber was no fine building, but Mr. Thomas Hooker's church at Newtown. It was a one-roomed building with no windows, whitewashed mud walls, a shake roof, and an earthen floor,

Solemn men. All the New England clergy had been called to attend. Some seemed full of hatred, some embarrassed, some ashamed as they sat there too close together, for no one wished to miss the court.

Mr. Hooker, bless him, had argued with me all the day before, being as they thought, and I, too, the most perceptive of them all. He had tried out of the depths of his heart to change my mind but I could not. I could not. He argued religion as legally as ever my lord Coke did argue the law in his day. So he and I spent ourselves in loving disagreement and prayed for each other's errors all that night.

We were so tired, tired in body, tired in soul, and the Father of Lights knows well, tired of our own and one another's argument. All that was left that morning in October when the wilderness outside the little door glowed, and a lovely breeze came within to ease the close-packed room, was for me to acknowledge that the charges were correct, so correct, always so correct by the time they come in every trial, before the judgement when all blood and sorrow has been leached out of them and they are only words.

I was not the first. There had been twenty before me who had offended with their brains, their consciences, and their mouths. I became that morning the twenty-first soul to be exiled back to England for what was in his mind. I sat waiting, as prisoners everywhere and at all times in the history of the world, waiting for those in power to change my life forever, when they hardly knew me, looked not into my eyes, not for shame but because they are always too busy, the High Court, the Chancery Court, the Star Chamber, the Sanhedrin, the General Court of the Massachusetts Bay Company in session. I had seen those faces before and for much of my life, the judges, impersonal, powerful, happy, and busy judges. I was part of a day's work for those who sat there above me, as they had sat in the Star Chamber, in the Privy Council.

There was something of pathos in it, the words so fine, so legal, the place so cold, though it was October, a cold-hearted place, except for Mr. Hooker who had urged on me the same argument that he gave me at Sempringham so long ago; he and Mr. Winthrop sat apart from the others and I prayed they would not cry. They were both so obviously close to tears.

I waited. Mary had cleaned my New Year's suit that Frances had give me, and she insisted I wear it. So, there I was in soft brown velvet in that pond of solemn black, with the only lace showing for the sake of those two dear women. I thought all the time of Mary who was with child, and my bones and my sinews twisted with cold and still I waited, while other matters of more importance came up, the finding of workmen for the fort, that settled, the paving of a road, that settled, the exile of an unwitting drunken child man, that settled and he led crying from the court by his mother, and then, to me. I had watched them all for so long that my name came as a relief.

So I stood and will until the Father of Lights releases me from the place of judgement by my fellowmen. Mary and I could not believe that it was happening, yet I knew at last when I stood there feeling as naked as my birthday that like a stone rolling downhill it would not be stopped.

"Whereas Mr. Roger Williams, one of the elders of the church of Salem, hath broached and divulged new and dangerous opinions against the authority of the magistrates; hath also wrote letters of defamation, both of the magistrates and churches here, and that before any conviction, and yet maintaineth the same without any retraction; it is therefore ordered that the said Mr. Williams shall depart out of this jurisdiction within six weeks next ensuing, which, if he neglect to perform, it shall be lawful for the governor and two of the magistrates to send him someplace out of this jurisdiction, not to return any more without license from the court."

Those words that I hold in my heart have been long forgotten by all except myself. How could I know, standing there, that they would show me my road, be my Golgotha, my reason for being? For I stood as all have stood since the beginning, persecuted for my thoughts and my words and not my actions. I had and have not ever broke the law, for my lord Coke long gave me such respect for it as the way for all us errant souls to live together in some kind of peace.

I stopped listening. I was saved once again by Bartholomew who is ever with me, and he told me then more clearly than the distant voice of my banishment, "Know you not, young Roger Williams, that only undeserved, unmerited punishment meted out by the cold-hearted in the name of God or the king or the high priest or the state can bring you closer to your Lord?"

So I would not tell a soul for it is the jewel of my life that while I heard the words my heart was filled with love and what is called grace by those who try to define it, bottle it, eat it at the mass, but never

never place themselves in the way of it for to act so led by God is fearful and brutal and marvelous and wonderful.

WHEN I LEFT the court it was still in session. I was dismissed, and alone, persona non grata by the law of Massachusetts, but by my soul, not by the Father of Lights. No one spoke to me, but one person. Mr. Hooker ran after me, and he touched my foot in the stirrup when I heard him and drew up. "I tried," the words of impotence throughout the world, the words of failure, "I tried," he sobbed, and the tears fell onto my shoe. He bowed his head and we prayed together though what we prayed for and what our silent prayers were I know not to this day. Not many months later Thomas Hooker led his own flock like Moses, a hundred of them on foot with their cattle and their goods, to a promised land among the Connecticuts.

None other soul came near me.

I rode slow on Chloe back toward Salem that day while it was still light. That wonderful and beautiful October day as it is only in New England, and I was filled with sad joy that it was so beautiful, and I condemned for what I had been give as a gift from God, to pursue the truth wherever it led and whatever it was. And have. All my life.

I took a road beyond the pale of Boston knowledge, one the Indians and the animals had long made through the great woods long ago as straight and wide as a highway. I wanted to meet no one and I knew that the coast road would be full of carts and drays and all, for it was the main protected way from Salem to Boston. I rode through an avenue of trees, some black firs for winter, some still in fall glory.

Like a hurt child who does not know why it is punished, I lingered on the terrible words "out of this jurisdiction." My sorrow for my boy self was almost unbearable to me, the man. Salem had been punished as well, with the only perfect weapon, for sheltering me. Until they finally agreed to cast me out from the church there, the Bay Colony held back permission for a tract of land much needed by Salem. God Land. God Land. It would ever be my near downfall, for it was God Land that drove Mr. William Harris, and God Power (and the devil Certainty) that drove Mr. John Cotton, and they both goaded me as if I were an ox in their traces.

I rode out of sorrow and into the rhythm of Chloe's hooves along the road, and a rhyme when I was a child came to my head and would not go, "Sticks and stones, sticks and stones," what now? I knew it then, "sticks and stones may break my bones but words will never hurt me." I tried to ride away from it. I urged Chloe into a canter and we were of a sudden beyond the grasping rhyme, the untrue rhyme, for words can stay forever and turn and turn like knives, and blows may leave scars but they hurt no longer.

I rode until I heard silence, and was a man again with the tears I had not known I had shed still wet upon my cheeks. I was filled with the blessing that came in silence, and I cantered along the road as eager and as full of joy as ever I did in the old days, once again like a boy in love, a cantering that has not stopped to this day, the joy and the silence, but only seldom. No man could stand that joy too often.

I pulled up near midnight in front of a house that was alight with torches and candles and lanterns and the fire and a crowd of those who were my friends, and in the street as I had rode by, my neighbors came, for they had been watching for me on the main road, and held on to my stirrups as Thomas Hooker had, God bless his soul, to welcome me and raise a furious brabble of dissent at what had happened. Richard Throckmorton had been within the little mud court, and had rode the main road fast with the news, while I had hid myself among the trees and found the silence at last and was ready to take what road was give me.

I found myself calming them and hugging my dear Mary, who held close to me, until at a nod, all the others left. They had brought their love, much of it, love and fury, and Mary and I must needs be free of both for a while.

We sat together most of the night, sometimes quiet, sometimes planning what we would do. I began to shiver and Mary gave me mulled wine to warm me but it drew forth a fury that I have forgot, even as soon as it happened, but Mary has told me, poor Mary with her mad crying raging husband, un-Christian, uncivilized, a wolf as I have seen the Indians turn wolf when they are pushed hard enough to lose dignity. They believe that loss, for them, is to lose a little of their lives.

She said I told her first about my ride along the trail in the forest and over and over, I told her, I found silence, heard it, heard silence and heard joy. And then she said, there was the rage which she welcomed

as a healthy thing in the face of the undeserved unkindness and thrusting forth for what was in my mind, for I had never done an act against
the civil law and had preached much about it, for the newcomers needed the words. No matter their age, they were often like children
released from school, anarchical at the first taste of freedom in their
lives.

There we sat in the near dark, Mary putting wood upon the fire to
give us light for each other's face, me drunk with wine and with fury
and with the un-Christian injustice of it. Finally, toward morning, she
said I asked her if she wished to go back to her father in England, for
we both knew I could not go, and we had discussed it together in low
times already.

We knew that Laud had ordered the awful punishment of Bastwick
and Burton and Prynne, their ears cut off, their faces scared with
branding, their jailing, the burning of their work. It was the first time
I heard of one who would be a friend—Freeborn Jack Lilburne, who
had been tied to a cart and lashed from Westminster to Paul's Cross for
smuggling religious tracts into England. And so who could know what
was in store for me? I thought I had seen much cruelty there in growing up, but it was less than the wild Protestant auto-da-fé of Laud, who
at every cruelty announced that he did God's will. If he could have
killed the colonies he would have, and for me to return to England was
to return to brutality worse than facing the wild forest and the
unknown paths.

Even as the morning came we began to plan, for no matter the cause,
liberation or condemnation or the brutality of men, there had to be
plans in order to survive. Must be. I could see St. Paul deciding what
he would most need to make his living and have some small homely
comfort upon the road to Ephesus.

But alas, as had happened twice before when I was backed to the corner by man's inhumanity, the first time Bartholomew, the second Lady
Lady Lady Joan Barrington, and now the third rejection of all my
hopes, I punished myself with the freezing illness as I had done before.
I lay there in that small cabin room unable to move and my soul crying aloud when I thought I slept.

Mary was in her ninth month. Three weeks later while I was still
frozen abed, she gave birth. I did not see them, Mary and our new

daughter Freeborne, for they were took to Throckmorton's house by his
dear wife and all the women of those who loved us came to that house
and helped her on the birthing stool.

But I did hear the first cry carried by the wind of late October in a
swirl of windblown leaves from that house to my bed, and thanked
God. I did hear that. So lay, waiting to accept in my body and my soul
and my mind what had happened to us. Had we not had those who
loved us beyond need or right, we would have perished then. So the
days passed, and the word came from Boston that since there was a new
child I could wait until spring to go beyond their, what was it? Their
jurisdiction. Jurisdiction. Translation. Translated to where they could
not pull me back by my hair, though they tried, by the Father of Lights
they tried for over thirty years after to flush me out.

Master Cotton, the beloved pastor, the Patriarch of New England
they called him, said it was God's punishment on me that I had fell so
ill. Translation. I would not, could not, will not let the loud and blar-
ing voice of their conscience drown out my own.

Mary sang the baby Freeborne to sleep by chanting when Adam
delved and Eve span until I told her not to sing so before anyone lest
we be reported as Familists, which then was the word that set forth
hysteria in Massachusetts Bay Colony, even more than land, land, land,
as if there were not enough for all reaching all the way to the sunset.

Mary made a list in the slow writing I had taught her, with her
feather in her mouth sucking it as she thought. Plow, harrow, picks,
shovels, seed, and on and on. We decided to mortgage our house when
the spring came to buy what was needed. Most who wanted to go with
us had ceased frequenting the closely watched church and met at home
to pray together.

In truth, and Mary heard me say this over and over, we were not to
be supplied by anyone but our own selves, and we did not desire any
to go with us as the Father of Lights knows and my soul too. My soul's
desire was to do the natives good, and to that end I had already learned
their language when I was at Plymouth and in the days we were in
Salem. I had no desire to be troubled with English company; Mary and
I discussed it much, and decided—oh that pathetic word, "decided,"
how man-made, how frail. We had decided to go on our own and may
be take a servant or two to help us settle, cut trees, help build a haven

for us. But friends begged to go with us, and I heard that duty as God's voice. So we all planned together how we would go in the spring, the men first to fell trees, plow and plant beyond the jurisdiction, beyond the pale, in the wilderness as the first man and woman.

There by the fire of December lighting our kitchen, with Mary nursing Freeborne who was a beautiful child, and I lying still troubled by spasm in my joints and back, we dreamed a house together as yokemates have done since Adam and Eve made theirselves a shelter in their wilderness.

We waited by the fire for spring, as the trees do and the animals, and the Natives in their swamp winter hiding places, for mankind in this wilderness has learned to put on winter as a garment. The days passed into January, grew longer with those blessed hopeful leaps as they do in the north, into light, while the winter still raged. They said it was one of the worst winters since the English came here.

Then, on a day in mid-January came Governor Winthrop's note to tell me that we were accused of having heretical religious meetings in our house. The visits of our friends, the companionship, the hopes together had all been suspect. The court had decided that I must be sent back to England at once as one too dangerous at spreading false doctrine and criticism of the authorities. They were sending me back to Laud who would finish the dirty work they had begun upon us. The note ended, "They send a pinnace for you to take you back to England at once. For the love of God, hide yourself. You have a little time with you for the pinnace is tied at Nantasket by contrary winds," he had wrote, and more advice on where to go as safest. "Go to Narragansett. . . ."

Long since Mr. Winthrop and I had bought together from my dearest Indian friend, old Canonicus, an island to raise goats. We called it Prudence as a kind of joke for we talked of what to do if the natives thrust us all back into the sea. I tried and failed to treat my going as casually as a day among the Indians. We kept forgetting things, to sell, to take, to leave for Mary to bring to wherever I was in the spring.

We could not keep my thrusting forth from our friends. John Throckmorton and his wife came to us as soon as they heard though how the news got beyond our door I know not. Before I left or was tore by my own hands away from Mary and she from me, I asked him to see to a mortgage for me, to be in charge of buying needs for the spring; I told Mary to wait and our friends would help her. Governor Endicott came running and panting down the road, and swore that Mary would be well took care of. Lord of Hosts, I hoped for and loved that iron-headed fat jovial man to the day of his death.

The little house was crowded with people, but I knew there had been and still was a Judas among us, for someone had reported our private plans and conversations in Boston. I had known that since I met my own words as accusations at my trial. In this new year so late in life, I know and have always known who it was, but had not proof and tried for so long a time to forgive and forget. It was William Harris, the Morris dancer who had come over on the boat with us, who begged to come to where I could find a place for the spring. Finally, as a way to stop his mouth I said he too could come if the others did, and make a new plantation beyond the borders of punishment for conscience.

He has never ceased to plague me through my life. He lied. He has lied through land fights and politics and sneaking and pretending. He accused me for forty years until his death of all the crimes that he would do had he been me. It is not true that I was employed by any, made Covenant with any, for daydreams and hopes and may bes and planning for a future that will never come as we foresee it, were not, to me and to Mary, a Covenant, a promise, an ironclad. By God's grace he was not there that afternoon for he had gone to find his cow which was ever running off. Finally John Throckmorton made them all leave, for he said Mary and I must be alone a little while. He was ever a thoughtful loving man until he became a Quaker all the years later.

Mary held me by the coat with one hand while she tilted Freeborne and nearly dropped her; little Mary kept dragging at her skirts. We clung together to gain strength and the quiet minds needed to survive.

I told Mary that I would set forth first to Massasoit, the sachem of the Pokanokets. We had become friends in my time at Plymouth. Massasoit had been the sachem who helped the Pilgrims stay alive their first year, and he had been a close friend to them ever since. I knew the way as the lines of my own hand for I had traveled much among them from Plymouth and from Salem, far inland from the coastal English. God was pleased to give me a love for them, though I was never fooled by them, for they had the honesty and the guile too of animals theirselves. They could be as treacherous as the wolves they felt themselves

akin to. God was pleased, too, to give me the painful patient spirit to
lodge with them in what to me were always their filthy smoke holes,
for I had been much spoiled by luxury in my life. Though I tried and
prayed for help to cast off such judgement. My Indian friends were our
hope, Mary's and mine, they and Governor Winthrop in secret for he
ever was torn between love and care for us and the demands of his position, his task, and his religion as he saw it.

By that late afternoon with the snow falling fast without, I was
ready. I had packed, and strapped the thongs of my bundle over my
shoulders, and could think of no more to do, but go. I bid my family
goodbye within the circle of their tears, for the children had caught the
sorrow and wailed with Mary and me. I promised, to quiet them, that
all would be well and reminded Mary of the Indian friends from the
Pokanokets and the Narragansetts who had been so often to our house.
I did not know how they would receive me when they knew I was an
exile, but I had to give her hope. All the time I wondered in that furious planning if I had all I could carry, dry cornmeal as I had eat often
with the Indian braves when they took me on their hunts, a Bible, a
change of linen and socks since I had to wade winter streams too fast
to freeze, my gun, and my dear compass, all to help me survive to my
own road to Ephesus.

Mary handed me a small note book I had been saving, two pencils
of lead, and my penknife. She did not need to say a word. They were
my weapons as much as the musket slung across my back.

The early evening came and the snow began to whiten under the rising moon. That one step out of my door, and the next. I still walk
them. I could not help myself, but kept looking back. Mary stood at
the door framed by the fire behind her for so long I thought she would
freeze there. My illness had left me weak, but I was able to move again
though my limbs and joints were rusty. I set out for the road I had
taken back from Boston and walked along the avenue within that virgin forest more benign to me than the company of rigid men. The
snow-white avenue was so clear and straight ahead that I could have
drove a carriage through it.

I let myself be guided as night came down upon me by Mr.
Winthrop's note that I had shared with no one but my Mary. He had
privately wrote me to steer my course to the Narragansett Bay and

Indians "for many high and heavenly and public ends," encouraging me by the freeness of the place from any English claims and patents. I kept the letter under my fur greatcoat in a leathern pocket Mary had made and could touch the paper he had wrote on as a comfort, for there was little other. I took his advice as a map, as a hint and a voice from God, and waving all other thoughts and motions I steered my course from Salem though the winter snow which I feel yet toward this blessed shore where I stand this morning, so long later, so short a time in my heart and soul.

Mary told me that when the soldiers came to fetch me four days later not one soul in Salem had any idea where I was.

Not a mile from Salem, and in the new darkness, I began to think of one step before the other to take me along a hope of survival in that emptiness so indifferent and so marvelously beautiful.

XXV

———————◆◆◆———————

We suppose they went to Rhode Island, for that is the recep-
tacle of all sorts of riff-raff people, and is nothing else but
the sewer (latrina) of New England. All the cranks of
New England retire thither. We suppose they will settle
there, as they are not tolerated by the Independents in any
other place.

— NEW NETHERLANDS MINISTER ON THE
REFUSAL TO ALLOW QUAKERS
IN NEW AMSTERDAM

SOMETIMES WHEN I SIGH, MARY SAYS I SIGH YEARS
long. How long, how hard the years were only we know. We wanted a
home. We founded a colony. We wanted to help the Indians as loving
neighbors so that we could all live together on the earth God gave us.
We have destroyed them, except for those few pathetic wandering souls
trying to eke out a day's food and drink, for the Indian is a natural victim of alcohol. God the Grace of my life, no matter what the hardship,
this was not meant to lead to their destruction when I set forth in the
cold darkness of that night to find a shelter where I could hide.

Every child here in Providence knows how I last saw my house as a
ghost blown by the wind, then fading into night, how I trudged and
fell and trudged and fell again in snowdrifts to my waist in a hell that
was frozen and white. But that, too often, is all they know, not why nor
how it happened.

I was afeared. Of course I was afeared. What man or woman born to
be among friends chooses the isolation, the thrusting forth, the ban-

ishment that comes to those who try to find out and tell what they see as truth, though it go against the mighty force of church and state and commonwealth and custom. Sometimes it is greater than can be held in one poor bosom. So the exiles gather in unknown cities or on wild shores as we did here. Who is not prepared to leave father mother friends lovers for conscience' sake must needs stay at home and accept the sorrow of not speaking out.

I walked on and on into the night, for hour after hour, for I thought to put as much distance between myself and the soldiers as I could, and in ways they would know not. The moon was bright, which meant that the night was at its coldest, for it is the strength of the full moon that draws the cold.

Its reflection lit the snow like some day in night. It was so bright it caste shadows. I could hear animals beyond the trees, and knew that I was watched, but only by the wild and not the civilized that would have destroyed me, oh not by honest tearing at my throat like the wild animals, but by law and dignity and the awful certainty of righteousness.

The wind blew ghosts in my path. I followed a crisscross of ways the Indians had showed me, through winter streams where the ice held me, natural fords when the water was still, ice jams where it had frozen in tumbling flow.

My path rose uphill so that twice I was able to watch an ocean of white snow on the cleared fields of the Indian villages. They were deserted, for the tribes had their winter secret places in the swamps, where like the animals they were so hidden that a man who knew not could walk within feet of their winter places and not know they were there. I knew they were there when I walked near the swamps, but it was so late in the night that I feared that the watchmen who sat awake atop the longhouses and scanned the bright snow for movement would not recognize me and would shoot me.

Day passed. Night passed. I sheltered where I could find a place out of the wind. There was only the rising of the sun and its lowering or the day storms or the night storms of snow, or the moon rise or those blessed nights under a black sky deep with stars. One tree or another, one abandoned lair or another, sometimes a cave, sometimes a tangle of shrubs where the small animals had made corridors for me to crawl within for warmth and safety's sake.

That was when friendly Indians of Massasoit's found me asleep one midday. It was the Indian way of dying, to go into the wilderness, to a place that they had chose long since, and there to die alone. Thanks be to God they did not leave me there and honor a choice I had not made.

I had traveled an hundred or so miles, who knows how much, like a ship's captain by the place of the sun, the growth and waning of the moon, reading the stars, and by the small compass which I still have, for it is ever in my pocket. That small metal disk has not ceased to remind me that the Father of Lights has watched over me all my life. There were times when I knew a comforter walked beside me, and I was not alone.

I found later that all through the tribes south of Boston the word had spread to look for me and guide me to Massasoit, for they knew better than the English how to find the lost and succor the weak, which I was then, witless, half frozen, beyond hunger, curled up like a child. They carried me to Massasoit's winter swamp village. It saved my life.

Massasoit flung his match coat over me, a great beaver cape that I had seen one of the squaws making for him in years before. But I was so cold that I struggled to get out of it and close to the fire that lit the longhouse for they had carried me there. Massasoit put his hand on my shoulder and pushed me down again. I thought in my despair that he was rejecting me. I found out the reason when they bathed my feet in cold water and then in warmer and then warmer. I have never felt so great a pain. They put me into their hot house, where I sat alone buck naked, as the English say of the Indians, and where I could not stop crying from the pain and from the evil that had exiled me from those that I loved.

Massasoit sent a message to Mary, that I was safe. I stayed with the tribe until the early spring when the world was deep in mud and the ice jams broke on the streams.

I bargained with Massasoit for land on the east shore of the Seekonk river so that I could make a place for Mary and the children. It was where Rehoboth is now. I expected only Mary and maybe a servant and farm hand, to come by land with our animals and goods as she had done before. Massasoit had promised an escort for her.

One day in early spring as I stood on the bank of the river I saw a two masted pinnace in the distance, and knew the soldiers had found me. I started up the bank to hide when I heard a wondrous voice, "What cheer Roger, my dear, heigh ho!" and other voices, "Ho, ho there. Ho!"

It was four young men who had promised to come and start a new free place as we had planned by the fire in a time that fall that seemed so long past. They were keeping their promise to find me in the spring. I cannot believe to this day that young William Harris was the first to jump from the boat to the shore and into my arms. Thomas Angel followed him, and John Smith, a miller who had been banished when I was, on the same day in the same court, he for the use of unseemly and ungodly language to his apprentice, Francis Weeks. He had brought Francis with him and spoke to him by habit as if he were a dog. Four of them, four angels, I thought then, and they were for there was no time or leisure then for argument and betrayal. We had to live.

They had come all the way from Salem by boat, for Massasoit had sent a message to Mary for me of where to find me beyond the jurisdiction of the Bay Colony as the law had demanded. They brought all we had planned. Throckmorton had kept his word to mortgage my house, and the boat was piled high with hand plows, shovels, bags of lime, seeds, and before God the largest cheese I have ever seen. And above all, axes! I think when I remember the beginning of things I will always hear the sound of the axe, a sound like turtles making love, the sound of our new world in the making.

Summer came on. We planted our first field and made a rude shelter. Mary wrote me in Throckmorton's hand for she was shy of her own writing. She sent her letters by Indian scout, for none of us trusted the English. Reassurance and love and the holding of those letters in my hands brought strength to me, those and the need to prepare for winter that began all through New England in the late spring and was the ever present topic of accord, discord, and habit.

Then, as if there had not been enough hardship for us all, came a letter from my ancient friend, Mr. Winslow, the governor of Plymouth, professing his own and other's love and respect for me but saying that the Massachusetts Bay authorities had decided Seekonk was within

Plymouth's bounds, and they were loath to displease the Bay on whom they depended for so much. He suggested that I move but to the other side, the west side of the water where we would be safe and free, for the Seekonk was the border, and we would be beyond any jurisdiction but the Narragansett's.

We lost then our first harvest, but there was no choice but to move still farther beyond the confines of what they considered the edge of the civilized world. Back and forth we rowed canoas with the seeds we had left, our tools, and wood that had already been cut and planed, all that five men had in the world on that day. We left the valuable pinnace at Plymouth, for we knew not yet a harbor to moor her safely.

I was at the prow of the first canoa, half standing to see if any had seen us and were awaiting our crossing. We had no idea whether the fierce Narragansetts would let us land. At least in four or five years, I had learned their language, not the private ones of each tribe yet, but that they use to treat with one another.

We scanned the west shore. They were waiting for us, five tall Narragansett warriors, standing together, their copper skin shining in the sun. Any one of them could have killed us and thrown us into the river, but thank God they were not painted for war.

I called out, "What cheer?" the only English most of them knew, and then their own word for friend, Netop. What cheer Netop! They guided us to a rock where there was a natural landing and I stepped ashore to this place where I am still. I had been there before when I lived in Plymouth. It was then I had found Canonicus, that shy, wise man who distrusted the new strangers with their skin, he said, as pale as a fish belly. All he feared for his tribal kingdom came to pass.

He was a taciturn old man, a bit of a curmudgeon, but somehow he trusted me. My attempts to learn the language softened his wary heart and sometimes even made the old man smile. I think, too, he was proud because I was so open in wanting to know about his people and how they lived. I learned to love him to his dying day and he let me come where few had ever dared within his old heart. On his last days he asked me to come and be with him and make his shroud of my own cloth.

So when the lookouts took me to him, he welcomed me by engulfing me in his arms so I could hardly breathe, for he was a large strong old man. They had been waiting for the boats to land, for of course he had heard what had happened, and had kept knowledge of my movements. My exile gave him a cause even beyond affection to help us, for he ever hated the Saints. He paced with me the land that would be our new Providence. It lay between two rivers, a fine peninsula jutting out into Narragansett Bay, with sandy bottoms on the rivers that bound it, and a high hill behind the shore that rose into the wilderness above.

We stood on the hill of what would be our town, seeing only the fine harbor, the confluence of two rivers, all the riches the earth could give, and that quickly. Behind us there was a barracade of virgin trees, maple, oak, sycamore, a few evergreens but not enough to sour the soil. To eat, to feed our families in time, we cut down some trees that first day to make small sunny patches for Indian planting, and girdled more for clearance of the fields to plant the next year in the English way. A girdled tree will bleed to death of its sap within a year. We left a few to make shelter for the cattle in hot weather.

There was no time within my mind then for any but daily task and practical dreams, a field, a house, a shelter for the beasts. Fencing to keep out the critters that could in one night eat our whole harvest for the winter. I see now that we, I, creature of expectations, was simply facing what most of the humans in the world face day after day year after year century after century. What we call the gifts of civilized man touch them not but are as clouds in the sky over their heads bringing war or peace.

I had had a trading business in Salem, and I took for granted that I could pick up my trading where I had left off. It had been my way of making a living. Canonicus told me the Narragansetts had begun to yearn for such luxuries the English brought as pots and pans and cloth the squaws had not wove theirselves. He sighed then, to match my sigh, and said the word they used for women and creatures and female animals altogether. For his part, he said, he would not accept money for the land, but if at any time he required sugar, he would accept my gift. Through the years I was bit often by Canonicus's sweet tooth.

But for a while I saw no way to trade. My exile had cut me off from the main harbor at Boston, and it was necessary that I make friends and allies with the Dutch at New Amsterdam to get supplies. Sometimes in all these decisions, troubles, daily pin pricks, axe blows, gnat bites that I thought exiled my soul from my Father of Lights as never before, I would stand and think that I had been guided to what some have called everyman, and others, more ironical, the facts of life. I saw myself as led by God to my fellowman to share his food, his hope, his fears, and his hunger.

Later in the year came three more of the men who had promised to join us: Throckmorton, my dearest friend of all of them, one Green, and Mr. Verin who was the son of one of the deacons of the Salem church, all old companions. They brought my Mary and my children and their own families. They came by land for none of them had yet been singled out for punishment by Boston.

We survived the summer, and the next winter. We survived war. Every person there, children and all, and there must have been thirty or so, was for all of the second summer in the worst danger until the burning of Providence so many years later. By the second year, thirty families had come to New Providence, for so I named the settlement, all with equal sharing out of the land I had bought of Canonicus. Rumor flew that the savage warlike Pequots were trying to gain allies among all the tribes to start a border war and rid themselves of what they termed the Yengee vermin. The Pequots were courting their long-time enemies, the Narragansetts, to join them as allies.

It brought me again to a task I was not prepared for, for true life never prepares us for the future; plans are child's toys in the face of the unknown. I took the first step to represent the English colonies in what would be years of negotiations with the tribes. Before God I saved many lives, and made many terrible mistakes, but I answered the cruelty of the Massachusetts Bay Colony with offering my protection to them. Revenge is not my way. I have never known how to do it. More than that, it had not been the grandees of Boston but plain people who had been lured by commercial promises to the new land, or chosen it as the only alternative to hopelessness, who would die. This I knew. I was trusted and they were not. I had made all the moves of friendship without arrogance, which I fear is an ever present trait among the island English, and not understood as the weakness it is by strangers.

So when I heard that there was a war council between the Pequots and the Narragansetts, and when at the same time letters from Governor Winthrop requested me to try and stop an alliance, to hinder the league labored for by the Pequots against us, the Lord guided me to quick action. I put my life in His hands. I scarce mentioned the danger to Mary. Alone in my canoa for there was no other boat or help without spreading war panic, I set out to cut through a stormy wind along the bay into great seas and finally to the house of Canonicus. He met me coldly for the first time since we had been friends, for he was very sour and accused the English of sending the plague among them and threatening to kill him.

Much of it had been told him by flatterers and our ill-willers. I knew I would have to stay until his soul was sweetened again. I posed to him that the English had caught the plague, too, and that God who made us all had struck us with death as well. He accused the Yengees of lying, stealing, idleness, and uncleanliness, and I told him they were sins of his own and all people, which he did not deny.

He took a stick and broke it into ten pieces for each broken word he harbored against us; I admit that he missed none, for it had been my struggle ever since I had first touched these shores to try and be the go-between who taught peace, and more than that, less prejudice, more honesty, and better manners, which would have saved so many lives.

I stayed three days, forced to lodge and mix with the bloody Pequot ambassadors, who came painted for war. There were times when my trial of friendliness stuck in my throat, for to me they reeked with the blood of my countrymen massacred on the Connecticut river. I knew I could nightly look for their bloody knives at my throat also.

God protected me and helped me to break to pieces the Pequots' negotiations, for Canonicus had never trusted them, they being blood enemies. The Narragansetts asked only that women and children be preserved when the English stormed the Pequot fort at Mystic, for that was their way in war. That was another promise unkept, and for my sins, I aided John Mason who led the assault by advice on how to surprise the fort, a shame of myself and my countrymen I carry to this day. I was told the way into the fort by a Narragansett friend who could spy upon their preparations.

The soldiers from Massachusetts Bay picked a night when the Mystic fort was more crowded than usual, and they took it, burned it with all the people within. Women, children, all, burned to death there, and the few who fled were picked off by the soldiers. And when the morning came and the Pequots were nearly wiped out in one night, like burning snakes in a rock pile, my countrymen from what they called Christendom knelt and thanked Almighty God for that slaughter. How could we who yearned for neighbor peace know that in the name of God when the Massachusetts Bay Colony negotiated with my neighbor Narragansetts they did it in bad faith?

If I had an excuse for being part of this it was to protect the families of those who had come to Providence and to Rhode Island, for they had begun coming in droves, all seeking the same thing, their freedom to worship as they would without danger to their lives, some land to farm for their families, and some daily peace without looking over their shoulders. Of course words were another matter. How they fought with one another and always have!

The Baptists fought the Familists, the Anglicans fought the Antinomians, I fought the Quakers who I thought a religiously lazy violent lot. Mrs. Hutchinson's followers fought Mr. Gorton's followers. I must say honestly, for I am far from saintly, that both of them pushed my tolerance almost to the breaking point and sometimes in the night in those dialogues we have alone in the dark I wished they had not come to our plantation.

There was even some humor in it all. When Mrs. Hutchinson's house was rattled by an earthquake and she announced to her followers that the Holy Ghost had shook it, I had to smile and shake my head for the Father of Lights when He gave me my road to travel did not relieve me of wit.

Mrs. Hutchinson was a civilized, witty woman who entertained as well as she could on the frontier, had a wonderful humor and levity, and heard voices. She and I spoke much, and had a fondness for one another, for we had made a friend in common, young Harry Vane, who had come to Massachusetts Bay and being one of the most important men in the government, with whom he did not get along, he was elected governor. Alas, he was far far too liberal in his thought and his religion for the Visible Saints. Once over their surprise at the turn of the voting, the Visible Saints rallied and got rid of him.

He had tried to protect Mrs. Hutchinson, and me as well, from their constant judgement. He had soon become too shocked by the lack of levity and the force of orthodoxy to stay. He had gone back to London and was to be one of the prides of the Long Parliament.

He rode often in the last months he was in Massachusetts Bay Colony to visit us and we became close friends. When he went back to England there grew between us a correspondence that drew us ever closer for we shared much in our hopes for purity of worship, and a new simplicity of faith that imitated the poor powerless Lord Christ Jesus and His followers and not Moses or the Pope of Rome.

Mrs. Hutchinson and her family and followers stayed too short a time, and they went on to Long Island among the Dutch, she said, to be out of hearing of Mr. Gorton's shouting. Mr. Gorton, on the other hand, shouted so loud and fought the world so hard that it took longer to be friends with him. He was usually right, but his extreme stands made mine seem mild, and he could, God my witness, make more noise than any man I have ever known.

So those were some of the people who came later and were our loving neighbors and there were many like them. There were the Jews who came from the Spanish America for they had word that we would not exile them. Most, when they arrived, had Spanish names for it had been against the law for them to use their Jewish names. So I had the honor, when one José changed his name back to his secret family one of Abraham Ben Ezra and remarried his wife in the Jewish way, to stand with them in that age-old ceremony and felt myself as one with the first Abraham and Isaac and Jacob who the Lord loved. I traveled, standing there, many centuries at the blessing and the breaking of the glass.

For two years we had survived hunger and war. Unlike the other colonies, which had been pushed near bankruptcy by the greed of their London owners, we owed no man, and were beholden to no man. But we had no right from London to be there, no charter, no grant of land from a king, for our land was bought fairly. But Connecticut and the Massachusetts Bay Colony gnawed at our borders, snipped at us for land and land and land, as if they had not enough.

Their pressure on our borders became too dangerous, far more than the Indian presence. It was considered that we were their menace; we had not only not suffered as meant for our wicked ways, but had gone ahead and made a home for ourselves and were reported, I gathered, even to be hospitable to anyone without judgement.

It was obvious we needed a charter to protect us. We all met and decided together, after long debate, what to do, for government by consensus meant that everyone's voice be heard. And heard. And heard. Finally it was decided that since I had connections in London, many of which I must say I was derided for as a braggart if I mentioned any London friend, that I should go to London to plead our cause.

Rumor and news from old England had for two years since the Long Parliament had first met been both ominous and wonderful. Harry Vane and his friends were in the Parliament, which the king had finally called far too late to repair the damage done in eleven years of autocratic rule. There was first whispering and then open traitorous talk.

The king was like a man attacked by sharks, throwing one piece of meat and then another to rid himself of their jaws. Stafford had been the first, others had followed. No one was safe from his panic. The court moved to Oxford away from the Parliament, abandoning London. The king gathered an army of the troops stationed in Ireland, and mercenaries from the old Protestant wars on the continent of Europe. He was the first in the civil war to raise his standard declaring war on the Parliament. It was done with much ceremony before Nottingham Castle, but since it was wet and muddy where the flag pole was stuck into the ground, it fell over.

There were signs and portents, storms and strange clouds in the heavens, all of them reported to us as ominous. Harry Vane was one of the leaders of a government cobbled together to raise an army and protect London. Rumor grew to monstrous size. The king was dead. Harry was dead. The king had won a battle. The Earl of Essex, the dour, fat son of that beautiful man who had entranced the old queen, was appointed to lead a Parliamentary army. Someone had made a rhyme that the world was turned upside down and it was quoted, sung, and became a part of swearing in the city. This was all the tangle of rumor, fact, hope, and fear that made up a country bursting into civil war. My letters of the time were as near to St. Stephen's chapel as they could be for they came from my dearest friend, Harry, and from his pious wife, and so I saw the events through their eyes which fitted as near my own as a pair of spectacles.

Money was gathered for me to go to London, God knows from poor pockets, not much, but enough to get me there. I went from Providence by pinnace with a Dutch trader to New Amsterdam to await a ship. I could not because of my banishment sail from Boston. That, as many things, I saw later as a blessing, for until I appeared in London and was much honored and bespoke to my surprise, I think the Massachusetts Bay proprietors hardly took into their plans that I was gone.

Mary, as always, took from my hands the practical decisions in my wanderings. Six children by then, no, five, all but one healthy and strong and stubborn, growing to people of their own souls and none of mine or Mary's.

I came to New Amsterdam when their own Indian troubles were beginning and I offered myself as interpreter for the trouble between the Mohawks and the Dutch since I spoke both languages, but it was to no avail. They wanted war, both of them, as hot as lusting men without the door of a whorehouse. Oh that blind need that lets nothing, no child, no land, no God, when men want war, and take that lust as the command of God.

As we sailed out of that beautiful port of New Amsterdam, I stood on the aft deck with the war-shocked Dutch families who had escaped New Amsterdam, the white sails full of the wind, and were going back to Holland. We watched the war begin.

Women and children, old men and their wives, were fleeing the burning boweries they had worked so hard to build. What had one day been the quiet town, so clean, so well built, so Dutch, was becoming an inferno, fire thrusting it back to the raw and untamed land. It was not until I returned two years gone that I found that sweet Anne Hutchinson and her family had perished on Long Island, sacrificed to blind war.

XXVI

In the New Testament the situation is this: the speaker, our Lord Jesus Christ, Himself absolutely expressing opposition, stands in a world which in turn absolutely expresses opposition to Him and His Teaching.

— SØREN KIERKEGAARD

I SIT WATCHING THE WATER OF THE SEEKONK FLOW by as I do so often, especially in such days as this in April, another April give to me by God for I did not die last winter as I had thought to do. The world is released from its ice prison, and the water flows quick, full, flung free from winter and rushing into spring. A new pale leaf has broke loose from its mama tree, and dances with the flow; a small branch caught by a breeze and flung into the water; the dash of a trout through the water ceiling to catch a dragonfly.

There was much peace like this at the beginning, sweet quietness, days of the soul's rest and the hands' work, then so much trouble for so long after. The Bay could not leave us alone. We were the itch it had to scratch.

That first voyage back home in 1642 was the most peaceful time I can remember, the finest sailing, the following of the trade winds, the ship cutting the water so it slid by the sides in white waves and joined the wake as if we were on a sleigh, silent as ghosts, the wake a white torrent, I as full of wonder as a child. Oh it was a grand thing to see the sails aloft and feel the living ship beneath my feet. The rigging and the sails sang as the sea chanties say. I would sit in my cabin and hear the creak and gentle groan of the living ship beneath us.

The captain took me to the crow's nest. We climbed hand over hand, I terrified, he so at home I thought him more agile than a monkey, a Dutch monkey, and it made me laugh so that I nearly lost my hold. He manhandled me into the crow's nest, and once I had got over the fear of being a bird rolling and pitching aloft, and made myself open my eyes and look to the horizon, I saw the ocean. Ocean, so much of earth, sometimes blue, some green, white veils, flashes of pure gold, silver white at evening, indigo at dawn, when the stars hung down over it so huge, so bright I thought that if I could fly I could touch them.

The whales spouted, the porpoises played, and once a sea monster drew even the sailors to the bow to watch it. It was as long as the ship, a Leviathan that could not be caught in a net. The sailors said it was an old bull wanting company, meaning us no harm. He followed the ship, swam beneath it, played it. One time his head surfaced before the prow, his tail thrashed behind the stern as if we rode Leviathan to England.

I had brought aboard a large skin pouch that held a tumble of bits of paper, bark, sailcloth, note books with the stains of weather blotting out words, a garbage of words to be sorted and made into the book I saw in my mind's eye. I hoped that I might turn them into pages of enough interest for a London bookseller to publish. I spent much time in my small cabin putting together a simple dictionary of the Indian language, for I ever thought that if we could speak together we could live together in loving friendship. I had dark times, of course, when I realized that the English in New England had no wish to speak among the savages, as they called them.

I thrust beyond my mind the troubles of the colony for at sea I could do nothing for them, and so had a short six weeks, a blessed time between, to complete a work I had gathered for several years at Cocumscussoc, where Canonicus had sold me land for my trading post. I had finally been able to get supplies from the Dutch and from what John Throckmorton could smuggle to me, for he had took over the pinnace and plied the coast for our needs.

From the green waters of America to the blue waters of the Bristol Channel, I stepped ashore at home, I thought. But it was nothing like the place we had left twelve years before. The dock at Bristol was crowded with soldiers, and one young man, Colonel Feinnes of the Parliamentary army, the son of Lord Saye and Sele, was in command. We had never met but he knew me, for he came forward to the gangplank with letters from Harry and welcomed me and invited me to dinner at the same inn where young John Winthrop and I had drunk Metheglin and planned so much.

Harry told me to get to London as best I could, and come to him at once. He thanked God, he said, for he ever needed my advice and comfort. It was easy to buy a nag strong enough to take me, for few of the regiments on either side were paying money. They simply stole and called it commandeering. I made my way to London through a country at war.

What were the signs? They were everywhere. Some villages had been burned by the king's troops scunning for pay. Parliamentary soldiers had commandeered what animals had not been hid, and gave paper tokens in some cynic pay. I was thrust off the road by soldiers passing, not knowing if they were king or Parliament. The inns were choked with people by evening for there were officers staying as well which made them safer.

God my Light this was no dear month of June as I remembered, not the glow, not the fertile fields, I was seeing what war does, even at its beginning, a pall of neglect over the countryside the color of sadness.

I went the other road by Windsor for I still could little bear passing Stoke House, though my dear lord Coke had been dead for nine years and I knew not who lived there. Beyond Windsor, London lay in the distance in the flat Thames valley downriver from Hampton Court. All this was so familiar that I knew where to rein in my horse on a high enough rise for my first look at my city after so long.

In the distance I saw a high wall that seemed to stretch for miles, a few gates in it manned by soldiers. It was London girdled for war. All around it for miles, all through its western approaches, and then to the north between Farrenden and the village of Islington, down the eastern side beyond Shoreditch, and across the Thames behind Southwark, a ten-mile-long trench had been dug by the people of London, old men, women, children, all working day to night without pay and sometimes without food, to save the city. The wall was nine feet high, behind the great moat, nine feet deep and nine feet wide.

It was manned already by the sentries from the trained bands, who had ever in London, since I was a child, dressed up as soldiers and paraded and practiced what they termed the arts of war, early in the mornings, in winter only once a week, in summer, a playing at arms each fine morning, kept together by expecting the Papists, for there was yet much fear of them. Then and always there were the Spanish, then the Dutch, for enemies. I knew them all, their colors, their uniforms, for they were made up of the guildsmen. My father was one of them, from the Merchant Tailors, proud of his pot, his armor, his musket, all of which he had kept gleaming since I could remember, a play soldier in a play field. Now it was real, and it was their own people, and they stood in small groups as men do who are at an accident, waiting.

I rode into Westminster and left my horse at an inn at Charing Cross. I remember simply standing there, my Indian book in the skin pouch upon my back, my small trunk at my feet, not knowing to go left or right, stunned. This was not my London, this war city, this gray, untended, wild place. Then, almost at once it was as if I had never left, never faced the sea and the wilderness, never gone west beyond Westminster. I was once again the boy I had been within my soul, unblooded by all that had happened to me. I was in my London, my great city.

By September the king's mercenaries, led by lords and knights and gentlemen and all, were winning the west and they seemed certain to connect their western and northern forces to surround and march on London, for who held London held the country, and so far it was the Parliament. The Parliamentary army had as many privileged and titled rich as the king's for the division was not one of class, though the royalists tried to say it was, but one of conviction.

Harry had wrote me that the Parliament had refused to let itself be dissolved. I knew that they had stood from the same constituencies as they had when closed by the king eleven years before. The members and their factions had seethed at the back of the stove until they were at bursting point. They had not changed a principle or a division. On his same throne of stubbornness, the king sat, as he would until he lost his poor blind privileged head. He never in all the war yielded one privilege, one gesture, one power, one honor, one bishop, one foot of what he called his own to rule.

But by Christ's heart it was a sweet time in London, a new place, a changed place where every man could speak his mind, and did, over and over, in ecstasies of new ideas tumbling over one another. The first battle had been fought to a draw, and all waited, and planned and hoped for a new life for all, as they do in time of revolution. My friends welcomed me, Sir William Masham, lovely John Milton, who took me to his printer, an Anabaptist called Webster, though it is strange to me to recall as a stranger a man who has since become for me a dearest neighbor and friend in need.

I published my dictionary, a simple work I thought it, only an introduction to the way my fellowmen, the natives, lived in the American wilderness. It was as organized as I could make it in the short time I had. I thought it a rude lump, and remembered much that I had left out when it was too late, which John Milton told me was ever a worry of writing men. I told the Indian words, as if there were a conversation between the reader and the Indians, and I added essays about how they lived, the gods they worshiped, their manners, and their morals, which I must say I pointed out were often better than ours, as their law of hospitality that saved many a Yengee life, including my own. I did not stint their wildness, their wolves' hearts, their savagery. I prayed that the good of them outweighed the danger of misunderstanding, which could end in bloodier war, not like the meeting of soldiers in fields of Mars, the civilized way of murder as in England, but hidden enemies, massacre, a wiping out as we had done to the Pequots. That was American war. I did not write of it.

I published my book in true humility. I simply wanted people to know how it was. No one was more shocked than I that it was a huge success. I was able to get money to live while I spoke with those in Parliament I hoped would back my cause. It was taken to the streets, the coffee houses, where the tracts were flying out like birds day after day, constant debate for a penny a sheet.

Officers of the Parliamentary army came within our favorite tavern, those known for the more radical element of diners. Fame had happened to me all of a sudden, and I was so unprepared that I made myself foolish with pride in my knowledge, the most pernicious kind of arrogance I know to this day. My little book was suddenly the talk of London. People I knew not came up to our table and greeted me as Watcheer Netop to show they had read my book.

It was fine. Everybody was young. God my Solace, how young we were. We talked of the future as if it were the present which is I believe the first mistake of revolution, for the turn is too rash, and quicker than the mind can follow. So like children, the fine crowds tire, and want their papa like children hoping for sleep without bad dreams, and all that is left of revolution is the residue of change.

I was welcomed as if I had gone abroad for a little while, instead of twelve years. To those in London I had been there, then I was not there, then there again, for it is a bounden certainty in London that if you are not there you are no place, and then when you return you are someplace again, London, the center of the world.

When I think of it, sometimes I am in a tavern. There is John Lilburne holding forth, and as they said of him, he fought the world with the Bible in one hand and the Reports of my lord Coke in the other. Those two, as we all considered, were our guides and outline for a peerless future. Freeborn Jack was ever in an argument. It was said of him that if there were no one else to challenge, Jack would argue with Lilburne and Lilburne with Jack. We often sat and drank together. I was took in among Harry's closest; Rainsborough, who was to become head of the Levelers, my friend Oliver Cromwell. We remembered one another from Otes. It was a new day in a new world, and God my strength, a new hope.

A dozen years dropped from my back, I soon caught the springing step of one at home in London's and Westminster's streets and taverns. I was welcomed at Harry Vane's as at my home. So war was all around us and within our speech and our hearts as we sat by the fire in Harry's study and rehearsed the past in New England. He was embittered against the Massachusetts men for they had treated him shabbily in the one year he had been governor, and he had tried and failed to defend both me and Mrs. Hutchinson whom he had found a charming witty loving woman. He had been the one man who was invited to her meet-

I , R O G E R W I L L I A M S

ings of women. So we sat there by the fire and brought her to life between us, not knowing then that she was already dead, killed by the Indians on Long Island in the Dutch war I had seen break out in the wake of the ship that had brought me to England.

Harry did banquet me royally; he brought together my Essex friends. I had last seen them, Sir William Masham and Sir Thomas Barrington, at the door of Otes when Mary and I fared forth to the unknown down the wet misty road. I was took to their hearts, all the Barrington and Cromwell and Whalley clan, as if I had been their brother, for they had forgot nothing of what I had stood for, and in the years had growed nearer to my thinking. Sir William Masham did raise laughter by remembering me the time I tried silent prayer and the maids thought I had forgot my lines. All those little things, all those moments of the happiness we had had to leave were welcomed again. Laud was in the Tower, the king at Oxford, London waiting to be besieged, and all of us young again drinking wine in the fire and candlelight, banging on the Turkey carpet that covered Harry's refectory table, and talking shouting agreeing, disputing far into the night. As the Father of Lights has ever led me into moments of happiness to sustain me, it was a blessed and would be a tragic time though we did not know it then.

I found that I could hold forth from my inmost thought as I had done so privily with Harry Vane, now with them all for they had grown young again, too, Oliver St. John who I had last seen at his marriage to Jug, Oliver Cromwell who sat a little sullen for he had come through rain to appear at the Parliament and banquet me. He roused himself from the darkness beyond the fire once or twice to ask questions about the Indians for they were all fascinated, not with our legal border troubles and our survival, but with the red men.

They treated me as if I were some Walter Raleigh instead of the country bumpkin I felt myself to be among them. I remembered what John Winthrop had said to me about my scholar's hands, and I watched those delicate hands of all my comrades, a little discreet lace at their wrists, holding fine wineglasses, that caught the beams of candlelight and threw them hither and yon as they gestured. I was embarrassed. I lost all thread of the argument and sat with my workworn hands in my lap. Then suddenly I laughed and it stopped the table riot. Sir Thomas Barrington was speaking, and he looked to me.

"You are amused, Roger?" He seemed annoyed.

"No, you and God forgive me. I was deep in a shameful thought, I mean ashamed when I should be proud, embarrassed when I should be dancing upon the table. Look, my loving friends, these are the hands that Mr. Winthrop once called scholar's hands and indeed they are. Scholar of rowing mile after mile, scholar of digging and plowing and surviving," and I placed my hands upon the table.

"Before our God dear Roger, they say it all." Harry Vane raised his glass and we drank and there was laughter all the way to the solemnities of Westminster.

It was indeed a blessed time, the first that I remember, when a man could speak his rathers without fear, and we thought God help us that that would last forever. But out beyond the warmth of Harry's table the worst of treasonous words was "toleration." The Scots Covenanters had come to an assembly at Westminster to decide on the form the new state church would take. They were holding Parliament to ransom, for they would not bring their needed army down to join the Parliamentary army without the certainty that toleration would not be brooked. All that those at Harry's table stood for, freedom of worship and conscience, was imperiled. The army was with us, for most of the officers were for toleration, many called Seekers, but the Parliament distrusted the army from the beginning. It was a teetering time.

The Westminster Assembly demanded no less than that the Parliament would pass an act to make a Presbyterian Church of England, Laud in broad Scots, Harry called it. He had been of the committee who had gone to Scotland to draw up a covenant and had managed only to add a clause and get it by the Scots that left a chink open in the door to toleration without their knowing it.

Oliver Cromwell had been asleep, his head upon the table, still wet, still dirty from his ride into London. He aroused himself when the inevitable word came up—toleration—and took over the evening. He pounded his fist on the table until the candles and the glasses jumped and the silver trenchers clanged; he made a music of his fury. "By the bowels of Christ it is blackmail! Evil Scots Presbyterian ignoble blackmail!" And he drifted off to sleep again. "That one was always since a boy either boisterous or in tears," Sir Thomas whispered, and all the cousins laughed as they had done for years at Oliver.

Harry interrupted for he was fond of Oliver, one of his closest friends. "I will say again what one of the members said when Oliver was called a sloven for his dress in the first year of the Long Parliament before the war began." He pointed to the sleeping Oliver and kept his finger there. "'That sloven,'" he quoted the familiar words, and went on pointing, "'that sloven whom you see before you hath no ornament in his speech; but that sloven, I say, if we should ever come to a breach with the king (which God forbid!) in such a case, I say, that sloven will be the greatest man in England.'"

The king's army finally began their march to a rendezvous to connect his forces of the north and the west to surround London. The city was in a riot, trained bands ordered westward, the apprentices flying to arms. I stood in the Strand and watched them pass, bright men-boys off to defend the reform against what they had been told were the forces of darkness headed by the king. It was a fine sight and I would then I could join them and what were the words we used? Fight for the right? But winter was coming, and it was growing cold. There were petitions to stop the war for the coal that kept London warm and dark and obscured by dirty smoke was in the hands of the king's army in the west, and the stalemate to open the supply was caused by the Scots they said, and their Presbyterian brothers in the Westminster Assembly who went on meeting and arguing and leaving the north unprotected.

I had long by then been useful, I hope, to the city for preaching to the troops when they needed me, and for taking in charge crews to go into the country to bring back wood for the poor of London who were without sea coal and had the winter before, stolen every post, pillar, bench, trough, pigpen, lattice that could be removed in the night to keep theirselves warm.

I had volunteered to organize forays into the countryside to gather wood for the poor, and I had been give a small troop of soldiers who had been woodsmen to help me, some wagons, axes, and orders to cut wood. I needed to be useful. All the praise and the cosseting and the dinners had assuaged my long starvation more than any food, but I needed to be part of the war, to work.

I had caught excitement as a spirit that gave me joy but unbeknownst to myself, I was catching war as a disease, a seduction. I know in my life war has been a necessity, but as a game of valor, it is a brutal seductive lie. I was drunk with events. In my soul and in my dreams, like other men, I wanted to be a soldier and fight.

XXVII

Democracy. I do not conceyve that ever God did ordeyne as
a fitt government either for church or commonwealth. . . .
As for Monarchy and aristocracy they are both of them
clearly approved, and directed in scripture yet so as (God)
referreth the sovereigntie to himself, and setteth up Theoc-
racy in both, as the best form of government.

— JOHN COTTON, CALLED
THE PATRIARCH OF NEW ENGLAND

All controversies concerning the church, ministry and worship, the last appeal must come to the bar of the people.

— ROGER WILLIAMS

THIS EARLY MORNING I AM STILL ABED, FOR MARY has
decided I have a cold and must needs put on the poultices and drink
the possets she knows for sure will cure me. So I stink of some herbs
and smell like a lady of others, and cannot speak a word for my voice
has departed this world which Mary says is God's blessing when she is
trying to get me well, for she does not have to listen to my complaints.

So I lie here unable to whine, which is the only pleasure in colds and
agues, and to make matters worse who should visit my mind as he does
so often but my old friend who called himself my enemy, Mr. John Cot-

ton. Never to his dying day did he forgive me for arguing with him. Now his son has took up the hatred and called me a servant of the devil, whoremonger, heretic, drunkard, etc., etc., and all such fribbling spite away beyond the accusations even of the orthodox and the Papists. Well, I can bear it for I hear he is a sloughing weak fellow, the product of too strong a father, and must spit his hate on somebody.

I must admit that for too long I saw his father as a soul-deceiving and soul-killing friend. He would not let me be. His admonishing letters followed me to Providence and then to Cocumscussoc until I sighed when I saw his writing. He was convinced he was trying to save my soul, but hatred burned his pages, that awful hatred that masks itself as Christian love. I answered them with all the humility I could muster within myself, which I admit was far short of pure meekness. Then he wrote words so terrible to me that I had no answer and never forgot them. I carried that last letter for so long under my jerkin. It lay in my sweat, waiting for the Father of Lights to tell me what to say. The words are ever with me when I think of him, "If you had perished in the wilderness your blood had been on your own head; it was your sin to procure it and your sorrow to suffer it."

It was at my beloved Cocumscussoc, my trading post uphill from the fine plain in the Narragansett country that reached down to the sea, where I wrote answers and tossed them away for they were too strong, too weak, not words but blunted weapons. The words were never right, and so I kept them in the same deerskin satchel where I kept the flotsam for my dictionary that I thought then would never see the light of day.

When I go back in my soul to those times, I am at my rough-hewn table that grew smoother with the hands, the copper pans, the cloth, the sugar and salt and pepper and nails, the pelts to pay, the to and fro across it. It is cleared, the door shut, and it is an evening in summer, not yet time for the pitch-pine torch nor the lantern nor the candle, the room smells of drying tobacco and summer herbs, and I am answering Mr. Cotton, my dearest enemy, a good solid target. In the hours that return to me I have one of those passionate monologues I think of as dialogues. So words on old paper bring back fine moon-washed nights where I hardly needed a lantern to work after the fires behind the skin walls of the wigwam villages had died down and I had the gift of choosing to be alone.

It was for me the saving of my spirit in a grand dream that sometimes I knew would not ever see the light of any eye other than my own, and sometimes the dream would be so strong I would think myself hollering for the right to follow the God's gift of one's own mind all the way across the fields and sea to Boston. I was so took up with zeal and cause. For the rest of my time I knew at least it must be wrote, must be, however long the wait, for it hounded me. I had been haunted ever since my exile from Massachusetts by the accusations sent ever after me across the borders of our haven. And am lost in silence and my mind. Am alone in a room filled with disputation, speaking, but when I raise my quill to my forehead and listen there is only silence, beloved silence, and I am in the woods of Cocumscussoc, alone.

Much interrupted, sometimes by months, sometimes by days, I worked on, arguing with ghosts. Many a morning I would go to the table before the first of the Indians came to me to trade, and write my disputation so furiously that when friends came, as Canonicus or Miantonomo, they would stand and wait so still I would not know they were there, for they had respect for my writing. They termed it war with the bird's feather. I was, of course, answering that letter I could never answer, when he had accused me of bringing my own death by my own act, had I perished in the winter of my flight.

When I think of it, I can see my own writing before me, smell the carbon ink, and the scent of fall leaves blowing in a faint wind, and have the faint hope that even in this wilderness retreat for my soul, nobody will interrupt me. God my witness and my love I was happy in that place. It was six or so miles by boat down the western shore of the bay from Providence, and it was, for my soul's peace, at the ends of the earth from that fuming and fighting and all the falls and snags of Providence.

Eastward before me lay a vast sweep of fields and meadows where the villages of my friends gently sloped to the water, and beyond, in the sea, our island of goats, our Prudence, and the one within the eye's scope we called Patience, where Dionysus, the billy goat, with his great horns and his stinking smell ruled his harem with the terrible dignity of a sultan.

It was a place where I could think, could speak to paper, could hold forth as if I spoke in the very Parliament in some sky commonwealth without interruption, and drop the words on paper. But never would I have the chance to do more than dream and write in private. At least I thought so then until my return to London, where the chance to speak out was dropped into my lap.

Clergy had been appointed and called to Westminster from all over England and Scotland to debate what form the Church of England should take, what words to use, what clothes to wear, what necessary brutality be relied on to bring the public to its proper place in their sight of God. There were five dissenters to speak for toleration—only five against the weight of hundreds of English clergy concerned about their livings, and the threat of the Scottish blackmail.

Much was spoke in admiration of Mr. Cotton among them. They invited him to the assembly as a spokesman and advisor for the New England way of shutting mouths, as it was when I was sent forth. They saw it as their duty to kill any hope of liberty of conscience which the fathers of the church (this time of the Kirk) saw as dangerous sedition.

That was in the sun of their thinking. In the shade, and all the way down into a dungeon of darkness, they wanted the king's power and no change other. Oh, the Pharisees, the fathers, hidebound, righteous, always with us! I find myself this late in life sometimes sliding into being one of them out of the impatience that comes, alas, with age. Right as the righteousness our Lord warned against, certain as the death of thinking, until I catch myself and let my youth of seeking come back to save me, and the devil's gift of certainty fades and blows away, and I know again that without search and trial no man attains right persuasion.

So there, in London, at last we came to the shock of battle, Mr. Cotton and I. He had used me unkindly, but that had been long ago, and the caring had become less sharp through the time. He pleaded age and did not come, but one of the more zealous of his tribe then made the mistake that opened the door wide for me to speak.

Mr. Cotton, who took his thoughts and writings with great solemnity, hardly ever wrote a letter, and certainly not one to me, that he did not make many copies to send to those who he considered needed more strength and argument to fight the awful libertine heresies that were

eating at the edges of his church. One of the Westminster clergy published one of Mr. Cotton's letters to me defending his orthodoxy and
the heavenly command for earthly punishment for heresy. It was a
long, well-constructed letter showing me as a sinner against his conscience, and deserving of any punishment meted out to me, to Anne
Hutchinson, poor saintly foolish woman, and to so many others. It was
all old history to me—Anabaptists flogged, the wild sects exiled—and
most to Rhode Island.

It was a letter that had been circulated for years among the Visible
Saints who nodded over it, all to explain their cause. When it, instead,
hoisted them on their own petard, they accused me of publishing it in
secret. It was not true. I had long forgot that one, for the letter ever
with me to this day was of that one terrible line, "Had you perished
. . ." Still it brings tears to my old eyes here snuggled in my bed in the
morning, that one should write so to another who had been a friend.

It set London in an uproar for the people were watching the Westminster Assembly and repeating any word that leaked out from the
flow of their argument. It had to be answered for the sake of those who
had gathered as Seekers and lovers of the freedom to worship by God's
word. I doubt whoever published Mr. Cotton's letter even knew I was
in London for they were so intent upon their own noses. I still cannot
believe the mistakes they made.

Harry Vane persuaded me to answer. We used without shame the
short and honeyed fame that my dictionary of the Indian language
brought me. It opened a door that was the miracle of why I was there
indeed for the quarrel focused the light of opinion on my colony and
what it stood for. So it was, I believe, within the walls of Westminster
that the decision was made to give me a charter to protect us from our
ravening, greedy neighbors. Harry was so practical about his hope for
answer, he said I should write what we had talked of for months, what
I had spoken of in my meetings with the Baptists and others whose
only hope was liberty of soul, for they had been much persecuted both
in Massachusetts and in old England.

It was a huge task, and I took from his house many notebooks and
wrote first an answer as a tract, which counted only to bring my name
to the public as a Seeker. It broke the ice jam of my mind I had hoped
and prayed for those many years. A barrage of words flowed, as if the

Father of Lights were telling me what to say and how to say it, a fountain of words, a flood of proofs from the Bible, as one who would write a case for Star Chamber as my lord Coke had so long ago taught me, "Plug up all holes in disputation. Leave no way for your adversaries to get within your argument."

I recalled as tools of writing all the paints and flourishes I had been taught to write and those who read it had been taught to read; I used all the pretenses of a formal dialogue, the erudition, the fine forms, the delicacies, to say a thing so simple and so lovely in its ways. I used the language of the mighty and it brought me to their eyes at the right time. It was enough to make this colony an example and a warning, I must needs add, for the rest of the new and brave, greedy English on these shores.

I called it *The Bloody Tenent of Persecution for Cause of Conscience.* It was too quickly written, too quickly published, too freighted with that polite and grand servility expected of a work in that formal way of saying, but I was finally able to answer John Cotton with thunder and passion and a cry to save the lives of those who would disagree with the orthodox whether in politics or in religion. It was my protection of the minority against the dead weight of custom. And it protects them still, at least here in Rhode Island. John Cotton is long dead and in the pit of rottenness. But sometimes, well sometimes I think I did not say enough to stop the ever vile and evil persecution for the cause of conscience for I have ever give my life to speaking out on it, ever on watch for weeds among the lilies, and swords in hand again, or the rope or the garrote. Why, not but a few years ago, the Quakers were hanged at Boston, and a woman taken in adultery in Connecticut.

The Bloody Tenent labeled John Cotton forever. Persecutor. Unmerciful. Oh that poor man who carried to his death my rancor. I clung to the dreadful certainty that I had heard God. I saw myself as innocent as the naked Indian boy who often guided me through the wilderness.

I took my notebooks and my satchel of rude notes with me wherever I went that fall, in the rain, along the axle-deep rutted roads, in chambers where we could find them, in cold, and in the fields, wherever there was a time and a snatch of quiet and peace, I wrote. When I see it now in the vision that brings me more pleasure than the words theirselves, I am in a thousand places . . . *yet David was holy and precious to*

God still (though like a jewel fallen in the dirt) whereas King Ahab, though acting his fasting and humiliation, was but Ahab still, though his act (in itselfe) was a duty and found success with God. Those words bring me not a book but the feel of my black lead pencil in my hand, while I wait in a field for the woodsmen to finish cutting a tree for the wood to be distributed among the poor of London, who already in that brutal winter were rioting for the war to be stopped. I remember hoping for a minute, a few more minutes before the troubles and noises of the world came down upon me.

It was in Essex that the local landowner and his servants used pitchforks and staves to try to run us out of his deer park. While I felt for him, I remember wishing he would go away, so I could snatch from all the hurry and flurry of war, a little time to think, to question, or to breathe in. That night in a low inn I remember writing, *in a free state no magistrate hath power over the bodies, goods, lands, liberties of a free people, but by their free consents.* I remember sitting awhile and staring at a dirty wall with writing upon it too faint to read, and the print of one bloody hand. I was wondering if I could sleep after such thinking, and made myself a note to explain the policy we had in Providence of earning the right to be a freeman and vote. I yawned and went to bed, and could not sleep until I had got up again and wrote in the dark, *Try all things. . . .*

I had begun it in Harry's house. *First, that the blood of so many hundred thousand soules of Protestants and Papists, split in the wars of present and former ages for their respective Consciences, is not required nor accepted by Jesus Christ, the Prince of Peace.* I saw it as a cry for mercy, a political tool, and God knows one of those flying objects set to rouse the world from its sleep, though in the long run, the world tends yet to weaken, turn over, and go to sleep again.

It was published in a London seething, a London changing, a London at civil war and in a panic to raise more trained bands to retake Bristol, for it had fallen almost without a fight a few days before. Long as it was, my book sold all over London and was much discussed, some in the churches, certainly in the taverns and the meetings of the sectarians who dared to meet. It had given them a voice and I thanked God for that. When it was time to sail again, with the charter in my pocket and atop the world with joy and success, I sailed from Southampton on a wilder voyage to reach my neighbors.

I carried with me a letter signed by the powerful Parliamentary committee for the colonies to allow me to land at Boston. I remember going through it alone seeing no one I knew, and taking boat to Plymouth when I could find someone to take me. But when I was brought into Plymouth there waiting for me was a flotilla of canoes and boats from Providence and from Rhode Island come to welcome me and carry me home. It was I think the most joyful day of my life.

While I was still at sea, my book was burned by the hangman at Paul's Cross by order of the Presbyterian majority in Parliament.

XVIII

If you please to ask me what my praescription is: I will not put you off to Christian moderation or Christian Humility, or Christian Prudence, or Christian Love, or Christian Selfedenyall, or Christian Contention or Patience. For I design a Civil, an humane and political medecine, which if the God of Heaven please to bless, you will find it Effectual. . . .

— LETTER TO MAJOR JOHN MASON
AND GOVERNOR THOMAS PRENCE
FROM ROGER WILLIAMS

*I*T IS WHAT WE CALL THE DEAD OF WINTER, AND IT IS so alive here on Foxes Hill that I wonder at the words. I have come out every year but those I spent in England at this time, in late January for it is then that I came to be myself so long ago in the white miles of snow. That was, let me see, by the old calendar it was 1635 still, by the new 1636, for the New Year since I was a baby boy was Lady Day; now it is the first of January. As if it mattered. I know, my soul knows, my heart knows that there was a time that the world was all in snow, and I the only one in it. Except for the thousand hidden and surviving, as they are now, even in this cleared and spacious meadow on Foxes Hill.

I am drawn here every year that I can climb the hill for it is the nearest place, far enough from all the stretching, yawning, first chores, first smiles, first sadness of the day, and near enough for this old old man to get to. Already the morning smoke rises from the hundred or so chimneys as if one great time called dawn, and that still late at this time of the year, is celebrated in the town. My town. The town I made. Free me for this holy time. It will be short.

I will be missed and one will come for me fussing and patting me down as if I were a dog escaped into the snow and threatening to track it into the clean house. And yet in these few minutes I am interrupted, as always, by daily sweet and sad matters that must be took care of. That little Lydia with child by a French sailor, that other one beat by her husband who quotes the Bible saying she takes too much time with God when she should be serving her husband. The violent damned man. Oh my Father of Lights the Bible hath caused much trouble.

I so love this world around me that I must celebrate when it began for me, reborn in the snow, in the silence of exile. For there is that in me which is forever exiled, must be, must be remembered so. It is so quiet, not a breeze, not an animal, only the path made by the children as they climb the hill to slide down that has led me to my bench. They have made it possible for me to come, preparing the way so I can hobble here, to my bench, my home from home, just for this time.

A fox or a wolf has killed and ate all but a red stain in the snow. Winter is a hungry time. The animals come almost to the doors of the houses. The deer are fed by the children when they can snatch enough from their plates to save for them. The bears sleep yet. The winter-thin wolves and foxes stalk for prey for it is for them the starving time. As it was for us when first we came here before we could grow enough, save enough, be wise enough to see ourselves through the winter. This winter. 1683 to the new bustling world. To an old man 1682.

So I am here again and it has been a shock that I have survived for so long beyond my friends, my enemies, and my use to others. It is so well to sit here on the bench I carved my own self for such purpose, for here away from the town and on Foxes Hill, let me think of my God and my hope, the same. Here in this blessed silence of the morning.

The dead come with me. So many. So much loss, my beloved John Winthrops, both of them, old Endicott. John Cotton. Even Will Harris, God rest his factionary soul. So many who came with me when this was not yet a treeless hill meadow. John Milton, Oliver, and my dearest friend of all, Harry Vane, who godfathered this colony as long as he could before the fine world we thought we lived in came down around us and the chains rebound us and broke our spirits.

I have survived to see the timeless shores of death so many times that it holds as little fear for me as the path to my front door. So much forgotten, my book gone up in flames that gave me leave to join all of those singled out by the fire for their beliefs, political fires, religious fires, I have at last seen them both as fires of language. We killed in a religious language but we killed politically. The same, whatever the cause, that blood of fury rising and overflowing into war one with another, one country with another, one tribe with another, the cause only the flint that lights the bonfire. Why is that killing fire called bon? Good?

Perhaps because sometimes when the fire is over, in the ashes of it there is left a small survival like a living ember. I have lived to see some of my words becomes rallying cries, for once tasted there are such thoughts that are not allowed to go up in flames. What I had hoped, has growed to a rallying cry in other voices, the ember long forgotten. Some still martyred for their conscience slip across the borders of the other colonies to ours, where they can breathe, speak, run riot, alas, while we labor to keep the peace.

In other years I went to Cocumscussoc to celebrate this time but it is gone for me. It is now a farm. The Indians I served there, that great nation, are gone, and those I meet are made servile by their hunger and their treatment. Only a few old ones are still there after the cleansing of the Narragansett country, the terrible sin we have to live with as a burden for our freedom.

I go sometimes to the few who are left, but it is all so changed that I could be anyplace beyond the towns. English farms divide the land, tilled and tilled again. Horses and cattle graze where the Indian villages were stretched in the distance all the way to the sea. It is domestic, safe, and peaceful and I am a stranger there, a visitor, an old man who maunders on remembering how it was when he can get anyone to listen.

But once, oh once I had a blessed retreat among them at my trading post, and was their friend and they mine, for the years before we pushed them to the insanity of suicide in King Philip's War.

It was a sacrifice to sell Cocumscussoc to pay for going once again to London to beg for the protection of a legal right to be here, for the first charter never stopped the gnashing at our borders, the insults, the demands; they crept to within our borders, for men have crazy dreams when there seems to be so much land for the taking. That time it was Mr. Coddington who decided that he owned the whole of that island we called Rhode Island, the island of roses. He was already a rich man when he came to our colony for the same reason that so many others came, to escape the Bay. But he went to London to claim the island and I suppose some oversleepy official gave him a charter to get rid of him, knowing or caring so little of where we were.

I had to go again to London. I looked not on that journey with any of the same joy that I had had before in the childhood of our hopes for a new Christian free land. The new hope had grown tired and old, failed, failed, and I saw it before my eyes when I went back among those I had known.

I was caught by change in London, and I had to stay that time near three years, away from home, away from those I loved, succoring those I loved there in the failing dream. The first time I went back I had been so at home, but this time I remained in my soul a stranger, even among comrades of so many years. Home in my mind had shifted across the great ocean at last. I thought myself American, as the children were who had never been anyplace but Providence since they were born.

Oliver was growing into a giant that no one could stand to. He was the unofficial leader of England, and everyone who had been betrayed by him knew it but no one dared say it, except Harry Vane.

Harry told me of the split between the Parliament and the army which grew more dangerous every day. It was, of course, seen as religious, orthodox against those who thought they too had fought for liberty of conscience. That in its time had become so familiar a slogan that it meant little, only what side you were on in a power struggle.

Oliver had already gone against his word and broke his cousin Whalley's regiment at Burford. He promised to meet and treat with them over their refusal to fight in Ireland. Harry showed me his broadsheet with the letter from their elected spokesmen, and it brought tears to us both. "What have we to do in Ireland, to fight and murder a people who have done us no harm. . . ." Oliver had the spokesmen shot, and sent the rest indentured to be auctioned off as servants in Virginia. He had found a strength in expediency. Ever the enemy of promise.

Why did we not know then that what seed had been planted was being trod on as it grew, while it was still young and spindly, and to most worthless, but not to me, and not to Harry Vane or John Milton, or thousands of the silent ones. I was there when Oliver walked into the Parliament in his shoddy morning clothes, dissolved it, and set the soldiers to shoo out the members as if they were chickens. When he stood in the middle of St. Stephen's chapel and announced that he was taking over with the army, Harry had called out, "This is unlawful," and he had already become immortal as the one who spoke while the rest stayed as silent as if Oliver Cromwell, standing there in his old clothes, was the anointed king of England. Oliver's only answer was, "Harry Vane! Harry Vane. God deliver me from Sir Harry Vane!" Harry had been for a time Oliver's dearest friend.

In all the years that I had sat in the visitors' gallery and studied the ways of the House of Commons, I never felt so chilled as at that moment looking down on Oliver, that unkempt mistaken man. We had all loved him and honored him. But we were in the way and God Expediency was the one he worshiped.

He appointed the men to sit in what the public called the Barebones Parliament. They were all, or most of them, from the army that worshiped him. His lordship, Oliver Cromwell, was set to rule England with as iron a hand as ever a king had done. Harry was put away from the government.

Most I had depended on put away. Oliver rid himself of those he had known too long. Not a single one of his huge family was left in power. It was so simple. The child within that strong and great man was beating his teasers and taunters and silencers at last, and what within him needed feeding was so hungry it needed the total power of the state to be himself to stanch it.

I would say, poor Oliver, and I should say, poor Oliver. But as we watched him, still fighting a boy's battle within a Parliament soon to go, among sectaries soon to be cast out, I feared for him and for the state. He lodged at Whitehall in the palace, and at Hampton Court. I saw him in both places. Hampton Court reminded me of Charterhouse in its lack of spirit after the gaudy court that I had seen there long

since. So many were cast aside, as the friends of the morning are rejected for the candlelit toadies of evening when a man is tired, and a country is tired. Oh what finally a parody of kingship it was to us who
hoped for more: the title, the command to call him "his highness," the
prison walls for those who dared to speak.

Oliver had a great soul; I know that and have always known, but he
had a weakness so fatal that the clay he sank in drowned his greatness.
He was a man completely without patience. I stayed awhile and
watched the tree die. Oh there were times that we were content, after-
noons, times with dear John, who beyond us all could speak the words
that cleansed my soul. For it was Milton himself who had loved him as
we had, and who had seen Oliver as our protection against the stone
rectitude of the Presbyterians, who wrote in 1652

> *. . . new foes arise,*
> *threatening to bind our souls with secular chains,*
> *Help us to save free Conscience from the paw*
> *Of hireling wolves whose Gospel is their maw.*

When I read it or hear it in my mind, I hear John's voice saying it
to me. Yet afterwards it was John in his blindness who saw more clearly than any of us what had happened when he said of his Satan, *"Myself
am hell."* I sat many a time by him beside his chair in his window for
he could still see light and dark when he sat there. He warned us all to
watch avarice, and above all to watch ambition's killing cure for early
disappointment as with Oliver. "For you may find that you have cher-
ished a more stubborn despot at home than ever you encountered in the
field of war."

God help us all. We had already fell back to speaking our thoughts
only in private and to those we trusted with our love. When Oliver
died, his weak son took over the reins of a tired and spavined horse. By
the Father of Lights we were all as a body singly minded. Were kept so
by what we held to, the cold dailiness of fact. By the time I left again
with only the promise of protection for our colony against its neighbors, Oliver was concerned with international fame. He was fighting a
war with the Dutch. Harry Vane had been imprisoned for speaking
out. There was strict censorship. Spies were everywhere. Then the book

burning began again. I think that men can be killed in passion, and the act blotted from memory, but the burning of books is ever the warning that there are those whose concern is to kill all minds that reflect not their own. And the words they burn live forever.

It was not Oliver who killed my lovely Harry Vane, no, he only broke his heart by his rejection of all that Harry stood for, loved, fought for. Harry was give the final relief of dying by the merry monarch Charles II who had him beheaded on Tower Green and surrounded him with drumbeats so that no one could hear Harry's dying words and make him an immortal flint to keep the fires alit. His words had long since been smuggled out and published, but kings are so above the common people that they know not what that murmur is they hear from time to time. Charles gave as his reason for denying the pleas of so many that Harry live when he signed Harry's death warrant. He said, "That man is too dangerous to live."

But I see Harry not beheaded on Tower Green, nor Oliver two years dead dug up, though some say it was another cadaver half rotted that was hanged at Tyburn and then drawn and quartered and thrown into the gutter. Oh how small and dull is revenge. How small, how mean the vengeful mind. To throw a corpse two years dead into the gutter. It is pitiful. No. I see them banqueting, the candles and the fire making the wine and glasses glow.

BY THE GRACE of my Father of Lights who hath beyond all others a sense of humor so towering, so mighty that we if we saw it much we would die of holy laughter, it was that king, that rascal, Charles II, who gave us finally here at Rhode Island the first royal charter ever granted that would keep us truly safe from predators, except our own selves. Against the advice of his Privy Council he it was who gave us the liberty of conscience and self-government, the separation of our churches and our civil government that we, I, had labored for for so long. I like to think he did it with a smile for he ever was bored with the solemn men who surrounded him and much preferred the playhouse.

So, finally, after nearly thirty years of trying, we have a jewel here in Providence, a sometime democracy that falls often into anarchy and brabble but somehow rights itself, where every man can speak his mind, and the majority rule and the minority be protected in their conscience and God knows to my impatience their ever shouting voices.

Oh Father of Lights if I still have a prayer within me, make them conscious of having bought truth so dear. We must not sell it cheap, not the least grain of it for the whole world. What I have learned and often forgot is to be a naysayer for I have seen those who have fallen into yea-saying for the sake of property, pleasure, or fear. It has been a bitter sweetening. For the broken bags of riches on eagles' wings, for a dream or land or gold or power any and all of these vanish on our deathbeds and leave tormenting stings behind them.

And I yet know this in my ever joyful heart and soul and have wrote it so; that every wind and cloud, and drop of rain and hail, every flake of snow, every leaf, every grass, every drop of water in the ocean and rivers, yea, every grain of corn and sand on the shore, is a voice or word and witness of God unto us. As for my banishment that began it all, first by the tiny lady in Essex, we all suffer many a banishment when childlike we offer our hearts to friends and lovers.

But keep the offering of being rejected I say. For this I was taught by Bartholomew, that only uncalled-for, undreamed-of, unmerited, unearned punishment for truth's sake can bring us nearer to our Jesus who walked the sandy roads of Galilee, and who suffered such an unearned foul and beastly death for our sakes. And we cannot, agree or not, ever forget that twisted bleeding man nailed there unhailed and deserted, pelted with stones, His privates exposed to all in loss of any dignity left, His guts pierced. A ragged wandering Jew we cannot ever ignore to our sometimes petty annoyance.

And this, too. Whatever the church, God give them grace and peace. Whether they are true or false they are very like unto a society or company of East India or Turkey merchants. They all may have records, disputes, dissentions, schisms, factions, break up, reform, break up again and again, appear and disappear. But yet the cities where we have our being together are nothing disturbed by these their troubles beyond a ripple. Well-being and peace is of the soul within the world, and from neighbor to neighbor, and door to door and the sun shines on all.

That I have learned and for the rest, may it be failure, may it be a seed that will sometime grow, that a conscience is a gift from God and cannot be persecuted whether the words of belief come from Moslem or Christian or Jew or Buddhist as Sydrach taught me long ago.

The root of the matter here in Providence is not about these children's toys of land, meadows, cattle, government. It is that all over this colony a great number of weak and distressed souls, scattered, are flying thither for shelter.

For me, though censured, threatened, persecuted, I must profess, while heaven and earth last, that no one tenent that either London, England, or the world harbors is so heretical, blasphemous, seditious, and dangerous to the corporal, to the spiritual, to the present, to the eternal good of all men as the bloody tenent (however washed and whited) of persecution for the cause of conscience. I, Roger Williams, have long been charged with folly for that freedom and liberty which I have always stood for, both in land and government. Such liberties for soul and body as were never enjoyed by any English men, nor any in the world yet I have heard of.

I must have spoke aloud. Mary has found me. She says I am ever quoting myself to myself and she need only listen for a while when I wander off to follow my disputations with the wind and the animals. She shouts and waves her arms across the meadow and tells me what I know, that it is cold and deep with snow.

Mind not, dear one. Mind not. Her voice is sweet and loving, then, listen! Like a trumpet it rises slowly as a fine music into a demanding hallow hallow you there you fool old man come in come in with me and get thyself warm.

Mary I have ever loved thee and burdened thee with much duty, and you have ever been stolid and forgiving, and by God's holy wisdom, jovial, which is the most important gift to me of all. Yet so I sit here (yes, Mary) with my behind in the snow and (yes Mary) it will mean an ague, and (yes Mary) you will care and fuss together over me. Oh by the Father of Lights I do love you so; this is always the time I must remind myself that if helpmeet and yokemate, if lover, if sweet one, if riches, if children, if friends, if cattle, if whatsoever increase, we must watch that the heart fly not loose upon them, lest we forget in daily blessings and strivings our own souls and the chisel that creates us from stone.

For a minute I am still. A minute more. Pretend not to hear or see her. Take another minute. Alone. As I was once in the snowblind wilderness that year, at home in that as nowhere else on earth or in time.

Laboring for the spiritual and caught by the hope of temporal peace, I have reached a place of silence at least within, and for the moment, a snow-white world even though the red blood stains it. To it all I say only Heigh Ho, if I perish I perish. It is, after all, but a shadow vanished, a bubble broke, a dream finished. Eternity will pay for all.

AFTERWORD

*M*any years ago I stood in the now-defunct Reading Room of the British Museum and cried. The book I searched for was not there. I knew I had to write it. The book was *O Beulah Land*.

But *O Beulah Land* was there, hidden in thousands of eighteenth-century papers, books, letters, put aside, catalogued, and protected by an army of paper savers through the years. There was the true picture of life as it was lived, seen, lied about, and honored at the time. Unimportant to the eighteenth-century lovers of the past, unlikely to those who were readers of the classics, there the fragments were, ready to be found again. Without such dedicated work in thousands of libraries we would still be barbarians.

So, for *I, Roger Williams,* I want to recognize and honor those who have saved the work of a man who could so easily have been forgotten. In the Alderman Library at the University of Virginia I found the complete works of Roger Williams, originally gathered and published by Narragansett Club Publications of Providence. There were the contemporary, almost complete notes of the two Parliaments that Sir Edward Coke led, both official and unofficial contemporary accounts of the reign of James I, and the contemporary history of the translation of the King James version of the Bible, to name only the most obvious sources I needed.

When I came to live in Vermont, I was able to find copies of most of the books I had left in Virginia at the Baker Library at Dartmouth College. So to the institutions who for years have prepared the way for me to work, I want to send thanks for their care, their help, and their generosity.

In Vermont I shared the kind of winter Roger Williams survived with his fellow refugees. But most of all, I shared his language. The University Press of New England in Hanover has kept in print, long beyond the call of literary duty, two volumes of his fascinating letters. These letters were written quickly, all too often with an Indian runner waiting to deliver them. He had little chance or reason to "correct" them, and so they carry the rhythms of his voice and his time as his more careful writing could not. He was trained at Charterhouse and at Pembroke College, Cambridge, to satisfy the contemporary idea of "good" writing: the polite servility, the stilted sentences, the quotes from the Bible, the Latin tags. To readers of our own time, much of his work is obscure. The letters are not. Neither is his passionate master-piece, *The Bloody Tenent of Persecution for Cause of Conscience,* also written on the run. Once the veil of the past is pulled away from our own minds, and we learn to read this work as we would another language, it is superb, America's first masterpiece, so radical, so sassy, that it was obscured by its orthodox enemies for years.

There are two fine American writers who have been my ever-present helpers, critics, and bulldogs for many years. Without them I might have given up at times; with them I have had a bulwark of recognition that has honored me, and so often given me strength.

For forty years, George Garrett, the one Renaissance gentleman I know, has been the writer whose wonderful novels that take place in the past have been my models. He is the most generous man of letters in this country. He has been my mentor, my advocate, and my dear friend. He was the first reader with whom I shared without fear the first hundred pages of *I, Roger Williams.* He recommended it to my present publisher. He has read almost every manuscript I have written, long before anyone else, and has given me the kind of valuable and impassioned criticism that is so necessary to a writer, and so rare in that delicate time of the first sharing of work. He has, for many writers, cre-ated an atmosphere much as it must have been in France in the nine-teenth century, when Turgenev is said to have written to his friend Flaubert, when he was castigated for *Madame Bovary,* "Courage, mon ami, tu es Flaubert, après tout."

For nearly twenty years the second of my mentors and first readers, never refusing, never delaying, has been the great critic, scholar, and essayist Roger Shattuck. He has given me some of the most valuable readings I have ever had, early enough for them to be useful in rewrite. He introduced me to Farrar, Straus & Giroux, and there, for three books, I had an almost ideal publisher/writer relationship.

So to two writers, all the librarians and paper savers from Thomason, who saved everything that he could find in print during the seventeenth-century English civil wars, to those who today put aside and catalogue what most of the world would think is politically suspect, socially unacceptable, and unimportant, I send my thanks, my recognition, and my love.

Available in Norton Paperback Fiction